THE NOVELS

AND RELATED WORKS OF

CHARLES BROCKDEN BROWN

BICENTENNIAL EDITION

Volume I

WIELAND

MEMOIRS OF CARWIN

CHARLES BROCKDEN BROWN
A portrait by James Sharples, probably dating from January 1798
Worcester Art Museum, Worcester, Mass.

CHARLES BROCKDEN BROWN

WIELAND
or
THE TRANSFORMATION
An American Tale

MEMOIRS OF CARWIN
THE BILOQUIST

Bicentennial Edition

KENT STATE UNIVERSITY PRESS

The Bicentennial Brown is a Publication of
KENT STATE UNIVERSITY

CENTER FOR EDITIONS OF
AMERICAN AUTHORS

AN APPROVED TEXT

MODERN LANGUAGE
ASSOCIATION OF AMERICA

®

Copyright © 1977 by the Kent State University Press
All rights reserved ISBN: 0-87338-160-2
Library of Congress Catalog Card Number: 74-79474
Manufactured in the United States of America
Designed by Harold Stevens

Library of Congress Cataloging in Publication Data

Brown, Charles Brockden, 1771-1810.
  The novels and related works of Charles Brockden Brown.

  Includes bibliographical references.
  CONTENTS: v. 1. Wieland. Memoirs of Carwin.
PZ3.B814Nr5 [PS1130]   813.2   74-79474
ISBN 0-87338-160-2 (v. 1)

EDITORS

SYDNEY J. KRAUSE	*General Editor*
S. W. REID	*Textual Editor*
ALEXANDER COWIE	*Contributing Editor*

Other Members of the Editorial Project

NORMAN S. GRABO	RUSSEL B. NYE
DONALD A. RINGE	MARVIN L. WILLIAMS, JR.

FOREWORD

This first volume in Kent State University's Bicentennial Edition of the Novels and Related Works of Charles Brockden Brown presents critical texts of Brown's first published novel, *Wieland,* and of the fragment, "Carwin," which he began in 1798 as a companion-piece to his novel. The texts are based on the first printings: the book edition of *Wieland* printed by T. and J. Swords in New York and published there by Hocquet Caritat in 1798, and the installments of "Carwin" that appeared in the *Literary Magazine* in Philadelphia in 1803, 1804, and 1805. The Historical Essay by Alexander Cowie, which follows the texts, discusses the facts surrounding the composition, publication, and reception of both works and their place in America's literary history, and the Textual Essay by S. W. Reid discusses the copy-texts for the present edition, the transmission of the texts, and the editorial decisions that have been based on these considerations. Also appended are photographs of the notebook pages containing Brown's "Outline" of *Wieland,* along with our transcription of it. Moreover, as the first in a series of volumes, this volume offers, as well, a note on the principles and procedures guiding the editing of all works in the Bicentennial Edition.

The editors are indebted to numerous institutions and individuals. First of all, for major assistance in the handling of loans and inquiries and permission to see, and in some instances to copy, manuscripts, first editions, and other Brown and Brown-related materials, we are especially grateful to:

Nicholas B. Wainwright, John D. Kilbourne, Henry Cadwalader, Frank W. Bobb, Harry Givens, Jane Butterfield, Paul Eustace, and Lucy Hrivnak of *The Historical Society of Pennsylvania.*
Edwin Wolf, 2nd, Lillian Tonkin, and Robert Kuncio of *The Library Company of Philadelphia.*
James J. Heslin and James Gregory of *The New York Historical Society.*
Warner Barnes, David Farmer and John R. Payne (Humanities Research Center) and June Moll of *The University of Texas* (Austin).
William H. Runge, the late John Cook Wyllie, Joan St. C. Crane, Julius Barclay, and Anne Freudenberg of *The University of Virginia.*
Also providing generous help with manuscripts and/or loans and inquiries were:
Marcus A. McCorison, Frederick E. Bauer, Jr., and John B. Hench, *American Antiquarian Society*; Herbert R. Brown, Robert L. Volz, Richard B. Reed, *Bowdoin College*; David Randall and Josiah Q. Bennett, *Indiana Univ.*; Matthew P. Lowman, II, and Karen S. Lennon, *Newberry Library*; Robert A. Tibbetts, *Ohio State Univ.*; Charles W. Mann, *Pennsylvania State Univ.*; Alexander P. Clark, Howard C. Rice, and Robert S. Fraser, *Princeton Univ.*; and Jane Allen, *Univ. of Cincinnati.*
And additionally:
Richard H. Shryock, Gertrude D. Hess, William Spawn, and Roy E. Goodman, *American Philosophical Society*; John Alden, *Boston Public Library*; Thomas R. Adams and Christine D. Hathaway, *Brown Univ.*; Kenneth A. Lohf and Hugh MacDonald, *Columbia Univ.*; V. Nelle Bellamy, *Church Historical Society* (Austin, Tex.); Dale Fields and Gladys M. Coghlan, *Delaware Historical Society*; William H. Bond, Roger E. Stoddard, Carolyn E. Jakeman, Donna Ferguson, and Linda Sklar, *Harvard Univ.*; Elizabeth B. Tritle and C. R. Thompson, *Haverford College*; James D. Mack, Mary E. Gruber and Brian Sanders, *Lehigh Univ.*; Phyliss Adams and David Frazier, *Library Company of*

Philadelphia; William Matheson, Frederick R. Goff, John C. Broderick, Robert H. Land and David Mearns, *Library of Congress*; James Tobin, Maude D. Cole, and Harold Merklen, *New York Public Library*; Theodore Grieder, *New York Univ.*; Serena Bradshaw and Jane W. Gallif, *Ohio State Univ.*; Amanda Smith, *Pennsylvania State Univ.*; John Mullane, *Public Library of Cincinnati*; Anthony S. Nicolosi, *Rutgers Univ.*; Dorothy G. Harris, *Swarthmore College*; Robert B. Downs, *Univ. of Illinois*; Lawrence F. London, *Univ. of North Carolina*; Flora D. Colton and Neda M. Westlake, *Univ. of Pennsylvania*; Mason Tolman, Darrel P. Welch, and Juliet F. Wolohan, *Univ. of the State of New York* (Albany); Edmund Berkeley and Margaret B. Sloss, *Univ. of Virginia*; and Peter Dzwonkoski, Madeline Stanton, Dorothy Bridgewater, and Concetta N. Sacco, *Yale Univ.*

Others who were helpful to us with similar requests, particularly inquiries, were:

Clyde E. Peterman, *Beloit College*; Sir Frank Francis and Mary Jane Miller, *British Museum*; William H. Loos, *Buffalo and Erie County Public Library*; Henry Grunder, *College of William and Mary*; Caroline T. Spicer, *Cornell Univ.*; Eugene L. Pike, *California State Library* (Sacramento); Evan Thompson, *Detroit Public Library*; Mary Isabel Fry, *Huntington Library*; John D. Cushing, *Massachusetts Historical Society*; Ann L. Wadsworth, *Library of the Boston Athenaeum*; Russell Maylone, *Northwestern Univ.*; Elizabeth Rumics, *Oberlin College*; Margaret Gleason, *State Historical Society of Wisconsin*; Marian M. Clarke, *Trinity College*; Jean F. Butt, *Tufts Univ.*; Brooke Whiting, *Univ. of California at Los Angeles*; Carol R. Kem, *Univ. of Florida*; Frank Paluka, *Univ. of Iowa*; Richard Gercken, *Univ. of Montana*; Lyman W. Riley, *Univ. of Pennsylvania*; George McM. Jones, *Univ. of Pittsburgh*; John Hostetter, *Univ. of South Carolina*; Sally Leach, *Univ. of Texas* (Austin); and Milton C. Russell, *Virginia State Library* (Richmond).

For various personal and professional assistance and encouragement, we also wish to recognize: Charles E. Bennett, Fredson Bowers, Matthew J. Bruccoli, Mrs. David Lee Clark, James E. Cronin, J. Maurice Duke, Gordon Hargraves, Harrison Hayford, Robert Hemenway, John S. Van E. Kohn, David Nordloh, Hershel Parker, J. Albert Robbins, and Rollo G. Silver.

Special thanks for extended book loans are due two of Brown's descendants: Dorothy Burr Thompson and Pamela Burr.

For support in establishing the Bibliographical and Textual Center and in assembling the materials needed to prepare the Brown edition, as well as for released time to work on it, we are deeply grateful to the Administration and the English Department of Kent State University. Kent State persons (present and former) who have in various ways assisted the project are: Glenn A. Olds, Bernard Hall, John J. Kamerick, F. Leslie Speir, Bruce Harkness, Hyman W. Kritzer, Dean H. Keller, the late Kenneth R. Pringle, Martin Nurmi, Howard P. Vincent, Thomas F. Marshall, Hilton Landry, Darlene Jordan, Lee Stockdale, Naomi Harrington, Helen Peoples and Linda Neloms. Our thanks are due, too, to our initial editorial assistants, Jane Pipes and Josephine Zuppan, and to our student assistants: James Caccamo, Deborah Conrad, Jay Czeck, Herman Holloway, Charles Jenkins, Rebecca A. Martin, Michael Schuldiner, Barbara Ward, and David Weymiller. We are appreciative as well of Paul H. Rohmann and Michael DiBattista of the Kent State University Press, and of our book designer, Harold M. Stevens.

Kent, Ohio   S.J.K.
December 1974   S.W.R.

CONTENTS

THE BICENTENNIAL TEXTS:
A NOTE

The Bicentennial Edition of the novels and related works of Charles Brockden Brown aims to provide accurate texts of the works which are as close as the extant documents permit to Brown's own final intentions. Thus it presents unmodernized critical texts that in each case reproduce Brown's original inscription and successive revision to the extent that these can be reconstructed from the evidence of the various authoritative documents in which the work has appeared, subject to normal editorial regulation. To provide such texts for the modern reader, the editors have adopted certain general principles and procedures in determining the exact forms of the text in the early documents and tracing the transmission of the text through them, in the editorial treatment of the authoritative texts, and in reporting the evidence used in editing each work. The present note discusses these general principles and procedures; the specific conditions to which they are applied in editing each work are examined in the Textual Essay in each volume.

To identify precisely for the Bicentennial Edition the most authoritative forms in which each work has appeared, there have been collations of the various editions[1] that were published in Brown's lifetime and of the early posthumous

---

[1] Throughout the present edition, the use of the terms edition, impression, issue, and state follows that recommended in Fredson Bowers, *Principles of Bibliographical Description* (Princeton, N.J.: Princeton Univ. Press, 1949).

editions that might contain new authority derived from his possible revisions of the work. Multiple copies of the first edition and of later editions selected for examination have been collated on the Hinman Collator or a similar machine to identify (1) changes arising between possible re-impressions of standing type, (2) variants occurring during any one printing, and (3) the exact readings of a single printing, illegible in any one copy because of bad inking, distortions in the paper, and the like. In addition, copies of these later editions have been hand-collated against copies of the first edition, and all substantive differences as well as such accidentals that might be attributed to a source other than the printers of the later edition recorded.

Although ideally intended to identify all significant varia-tion, the completeness of the information actually gathered by this process is limited by practical considerations and is likely to be different for different works. The copies of an edition that are available to an editorial project inevitably determine what information becomes available to the editors, and chance may have it that a certain variant or group of variants occurs in none of the exemplars examined.[2] To minimize the chance of authoritative read-ings remaining undiscovered, usually five or more copies of the authoritative editions of each work have been machine-collated; when it has not been possible to collate certain copies in this way, they have been scrupulously hand-collated. These collations have been repeated one or more times by different operators. Moreover, since the main problem is to discover variants arising during con-cealed re-impressions of a single typesetting, there has been an attempt to make single collations of four or five other copies of the editions examined.[3] The hand-collations of different editions have also been repeated. In general, all

[2] For instance, since only four copies of the 1804 *Jane Talbot* are now known, the collation of this edition must be less thorough than that of the 1798 *Wieland,* represented by over thirty copies.

[3] If variants have been found in a copy collated once, the collation has also been repeated.

editions selected for examination have undergone both types of collation. But when initial collations have shown that a certain edition contains only the textual corruption commonly incidental to mere reprinting, the thorough collation of multiple copies has been discontinued in favor of concentrating on those editions that appear to be more than mere reprints. Because eighteenth-century magazines were sometimes reset or re-impressed and because those Brown was connected with were possibly issued quarterly or annually (bound) as well as weekly or monthly (unbound), the standards applied to the collation of works appearing in book form have also been applied to initial appearances of Brown's works in magazines.

By means of these collations and the conflation of the results in one record of variation, the evidence has been gathered that is necessary to making decisions about the authority of the various extant documents. On the basis of this internal evidence, together with whatever external evidence proves to be pertinent, the line of textual transmission from document to document can be traced and those editions that merely reprint a previous edition can be isolated from those that most directly derive in whole or in part from authorial manuscripts and are therefore the authoritative documents on which the Bicentennial text must be based.[4]

Once the exact forms of the authoritative texts and their relationships to one another have been thus identified, one of them is chosen to serve as copy-text (as the basis for this edition). The selection of the copy-text conforms to the

[4] Ordinarily new authority in an edition subsequent to the first would enter by means of a copy of a previous edition annotated with revised readings; hence, the later edition might derive only partly from an independent authorial manuscript. The annotation might have been done by the author or (especially in the case of a posthumous printing) by someone else using a manuscript, a list of changes, or even another copy marked up by the author. However, it is conceivable that a later edition might derive wholly from an independent manuscript (as seems to be the case with *Alcuin*). The principles for dealing with such revision and corrections are discussed below.

practices of modern textual criticism and, specifically, to the principles explained by Sir Walter Greg.[5] Although the actual choice depends on particular conditions that may vary from work to work, the guiding principle is to choose as copy-text the single form which provides the best means of recovering the details of the text of the autograph manuscript behind the extant documents.

When only the first edition is found to have authority, it must serve as copy-text. The editorial treatment of this single authority consists of corrective emendation such as that described below.

If two or more editions of a single version of a work are authoritative, the double authority distinguished by Greg is recognized. Greg discriminates between the authority of the "substantives" (those readings that affect the author's meaning or the essence of his expression) and of the "accidentals" of a text (those that affect only its formal presentation). An edition (usually only the first) set from an autograph manuscript possesses general authority for the accidentals of the text (that is, serves as the best evidence of the spelling, punctuation, capitalization, word-division, and paragraphing of the lost autograph manuscript),[6] whereas the substantives of the first edition and the substantive revisions in any later edition both have authority, though the authority of the later authorial variants is superior to

[5] "The Rationale of Copy-Text," *Studies in Bibliography*, 3 (1950-51), 19-36; rpt. Greg, *Collected Papers*, ed. J. C. Maxwell (Oxford: Clarendon Press, 1966), pp. 374-391.

[6] Theoretically, of course, any changes in the accidentals of the later, revised text that derive from the author also possess authority, but in actual practice identifying the relatively few which occur among numerous printing-house changes is usually impossible. (See Fredson Bowers, "Current Theories of Copy-Text, with an Illustration from Dryden," *Modern Philology*, 48 (1950), 12-20.) Hence, unless certainty in this matter is obtainable, it is better to retain the accidentals of the copy-text than to substitute those that may or may not be authoritative (even though some of these may seem to conform to Brown's habits more than those of the copy-text). Since Brown apparently was somewhat inattentive to such matters, a prima-facie case exists for conservative revisory emendation of the accidentals of the copy-text.

that of the earlier.[7] In such a case, the first edition (or that set as a whole from autograph) must still be chosen as the copy-text, but the variant substantive readings in the later edition that presumably originated with the author are substituted for those of the copy-text. The principal editorial problem then becomes distinguishing those readings in the later authority that are corruptions resulting from reprinting from those that are genuine authorial revisions. Only the authorial alterations need be incorporated in the established text,[8] and when they are incorporated they are made to conform in their accidentals to the general formal features of the text reconstructed from the copy-text.

If two or more authoritative documents in collateral relationship are found to be independent witnesses deriving immediately from a lost common ancestor, they are used to reconstruct the text of the lost document; the copy-text is that single authority which serves as the most practical basis for an apparatus recording the variants in all authoritative documents. When documents in collateral relationship are not equidistant from an autograph manuscript, or cannot be used to reconstruct the text of a lost common ancestor, the copy-text is that one which derives most directly from autograph and is the best witness to Brown's accidentals; the other documents are used as sources of corrective

[7] This, of course, assumes a direct relationship between the chronological order of the printings and the order of the variants in the copy behind these printings. It is, however, possible (as in the case of *Alcuin*) for the relationship to be reversed, for the earlier printing to contain the later readings; in such a case, the revisions in the earlier edition have superior authority and must be chosen.

[8] Once identified as authorial, these revisions are chosen even if some seem to the editors literarily inferior to the earlier readings. (Of course, the question of literary value inevitably enters into the original decision about whether the author is behind the changes in the later text; the point is that once the general character of the changes is assessed and the author assigned as their source, all the author's revisions must be accepted.) However, one exception to this rule is observed: if the changes were made by Brown but are judged to have been made not for literary reasons but merely because of external pressures (editorial, financial, political, and so on), they may be regarded as censorship (even though self-imposed) and rejected.

emendation of the copy-text. In all cases, those variant substantive readings in the documents that represent Brown's latest intentions are adopted and incorporated in the Bicentennial text.[9]

In addition to incorporating revisions in its texts, the Bicentennial Edition includes emendations of the copy-text undertaken to clear it of error and of such nonauthorial mechanical irregularities as may unnecessarily distract the reader. Basically such corrective emendation deals with errors not altered in proof. Brown, when he concerned himself with proofreading at all, seems to have been a rather careless correcter of his printers. Indeed, his concern with the correctness of the printer's copy itself is difficult to define. At one time, he commented on his need to transcribe his "hasty and inaccurate" first drafts before submitting them to the printer, but at another, he seems to have defended his manner of composition when remarking that "rapidity" added to the excellence of the "execution" of a main plan, while it produced some "slighter inaccuracies of grammar, orthography, and punctuation." Since apparently none of his literary manuscripts in prose survives, the only internal evidence that exists is in the first editions themselves, and these indicate that Brown did not always successfully translate into action his intention to correct infelicities of presentation when transcribing his manuscripts and that this concern did not necessarily extend to proofreading. Hence correction of errors—as distinguished from authorial infelicities—which he himself would presumably have changed had he been aware of them is necessary.[10]

[9] For a more extensive discussion of the principles followed here, see Fredson Bowers, "Multiple Authority: New Problems and Concepts of Copy-Text," *The Library*, 5th Ser., 27 (1972), 81-115.

[10] See William Dunlap, *Life of Charles Brockden Brown* (Philadelphia: Parke, 1815), I, 107; Brown to Bringhurst, 20 May 1792, quoted in Herbert R. Brown, "Charles Brockden Brown's 'The Story of Julius': Rousseau and Richardson 'Improved'," in *Essays Mostly on Periodical Publishing in America*, ed. James Woodress (Durham, N.C.: Duke Univ. Press, 1973), p. 40. The evidence for the conclusion regarding Brown's proof-

THE BICENTENNIAL TEXTS: A NOTE

In addition, several other types of emendation of the copy-text are undertaken. Unintentional ambiguities resulting from deficient formal presentation (chiefly punctuation missing or misplaced) are resolved as the context warrants.[11] Other punctuation or spelling in the copy-text is retained unless a change can be justified logically by passing these three tests: (1) it should restore spelling or punctuation that was, on the available evidence, habitual with Brown and hence very probably present in his lost manuscript; (2) it should restore spelling or pointing which the printer of the copy-text habitually rejected in favor of that present in the copy-text; and (3) it should not vary markedly from the over-all usage of the copy-text.[12] Not only does very little of Brown's literary work (prose or verse) survive in manuscript, but the letters and notebooks that are extant do not provide a case exactly parallel to literary works intended for publication; moreover, his own usage in his manuscripts is often inconsistent, and the practices of his printers cannot always be determined. Therefore, the emendation of these accidentals of the copy-text is, in effect, very conservative and consists chiefly of resolving

reading is mainly internal, chiefly the numerous errors in most first editions for which Brown alone was responsible as compared to the relative cleanness of *Wieland* (1798), proofread in part by Elihu Hubbard Smith and William Johnson, as well as Brown. See also Brown's letter to an unknown correspondent, 8 May 1801 (ALS, Haverford College Library), which indicates Brown's concern with the typographical appearance of his books.

[11] The operative words here are "as the context warrants"; this applies to the immediate context that determines the kind of emendation that is appropriate given the passage's meaning, and the larger context of the entire work that determines the exact form to be chosen for the emendation. In this edition it is assumed that because the accidentals of the copy-text cannot be superseded altogether by thorough emendation that restores Brown's own usage, the copy-text remains the only real authority for the general formal texture of the work, and all emendations, accidental as well as substantive, must retain the general character of these formal features for a consistent text to be logically established.

[12] To gather facts for the first test, Brown's extant manuscripts have been searched; for the second, editions contemporaneous with the copy-text have been consulted to identify the practices of each printer; for the third, the usage of the copy-text has been recorded.

xxi

inconsistencies in the copy-text when one of the variant forms is known to conform to Brown's habitual usage and the other obviously represents the printer's imperfectly realized attempt at styling contrary to Brown's intentions.

This conservative treatment of the spellings of the copy-text does not extend to misspellings, however; when there are spellings which seem inadvertent on Brown's part and which can be defined as positively wrong in his time,[13] they are corrected. But the same general principles do extend to the capitalization and word-division of the copy-text. If each is inconsistent but acceptable, it is allowed to stand, unless Brown's own usage requires choosing a certain form for a given word or compound; if wrong, it is corrected. When the components of a compound divide at the break between lines of the copy-text, the form used a majority of the time in the copy-text is chosen, unless it clearly contravenes Brown's habitual preference while the minority form agrees with his preference (in which case the minority form is of course chosen).

Although these types of corrective emendation may be made, there is no attempt to correct grammatical constructions wrong by modern standards but not obviously wrong in Brown's time. Thus, the frequent, apparently authorial lack of agreement between noun and verb in clauses such as 'My folly and rashness has left me' (*Wieland,* 137.20-21) and other such "inaccuracies of grammar" are retained. Also

[13] In addition to the normal authorities (e.g., *OED, DAE*), the following sources have been consulted to determine acceptable usage: Brown's copy (in the Barrett Collection at the University of Virginia) of Samuel Johnson's *Dictionary of the English Language* (London: Strahan, 1783); Noah Webster, *A Compendious Dictionary of the English Language* (New Haven, Conn.: Hudson and Goodwin, 1806); Thomas Dilworth, *A New Guide to the English Tongue* (Philadelphia: Crukshank, 1789); Webster, *A Grammatical Institute of the English Language, Part I* (1783; rpt. Menston, Yorks.: Scolar Press, 1968); Webster, *The American Spelling Book* (Hartford, Conn.: Hudson and Goodwin, 1804), revision of *A Grammatical Institute;* George Fox, *Instructions for Right Spelling, and Plain Directions for Reading and Writing True English* (Boston: Roger and Fowle, 1743), a standard in Quaker schools; Robert Lowth, *A Short Introduction to English Grammar* (1762; rpt. Menston: Scolar Press, 1967); Lindley Murray, *English Grammar* (1795; rpt. Menston: Scolar Press, 1968).

retained are variant names for Brown's characters. These almost certainly represent his own practice. Hence, *Constance/Constantia* and *Hellen/Helena (Ormond)* are reproduced.

The practice of presenting both direct and indirect discourse which is followed in the various editions of Brown's works constitutes a special problem. His own usage is difficult to determine, but his first editions (the only surviving evidence) suggest that Brown was not fully conscious of our modern distinction between the two. The various typographical devices used by some of his printers (including dashes, colons, semicolons, and successive dots, as well as quotation marks and commas) indicate a similar attitude on the part of some of his contemporaries. Under these circumstances, this edition adopts the copy-text's dominant system (if any) of presenting direct and indirect discourse in a given work and follows it throughout, emending the copy-text where it clearly misrepresents Brown's intentions. Generally, the system of the copy-text and the emendatory practice of this edition are described in the respective Textual Essays, and all alterations of this type are reported in one list, either as a footnote or as a discrete part of the Emendations list described below.

Silent (that is, unreported) alterations of the document serving as copy-text occur during the printing of this edition. For instance, the long *s* appearing in some first editions is uniformly reduced to the short (modern) *s*. Typographical irregularities in apostrophes and dashes are regularized. Successive dots which are used for dramatic pause or to introduce or terminate quotations (but which are merely compositorial in their number and spacing) are printed as spaced periods (. . .). Other mere mechanical details of the original documents—such as pagination, lineation, use of display capitals at the beginning of chapters, punctuation and capitalization in running-titles and chapter-headings—are normalized. Finally, typographical errors, such as turned letters, wrong font, or misplaced types (e.g., 'foundh er') are silently emended.

It is perhaps obvious from the discussion of the handling of quotations that, with the exceptions already enumerated, there is no attempt to impose a uniform style on the texts included in this edition. The intent is to reconstruct the texts logically from the evidence of the authoritative documents, and since these differ in many minute respects, the reconstructed texts must also differ. Revisory emendation of the copy-text is admitted only from authoritative documents; corrective emendation is admitted from any source, including unauthoritative reprints, other scholarly editions, and independent editorial judgment. With the exception of such silent emendation as has just been discussed, all emendation (revisory or corrective) is noted in appendixes, where the interested reader may have access to the significant textual evidence available to the editors in emending the copy-text and determining the general authority of the relevant documents; with these notes he may for himself reconstruct from the edited text both the copy-text and the substantive readings of any other document examined.

The basis for each note is the numbers of the page and line of the established text in this edition; that is, 15.10 means the reading occurs on page 15, at line 10, in this edition. These numbers are followed by the exact intended form of the reading of the established text, succeeded usually by a square bracket. Since the purpose of these notes is to inform the reader about editorial decisions, the reading is always in the form intended for the established text, even though chance may have it that the word is divided between two lines in the present edition; thus all divisions between lines (e.g., *mas-|ter*), even in possible compounds (e.g., *me-|thinks*),[14] go unrecorded in the lemma itself. What follows the lemma depends on the function of the particular appendix. Unless unusual circumstances call for additional

[14] A full report on these may be found in the list described below; how we call the reader's attention to this edition's fortuitous division of the reading in the lemma, and thus refer him to this list, is discussed in the following descriptions of each appendix.

information, there are ordinarily four appendixes on strictly textual matters.

Textual Notes. These discuss emendations adopted or not adopted, when some explanation of the editorial decision seems desirable.

List of Emendations. Both substantives and accidentals of the copy-text altered in this edition (with the exceptions enumerated above) are recorded and the sources of the emendations noted. Each note provides the basic information on the emendation and ignores everything but the earliest use of the adopted reading and the history of the rejected reading up to the time of its alteration to the adopted reading.[15]

In these notes, following the lemma with the square bracket there is a siglum identifying the earliest source of the emendation (that is, the earliest among those editions examined). A semicolon succeeds this notation and is followed by the rejected copy-text reading with the sigla identifying the pertinent editions in which the reading occurs. Further variants, if any, are noted in a similar manner following these sigla and an appended semicolon. The sigla used to denote the editions referred to are explained in each Textual Essay; generally, "A" signifies American book editions, and "E" English ones. Throughout "B" identifies emendations made for the first time in the Bicentennial Edition (that is, readings not appearing in the editions examined). Thus the note

25.10 belief] E2; relief A,E1

means that the *belief* reading of the Bicentennial text has been adopted from the second English edition, whereas the copy-text, the American edition (A), has *relief*, the reading also of the first English edition (E1). Other arbitrary symbols appear in such notes throughout this edition. A wavy

[15] The practice of noting the first occurrence of an emendation, even though the edition cited is a mere reprint, is followed as a matter of convenience and frankness with the reader, and is not meant to imply a kind of secondary authority.

dash ($\sim$) occurs in place of a repeated word associated with pointing when the variant at issue is the punctuation and not the word. An inferior caret ($_\wedge$) indicates that punctuation is lacking and that this lack is the variant being recorded. Three dots (. . .) mean that one or more words in a series are omitted from the note. A vertical stroke (|) marks the break between two lines when possible compounds are divided between lines in the copy-text. An asterisk (*) preceding the lemma directs the reader to the discussion of the emendation in the Textual Notes. Finally, a dagger (†) precedes the lemma when the reading of the lemma is a possible compound and is divided and hyphenated between two lines in the present edition; the dagger also serves as a cross-reference to Part B of the following appendix, where the reader can consult additional notes on the division of such words.

End-of-Line Word-Division. The intended form of a compound must be inferred by editors or readers or both when the components of the compound are coincidentally printed in two lines with a hyphen at the end of the first. To record the editorial decisions about the exact forms of compounds the components of which could be divided in Brown's day and which happen to be hyphenated at a break between lines in the copy-text, Part A of this appendix lists such compounds, but omits mere compositorial syllabication (e.g., *judge-|ment, to-mor-|row*) and hyphenation joining capitalized elements in compounds (e.g., *North-|American*), about which there can be no ambiguity. As always, the reading listed is that of the established text, regardless of the lineation of the present edition, but nothing need follow it. If in a few rare cases the compound also is inadvertently hyphenated at the end of a line in the present edition, that fact is noted by printing before the page-line reference a double dagger (‡), which also serves as a cross-reference to Part B of this appendix.

Part B lists (in the same form as Part A) those compounds—and only those—that are intended to be hyphenated in the established text and that also happen to be divided and hyphenated between two lines in the present edition. Thus the absence of a word which is hyphenated and divided in the present edition implies that it should be read as unhyphenated in the established text, whereas the presence of a word in this list shows that it is a hyphenated compound in the established text. In all cases the reading may be regarded as identical with that of the copy-text as well as the established text, except when (1) the copy-text has been emended, or (2) the copy-text also has the word hyphenated and divided at the end of a line. A dagger (†) precedes the first type of exception and directs the reader to the List of Emendations; a double dagger (‡) precedes the second type, about which, necessarily, there has also been editorial decision, and refers the reader to Part A of this appendix.

Historical List of Substantive Variants. This appendix provides information on all substantive variation among the editions examined. Mere accidental variation is ignored. In a given entry, the reading in question is cited in the same manner as in the List of Emendations, but following the bracket appear only (1) the variants from the reading of the established text cited in the lemma and (2) the sigla for the editions in which the variants occur. Thus it is assumed that the editions consulted but not cited in a given note agree in reading with the established text (i.e., omission of sigla implies agreement). For example, in the following note,

beliefs] belief A2; relief E1-2

beliefs is the reading of the Bicentennial text and of the first American edition (A1, the copy-text), whereas the second American edition (A2) reads *belief.* The first English edition (E1) and its descendant, the second (E2), agree in reading *relief.*

The *Record of Collations and Copies Consulted* gives an account of the collation and other consultation of the textual documents which were performed in preparing this edition; this appendix also identifies the copies consulted.

Proof for this edition has been read at least five times and at least once by each of the editors involved. It has been checked in such a way as to ensure that no editorially unauthorized changes have been introduced by the printers after proofs have been pulled.

S.W.R.

WIELAND;
or
THE TRANSFORMATION
An American Tale

From Virtue's blissful paths away
The double-tongued are sure to stray;
Good is a forth-right journey still,
And mazy paths but lead to ill.

WIELAND;

OR THE

TRANSFORMATION.

AN

AMERICAN TALE.

From Virtue's blifsful paths away
The double-tongued are fure to ftray;
Good is a forth-right journey ftill,
And mazy paths but lead to ill.

COPY-RIGHT SECURED.

NEW-YORK:

Printed by T. & J. SWORDS, for H. CARITAT.
—1798.—

Title-page of the first edition of *Wieland*
Facsimile of a copy at Kent State University

ADVERTISEMENT

THE following Work is delivered to the world as the first of a series of performances, which the favorable reception of this will induce the Writer to publish. His purpose is neither selfish nor temporary, but aims at the illustration of some important branches of the moral constitution of man. Whether this tale will be classed with the ordinary or frivolous sources of amusement, or be ranked with the few productions whose usefulness secures to them a lasting reputation, the reader must be permitted to decide.

The incidents related are extraordinary and rare. Some of them, perhaps, approach as nearly to the nature of miracles as can be done by that which is not truly miraculous. It is hoped that intelligent readers will not disapprove of the manner in which appearances are solved, but that the solution will be found to correspond with the known principles of human nature. The power which the principal person is said to possess can scarcely be denied to be real. It must be acknowledged to be extremely rare; but no fact, equally uncommon, is supported by the same strength of historical evidence.

Some readers may think the conduct of the younger Wieland impossible. In support of its possibility the Writer must appeal to Physicians and to men conversant with the latent springs and occasional perversions of the human mind. It will not be objected that the instances of similar delusion are rare, because it is the business of moral painters to exhibit their subject in its most instructive and memorable forms. If history furnishes one parallel fact, it is a sufficient vindication of the Writer; but most readers will probably recollect an authentic case, remarkably similar to that of Wieland.

It will be necessary to add, that this narrative is addressed, in an epistolary form, by the Lady whose story it contains, to a small number of friends, whose curiosity, with regard to it, had been greatly awakened. It may likewise be mentioned, that these events took place between the conclusion of the French and the beginning of the revolutionary war. The memoirs of Carwin, alluded to at the conclusion of the work, will be published or suppressed according to the reception which is given to the present attempt.

C.B.B.

September 3, 1798.

WIELAND; OR THE TRANSFORMATION

CHAPTER I

I FEEL little reluctance in complying with your request. You know not fully the cause of my sorrows. You are a stranger to the depth of my distresses. Hence your efforts at consolation must necessarily fail. Yet the tale that I am going to tell is not intended as a claim upon your sympathy. In the midst of my despair, I do not disdain to contribute what little I can to the benefit of mankind. I acknowledge your right to be informed of the events that have lately happened in my family. Make what use of the tale you shall think proper. If it be communicated to the world, it will inculcate the duty of avoiding deceit. It will exemplify the force of early impressions, and show the immeasurable evils that flow from an erroneous or imperfect discipline.

My state is not destitute of tranquillity. The sentiment that dictates my feelings is not hope. Futurity has no power over my thoughts. To all that is to come I am perfectly indifferent. With regard to myself, I have nothing more to fear. Fate has done its worst. Henceforth, I am callous to misfortune.

I address no supplication to the Deity. The power that governs the course of human affairs has chosen his path. The decree that ascertained the condition of my life, admits of no recal. No doubt it squares with the maxims of eternal equity. That is neither to be questioned nor denied by me. It suffices that the past is exempt from mutation. The storm that tore up our happiness, and changed into dreariness

5

and desert the blooming scene of our existence, is lulled
into grim repose; but not until the victim was transfixed and
mangled; till every obstacle was dissipated by its rage; till
every remnant of good was wrested from our grasp and
exterminated.

How will your wonder, and that of your companions, be
excited by my story! Every sentiment will yield to your
amazement. If my testimony were without corroborations,
you would reject it as incredible. The experience of no
human being can furnish a parallel: That I, beyond the rest
of mankind, should be reserved for a destiny without allevi-
ation, and without example! Listen to my narrative, and
then say what it is that has made me deserve to be placed on
this dreadful eminence, if, indeed, every faculty be not
suspended in wonder that I am still alive, and am able to
relate it.

My father's ancestry was noble on the paternal side; but
his mother was the daughter of a merchant. My grand-
father was a younger brother, and a native of Saxony. He
was placed, when he had reached the suitable age, at a German college. During the vacations, he employed himself in
traversing the neighbouring territory. On one occasion it
was his fortune to visit Hamburg. He formed an acquaintance with Leonard Weise, a merchant of that city, and was
a frequent guest at his house. The merchant had an only
daughter, for whom his guest speedily contracted an affection; and, in spite of parental menaces and prohibitions, he,
in due season, became her husband.

By this act he mortally offended his relations. Thence-
forward he was entirely disowned and rejected by them.
They refused to contribute any thing to his support. All
intercourse ceased, and he received from them merely that
treatment to which an absolute stranger, or detested
enemy, would be entitled.

He found an asylum in the house of his new father, whose
temper was kind, and whose pride was flattered by this
alliance. The nobility of his birth was put in the balance
against his poverty. Weise conceived himself, on the whole,
to have acted with the highest discretion, in thus disposing

of his child. My grand-father found it incumbent on him to search out some mode of independent subsistence. His youth had been eagerly devoted to literature and music. These had hitherto been cultivated merely as sources of amusement. They were now converted into the means of gain. At this period there were few works of taste in the Saxon dialect. My ancestor may be considered as the founder of the German Theatre. The modern poet of the same name is sprung from the same family, and, perhaps, surpasses but little, in the fruitfulness of his invention, or the soundness of his taste, the elder Wieland. His life was spent in the composition of sonatas and dramatic pieces. They were not unpopular, but merely afforded him a scanty subsistence. He died in the bloom of his life, and was quickly followed to the grave by his wife. Their only child was taken under the protection of the merchant. At an early age he was apprenticed to a London trader, and passed seven years of mercantile servitude.

My father was not fortunate in the character of him under whose care he was now placed. He was treated with rigor, and full employment was provided for every hour of his time. His duties were laborious and mechanical. He had been educated with a view to this profession, and, therefore, was not tormented with unsatisfied desires. He did not hold his present occupations in abhorrence, because they withheld him from paths more flowery and more smooth, but he found in unintermitted labour, and in the sternness of his master, sufficient occasions for discontent. No opportunities of recreation were allowed him. He spent all his time pent up in a gloomy apartment, or traversing narrow and crowded streets. His food was coarse, and his lodging humble.

His heart gradually contracted a habit of morose and gloomy reflection. He could not accurately define what was wanting to his happiness. He was not tortured by comparisons drawn between his own situation and that of others. His state was such as suited his age and his views as to fortune. He did not imagine himself treated with extraordinary or unjustifiable rigor. In this respect he supposed the condition of others, bound like himself to mercantile service, to resemble his own; yet every engagement was irksome, and every hour tedious in its lapse.

In this state of mind he chanced to light upon a book written by one of the teachers of the Albigenses, or French Protestants. He entertained no relish for books, and was wholly unconscious of any power they possessed to delight or instruct. This volume had lain for years in a corner of his garret, half buried in dust and rubbish. He had marked it as it lay; had thrown it, as his occasions required, from one spot to another; but had felt no inclination to examine its contents, or even to inquire what was the subject of which it treated.

One Sunday afternoon, being induced to retire for a few minutes to his garret, his eye was attracted by a page of this book, which, by some accident, had been opened and placed full in his view. He was seated on the edge of his bed, and was employed in repairing a rent in some part of his clothes. His eyes were not confined to his work, but occasionally wandering, lighted at length upon the page. The words "Seek and ye shall find," were those that first offered themselves to his notice. His curiosity was roused by these so far as to prompt him to proceed. As soon as he finished his work, he took up the book and turned to the first page. The further he read, the more inducement he found to continue, and he regretted the decline of the light which obliged him for the present to close it.

The book contained an exposition of the doctrine of the sect of Camissards, and an historical account of its origin. His mind was in a state peculiarly fitted for the reception of devotional sentiments. The craving which had haunted him was now supplied with an object. His mind was at no loss for a theme of meditation. On days of business, he rose at the dawn, and retired to his chamber not till late at night. He now supplied himself with candles, and employed his nocturnal and Sunday hours in studying this book. It, of course, abounded with allusions to the Bible. All its conclusions were deduced from the sacred text. This was the fountain, beyond which it was unnecessary to trace the

8

stream of religious truth; but it was his duty to trace it thus
far.

A Bible was easily procured, and he ardently entered on
the study of it. His understanding had received a particular
direction. All his reveries were fashioned in the same
mould. His progress towards the formation of his creed was
rapid. Every fact and sentiment in this book were viewed
through a medium which the writings of the Camissard
apostle had suggested. His constructions of the text were
hasty, and formed on a narrow scale. Every thing was
viewed in a disconnected position. One action and one
precept were not employed to illustrate and restrict the
meaning of another. Hence arose a thousand scruples to
which he had hitherto been a stranger. He was alternately
agitated by fear and by ecstacy. He imagined himself beset
by the snares of a spiritual foe, and that his security lay in
ceaseless watchfulness and prayer.

His morals, which had never been loose, were now modelled by a stricter standard. The empire of religious duty
extended itself to his looks, gestures, and phrases. All
levities of speech, and negligences of behaviour, were pro-
scribed. His air was mournful and contemplative. He
laboured to keep alive a sentiment of fear, and a belief of
the awe-creating presence of the Deity. Ideas foreign to this
were sedulously excluded. To suffer their intrusion was a
crime against the Divine Majesty inexpiable but by days and
weeks of the keenest agonies.

No material variation had occurred in the lapse of two
years. Every day confirmed him in his present modes of
thinking and acting. It was to be expected that the tide of his
emotions would sometimes recede, that intervals of despondency and doubt would occur; but these gradually
were more rare, and of shorter duration; and he, at last,
arrived at a state considerably uniform in this respect.

His apprenticeship was now almost expired. On his arrival of age he became entitled, by the will of my grand-
father, to a small sum. This sum would hardly suffice to set
him afloat as a trader in his present situation, and he had
nothing to expect from the generosity of his master. Resi-

dence in England had, besides, become almost impossible, on account of his religious tenets. In addition to these motives for seeking a new habitation, there was another of the most imperious and irresistable necessity. He had imbibed an opinion that it was his duty to disseminate the truths of the gospel among the unbelieving nations. He was terrified at first by the perils and hardships to which the life of a missionary is exposed. This cowardice made him diligent in the invention of objections and excuses; but he found it impossible wholly to shake off the belief that such was the injunction of his duty. The belief, after every new conflict with his passions, acquired new strength; and, at length, he formed a resolution of complying with what he deemed the will of heaven.

The North-American Indians naturally presented themselves as the first objects for this species of benevolence. As soon as his servitude expired, he converted his little fortune into money, and embarked for Philadelphia. Here his fears were revived, and a nearer survey of savage manners once more shook his resolution. For a while he relinquished his purpose, and purchasing a farm on Schuylkill, within a few miles of the city, set himself down to the cultivation of it. The cheapness of land, and the service of African slaves, which were then in general use, gave him who was poor in Europe all the advantages of wealth. He passed fourteen years in a thrifty and laborious manner. In this time new objects, new employments, and new associates appeared to have nearly obliterated the devout impressions of his youth. He now became acquainted with a woman of a meek and quiet disposition, and of slender acquirements like himself. He proffered his hand and was accepted.

His previous industry had now enabled him to dispense with personal labour, and direct attention to his own concerns. He enjoyed leisure, and was visited afresh by devotional contemplation. The reading of the scriptures, and other religious books, became once more his favorite employment. His ancient belief relative to the conversion of the savage tribes, was revived with uncommon energy. To the former obstacles were now added the pleadings of parental and conjugal love. The struggle was long and vehement; but his sense of duty would not be stifled or enfeebled, and finally triumphed over every impediment.

His efforts were attended with no permanent success. His exhortations had sometimes a temporary power, but more frequently were repelled with insult and derision. In pursuit of this object he encountered the most imminent perils, and underwent incredible fatigues, hunger, sickness, and solitude. The licence of savage passion, and the artifices of his depraved countrymen, all opposed themselves to his progress. His courage did not forsake him till there appeared no reasonable ground to hope for success. He desisted not till his heart was relieved from the supposed obligation to persevere. With a constitution somewhat decayed, he at length returned to his family. An interval of tranquillity succeeded. He was frugal, regular, and strict in the performance of domestic duties. He allied himself with no sect, because he perfectly agreed with none. Social worship is that by which they are all distinguished; but this article found no place in his creed. He rigidly interpreted that precept which enjoins us, when we worship, to retire into solitude, and shut out every species of society. According to him devotion was not only a silent office, but must be performed alone. An hour at noon, and an hour at midnight were thus appropriated.

At the distance of three hundred yards from his house, on the top of a rock whose sides were steep, rugged, and encumbered with dwarf cedars and stony asperities, he built what to a common eye would have seemed a summer-house. The eastern verge of this precipice was sixty feet above the river which flowed at its foot. The view before it consisted of a transparent current, fluctuating and rippling in a rocky channel, and bounded by a rising scene of corn-fields and orchards. The edifice was slight and airy. It was no more than a circular area, twelve feet in diameter, whose flooring was the rock, cleared of moss and shrubs, and exactly levelled, edged by twelve Tuscan columns, and covered by an undulating dome. My father furnished the dimensions and outlines, but allowed the artist whom he employed to complete the structure on his own plan. It was without seat, table, or ornament of any kind.

This was the temple of his Deity. Twice in twenty-four hours he repaired hither, unaccompanied by any human being. Nothing but physical inability to move was allowed to obstruct or postpone this visit. He did not exact from his family compliance with his example. Few men, equally sincere in their faith, were as sparing in their censures and restrictions, with respect to the conduct of others, as my father. The character of my mother was no less devout; but her education had habituated her to a different mode of worship. The loneliness of their dwelling prevented her from joining any established congregation; but she was punctual in the offices of prayer, and in the performance of hymns to her Saviour, after the manner of the disciples of Zinzendorf. My father refused to interfere in her arrangements. His own system was embraced not, accurately speaking, because it was the best, but because it had been expressly prescribed to him. Other modes, if practised by other persons, might be equally acceptable.

His deportment to others was full of charity and mildness. A sadness perpetually overspread his features, but was unmingled with sternness or discontent. The tones of his voice, his gestures, his steps were all in tranquil unison. His conduct was characterised by a certain forbearance and humility, which secured the esteem of those to whom his tenets were most obnoxious. They might call him a fanatic and a dreamer, but they could not deny their veneration to his invincible candour and invariable integrity. His own belief of rectitude was the foundation of his happiness. This, however, was destined to find an end.

Suddenly the sadness that constantly attended him was deepened. Sighs, and even tears, sometimes escaped him. To the expostulations of his wife he seldom answered any thing. When he deigned to be communicative, he hinted that his peace of mind was flown, in consequence of deviation from his duty. A command had been laid upon him, which he had delayed to perform. He felt as if a certain period of hesitation and reluctance had been allowed him, but that this period was passed. He was no longer permitted to obey. The duty assigned to him was transferred, in consequence of his disobedience, to another, and all that remained was to endure the penalty.

He did not describe this penalty. It appeared to be nothing more for some time than a sense of wrong. This was sufficiently acute, and was aggravated by the belief that his offence was incapable of expiation. No one could contemplate the agonies which he seemed to suffer without the deepest compassion. Time, instead of lightening the burthen, appeared to add to it. At length he hinted to his wife, that his end was near. His imagination did not prefigure the mode or the time of his decease, but was fraught with an incurable persuasion that his death was at hand. He was likewise haunted by the belief that the kind of death that awaited him was strange and terrible. His anticipations were thus far vague and indefinite; but they sufficed to poison every moment of his being, and devote him to ceaseless anguish.

CHAPTER II

EARLY in the morning of a sultry day in August, he left Mettingen, to go to the city. He had seldom passed a day from home since his return from the shores of the Ohio. Some urgent engagements at this time existed, which would not admit of further delay. He returned in the evening, but appeared to be greatly oppressed with fatigue. His silence and dejection were likewise in a more than ordinary degree conspicuous. My mother's brother, whose profession was that of a surgeon, chanced to spend this night at our house. It was from him that I have frequently received an exact account of the mournful catastrophe that followed.

As the evening advanced, my father's inquietudes increased. He sat with his family as usual, but took no part in their conversation. He appeared fully engrossed by his own reflections. Occasionally his countenance exhibited tokens of alarm; he gazed stedfastly and wildly at the ceiling; and the exertions of his companions were scarcely sufficient to interrupt his reverie. On recovering from these fits, he expressed no surprize; but pressing his hand to his head, complained, in a tremulous and terrified tone, that his brain was scorched to cinders. He would then betray marks of insupportable anxiety.

My uncle perceived, by his pulse, that he was indisposed, but in no alarming degree, and ascribed appearances chiefly to the workings of his mind. He exhorted him to recollection and composure, but in vain. At the hour of repose he readily retired to his chamber. At the persuasion of my mother he even undressed and went to bed. Nothing could abate his restlessness. He checked her tender expostulations with some sternness. "Be silent," said he, "for that which I feel there is but one cure, and that will shortly come. You can help me nothing. Look to your own condition, and pray to God to strengthen you under the calamities that await you." "What am I to fear?" she answered. "What terrible disaster is it that you think of?" "Peace—as yet I know it not myself, but come it will, and shortly." She repeated her inquiries and doubts; but he suddenly put an end to the discourse, by a stern command to be silent.

She had never before known him in this mood. Hitherto all was benign in his deportment. Her heart was pierced with sorrow at the contemplation of this change. She was utterly unable to account for it, or to figure to herself the species of disaster that was menaced.

Contrary to custom, the lamp, instead of being placed on the hearth, was left upon the table. Over it against the wall there hung a small clock, so contrived as to strike a very hard stroke at the end of every sixth hour. That which was now approaching was the signal for retiring to the fane at which he addressed his devotions. Long habit had occasioned him to be always awake at this hour, and the toll was instantly obeyed.

Now frequent and anxious glances were cast at the clock. Not a single movement of the index appeared to escape his notice. As the hour verged towards twelve his anxiety visibly augmented. The trepidations of my mother kept pace with those of her husband; but she was intimidated into silence. All that was left to her was to watch every change of his features, and give vent to her sympathy in tears.

At length the hour was spent, and the clock tolled. The sound appeared to communicate a shock to every part of my father's frame. He rose immediately, and threw over himself a loose gown. Even this office was performed with difficulty, for his joints trembled, and his teeth chattered with dismay. At this hour his duty called him to the rock, and my mother naturally concluded that it was thither he

15

intended to repair. Yet these incidents were so uncommon, as to fill her with astonishment and foreboding. She saw him leave the room, and heard his steps as they hastily descended the stairs. She half resolved to rise and pursue him, but the wildness of the scheme quickly suggested itself. He was going to a place whither no power on earth could induce him to suffer an attendant.

The window of her chamber looked toward the rock. The atmosphere was clear and calm, but the edifice could not be discovered at that distance through the dusk. My mother's anxiety would not allow her to remain where she was. She rose, and seated herself at the window. She strained her sight to get a view of the dome, and of the path that led to it. The first painted itself with sufficient distinctness on her fancy, but was undistinguishable by the eye from the rocky mass on which it was erected. The second could be imperfectly seen; but her husband had already passed, or had taken a different direction.

What was it that she feared? Some disaster impended over her husband or herself. He had predicted evils, but professed himself ignorant of what nature they were. When were they to come? Was this night, or this hour to witness the accomplishment? She was tortured with impatience, and uncertainty. All her fears were at present linked to his person, and she gazed at the clock, with nearly as much eagerness as my father had done, in expectation of the next hour.

An half hour passed away in this state of suspence. Her eyes were fixed upon the rock; suddenly it was illuminated. A light proceeding from the edifice, made every part of the scene visible. A gleam diffused itself over the intermediate space, and instantly a loud report, like the explosion of a mine, followed. She uttered an involuntary shriek, but the new sounds that greeted her ear, quickly conquered her surprise. They were piercing shrieks, and uttered without intermission. The gleams which had diffused themselves far and wide were in a moment withdrawn, but the interior of the edifice was filled with rays.

The first suggestion was that a pistol was discharged, and

that the structure was on fire. She did not allow herself time to meditate a second thought, but rushed into the entry and knocked loudly at the door of her brother's chamber. My uncle had been previously roused by the noise, and instantly flew to the window. He also imagined what he saw to be fire. The loud and vehement shrieks which succeeded the first explosion, seemed to be an invocation of succour. The incident was inexplicable; but he could not fail to perceive the propriety of hastening to the spot. He was unbolting the door, when his sister's voice was heard on the outside conjuring him to come forth.

He obeyed the summons with all the speed in his power. He stopped not to question her, but hurried down stairs and across the meadow which lay between the house and the rock. The shrieks were no longer to be heard; but a blazing light was clearly discernible between the columns of the temple. Irregular steps, hewn in the stone, led him to the summit. On three sides, this edifice touched the very verge of the cliff. On the fourth side, which might be regarded as the front, there was an area of small extent, to which the rude staircase conducted you. My uncle speedily gained this spot. His strength was for a moment exhausted by his haste. He paused to rest himself. Meanwhile he bent the most vigilant attention towards the object before him.

Within the columns he beheld what he could no better describe, than by saying that it resembled a cloud impregnated with light. It had the brightness of flame, but was without its upward motion. It did not occupy the whole area, and rose but a few feet above the floor. No part of the building was on fire. This appearance was astonishing. He approached the temple. As he went forward the light retired, and, when he put his feet within the apartment, utterly vanished. The suddenness of this transition increased the darkness that succeeded in a tenfold degree. Fear and wonder rendered him powerless. An occurrence like this, in a place assigned to devotion, was adapted to intimidate the stoutest heart.

His wandering thoughts were recalled by the groans of one near him. His sight gradually recovered its power, and he was able to discern my father stretched on the floor. At that moment, my mother and servants arrived with a lanthorn, and enabled my uncle to examine more closely this scene. My father, when he left the house, besides a loose upper vest and slippers, wore a shirt and drawers. Now he was naked; his skin throughout the greater part of his body was scorched and bruised. His right arm exhibited marks as of having been struck by some heavy body. His clothes had been removed, and it was not immediately perceived that they were reduced to ashes. His slippers and his hair were untouched.

He was removed to his chamber, and the requisite attention paid to his wounds, which gradually became more painful. A mortification speedily shewed itself in the arm, which had been most hurt. Soon after, the other wounded parts exhibited the like appearance.

Immediately subsequent to this disaster, my father seemed nearly in a state of insensibility. He was passive under every operation. He scarcely opened his eyes, and was with difficulty prevailed upon to answer the questions that were put to him. By his imperfect account, it appeared, that while engaged in silent orisons, with thoughts full of confusion and anxiety, a faint gleam suddenly shot athwart the apartment. His fancy immediately pictured to itself, a person bearing a lamp. It seemed to come from behind. He was in the act of turning to examine the visitant, when his right arm received a blow from a heavy club. At the same instant, a very bright spark was seen to light upon his clothes. In a moment, the whole was reduced to ashes. This was the sum of the information which he chose to give. There was somewhat in his manner that indicated an imperfect tale. My uncle was inclined to believe that half the truth had been suppressed.

Meanwhile, the disease thus wonderfully generated, betrayed more terrible symptoms. Fever and delirium terminated in lethargic slumber, which, in the course of two hours, gave place to death. Yet not till insupportable exhalations and crawling putrefaction had driven from his chamber and the house every one whom their duty did not detain.

18

Such was the end of my father. None surely was ever more mysterious. When we recollect his gloomy anticipations and unconquerable anxiety; the security from human malice which his character, the place, and the condition of the times, might be supposed to confer; the purity and cloudlessness of the atmosphere, which rendered it impossible that lightning was the cause; what are the conclusions that we must form?

The prelusive gleam, the blow upon his arm, the fatal spark, the explosion heard so far, the fiery cloud that environed him, without detriment to the structure though composed of combustible materials, the sudden vanishing of this cloud at my uncle's approach—what is the inference to be drawn from these facts? Their truth cannot be doubted. My uncle's testimony is peculiarly worthy of credit, because no man's temper is more sceptical, and his belief is unalterably attached to natural causes.

I was at this time a child of six years of age. The impressions that were then made upon me, can never be effaced. I was ill qualified to judge respecting what was then passing; but as I advanced in age, and became more fully acquainted with these facts, they oftener became the subject of my thoughts. Their resemblance to recent events revived them with new force in my memory, and made me more anxious to explain them. Was this the penalty of disobedience? this the stroke of a vindictive and invisible hand? Is it a fresh proof that the Divine Ruler interferes in human affairs, meditates an end, selects and commissions his agents, and enforces, by unequivocal sanctions, submission to his will? Or, was it merely the irregular expansion of the fluid that imparts warmth to our heart and our blood, caused by the fatigue of the preceding day, or flowing, by established laws, from the condition of his thoughts?*

---

* A case, in its symptoms exactly parallel to this, is published in one of the Journals of Florence. See, likewise, similar cases reported by Messrs. Merille and Muraire, in the "Journal de Medicine," for February and May, 1783. The researches of Maffei and Fontana have thrown some light upon this subject.

CHAPTER III

THE shock which this disastrous occurrence occasioned to my mother, was the foundation of a disease which carried her, in a few months, to the grave. My brother and myself were children at this time, and were now reduced to the condition of orphans. The property which our parents left was by no means inconsiderable. It was entrusted to faithful hands, till we should arrive at a suitable age. Meanwhile, our education was assigned to a maiden aunt who resided in the city, and whose tenderness made us in a short time cease to regret that we had lost a mother.

The years that succeeded were tranquil and happy. Our lives were molested by few of those cares that are incident to childhood. By accident more than design, the indulgence and yielding temper of our aunt was mingled with resolution and stedfastness. She seldom deviated into either extreme of rigour or lenity. Our social pleasures were subject to no unreasonable restraints. We were instructed in most branches of useful knowledge, and were saved from the corruption and tyranny of colleges and boarding-schools.

Our companions were chiefly selected from the children of our neighbours. Between one of these and my brother, there quickly grew the most affectionate intimacy. Her name was Catharine Pleyel. She was rich, beautiful, and contrived to blend the most bewitching softness with the most exuberant vivacity. The tie by which my brother and she were united, seemed to add force to the love which I bore her, and which was amply returned. Between her and myself there was every circumstance tending to produce and foster friendship. Our sex and age were the same. We lived within sight of each other's abode. Our tempers were remarkably congenial, and the superintendants of our education not only prescribed to us the same pursuits, but allowed us to cultivate them together.

Every day added strength to the triple bonds that united us. We gradually withdrew ourselves from the society of others, and found every moment irksome that was not devoted to each other. My brother's advance in age made no change in our situation. It was determined that his profession should be agriculture. His fortune exempted him from the necessity of personal labour. The task to be performed by him was nothing more than superintendance. The skill that was demanded by this was merely theoretical, and was furnished by casual inspection, or by closet study. The attention that was paid to this subject did not seclude him for any long time from us, on whom time had no other effect than to augment our impatience in the absence of each other and of him. Our tasks, our walks, our music, were seldom performed but in each other's company.

It was easy to see that Catharine and my brother were born for each other. The passion which they mutually entertained quickly broke those bounds which extreme youth had set to it; confessions were made or extorted, and their union was postponed only till my brother had passed his minority. The previous lapse of two years was constantly and usefully employed.

O my brother! But the task I have set myself let me perform with steadiness. The felicity of that period was marred by no gloomy anticipations. The future, like the present, was serene. Time was supposed to have only new delights in store. I mean not to dwell on previous incidents longer than is necessary to illustrate or explain the great events that have since happened. The nuptial day at length arrived. My brother took possession of the house in which he was born, and here the long protracted marriage was solemnized.

My father's property was equally divided between us. A neat dwelling, situated on the bank of the river, three quarters of a mile from my brother's, was now occupied by me. These domains were called, from the name of the first possessor, Mettingen. I can scarcely account for my refusing to take up my abode with him, unless it were from a disposition to be an economist of pleasure. Self-denial, seasonably exercised, is one means of enhancing our gratifications. I was, beside, desirous of administering a fund, and regulating an household, of my own. The short distance allowed us to exchange visits as often as we pleased. The walk from one mansion to the other was no undelightful prelude to our interviews. I was sometimes their visitant, and they, as frequently, were my guests.

Our education had been modelled by no religious standard. We were left to the guidance of our own understanding, and the casual impressions which society might make upon us. My friend's temper, as well as my own, exempted us from much anxiety on this account. It must not be supposed that we were without religion, but with us it was the product of lively feelings, excited by reflection on our own happiness, and by the grandeur of external nature. We sought not a basis for our faith, in the weighing of proofs, and the dissection of creeds. Our devotion was a mixed and casual sentiment, seldom verbally expressed, or solicitously sought, or carefully retained. In the midst of present enjoyment, no thought was bestowed on the future. As a consolation in calamity religion is dear. But calamity was yet at a distance, and its only tendency was to heighten enjoyments which needed not this addition to satisfy every craving.

My brother's situation was somewhat different. His deportment was grave, considerate, and thoughtful. I will not say whether he was indebted to sublimer views for this disposition. Human life, in his opinion, was made up of changeable elements, and the principles of duty were not easily unfolded. The future, either as anterior, or subse-

22

quent to death, was a scene that required some preparation and provision to be made for it. These positions we could not deny, but what distinguished him was a propensity to ruminate on these truths. The images that visited us were blithsome and gay, but those with which he was most familiar were of an opposite hue. They did not generate affliction and fear, but they diffused over his behaviour a certain air of forethought and sobriety. The principal effect of this temper was visible in his features and tones. These, in general, bespoke a sort of thrilling melancholy. I scarcely ever knew him to laugh. He never accompanied the lawless mirth of his companions with more than a smile, but his conduct was the same as ours.

He partook of our occupations and amusements with a zeal not less than ours, but of a different kind. The diversity in our temper was never the parent of discord, and was scarcely a topic of regret. The scene was variegated, but not tarnished or disordered, by it. It hindered the element in which we moved from stagnating. Some agitation and concussion is requisite to the due exercise of human understanding. In his studies, he pursued an austerer and more arduous path. He was much conversant with the history of religious opinions, and took pains to ascertain their validity. He deemed it indispensable to examine the ground of his belief, to settle the relation between motives and actions, the criterion of merit, and the kinds and properties of evidence.

There was an obvious resemblance between him and my father, in their conceptions of the importance of certain topics, and in the light in which the vicissitudes of human life were accustomed to be viewed. Their characters were similar, but the mind of the son was enriched by science, and embellished with literature.

The temple was no longer assigned to its ancient use. From an Italian adventurer, who erroneously imagined that he could find employment for his skill, and sale for his sculptures in America, my brother had purchased a bust of Cicero. He professed to have copied this piece from an antique dug up with his own hands in the environs of

23

Modena. Of the truth of his assertions we were not qualified to judge; but the marble was pure and polished, and we were contented to admire the performance, without waiting for the sanction of connoisseurs. We hired the same artist to hew a suitable pedestal from a neighbouring quarry. This was placed in the temple, and the bust rested upon it. Opposite to this was a harpsichord, sheltered by a temporary roof from the weather. This was the place of resort in the evenings of summer. Here we sung, and talked, and read, and occasionally banqueted. Every joyous and tender scene most dear to my memory, is connected with this edifice. Here the performances of our musical and poetical ancestor were rehearsed. Here my brother's children received the rudiments of their education; here a thousand conversations, pregnant with delight and improvement, took place; and here the social affections were accustomed to expand, and the tear of delicious sympathy to be shed.

My brother was an indefatigable student. The authors whom he read were numerous, but the chief object of his veneration was Cicero. He was never tired of conning and rehearsing his productions. To understand them was not sufficient. He was anxious to discover the gestures and cadences with which they ought to be delivered. He was very scrupulous in selecting a true scheme of pronunciation for the Latin tongue, and in adapting it to the words of his darling writer. His favorite occupation consisted in embellishing his rhetoric with all the proprieties of gesticulation and utterance.

Not contented with this, he was diligent in settling and restoring the purity of the text. For this end, he collected all the editions and commentaries that could be procured, and employed months of severe study in exploring and comparing them. He never betrayed more satisfaction than when he made a discovery of this kind.

It was not till the addition of Henry Pleyel, my friend's only brother, to our society, that his passion for Roman eloquence was countenanced and fostered by a sympathy of tastes. This young man had been some years in Europe. We

24

had separated at a very early age, and he was now returned to spend the remainder of his days among us.

Our circle was greatly enlivened by the accession of a new member. His conversation abounded with novelty. His gaiety was almost boisterous, but was capable of yielding to a grave deportment, when the occasion required it. His discernment was acute, but he was prone to view every object merely as supplying materials for mirth. His conceptions were ardent but ludicrous, and his memory, aided, as he honestly acknowledged, by his invention, was an inexhaustible fund of entertainment.

His residence was at the same distance below the city as ours was above, but there seldom passed a day without our being favoured with a visit. My brother and he were endowed with the same attachment to the Latin writers; and Pleyel was not behind his friend in his knowledge of the history and metaphysics of religion. Their creeds, however, were in many respects opposite. Where one discovered only confirmations of his faith, the other could find nothing but reasons for doubt. Moral necessity, and calvinistic inspiration, were the props on which my brother thought proper to repose. Pleyel was the champion of intellectual liberty, and rejected all guidance but that of his reason. Their discussions were frequent, but, being managed with candour as well as with skill, they were always listened to by us with avidity and benefit.

Pleyel, like his new friends, was fond of music and poetry. Henceforth our concerts consisted of two violins, an harpsichord, and three voices. We were frequently reminded how much happiness depends upon society. This new friend, though, before his arrival, we were sensible of no vacuity, could not now be spared. His departure would occasion a void which nothing could fill, and which would produce insupportable regret. Even my brother, though his opinions were hourly assailed, and even the divinity of Cicero contested, was captivated with his friend, and laid aside some part of his ancient gravity at Pleyel's approach.

CHAPTER IV

SIX years of uninterrupted happiness had rolled away, since my brother's marriage. The sound of war had been heard, but it was at such a distance as to enhance our enjoyment by affording objects of comparison. The Indians were repulsed on the one side, and Canada was conquered on the other. Revolutions and battles, however calamitous to those who occupied the scene, contributed in some sort to our happiness, by agitating our minds with curiosity, and furnishing causes of patriotic exultation. Four children, three of whom were of an age to compensate, by their personal and mental progress, the cares of which they had been, at a more helpless age, the objects, exercised my brother's tenderness. The fourth was a charming babe that promised to display the image of her mother, and enjoyed perfect health. To these were added a sweet girl fourteen years old, who was loved by all of us, with an affection more than parental.

Her mother's story was a mournful one She had come hither from England, when this child was an infant, alone, without friends, and without money. She appeared to have embarked in a hasty and clandestine manner. She passed three years of solitude and anguish under my aunt's protection, and died a martyr to woe; the source of which she could, by no importunities, be prevailed upon to unfold. Her education and manners bespoke her to be of no mean birth. Her last moments were rendered serene, by the assurances she received from my aunt, that her daughter should experience the same protection that had been extended to herself.

On my brother's marriage, it was agreed that she should make a part of his family. I cannot do justice to the attractions of this girl. Perhaps the tenderness she excited might partly originate in her personal resemblance to her mother, whose character and misfortunes were still fresh in our remembrance. She was habitually pensive, and this circumstance tended to remind the spectator of her friendless condition; and yet that epithet was surely misapplied in this case. This being was cherished by those with whom she now resided, with unspeakable fondness. Every exertion was made to enlarge and improve her mind. Her safety was the object of a solicitude that almost exceeded the bounds of discretion. Our affection indeed could scarcely transcend her merits. She never met my eye, or occurred to my reflections, without exciting a kind of enthusiasm. Her softness, her intelligence, her equanimity, never shall I see surpassed. I have often shed tears of pleasure at her approach, and pressed her to my bosom in an agony of fondness.

While every day was adding to the charms of her person, and the stores of her mind, there occurred an event which threatened to deprive us of her. An officer of some rank, who had been disabled by a wound at Quebec, had employed himself, since the ratification of peace, in travelling through the colonies. He remained a considerable period at Philadelphia, but was at last preparing for his departure. No one had been more frequently honoured with his visits than Mrs. Baynton, a worthy lady with whom our family were intimate. He went to her house with a view to perform a farewell visit, and was on the point of taking his leave, when I and my young friend entered the apartment. It is impossible to describe the emotions of the stranger, when he fixed his eyes upon my companion. He was motionless with surprise. He was unable to conceal his feelings, but sat silently gazing at the spectacle before him. At length he turned to Mrs. Baynton, and more by his looks and gestures than by words, besought her for an explanation of the scene. He seized the hand of the girl, who, in her turn, was surprised by his behaviour, and drawing her forward, said in an eager and faultering tone, "Who is she? whence does she come? what is her name?"

The answers that were given only increased the confusion of his thoughts. He was successively told, that she was the daughter of one whose name was Louisa Conway, who arrived among us at such a time, who sedulously concealed her parentage, and the motives of her flight, whose incurable griefs had finally destroyed her, and who had left this child under the protection of her friends. Having heard the tale, he melted into tears, eagerly clasped the young lady in his arms, and called himself her father. When the tumults excited in his breast by this unlooked-for meeting were somewhat subsided, he gratified our curiosity by relating the following incidents.

Miss Conway was the only daughter of a banker in London, who discharged towards her every duty of an affectionate father. He had chanced to fall into her company, had been subdued by her attractions, had tendered her his hand, and been joyfully accepted both by parent and child. His wife had given him every proof of the fondest attachment. Her father, who possessed immense wealth, treated him with distinguished respect, liberally supplied his wants, and had made one condition of his consent to their union, a resolution to take up their abode with him.

They had passed three years of conjugal felicity, which had been augmented by the birth of this child, when his professional duty called him into Germany. It was not without an arduous struggle, that she was persuaded to relinquish the design of accompanying him through all the toils and perils of war. No parting was ever more distressful. They strove to alleviate, by frequent letters, the evils of their lot. Those of his wife, breathed nothing but anxiety for his safety, and impatience of his absence. At length, a new arrangement was made, and he was obliged to repair from Westphalia to Canada. One advantage attended this change. It afforded him an opportunity of meeting his family. His wife anticipated this interview, with no less rapture than himself. He hurried to London, and the moment he alighted from the stage-coach, ran with all speed to Mr. Conway's house.

It was an house of mourning. His father was overwhelmed with grief, and incapable of answering his inquiries. The servants, sorrowful and mute, were equally refractory. He explored the house, and called on the names of his wife and daughter, but his summons was fruitless. At length, this new disaster was explained. Two days before his arrival, his wife's chamber was found empty. No search, however diligent and anxious, could trace her steps. No cause could be assigned for her disappearance. The mother and child had fled away together.

New exertions were made, her chamber and cabinets were ransacked, but no vestige was found serving to inform them as to the motives of her flight, whether it had been voluntary or otherwise, and in what corner of the kingdom or of the world she was concealed. Who shall describe the sorrow and amazement of the husband? His restlessness, his vicissitudes of hope and fear, and his ultimate despair? His duty called him to America. He had been in this city, and had frequently passed the door of the house in which his wife, at that moment, resided. Her father had not remitted his exertions to elucidate this painful mystery, but they had failed. This disappointment hastened his death; in consequence of which, Louisa's father became possessor of his immense property.

This tale was a copious theme of speculation. A thousand questions were started and discussed in our domestic circle, respecting the motives that influenced Mrs. Stuart to abandon her country. It did not appear that her proceeding was involuntary. We recalled and reviewed every particular that had fallen under our own observation. By none of these were we furnished with a clue. Her conduct, after the most rigorous scrutiny, still remained an impenetrable secret. On a nearer view, Major Stuart proved himself a man of most amiable character. His attachment to Louisa appeared hourly to increase. She was no stranger to the sentiments suitable to her new character. She could not but readily embrace the scheme which was proposed to her, to return with her father to England. This scheme his regard for her induced him, however, to postpone. Some time was necessary to prepare her for so great a change and enable her to think without agony of her separation from us.

I was not without hopes of prevailing on her father entirely to relinquish this unwelcome design. Meanwhile, he pursued his travels through the southern colonies, and his daughter continued with us. Louisa and my brother frequently received letters from him, which indicated a mind of no common order. They were filled with amusing details, and profound reflections. While here, he often partook of our evening conversations at the temple; and since his departure, his correspondence had frequently supplied us with topics of discourse.

One afternoon in May, the blandness of the air, and brightness of the verdure, induced us to assemble, earlier than usual, in the temple. We females were busy at the needle, while my brother and Pleyel were bandying quotations and syllogisms. The point discussed was the merit of the oration for Cluentius, as descriptive, first, of the genius of the speaker; and, secondly, of the manners of the times. Pleyel laboured to extenuate both these species of merit, and tasked his ingenuity, to shew that the orator had embraced a bad cause; or, at least, a doubtful one. He urged, that to rely on the exaggerations of an advocate, or to make the picture of a single family a model from which to sketch the condition of a nation, was absurd. The controversy was suddenly diverted into a new channel, by a misquotation. Pleyel accused his companion of saying *"polliceatur"* when he should have said *"polliceretur."* Nothing would decide the contest, but an appeal to the volume. My brother was returning to the house for this purpose, when a servant met him with a letter from Major Stuart. He immediately returned to read it in our company.

Besides affectionate compliments to us, and paternal benedictions on Louisa, his letter contained a description of a waterfall on the Monongahela. A sudden gust of rain falling, we were compelled to remove to the house. The storm passed away, and a radiant moon-light succeeded.

30

There was no motion to resume our seats in the temple. We therefore remained where we were, and engaged in sprightly conversation. The letter lately received naturally suggested the topic. A parallel was drawn between the cataract there described, and one which Pleyel had discovered among the Alps of Glarus. In the state of the former, some particular was mentioned, the truth of which was questionable. To settle the dispute which thence arose, it was proposed to have recourse to the letter. My brother searched for it in his pocket. It was no where to be found. At length, he remembered to have left it in the temple, and he determined to go in search of it. His wife, Pleyel, Louisa, and myself, remained where we were.

In a few minutes he returned. I was somewhat interested in the dispute, and was therefore impatient for his return; yet, as I heard him ascending the stairs, I could not but remark, that he had executed his intention with remarkable dispatch. My eyes were fixed upon him on his entrance. Methought he brought with him looks considerably different from those with which he departed. Wonder, and a slight portion of anxiety were mingled in them. His eyes seemed to be in search of some object. They passed quickly from one person to another, till they rested on his wife. She was seated in a careless attitude on the sofa, in the same spot as before. She had the same muslin in her hand, by which her attention was chiefly engrossed.

The moment he saw her, his perplexity visibly increased. He quietly seated himself, and fixing his eyes on the floor, appeared to be absorbed in meditation. These singularities suspended the inquiry which I was preparing to make respecting the letter. In a short time, the company relinquished the subject which engaged them, and directed their attention to Wieland. They thought that he only waited for a pause in the discourse, to produce the letter. The pause was uninterrupted by him. At length Pleyel said, "Well, I suppose you have found the letter."

"No," said he, without any abatement of his gravity, and looking stedfastly at his wife, "I did not mount the hill."—"Why not?"—"Catherine, have you not moved from

31

that spot since I left the room?"—She was affected with the solemnity of his manner, and laying down her work, answered in a tone of surprise, "No; Why do you ask that question?"—His eyes were again fixed upon the floor, and he did not immediately answer. At length, he said, looking round upon us, "Is it true that Catharine did not follow me to the hill? That she did not just now enter the room?"—We assured him, with one voice, that she had not been absent for a moment, and inquired into the motive of his questions.

"Your assurances," said he, "are solemn and unanimous; and yet I must deny credit to your assertions, or disbelieve the testimony of my senses, which informed me, when I was half way up the hill, that Catharine was at the bottom."

We were confounded at this declaration. Pleyel rallied him with great levity on his behaviour. He listened to his friend with calmness, but without any relaxation of features.

"One thing," said he with emphasis, "is true; either I heard my wife's voice at the bottom of the hill, or I do not hear your voice at present."

"Truly," returned Pleyel, "it is a sad dilemma to which you have reduced yourself. Certain it is, if our eyes can give us certainty, that your wife has been sitting in that spot during every moment of your absence. You have heard her voice, you say, upon the hill. In general, her voice, like her temper, is all softness. To be heard across the room, she is obliged to exert herself. While you were gone, if I mistake not, she did not utter a word. Clara and I had all the talk to ourselves. Still it may be that she held a whispering conference with you on the hill; but tell us the particulars."

"The conference," said he, "was short; and far from being carried on in a whisper. You know with what intention I left the house. Half way to the rock, the moon was for a moment hidden from us by a cloud. I never knew the air to be more bland and more calm. In this interval I glanced at the temple, and thought I saw a glimmering between the columns. It was so faint, that it would not perhaps have been visible, if the moon had not been shrouded. I looked again, but saw nothing. I never visit this building alone, or at night, without being reminded of the fate of my father. There was nothing wonderful in this appearance; yet it suggested something more than mere solitude and darkness in the same place would have done.

"I kept on my way. The images that haunted me were solemn; and I entertained an imperfect curiosity, but no fear, as to the nature of this object. I had ascended the hill little more than half way, when a voice called me from behind. The accents were clear, distinct, powerful, and were uttered, as I fully believed, by my wife. Her voice is not commonly so loud. She has seldom occasion to exert it, but, nevertheless, I have sometimes heard her call with force and eagerness. If my ear was not deceived, it was her voice which I heard.

"'Stop, go no further. There is danger in your path.' The suddenness and unexpectedness of this warning, the tone of alarm with which it was given, and, above all, the persuasion that it was my wife who spoke, were enough to disconcert and make me pause. I turned and listened to assure myself that I was not mistaken. The deepest silence succeeded. At length, I spoke in my turn. 'Who calls? is it you, Catharine?' I stopped and presently received an answer. 'Yes, it is I; go not up; return instantly; you are wanted at the house.' Still the voice was Catharine's, and still it proceeded from the foot of the stairs.

"What could I do? The warning was mysterious. To be uttered by Catharine at a place, and on an occasion like these, enhanced the mystery. I could do nothing but obey. Accordingly, I trod back my steps, expecting that she waited for me at the bottom of the hill. When I reached the bottom, no one was visible. The moon-light was once more universal and brilliant, and yet, as far as I could see no human or moving figure was discernable. If she had returned to the house, she must have used wonderous expedition to have passed already beyond the reach of my eye. I exerted my voice, but in vain. To my repeated exclamations, no answer was returned.

"Ruminating on these incidents, I returned hither.

33

There was no room to doubt that I had heard my wife's voice; attending incidents were not easily explained; but you now assure me that nothing extraordinary has happened to urge my return, and that my wife has not moved from her seat."

Such was my brother's narrative. It was heard by us with different emotions. Pleyel did not scruple to regard the whole as a deception of the senses. Perhaps a voice had been heard; but Wieland's imagination had misled him in supposing a resemblance to that of his wife, and giving such a signification to the sounds. According to his custom he spoke what he thought. Sometimes, he made it the theme of grave discussion, but more frequently treated it with ridicule. He did not believe that sober reasoning would convince his friend, and gaiety, he thought, was useful to take away the solemnities which, in a mind like Wieland's, an accident of this kind was calculated to produce.

Pleyel proposed to go in search of the letter. He went and speedily returned, bearing it in his hand. He had found it open on the pedestal; and neither voice nor visage had risen to impede his design.

Catharine was endowed with an uncommon portion of good sense; but her mind was accessible, on this quarter, to wonder and panic. That her voice should be thus inexplicably and unwarrantably assumed, was a source of no small disquietude. She admitted the plausibility of the arguments by which Pleyel endeavoured to prove, that this was no more than an auricular deception; but this conviction was sure to be shaken, when she turned her eyes upon her husband, and perceived that Pleyel's logic was far from having produced the same effect upon him.

As to myself, my attention was engaged by this occurrence. I could not fail to perceive a shadowy resemblance between it and my father's death. On the latter event, I had frequently reflected; my reflections never conducted me to certainty, but the doubts that existed were not of a tormenting kind. I could not deny that the event was miraculous, and yet I was invincibly averse to that method of solution. My wonder was excited by the inscrutableness of the cause, but my wonder was unmixed with sorrow or fear. It begat in me a thrilling, and not unpleasing solemnity. Similar to these were the sensations produced by the recent adventure.

But its effect upon my brother's imagination was of chief moment. All that was desirable was, that it should be regarded by him with indifference. The worst effect that could flow, was not indeed very formidable. Yet I could not bear to think that his senses should be the victims of such delusion. It argued a diseased condition of his frame, which might show itself hereafter in more dangerous symptoms. The will is the tool of the understanding, which must fashion its conclusions on the notices of sense. If the senses be depraved, it is impossible to calculate the evils that may flow from the consequent deductions of the understanding.

I said, this man is of an ardent and melancholy character. Those ideas which, in others, are casual or obscure, which are entertained in moments of abstraction and solitude, and easily escape when the scene is changed, have obtained an immoveable hold upon his mind. The conclusions which long habit has rendered familiar, and, in some sort, palpable to his intellect, are drawn from the deepest sources. All his actions and practical sentiments are linked with long and abstruse deductions from the system of divine government and the laws of our intellectual constitution. He is, in some respects, an enthusiast, but is fortified in his belief by innumerable arguments and subtilties.

His father's death was always regarded by him as flowing from a direct and supernatural decree. It visited his meditations oftener than it did mine. The traces which it left were more gloomy and permanent. This new incident had a visible effect in augmenting his gravity. He was less disposed than formerly to converse and reading. When we sifted his thoughts, they were generally found to have a relation, more or less direct, with this incident. It was difficult to ascertain the exact species of impression which it made upon him. He never introduced the subject into conversation, and listened with a silent and half-serious smile to the satirical effusions of Pleyel.

One evening we chanced to be alone together in the temple. I seized that opportunity of investigating the state of his thoughts. After a pause, which he seemed in no wise inclined to interrupt, I spoke to him—"How almost palpable is this dark; yet a ray from above would dispel it." "Ay," said Wieland, with fervor, "not only the physical, but moral night would be dispelled." "But why," said I, "must the Divine Will address its precepts to the eye?" He smiled significantly. "True," said he, "the understanding has other avenues." "You have never," said I, approaching nearer to the point—"you have never told me in what way you considered the late extraordinary incident." "There is no determinate way in which the subject can be viewed. Here is an effect, but the cause is utterly inscrutable. To suppose a deception will not do. Such is possible, but there are twenty other suppositions more probable. They must all be set aside before we reach that point." "What are these twenty suppositions?" "It is needless to mention them. They are only less improbable than Pleyel's. Time may convert one of them into certainty. Till then it is useless to expatiate on them."

CHAPTER V

S OME time had elapsed when there happened another occurrence, still more remarkable. Pleyel, on his return from Europe, brought information of considerable importance to my brother. My ancestors were noble Saxons, and possessed large domains in Lusatia. The Prussian wars had destroyed those persons whose right to these estates precluded my brother's. Pleyel had been exact in his inquiries, and had discovered that, by the law of male-primogeniture, my brother's claims were superior to those of any other person now living. Nothing was wanting but his presence in that country, and a legal application to establish this claim.

Pleyel strenuously recommended this measure. The advantages, he thought, attending it were numerous, and it would argue the utmost folly to neglect them. Contrary to his expectation he found my brother averse to the scheme. Slight efforts, he, at first, thought would subdue his reluctance; but he found this aversion by no means slight. The interest that he took in the happiness of his friend and his sister, and his own partiality to the Saxon soil, from which he had likewise sprung, and where he had spent several years of his youth, made him redouble his exertions to win Wieland's consent. For this end he employed every argument that his invention could suggest. He painted, in attractive colours, the state of manners and government in that country, the security of civil rights, and the freedom of religious sentiments. He dwelt on the privileges of wealth and rank, and drew from the servile condition of one class, an argument in favor of his scheme, since the revenue and power annexed to a German principality afford so large a field for benevolence. The evil flowing from this power, in malignant hands, was proportioned to the good that would arise from the virtuous use of it. Hence, Wieland, in forbearing to claim his own, withheld all the positive felicity that would accrue to his vassals from his success, and hazarded all the misery that would redound from a less enlightened proprietor.

It was easy for my brother to repel these arguments, and to shew that no spot on the globe enjoyed equal security and liberty to that which he at present inhabited. That if the Saxons had nothing to fear from mis-government, the external causes of havoc and alarm were numerous and manifest. The recent devastations committed by the Prussians furnished a specimen of these. The horrors of war would always impend over them, till Germany were seized and divided by Austrian and Prussian tyrants; an event which he strongly suspected was at no great distance. But setting these considerations aside, was it laudable to grasp at wealth and power even when they were within our reach? Were not these the two great sources of depravity? What security had he, that in this change of place and condition, he should not degenerate into a tyrant and voluptuary? Power and riches were chiefly to be dreaded on account of their tendency to deprave the possessor. He held them in abhorrence, not only as instruments of misery to others, but to him on whom they were conferred. Besides, riches were comparative, and was he not rich already? He lived at present in the bosom of security and luxury. All the instruments of pleasure, on which his reason or imagination set any value, were within his reach. But these he must forego, for the sake of advantages which, whatever were their value, were as yet uncertain. In pursuit of an imaginary addition to his wealth, he must reduce himself to poverty, he must exchange present certainties for what was distant and contingent; for who knows not that the law is a system of expence, delay and uncertainty? If he should embrace this

38

scheme, it would lay him under the necessity of making a voyage to Europe, and remaining for a certain period, separate from his family. He must undergo the perils and discomforts of the ocean; he must divest himself of all domestic pleasures; he must deprive his wife of her companion, and his children of a father and instructor, and all for what? For the ambiguous advantages which overgrown wealth and flagitious tyranny have to bestow? For a precarious possession in a land of turbulence and war? Advantages, which will not certainly be gained, and of which the acquisition, if it were sure, is necessarily distant.

Pleyel was enamoured of his scheme on account of its instrinsic benefits, but, likewise, for other reasons. His abode at Leipsig made that country appear to him like home. He was connected with this place by many social ties. While there he had not escaped the amorous contagion. But the lady, though her heart was impressed in his favor, was compelled to bestow her hand upon another. Death had removed this impediment, and he was now invited by the lady herself to return. This he was of course determined to do, but was anxious to obtain the company of Wieland; he could not bear to think of an eternal separation from his present associates. Their interest, he thought, would be no less promoted by the change than his own. Hence he was importunate and indefatigable in his arguments and solicitations.

He knew that he could not hope for mine or his sister's ready concurrence in this scheme. Should the subject be mentioned to us, we should league our efforts against him, and strengthen that reluctance in Wieland which already was sufficiently difficult to conquer. He, therefore, anxiously concealed from us his purpose. If Wieland were previously enlisted in his cause, he would find it a less difficult task to overcome our aversion. My brother was silent on this subject, because he believed himself in no danger of changing his opinion, and he was willing to save us from any uneasiness. The mere mention of such a scheme and the possibility of his embracing it, he knew, would considerably impair our tranquillity.

One day, about three weeks subsequent to the mysterious call, it was agreed that the family should be my guests. Seldom had a day been passed by us, of more serene enjoyment. Pleyel had promised us his company, but we did not see him till the sun had nearly declined. He brought with him a countenance that betokened disappointment and vexation. He did not wait for our inquiries, but immediately explained the cause. Two days before a packet had arrived from Hamburgh, by which he had flattered himself with the expectation of receiving letters, but no letters had arrived. I never saw him so much subdued by an untoward event. His thoughts were employed in accounting for the silence of his friends. He was seized with the torments of jealousy, and suspected nothing less than the infidelity of her to whom he had devoted his heart. The silence must have been concerted. Her sickness, or absence, or death, would have increased the certainty of some one's having written. No supposition could be formed but that his mistress had grown indifferent, or that she had transferred her affections to another. The miscarriage of a letter was hardly within the reach of possibility. From Leipsig to Hamburgh, and from Hamburgh hither, the conveyance was exposed to no hazard.

He had been so long detained in America chiefly in consequence of Wieland's aversion to the scheme which he proposed. He now became more impatient than ever to return to Europe. When he reflected that, by his delays, he had probably forfeited the affections of his mistress, his sensations amounted to agony. It only remained, by his speedy departure, to repair, if possible, or prevent so intolerable an evil. Already he had half resolved to embark in this very ship which, he was informed, would set out in a few weeks on her return.

Meanwhile he determined to make a new attempt to shake the resolution of Wieland. The evening was somewhat advanced when he invited the latter to walk abroad with him. The invitation was accepted, and they left Catharine, Louisa and me, to amuse ourselves by the best means in our power. During this walk, Pleyel renewed the

40

subject that was nearest his heart. He re-urged all his former arguments, and placed them in more forcible lights.

They promised to return shortly; but hour after hour passed, and they made not their appearance. Engaged in sprightly conversation, it was not till the clock struck twelve that we were reminded of the lapse of time. The absence of our friends excited some uneasy apprehensions. We were expressing our fears, and comparing our conjectures as to what might be the cause, when they entered together. There were indications in their countenances that struck me mute. These were unnoticed by Catharine, who was eager to express her surprize and curiosity at the length of their walk. As they listened to her, I remarked that their surprize was not less than ours. They gazed in silence on each other, and on her. I watched their looks, but could not understand the emotions that were written in them.

These appearances diverted Catharine's inquiries into a new channel. What did they mean, she asked, by their silence, and by their thus gazing wildly at each other, and at her? Pleyel profited by this hint, and assuming an air of indifference, framed some trifling excuse, at the same time darting significant glances at Wieland, as if to caution him against disclosing the truth. My brother said nothing, but delivered himself up to meditation. I likewise was silent, but burned with impatience to fathom this mystery. Presently my brother and his wife, and Louisa, returned home. Pleyel proposed, of his own accord, to be my guest for the night. This circumstance, in addition to those which preceded, gave new edge to my wonder.

As soon as we were left alone, Pleyel's countenance assumed an air of seriousness, and even consternation, which I had never before beheld in him. The steps with which he measured the floor betokened the trouble of his thoughts. My inquiries were suspended by the hope that he would give me the information that I wanted without the importunity of questions. I waited some time, but the confusion of his thoughts appeared in no degree to abate. At length I mentioned the apprehensions which their unusual absence had occasioned, and which were increased by their behaviour since their return, and solicited an explanation. He stopped when I began to speak, and looked stedfastly at me. When I had done, he said, to me, in a tone which faultered through the vehemence of his emotions, "How were you employed during our absence?" "In turning over the Della Crusca dictionary, and talking on different subjects; but just before your entrance, we were tormenting ourselves with omens and prognosticks relative to your absence." "Catharine was with you the whole time?" "Yes." "But are you sure?" "Most sure. She was not absent a moment." He stood, for a time, as if to assure himself of my sincerity. Then, clenching his hands, and wildly lifting them above his head, "Lo," cried he, "I have news to tell you. The Baroness de Stolberg is dead!"

This was her whom he loved. I was not surprised at the agitations which he betrayed. But how was the information procured? How was the truth of this news connected with the circumstance of Catharine's remaining in our company? He was for some time inattentive to my questions. When he spoke, it seemed merely a continuation of the reverie into which he had been plunged.

"And yet it might be a mere deception. But could both of us in that case have been deceived? A rare and prodigious coincidence! Barely not impossible. And yet, if the accent be oracular—Theresa is dead. No, no," continued he, covering his face with his hands, and in a tone half broken into sobs, "I cannot believe it. She has not written, but if she were dead, the faithful Bertrand would have given me the earliest information. And yet if he knew his master, he must have easily guessed at the effect of such tidings. In pity to me he was silent.

"Clara, forgive me; to you, this behaviour is mysterious. I will explain as well as I am able. But say not a word to Catharine. Her strength of mind is inferior to your's. She will, besides, have more reason to be startled. She is Wieland's angel."

Pleyel proceeded to inform me, for the first time, of the scheme which he had pressed, with so much earnestness, on my brother. He enumerated the objections which had been made, and the industry with which he had endeavoured to confute them. He mentioned the effect upon his resolutions produced by the failure of a letter. "During our late walk," continued he, "I introduced the subject that was nearest my heart. I re-urged all my former arguments, and placed them in more forcible lights. Wieland was still refractory. He expatiated on the perils of wealth and power, on the sacredness of conjugal and parental duties, and the happiness of mediocrity.

"No wonder that the time passed, unperceived, away. Our whole souls were engaged in this cause. Several times we came to the foot of the rock; as soon as we perceived it, we changed our course, but never failed to terminate our circuitous and devious ramble at this spot. At length your brother observed, 'We seem to be led hither by a kind of fatality. Since we are so near, let us ascend and rest ourselves a while. If you are not weary of this argument we will resume it there.'

"I tacitly consented. We mounted the stairs, and drawing the sofa in front of the river, we seated ourselves upon it. I took up the thread of our discourse where we had dropped it. I ridiculed his dread of the sea, and his attachment to home. I kept on in this strain, so congenial with my disposition, for some time, uninterrupted by him. At length, he said to me, 'Suppose now that I, whom argument has not convinced, should yield to ridicule, and should agree that your scheme is eligible; what will you have gained? Nothing. You have other enemies beside myself to encounter. When you have vanquished me, your toil has scarcely begun. There are my sister and wife, with whom it will remain for you to maintain the contest. And trust me, they are adversaries whom all your force and stratagem will never subdue.' I insinuated that they would model themselves by his will: that Catharine would think obedience her duty. He answered, with some quickness, 'You mistake. Their concurrence is indispensable. It is not my custom to exact sacrifices of this kind. I live to be their protector and friend, and not their tyrant and foe. If my wife shall deem her happiness, and that of her children, most consulted by remaining where she is, here she shall remain.' 'But,' said I, 'when she knows your pleasure, will she not conform to it?' Before my friend had time to answer this question, a negative was clearly and distinctly uttered from another quarter. It did not come from one side or the other, from before us or behind. Whence then did it come? By whose organs was it fashioned?

"If any uncertainty had existed with regard to these particulars, it would have been removed by a deliberate and equally distinct repetition of the same monosyllable, 'No.' The voice was my sister's. It appeared to come from the roof. I started from my seat. 'Catharine,' exclaimed I, 'where are you?' No answer was returned. I searched the room, and the area before it, but in vain. Your brother was motionless in his seat. I returned to him, and placed myself again by his side. My astonishment was not less than his.

"'Well,' said he, at length, 'What think you of this? This is the self-same voice which I formerly heard; you are now convinced that my ears were well informed.'

"'Yes,' said I, 'this, it is plain, is no fiction of the fancy.' We again sunk into mutual and thoughtful silence. A recollection of the hour, and of the length of our absence, made me at last propose to return. We rose up for this purpose. In doing this, my mind reverted to the contemplation of my own condition. 'Yes,' said I aloud, but without particularly addressing myself to Wieland, 'my resolution is taken. I cannot hope to prevail with my friends to accompany me. They may doze away their days on the banks of Schuylkill, but as to me, I go in the next vessel; I will fly to her presence, and demand the reason of this extraordinary silence.'

"I had scarcely finished the sentence, when the same mysterious voice exclaimed, 'You shall not go. The seal of death is on her lips. Her silence is the silence of the tomb.' Think of the effects which accents like these must have had upon me. I shuddered as I listened. As soon as I recovered from my first amazement, 'Who is it that speaks?' said I, 'whence did you procure these dismal tidings?' I did not wait long for an answer. 'From a source that cannot fail. Be satisfied. She is dead.' You may justly be surprised, that, in the circumstances in which I heard the tidings, and notwithstanding the mystery which environed him by whom they were imparted, I could give an undivided attention to the facts, which were the subject of our dialogue. I eagerly inquired, when and where did she die? What was the cause of her death? Was her death absolutely certain? An answer was returned only to the last of these questions. 'Yes,' was pronounced by the same voice; but it now sounded from a greater distance, and the deepest silence was all the return made to my subsequent interrogatories.

"It was my sister's voice; but it could not be uttered by her; and yet, if not by her, by whom was it uttered? When we returned hither, and discovered you together, the doubt that had previously existed was removed. It was manifest that the intimation came not from her. Yet if not from her, from whom could it come? Are the circumstances attending the imparting of this news proof that the tidings are true? God forbid that they should be true."

Here Pleyel sunk into anxious silence, and gave me leisure to ruminate on this inexplicable event. I am at a loss to describe the sensations that affected me. I am not fearful of shadows. The tales of apparitions and enchantments did not possess that power over my belief which could even render them interesting. I saw nothing in them but ignorance and folly, and was a stranger even to that terror which is pleasing. But this incident was different from any that I had ever before known. Here were proofs of a sensible and intelligent existence, which could not be denied. Here was information obtained and imparted by means unquestionably super-human.

That there are conscious beings, beside ourselves, in existence, whose modes of activity and information surpass our own, can scarcely be denied. Is there a glimpse afforded us into a world of these superior beings? My heart was scarcely large enough to give admittance to so swelling a thought. An awe, the sweetest and most solemn that imagination can conceive, pervaded my whole frame. It forsook me not when I parted from Pleyel and retired to my chamber. An impulse was given to my spirits utterly incompatible with sleep. I passed the night wakeful and full of meditation. I was impressed with the belief of mysterious, but not of malignant agency. Hitherto nothing had occurred to persuade me that this airy minister was busy to evil rather than to good purposes. On the contrary, the idea of superior virtue had always been associated in my mind with that of superior power. The warnings that had thus been heard appeared to have been prompted by beneficent intentions. My brother had been hindered by this voice from ascending the hill. He was told that danger lurked in his path, and his obedience to the intimation had perhaps saved him from a destiny similar to that of my father.

Pleyel had been rescued from tormenting uncertainty, and from the hazards and fatigues of a fruitless voyage, by the same interposition. It had assured him of the death of his Theresa.

This woman was then dead. A confirmation of the tidings, if true, would speedily arrive. Was this confirmation to be deprecated or desired? By her death, the tie that attached him to Europe, was taken away. Henceforward every motive would combine to retain him in his native country, and we were rescued from the deep regrets that would accompany his hopeless absence from us. Propitious was the spirit that imparted these tidings. Propitious he would perhaps have been, if he had been instrumental in producing, as well as in communicating the tidings of her death. Propitious to us, the friends of Pleyel, to whom has thereby been secured the enjoyment of his society; and not unpropitious to himself; for though this object of his love be snatched away, is there not another who is able and willing to console him for her loss?

Twenty days after this, another vessel arrived from the same port. In this interval, Pleyel, for the most part, estranged himself from his old companions. He was become the prey of a gloomy and unsociable grief. His walks were limited to the bank of the Delaware. This bank is an artificial one. Reeds and the river are on one side, and a watery marsh on the other, in that part which bounded his lands, and which extended from the mouth of Hollander's creek

46

to that of Schuylkill. No scene can be imagined less enticing to a lover of the picturesque than this. The shore is deformed with mud, and incumbered with a forest of reeds. The fields, in most seasons, are mire; but when they afford a firm footing, the ditches by which they are bounded and intersected, are mantled with stagnating green, and emit the most noxious exhalations. Health is no less a stranger to those seats than pleasure. Spring and autumn are sure to be accompanied with agues and bilious remittents.

The scenes which environed our dwellings at Mettingen constituted the reverse of this. Schuylkill was here a pure and translucid current, broken into wild and ceaseless music by rocky points, murmuring on a sandy margin, and reflecting on its surface, banks of all varieties of height and degrees of declivity. These banks were chequered by patches of dark verdure and shapeless masses of white marble, and crowned by copses of cedar, or by the regular magnificence of orchards, which, at this season, were in blossom and were prodigal of odours. The ground which receded from the river was scooped into valleys and dales. Its beauties were enhanced by the horticultural skill of my brother, who bedecked this exquisite assemblage of slopes and risings with every species of vegetable ornament, from the giant arms of the oak to the clustering tendrils of the honey-suckle.

To screen him from the unwholesome airs of his own residence, it had been proposed to Pleyel to spend the months of spring with us. He had apparently acquiesced in this proposal; but the late event induced him to change his purpose. He was only to be seen by visiting him in his retirements. His gaiety had flown, and every passion was absorbed in eagerness to procure tidings from Saxony. I have mentioned the arrival of another vessel from the Elbe. He descried her early one morning as he was passing along the skirt of the river. She was easily recognized, being the ship in which he had performed his first voyage to Germany. He immediately went on board, but found no letters directed to him. This omission was, in some degree, compensated by meeting with an old acquaintance among the passengers, who had till lately been a resident in Leipsig. This person put an end to all suspense respecting the fate of Theresa, by relating the particulars of her death and funeral.

Thus was the truth of the former intimation attested. No longer devoured by suspense, the grief of Pleyel was not long in yielding to the influence of society. He gave himself up once more to our company. His vivacity had indeed been damped; but even in this respect he was a more acceptable companion than formerly, since his seriousness was neither incommunicative nor sullen.

These incidents, for a time, occupied all our thoughts. In me they produced a sentiment not unallied to pleasure, and more speedily than in the case of my friends were intermixed with other topics. My brother was particularly affected by them. It was easy to perceive that most of his meditations were tinctured from this source. To this was to be ascribed a design in which his pen was, at this period, engaged, of collecting and investigating the facts which relate to that mysterious personage, the Dæmon of Socrates.

My brother's skill in Greek and Roman learning was exceeded by that of few, and no doubt the world would have accepted a treatise upon this subject from his hand with avidity; but alas! this and every other scheme of felicity and honor, were doomed to sudden blast and hopeless extermination.

CHAPTER VI

I NOW come to the mention of a person with whose name the most turbulent sensations are connected. It is with a shuddering reluctance that I enter on the province of describing him. Now it is that I begin to perceive the difficulty of the task which I have undertaken; but it would be weakness to shrink from it. My blood is congealed: and my fingers are palsied when I call up his image. Shame upon my cowardly and infirm heart! Hitherto I have proceeded with some degree of composure, but now I must pause. I mean not that dire remembrance shall subdue my courage or baffle my design, but this weakness cannot be immediately conquered. I must desist for a little while.

I have taken a few turns in my chamber, and have gathered strength enough to proceed. Yet have I not projected a task beyond my power to execute? If thus, on the very threshold of the scene, my knees faulter and I sink, how shall I support myself, when I rush into the midst of horrors such as no heart has hitherto conceived, nor tongue related? I sicken and recoil at the prospect, and yet my irresolution is momentary. I have not formed this design upon slight grounds, and though I may at times pause and hesitate, I will not be finally diverted from it.

And thou, O most fatal and potent of mankind, in what terms shall I describe thee? What words are adequate to the just delineation of thy character? How shall I detail the means which rendered the secrecy of thy purposes unfathomable? But I will not anticipate. Let me recover if possible, a sober strain. Let me keep down the flood of passion that would render me precipitate or powerless. Let me stifle the agonies that are awakened by thy name. Let me, for a time, regard thee as a being of no terrible attributes. Let me tear myself from contemplation of the evils of which it is but too certain that thou wast the author, and limit my view to those harmless appearances which attended thy entrance on the stage.

One sunny afternoon, I was standing in the door of my house, when I marked a person passing close to the edge of the bank that was in front. His pace was a careless and lingering one, and had none of that gracefulness and ease which distinguish a person with certain advantages of education from a clown. His gait was rustic and aukward. His form was ungainly and disproportioned. Shoulders broad and square, breast sunken, his head drooping, his body of uniform breadth, supported by long and lank legs, were the ingredients of his frame. His garb was not ill adapted to such a figure. A slouched hat, tarnished by the weather, a coat of thick grey cloth, cut and wrought, as it seemed, by a country tailor, blue worsted stockings, and shoes fastened by thongs, and deeply discoloured by dust, which brush had never disturbed, constituted his dress.

There was nothing remarkable in these appearances; they were frequently to be met with on the road, and in the harvest field. I cannot tell why I gazed upon them, on this occasion, with more than ordinary attention, unless it were that such figures were seldom seen by me, except on the road or field. This lawn was only traversed by men whose views were directed to the pleasures of the walk, or the grandeur of the scenery.

He passed slowly along, frequently pausing, as if to examine the prospect more deliberately, but never turning his eye towards the house, so as to allow me a view of his countenance. Presently, he entered a copse at a small distance, and disappeared. My eye followed him while he remained in sight. If his image remained for any duration in my fancy after his departure, it was because no other object occurred sufficient to expel it.

I continued in the same spot for half an hour, vaguely, and by fits, contemplating the image of this wanderer, and drawing, from outward appearances, those inferences with respect to the intellectual history of this person, which experience affords us. I reflected on the alliance which commonly subsists between ignorance and the practice of agriculture, and indulged myself in airy speculations as to the influence of progressive knowledge in dissolving this alliance, and embodying the dreams of the poets. I asked why the plough and the hoe might not become the trade of every human being, and how this trade might be made conducive to, or, at least, consistent with the acquisition of wisdom and eloquence.

Weary with these reflections, I returned to the kitchen to perform some household office. I had usually but one servant, and she was a girl about my own age. I was busy near the chimney, and she was employed near the door of the apartment, when some one knocked. The door was opened by her, and she was immediately addressed with "Pry'thee, good girl, canst thou supply a thirsty man with a glass of buttermilk?" She answered that there was none in the house. "Aye, but there is some in the dairy yonder. Thou knowest as well as I, though Hermes never taught thee, that though every dairy be an house, every house is not a dairy." To this speech, though she understood only a part of it, she replied by repeating her assurances, that she had none to give. "Well then," rejoined the stranger, "for charity's sweet sake, hand me forth a cup of cold water." The girl said she would go to the spring and fetch it. "Nay, give me the cup, and suffer me to help myself. Neither manacled nor lame, I should merit burial in the maw of carrion crows, if I laid this task upon thee." She gave him the cup, and he turned to go to the spring.

I listened to this dialogue in silence. The words uttered by the person without, affected me as somewhat singular, but what chiefly rendered them remarkable, was the tone that accompanied them. It was wholly new. My brother's voice and Pleyel's were musical and energetic. I had fondly imagined, that, in this respect, they were surpassed by none. Now my mistake was detected. I cannot pretend to communicate the impression that was made upon me by these accents, or to depict the degree in which force and sweetness were blended in them. They were articulated with a distinctness that was unexampled in my experience. But this was not all. The voice was not only mellifluent and clear, but the emphasis was so just, and the modulation so impassioned, that it seemed as if an heart of stone could not fail of being moved by it. It imparted to me an emotion altogether involuntary and incontroulable. When he uttered the words "for charity's sweet sake," I dropped the cloth that I held in my hand, my heart overflowed with sympathy, and my eyes with unbidden tears.

This description will appear to you trifling or incredible. The importance of these circumstances will be manifested in the sequel. The manner in which I was affected on this occasion, was, to my own apprehension, a subject of astonishment. The tones were indeed such as I never heard before; but that they should, in an instant, as it were, dissolve me in tears, will not easily be believed by others, and can scarcely be comprehended by myself.

It will be readily supposed that I was somewhat inquisitive as to the person and demeanour of our visitant. After a moment's pause, I stepped to the door and looked after him. Judge my surprize, when I beheld the self-same figure that had appeared an half hour before upon the bank. My fancy had conjured up a very different image. A form, and attitude, and garb, were instantly created worthy to accompany such elocution; but this person was, in all visible respects, the reverse of this phantom. Strange as it may seem, I could not speedily reconcile myself to this disappointment. Instead of returning to my employment, I threw myself in a chair that was placed opposite the door, and sunk into a fit of musing.

My attention was, in a few minutes, recalled by the stranger, who returned with the empty cup in his hand. I had not thought of the circumstance, or should certainly have chosen a different seat. He no sooner shewed himself, than a confused sense of impropriety, added to the suddenness of the interview, for which, not having foreseen it, I had made no preparation, threw me into a state of the most painful embarrassment. He brought with him a placid brow; but no sooner had he cast his eyes upon me, than his face was as glowingly suffused as my own. He placed the cup upon the bench, stammered out thanks, and retired.

It was some time before I could recover my wonted composure. I had snatched a view of the stranger's countenance. The impression that it made was vivid and indelible. His cheeks were pallid and lank, his eyes sunken, his forehead overshadowed by coarse straggling hairs, his teeth large and irregular, though sound and brilliantly white, and his chin discoloured by a tetter. His skin was of coarse grain, and sallow hue. Every feature was wide of beauty, and the outline of his face reminded you of an inverted cone.

And yet his forehead, so far as shaggy locks would allow it to be seen, his eyes lustrously black, and possessing, in the midst of haggardness, a radiance inexpressibly serene and potent, and something in the rest of his features, which it would be in vain to describe, but which served to betoken a mind of the highest order, were essential ingredients in the portrait. This, in the effects which immediately flowed from it, I count among the most extraordinary incidents of my life. This face, seen for a moment, continued for hours to occupy my fancy, to the exclusion of almost every other image. I had purposed to spend the evening with my brother, but I could not resist the inclination of forming a sketch upon paper of this memorable visage. Whether my hand was aided by any peculiar inspiration, or I was deceived by my own fond conceptions, this portrait, though hastily executed, appeared unexceptionable to my own taste.

I placed it at all distances, and in all lights; my eyes were rivetted upon it. Half the night passed away in wakefulness and in contemplation of this picture. So flexible, and yet so stubborn, is the human mind. So obedient to impulses the most transient and brief, and yet so unalterably observant

53

of the direction which is given to it! How little did I then foresee the termination of that chain, of which this may be regarded as the first link?

Next day arose in darkness and storm. Torrents of rain fell during the whole day, attended with incessant thunder, which reverberated in stunning echoes from the opposite declivity. The inclemency of the air would not allow me to walk out. I had, indeed, no inclination to leave my apartment. I betook myself to the contemplation of this portrait, whose attractions time had rather enhanced than diminished. I laid aside my usual occupations, and seating myself at a window, consumed the day in alternately looking out upon the storm, and gazing at the picture which lay upon a table before me. You will, perhaps, deem this conduct somewhat singular, and ascribe it to certain peculiarities of temper. I am not aware of any such peculiarities. I can account for my devotion to this image no otherwise, than by supposing that its properties were rare and prodigious. Perhaps you will suspect that such were the first inroads of a passion incident to every female heart, and which frequently gains a footing by means even more slight, and more improbable than these. I shall not controvert the reasonableness of the suspicion, but leave you at liberty to draw, from my narrative, what conclusions you please.

Night at length returned, and the storm ceased. The air was once more clear and calm, and bore an affecting contrast to that uproar of the elements by which it had been preceded. I spent the darksome hours, as I spent the day, contemplative and seated at the window. Why was my mind absorbed in thoughts ominous and dreary? Why did my bosom heave with sighs, and my eyes overflow with tears? Was the tempest that had just past a signal of the ruin which impended over me? My soul fondly dwelt upon the images of my brother and his children, yet they only increased the mournfulness of my contemplations. The smiles of the charming babes were as bland as formerly. The same dignity sat on the brow of their father, and yet I thought of them with anguish. Something whispered that the happiness we at present enjoyed was set on mutable foundations.

Death must happen to all. Whether our felicity was to be subverted by it to-morrow, or whether it was ordained that we should lay down our heads full of years and of honor, was a question that no human being could solve. At other times, these ideas seldom intruded. I either forbore to reflect upon the destiny that is reserved for all men, or the reflection was mixed up with images that disrobed it of terror; but now the uncertainty of life occurred to me without any of its usual and alleviating accompaniments. I said to myself, we must die. Sooner or later, we must disappear for ever from the face of the earth. Whatever be the links that hold us to life, they must be broken. This scene of existence is, in all its parts, calamitous. The greater number is oppressed with immediate evils, and those, the tide of whose fortunes is full, how small is their portion of enjoyment, since they know that it will terminate.

For some time I indulged myself, without reluctance, in these gloomy thoughts; but at length, the dejection which they produced became insupportably painful. I endeavoured to dissipate it with music. I had all my grand-father's melody as well as poetry by rote. I now lighted by chance on a ballad, which commemorated the fate of a German Cavalier, who fell at the siege of Nice under Godfrey of Bouillon. My choice was unfortunate, for the scenes of violence and carnage which were here wildly but forcibly pourtrayed, only suggested to my thoughts a new topic in the horrors of war.

I sought refuge, but ineffectually, in sleep. My mind was thronged by vivid, but confused images, and no effort that I made was sufficient to drive them away. In this situation I heard the clock, which hung in the room, give the signal for twelve. It was the same instrument which formerly hung in my father's chamber, and which, on account of its being his workmanship, was regarded, by every one of our family, with veneration. It had fallen to me, in the division of his property, and was placed in this asylum. The sound awakened a series of reflections, respecting his death. I was not allowed to pursue them; for scarcely had the vibrations ceased, when my attention was attracted by a whisper, which, at first, appeared to proceed from lips that were laid close to my ear.

No wonder that a circumstance like this startled me. In the first impulse of my terror, I uttered a slight scream, and shrunk to the opposite side of the bed. In a moment, however, I recovered from my trepidation. I was habitually indifferent to all the causes of fear, by which the majority are afflicted. I entertained no apprehension of either ghosts or robbers. Our security had never been molested by either, and I made use of no means to prevent or counter-work their machinations. My tranquillity, on this occasion, was quickly retrieved. The whisper evidently proceeded from one who was posted at my bed-side. The first idea that suggested itself was, that it was uttered by the girl who lived with me as a servant. Perhaps, somewhat had alarmed her, or she was sick, and had come to request my assistance. By whispering in my ear, she intended to rouse without alarming me.

Full of this persuasion, I called; "Judith," said I, "is it you? What do you want? Is there any thing the matter with you?" No answer was returned. I repeated my inquiry, but equally in vain. Cloudy as was the atmosphere, and curtained as my bed was, nothing was visible. I withdrew the curtain, and leaning my head on my elbow, I listened with the deepest attention to catch some new sound. Meanwhile, I ran over in my thoughts, every circumstance that could assist my conjectures.

My habitation was a wooden edifice, consisting of two stories. In each story were two rooms, separated by an entry, or middle passage, with which they communicated by opposite doors. The passage, on the lower story, had doors at the two ends, and a stair-case. Windows answered to the doors on the upper story. Annexed to this, on the eastern side, were wings, divided, in like manner, into an upper and lower room; one of them comprized a kitchen, and chamber above it for the servant, and communicated, on both stories, with the parlour adjoining it below, and the chamber adjoining it above. The opposite wing is of smaller dimensions, the rooms not being above eight feet square.

The lower of these was used as a depository of household implements, the upper was a closet in which I deposited my books and papers. They had but one inlet, which was from the room adjoining. There was no window in the lower one, and in the upper, a small aperture which communicated light and air, but would scarcely admit the body. The door which led into this, was close to my bed-head, and was always locked, but when I myself was within. The avenues below were accustomed to be closed and bolted at nights.

The maid was my only companion, and she could not reach my chamber without previously passing through the opposite chamber, and the middle passage, of which, however, the doors were usually unfastened. If she had occasioned this noise, she would have answered my repeated calls. No other conclusion, therefore, was left me, but that I had mistaken the sounds, and that my imagination had transformed some casual noise into the voice of a human creature. Satisfied with this solution, I was preparing to relinquish my listening attitude, when my ear was again saluted with a new and yet louder whispering. It appeared, as before, to issue from lips that touched my pillow. A second effort of attention, however, clearly shewed me, that the sounds issued from within the closet, the door of which was not more than eight inches from my pillow.

This second interruption occasioned a shock less vehement than the former. I started, but gave no audible token of alarm. I was so much mistress of my feelings, as to continue listening to what should be said. The whisper was distinct, hoarse, and uttered so as to shew that the speaker was desirous of being heard by some one near, but, at the same time, studious to avoid being overheard by any other.

"Stop, stop, I say; madman as you are! there are better means than that. Curse upon your rashness! There is no need to shoot."

Such were the words uttered in a tone of eagerness and anger, within so small a distance of my pillow. What construction could I put upon them? My heart began to palpitate with dread of some unknown danger. Presently, another voice, but equally near me, was heard whispering in answer. "Why not? I will draw a trigger in this business, but perdition be my lot if I do more." To this, the first voice returned, in a tone which rage had heightened in a small degree above a whisper, "Coward! stand aside, and see me do it. I will grasp her throat; I will do her business in an instant; she shall not have time so much as to groan." What wonder that I was petrified by sounds so dreadful! Murderers lurked in my closet. They were planning the means of my destruction. One resolved to shoot, and the other menaced suffocation. Their means being chosen, they would forthwith break the door. Flight instantly suggested itself as most eligible in circumstances so perilous. I deliberated not a moment; but, fear adding wings to my speed, I leaped out of bed, and scantily robed as I was, rushed out of the chamber, down stairs, and into the open air. I can hardly recollect the process of turning keys, and withdrawing bolts. My terrors urged me forward with almost a mechanical impulse. I stopped not till I reached my brother's door. I had not gained the threshold, when, exhausted by the violence of my emotions, and by my speed, I sunk down in a fit.

How long I remained in this situation I know not. When I recovered, I found myself stretched on a bed, surrounded by my sister and her female servants. I was astonished at the scene before me, but gradually recovered the recollection of what had happened. I answered their importunate inquiries as well as I was able. My brother and Pleyel, whom the storm of the preceding day chanced to detain here, informing themselves of every particular, proceeded with lights and weapons to my deserted habitation. They entered my chamber and my closet, and found every thing in its proper place and customary order. The door of the closet was locked, and appeared not to have been opened in my absence. They went to Judith's apartment. They found her asleep and in safety. Pleyel's caution induced him to forbear alarming the girl; and finding her wholly ignorant of what had passed, they directed her to return to her chamber. They then fastened the doors, and returned.

My friends were disposed to regard this transaction as a

dream. That persons should be actually immured in this closet, to which, in the circumstances of the time, access from without or within was apparently impossible, they could not seriously believe. That any human beings had intended murder, unless it were to cover a scheme of pillage, was incredible; but that no such design had been formed, was evident from the security in which the furniture of the house and the closet remained.

I revolved every incident and expression that had occurred. My senses assured me of the truth of them, and yet their abruptness and improbability made me, in my turn, somewhat incredulous. The adventure had made a deep impression on my fancy, and it was not till after a week's abode at my brother's, that I resolved to resume the possession of my own dwelling.

There was another circumstance that enhanced the mysteriousness of this event. After my recovery it was obvious to inquire by what means the attention of the family had been drawn to my situation. I had fallen before I had reached the threshold, or was able to give any signal. My brother related, that while this was transacting in my chamber, he himself was awake, in consequence of some slight indisposition, and lay, according to his custom, musing on some favorite topic. Suddenly the silence, which was remarkably profound, was broken by a voice of most piercing shrillness, that seemed to be uttered by one in the hall below his chamber. "Awake! arise!" it exclaimed: "hasten to succour one that is dying at your door."

This summons was effectual. There was no one in the house who was not roused by it. Pleyel was the first to obey, and my brother overtook him before he reached the hall. What was the general astonishment when your friend was discovered stretched upon the grass before the door, pale, ghastly, and with every mark of death!

This was the third instance of a voice, exerted for the benefit of this little community. The agent was no less inscrutable in this, than in the former case. When I ruminated upon these events, my soul was suspended in wonder and awe. Was I really deceived in imagining that I heard the closet conversation? I was no longer at liberty to question the reality of those accents which had formerly recalled my brother from the hill; which had imparted tidings of the death of the German lady to Pleyel; and which had lately summoned them to my assistance.

But how was I to regard this midnight conversation? Hoarse and manlike voices conferring on the means of death, so near my bed, and at such an hour! How had my ancient security vanished! That dwelling, which had hitherto been an inviolate asylum, was now beset with danger to my life. That solitude, formerly so dear to me, could no longer be endured. Pleyel, who had consented to reside with us during the months of spring, lodged in the vacant chamber, in order to quiet my alarms. He treated my fears with ridicule, and in a short time very slight traces of them remained: but as it was wholly indifferent to him whether his nights were passed at my house or at my brother's, this arrangement gave general satisfaction.

CHAPTER VII

I WILL not enumerate the various inquiries and conjectures which these incidents occasioned. After all
our efforts, we came no nearer to dispelling the mist
in which they were involved; and time, instead of facilitat-
ing a solution, only accumulated our doubts.

In the midst of thoughts excited by these events, I was not
unmindful of my interview with the stranger. I related the
particulars, and shewed the portrait to my friends. Pleyel
recollected to have met with a figure resembling my description in the city; but neither his face or garb made the
same impression upon him that it made upon me. It was a
hint to rally me upon my prepossessions, and to amuse us
with a thousand ludicrous anecdotes which he had collected
in his travels. He made no scruple to charge me with being
in love; and threatened to inform the swain, when he met
him, of his good fortune.

Pleyel's temper made him susceptible of no durable impressions. His conversation was occasionally visited by
gleams of his ancient vivacity; but, though his impetuosity
was sometimes inconvenient, there was nothing to dread
from his malice. I had no fear that my character or dignity
would suffer in his hands, and was not heartily displeased
when he declared his intention of profiting by his first
meeting with the stranger to introduce him to our acquaintance.

Some weeks after this I had spent a toilsome day, and, as
the sun declined, found myself disposed to seek relief in a

walk. The river bank is, at this part of it, and for some considerable space upward, so rugged and steep as not to be easily descended. In a recess of this declivity, near the southern verge of my little demesne, was placed a slight building, with seats and lattices. From a crevice of the rock, to which this edifice was attached, there burst forth a stream of the purest water, which, leaping from ledge to ledge, for the space of sixty feet, produced a freshness in the air, and a murmur, the most delicious and soothing imaginable. These, added to the odours of the cedars which embowered it, and of the honey-suckle which clustered among the lattices, rendered this my favorite retreat in summer.

On this occasion I repaired hither. My spirits drooped through the fatigue of long attention, and I threw myself upon a bench, in a state, both mentally and personally, of the utmost supineness. The lulling sounds of the waterfall, the fragrance and the dusk combined to becalm my spirits, and, in a short time, to sink me into sleep. Either the uneasiness of my posture, or some slight indisposition molested my repose with dreams of no cheerful hue. After various incoherences had taken their turn to occupy my fancy, I at length imagined myself walking, in the evening twilight, to my brother's habitation. A pit, methought, had been dug in the path I had taken, of which I was not aware. As I carelessly pursued my walk, I thought I saw my brother, standing at some distance before me, beckoning and calling me to make haste. He stood on the opposite edge of the gulph. I mended my pace, and one step more would have plunged me into this abyss, had not some one from behind caught suddenly my arm, and exclaimed, in a voice of eagerness and terror, "Hold! hold!"

The sound broke my sleep, and I found myself, at the next moment, standing on my feet, and surrounded by the deepest darkness. Images so terrific and forcible disabled me, for a time, from distinguishing between sleep and wakefulness, and withheld from me the knowledge of my actual condition. My first panics were succeeded by the perturbations of surprize, to find myself alone in the open air, and immersed in so deep a gloom. I slowly recollected the incidents of the afternoon, and how I came hither. I could not estimate the time, but saw the propriety of returning with speed to the house. My faculties were still too confused, and the darkness too intense, to allow me immediately to find my way up the steep. I sat down, therefore, to recover myself, and to reflect upon my situation.

This was no sooner done, than a low voice was heard from behind the lattice, on the side where I sat. Between the rock and the lattice was a chasm not wide enough to admit a human body; yet, in this chasm he that spoke appeared to be stationed. "Attend! attend! but be not terrified."

I started and exclaimed, "Good heavens! what is that? Who are you?"

"A friend; one come, not to injure, but to save you; fear nothing."

This voice was immediately recognized to be the same with one of those which I had heard in the closet; it was the voice of him who had proposed to shoot, rather than to strangle, his victim. My terror made me, at once, mute and motionless. He continued, "I leagued to murder you. I repent. Mark my bidding, and be safe. Avoid this spot. The snares of death encompass it. Elsewhere danger will be distant; but this spot, shun it as you value your life. Mark me further; profit by this warning, but divulge it not. If a syllable of what has passed escape you, your doom is sealed. Remember your father, and be faithful."

Here the accents ceased, and left me overwhelmed with dismay. I was fraught with the persuasion, that during every moment I remained here, my life was endangered; but I could not take a step without hazard of falling to the bottom of the precipice. The path, leading to the summit, was short, but rugged and intricate. Even star-light was excluded by the umbrage, and not the faintest gleam was afforded to guide my steps. What should I do? To depart or remain was equally and eminently perilous.

In this state of uncertainty, I perceived a ray flit across the gloom and disappear. Another succeeded, which was stronger, and remained for a passing moment. It glittered on the shrubs that were scattered at the entrance, and gleam continued to succeed gleam for a few seconds, till they, finally, gave place to unintermitted darkness.

The first visitings of this light called up a train of horrors in my mind; destruction impended over this spot; the voice which I had lately heard had warned me to retire, and had menaced me with the fate of my father if I refused. I was desirous, but unable, to obey; these gleams were such as preluded the stroke by which he fell; the hour, perhaps, was the same—I shuddered as if I had beheld, suspended over me, the exterminating sword.

Presently a new and stronger illumination burst through the lattice on the right hand, and a voice, from the edge of the precipice above, called out my name. It was Pleyel. Joyfully did I recognize his accents; but such was the tumult of my thoughts that I had not power to answer him till he had frequently repeated his summons. I hurried, at length, from the fatal spot, and, directed by the lanthorn which he bore, ascended the hill.

Pale and breathless, it was with difficulty I could support myself. He anxiously inquired into the cause of my affright, and the motive of my unusual absence. He had returned from my brother's at a late hour, and was informed by Judith, that I had walked out before sun-set, and had not yet returned. This intelligence was somewhat alarming. He waited some time; but, my absence continuing, he had set out in search of me. He had explored the neighbourhood with the utmost care, but, receiving no tidings of me, he was preparing to acquaint my brother with this circumstance, when he recollected the summer-house on the bank, and conceived it possible that some accident had detained me there. He again inquired into the cause of this detention, and of that confusion and dismay which my looks testified.

I told him that I had strolled hither in the afternoon, that sleep had overtaken me as I sat, and that I had awakened a few minutes before his arrival. I could tell him no more. In the present impetuosity of my thoughts, I was almost dubious, whether the pit, into which my brother had endeavoured to entice me, and the voice that talked through the lattice, were not parts of the same dream. I remembered, likewise, the charge of secrecy, and the penalty denounced, if I should rashly divulge what I had heard. For these reasons, I was silent on that subject, and shutting myself in my chamber, delivered myself up to contemplation.

What I have related will, no doubt, appear to you a fable. You will believe that calamity has subverted my reason, and that I am amusing you with the chimeras of my brain, instead of facts that have really happened. I shall not be surprized or offended, if these be your suspicions. I know not, indeed, how you can deny them admission. For, if to me, the immediate witness, they were fertile of perplexity and doubt, how must they affect another to whom they are recommended only by my testimony? It was only by subsequent events, that I was fully and incontestibly assured of the veracity of my senses.

Meanwhile what was I to think? I had been assured that a design had been formed against my life. The ruffians had leagued to murder me. Whom had I offended? Who was there with whom I had ever maintained intercourse, who was capable of harbouring such atrocious purposes?

My temper was the reverse of cruel and imperious. My heart was touched with sympathy for the children of misfortune. But this sympathy was not a barren sentiment. My purse, scanty as it was, was ever open, and my hands ever active, to relieve distress. Many were the wretches whom my personal exertions had extricated from want and disease, and who rewarded me with their gratitude. There was no face which lowered at my approach, and no lips which uttered imprecations in my hearing. On the contrary, there was none, over whose fate I had exerted any influence, or to whom I was known by reputation, who did not greet me with smiles, and dismiss me with proofs of veneration; yet did not my senses assure me that a plot was laid against my life?

I am not destitute of courage. I have shewn myself deliberative and calm in the midst of peril. I have hazarded my own life, for the preservation of another, but now was I confused and panic-struck. I have not lived so as to fear death, yet to perish by an unseen and secret stroke, to be mangled by the knife of an assassin, was a thought at which I shuddered; what had I done to deserve to be made the victim of malignant passions?

But soft! was I not assured, that my life was safe in all places but one? And why was the treason limited to take effect in this spot? I was every where equally defenceless. My house and chamber were, at all times, accessible. Danger still impended over me; the bloody purpose was still entertained, but the hand that was to execute it, was powerless in all places but one!

Here I had remained for the last four or five hours, without the means of resistance or defence, yet I had not been attacked. A human being was at hand, who was conscious of my presence, and warned me hereafter to avoid this retreat. His voice was not absolutely new, but had I never heard it but once before? But why did he prohibit me from relating this incident to others, and what species of death will be awarded if I disobey?

He talked of my father. He intimated, that disclosure would pull upon my head, the same destruction. Was then the death of my father, portentous and inexplicable as it was, the consequence of human machinations? It should seem, that this being is apprised of the true nature of this event, and is conscious of the means that led to it. Whether it shall likewise fall upon me, depends upon the observance of silence. Was it the infraction of a similar command, that brought so horrible a penalty upon my father?

Such were the reflections that haunted me during the night, and which effectually deprived me of sleep. Next morning, at breakfast, Pleyel related an event which my disappearance had hindered him from mentioning the night before. Early the preceding morning, his occasions called him to the city; he had stepped into a coffee-house to while away an hour; here he had met a person whose appearance instantly bespoke him to be the same whose hasty visit I have mentioned, and whose extraordinary visage and tones had so powerfully affected me. On an attentive survey, however, he proved, likewise, to be one with whom my friend had had some intercourse in Europe. This authorised the liberty of accosting him, and after some conversation, mindful, as Pleyel said, of the footing which this stranger had gained in my heart, he had ventured to invite him to Mettingen. The invitation had been cheerfully accepted, and a visit promised on the afternoon of the next day.

This information excited no sober emotions in my breast. I was, of course, eager to be informed as to the circumstances of their ancient intercourse. When, and where had they met? What knew he of the life and character of this man?

In answer to my inquiries, he informed me that, three years before, he was a traveller in Spain. He had made an excursion from Valencia to Murviedro, with a view to inspect the remains of Roman magnificence, scattered in the environs of that town. While traversing the scite of the theatre of old Saguntum, he lighted upon this man, seated on a stone, and deeply engaged in perusing the work of the deacon Marti. A short conversation ensued, which proved the stranger to be English. They returned to Valencia together.

His garb, aspect, and deportment, were wholly Spanish. A residence of three years in the country, indefatigable attention to the language, and a studious conformity with the customs of the people, had made him indistinguishable from a native, when he chose to assume that character. Pleyel found him to be connected, on the footing of friendship and respect, with many eminent merchants in that city. He had embraced the catholic religion, and adopted a Spanish name instead of his own, which was CARWIN, and devoted himself to the literature and religion of his new country. He pursued no profession, but subsisted on remittances from England.

While Pleyel remained in Valencia, Carwin betrayed no aversion to intercourse, and the former found no small attractions in the society of this new acquaintance. On general topics he was highly intelligent and communicative. He had visited every corner of Spain, and could furnish the most accurate details respecting its ancient and present state. On topics of religion and of his own history, previous to his *transformation* into a Spaniard, he was invariably silent. You could merely gather from his discourse that he was English, and that he was well acquainted with the neighbouring countries.

His character excited considerable curiosity in this observer. It was not easy to reconcile his conversion to the Romish faith, with those proofs of knowledge and capacity that were exhibited by him on different occasions. A suspicion was, sometimes, admitted, that his belief was counterfeited for some political purpose. The most careful observation, however, produced no discovery. His manners were, at all times, harmless and inartificial, and his habits those of a lover of contemplation and seclusion. He appeared to have contracted an affection for Pleyel, who was not slow to return it.

My friend, after a month's residence in this city, returned into France, and, since that period, had heard nothing concerning Carwin till his appearance at Mettingen.

On this occasion Carwin had received Pleyel's greeting with a certain distance and solemnity to which the latter had not been accustomed. He had waved noticing the inquiries of Pleyel respecting his desertion of Spain, in which he had formerly declared that it was his purpose to spend his life. He had assiduously diverted the attention of the latter to indifferent topics, but was still, on every theme, as eloquent and judicious as formerly. Why he had assumed the garb of a rustic, Pleyel was unable to conjecture. Perhaps it might be poverty, perhaps he was swayed by motives which it was his interest to conceal, but which were connected with consequences of the utmost moment.

Such was the sum of my friend's information. I was not sorry to be left alone during the greater part of this day. Every employment was irksome which did not leave me at liberty to meditate. I had now a new subject on which to exercise my thoughts. Before evening I should be ushered into his presence, and listen to those tones whose magical and thrilling power I had already experienced. But with what new images would he then be accompanied?

Carwin was an adherent to the Romish faith, yet was an Englishman by birth, and, perhaps, a protestant by education. He had adopted Spain for his country, and had intimated a design to spend his days there, yet now was an inhabitant of this district, and disguised by the habiliments of a clown! What could have obliterated the impressions of his youth, and made him abjure his religion and his country? What subsequent events had introduced so total a change in his plans? In withdrawing from Spain, had he reverted to the religion of his ancestors; or was it true, that his former conversion was deceitful, and that his conduct had been swayed by motives which it was prudent to conceal?

Hours were consumed in revolving these ideas. My meditations were intense; and, when the series was broken, I began to reflect with astonishment on my situation. From the death of my parents, till the commencement of this year, my life had been serene and blissful, beyond the ordinary portion of humanity; but, now, my bosom was corroded by anxiety. I was visited by dread of unknown dangers, and the future was a scene over which clouds rolled, and thunders muttered. I compared the cause with the effect, and they seemed disproportioned to each other. All unaware, and in a manner which I had no power to explain, I was pushed from my immoveable and lofty station, and cast upon a sea of troubles.

I determined to be my brother's visitant on this evening, yet my resolves were not unattended with wavering and reluctance. Pleyel's insinuations that I was in love, affected, in no degree, my belief, yet the consciousness that this was the opinion of one who would, probably, be present at our introduction to each other, would excite all that confusion which the passion itself is apt to produce. This would confirm him in his error, and call forth new railleries. His mirth, when exerted upon this topic, was the source of the bitterest vexation. Had he been aware of its influence upon my happiness, his temper would not have allowed him to persist; but this influence, it was my chief endeavour to conceal. That the belief of my having bestowed my heart upon another, produced in my friend none but ludicrous sensations, was the true cause of my distress; but if this had been discovered by him, my distress would have been unspeakably aggravated.

CHAPTER VIII

AS soon as evening arrived, I performed my visit. Carwin made one of the company, into which I was ushered. Appearances were the same as when I before beheld him. His garb was equally negligent and rustic. I gazed upon his countenance with new curiosity. My situation was such as to enable me to bestow upon it a deliberate examination. Viewed at more leisure, it lost none of its wonderful properties. I could not deny my homage to the intelligence expressed in it, but was wholly uncertain, whether he were an object to be dreaded or adored, and whether his powers had been exerted to evil or to good.

He was sparing in discourse; but whatever he said was pregnant with meaning, and uttered with rectitude of articulation, and force of emphasis, of which I had entertained no conception previously to my knowledge of him. Notwithstanding the uncouthness of his garb, his manners were not unpolished. All topics were handled by him with skill, and without pedantry or affectation. He uttered no sentiment calculated to produce a disadvantageous impression: on the contrary, his observations denoted a mind alive to every generous and heroic feeling. They were introduced without parade, and accompanied with that degree of earnestness which indicates sincerity.

He parted from us not till late, refusing an invitation to spend the night here, but readily consented to repeat his visit. His visits were frequently repeated. Each day introduced us to a more intimate acquaintance with his sentiments, but left us wholly in the dark, concerning that about which we were most inquisitive. He studiously avoided all mention of his past or present situation. Even the place of his abode in the city he concealed from us.

Our sphere, in this respect, being somewhat limited, and the intellectual endowments of this man being indisputably great, his deportment was more diligently marked, and copiously commented on by us, than you, perhaps, will think the circumstances warranted. Not a gesture, or glance, or accent, that was not, in our private assemblies, discussed, and inferences deduced from it. It may well be thought that he modelled his behaviour by an uncommon standard, when, with all our opportunities and accuracy of observation, we were able, for a long time, to gather no satisfactory information. He afforded us no ground on which to build even a plausible conjecture.

There is a degree of familiarity which takes place between constant associates, that justifies the negligence of many rules of which, in an earlier period of their intercourse, politeness requires the exact observance. Inquiries into our condition are allowable when they are prompted by a disinterested concern for our welfare; and this solicitude is not only pardonable, but may justly be demanded from those who chuse us for their companions. This state of things was more slow to arrive on this occasion than on most others, on account of the gravity and loftiness of this man's behaviour.

Pleyel, however, began, at length, to employ regular means for this end. He occasionally alluded to the circumstances in which they had formerly met, and remarked the incongruousness between the religion and habits of a Spaniard, with those of a native of Britain. He expressed his astonishment at meeting our guest in this corner of the globe, especially as, when they parted in Spain, he was taught to believe that Carwin should never leave that country. He insinuated, that a change so great must have been prompted by motives of a singular and momentous kind.

No answer, or an answer wide of the purpose, was generally made to these insinuations. Britons and Spaniards, he said, are votaries of the same Deity, and square their faith by the same precepts; their ideas are drawn from the same fountains of literature, and they speak dialects of the same tongue; their government and laws have more resemblances than differences; they were formerly provinces of the same civil, and till lately, of the same religious, Empire.

As to the motives which induce men to change the place of their abode, these must unavoidably be fleeting and mutable. If not bound to one spot by conjugal or parental ties, or by the nature of that employment to which we are indebted for subsistence, the inducements to change are far more numerous and powerful, than opposite inducements.

He spoke as if desirous of shewing that he was not aware of the tendency of Pleyel's remarks; yet, certain tokens were apparent, that proved him by no means wanting in penetration. These tokens were to be read in his countenance, and not in his words. When any thing was said, indicating curiosity in us, the gloom of his countenance was deepened, his eyes sunk to the ground, and his wonted air was not resumed without visible struggle. Hence, it was obvious to infer, that some incidents of his life were reflected on by him with regret; and that, since these incidents were carefully concealed, and even that regret which flowed from them laboriously stifled, they had not been merely disastrous. The secrecy that was observed appeared not designed to provoke or baffle the inquisitive, but was prompted by the shame, or by the prudence of guilt.

These ideas, which were adopted by Pleyel and my brother, as well as myself, hindered us from employing more direct means for accomplishing our wishes. Questions might have been put in such terms, that no room should be left for the pretence of misapprehension, and if modesty merely had been the obstacle, such questions would not have been wanting; but we considered, that, if the disclosure were productive of pain or disgrace, it was inhuman to extort it.

Amidst the various topics that were discussed in his presence, allusions were, of course, made to the inexplicable events that had lately happened. At those times, the words and looks of this man were objects of my particular attention. The subject was extraordinary; and any one whose experience or reflections could throw any light upon it, was entitled to my gratitude. As this man was enlightened by reading and travel, I listened with eagerness to the remarks which he should make.

At first, I entertained a kind of apprehension, that the tale would be heard by him with incredulity and secret ridicule. I had formerly heard stories that resembled this in some of their mysterious circumstances, but they were, commonly, heard by me with contempt. I was doubtful, whether the same impression would not now be made on the mind of our guest; but I was mistaken in my fears.

He heard them with seriousness, and without any marks either of surprize or incredulity. He pursued, with visible pleasure, that kind of disquisition which was naturally suggested by them. His fancy was eminently vigorous and prolific, and if he did not persuade us, that human beings are, sometimes, admitted to a sensible intercourse with the author of nature, he, at least, won over our inclination to the cause. He merely deduced, from his own reasonings, that such intercourse was probable; but confessed that, though he was acquainted with many instances somewhat similar to those which had been related by us, none of them were perfectly exempted from the suspicion of human agency.

On being requested to relate these instances, he amused us with many curious details. His narratives were constructed with so much skill, and rehearsed with so much energy, that all the effects of a dramatic exhibition were frequently produced by them. Those that were most coherent and most minute, and, of consequence, least entitled to credit, were yet rendered probable by the exquisite art of this rhetorician. For every difficulty that was suggested, a ready and plausible solution was furnished. Mysterious voices had always a share in producing the catastrophe, but they were always to be explained on some known principles, either as reflected into a focus, or communicated through a tube. I could not but remark that his narratives, however complex or marvellous, contained no instance sufficiently parallel to those that had befallen ourselves, and in which the solution was applicable to our own case.

My brother was a much more sanguine reasoner than our guest. Even in some of the facts which were related by Carwin, he maintained the probability of celestial interference, when the latter was disposed to deny it, and had found, as he imagined, footsteps of an human agent. Pleyel was by no means equally credulous. He scrupled not to deny faith to any testimony but that of his senses, and allowed the facts which had lately been supported by this testimony, not to mould his belief, but merely to give birth to doubts.

It was soon observed that Carwin adopted, in some degree, a similar distinction. A tale of this kind, related by others, he would believe, provided it was explicable upon known principles; but that such notices were actually communicated by beings of an higher order, he would believe only when his own ears were assailed in a manner which could not be otherwise accounted for. Civility forbad him to contradict my brother or myself, but his understanding refused to acquiesce in our testimony. Besides, he was disposed to question whether the voices heard in the temple, at the foot of the hill, and in my closet, were not really uttered by human organs. On this supposition he was desired to explain how the effect was produced.

He answered, that the power of mimickry was very common. Catharine's voice might easily be imitated by one at the foot of the hill, who would find no difficulty in eluding, by flight, the search of Wieland. The tidings of the death of the Saxon lady were uttered by one near at hand, who overheard the conversation, who conjectured her death, and whose conjecture happened to accord with the truth. That the voice appeared to come from the cieling was to be considered as an illusion of the fancy. The cry for help, heard in the hall on the night of my adventure, was to be ascribed to an human creature, who actually stood in the hall when he uttered it. It was of no moment, he said, that we could not explain by what motives he that made the signal was led hither. How imperfectly acquainted were we with the condition and designs of the beings that surrounded us? The city was near at hand, and thousands might there exist whose powers and purposes might easily explain whatever was mysterious in this transaction. As to the closet dialogue, he was obliged to adopt one of two suppositions, and affirm either that it was fashioned in my own fancy, or that it actually took place between two persons in the closet.

Such was Carwin's mode of explaining these appearances. It is such, perhaps, as would commend itself as most plausible to the most sagacious minds, but it was insufficient to impart conviction to us. As to the treason that was meditated against me, it was doubtless just to conclude that it was either real or imaginary; but that it was real was attested by the mysterious warning in the summer-house, the secret of which I had hitherto locked up in my own breast.

A month passed away in this kind of intercourse. As to Carwin, our ignorance was in no degree enlightened respecting his genuine character and views. Appearances were uniform. No man possessed a larger store of knowledge, or a greater degree of skill in the communication of it to others: Hence he was regarded as an inestimable addition to our society. Considering the distance of my brother's house from the city, he was frequently prevailed upon to pass the night where he spent the evening. Two days seldom elapsed without a visit from him; hence he was regarded as a kind of inmate of the house. He entered and departed without ceremony. When he arrived he received an unaffected welcome, and when he chose to retire, no importunities were used to induce him to remain.

The temple was the principal scene of our social enjoyments; yet the felicity that we tasted when assembled in this asylum, was but the gleam of a former sun-shine. Carwin never parted with his gravity. The inscrutableness of his character, and the uncertainty whether his fellowship tended to good or to evil, were seldom absent from our minds. This circumstance powerfully contributed to sadden us.

My heart was the seat of growing disquietudes. This change in one who had formerly been characterized by all the exuberances of soul, could not fail to be remarked by my friends. My brother was always a pattern of solemnity. My sister was clay, moulded by the circumstances in which she happened to be placed. There was but one whose deportment remains to be described as being of importance to our happiness. Had Pleyel likewise dismissed his vivacity?

He was as whimsical and jestful as ever, but he was not happy. The truth, in this respect, was of too much importance to me not to make me a vigilant observer. His mirth was easily perceived to be the fruit of exertion. When his thoughts wandered from the company, an air of dissatisfaction and impatience stole across his features. Even the punctuality and frequency of his visits were somewhat lessened. It may be supposed that my own uneasiness was heightened by these tokens; but, strange as it may seem, I found, in the present state of my mind, no relief but in the persuasion that Pleyel was unhappy.

That unhappiness, indeed, depended, for its value, in my eyes, on the cause that produced it. It did not arise from the death of the Saxon lady: it was not a contagious emanation from the countenances of Wieland or Carwin. There was but one other source whence it could flow. A nameless ecstacy thrilled through my frame when any new proof occurred that the ambiguousness of my behaviour was the cause.

CHAPTER IX

MY brother had received a new book from Germany. It was a tragedy, and the first attempt of a Saxon poet, of whom my brother had been taught to entertain the highest expectations. The exploits of Zisca, the Bohemian hero, were woven into a dramatic series and connection. According to German custom, it was minute and diffuse, and dictated by an adventurous and lawless fancy. It was a chain of audacious acts, and unheard-of disasters. The moated fortress, and the thicket; the ambush and the battle; and the conflict of headlong passions, were pourtrayed in wild numbers, and with terrific energy. An afternoon was set apart to rehearse this performance. The language was familiar to all of us but Carwin, whose company, therefore, was tacitly dispensed with.

The morning previous to this intended rehearsal, I spent at home. My mind was occupied with reflections relative to my own situation. The sentiment which lived with chief energy in my heart, was connected with the image of Pleyel. In the midst of my anguish, I had not been destitute of consolation. His late deportment had given spring to my hopes. Was not the hour at hand, which should render me the happiest of human creatures? He suspected that I looked with favorable eyes upon Carwin. Hence arose disquietudes, which he struggled in vain to conceal. He loved me, but was hopeless that his love would be compensated. Is it not time, said I, to rectify this error? But by what means is

this to be effected? It can only be done by a change of
deportment in me; but how must I demean myself for this
purpose?

I must not speak. Neither eyes, nor lips, must impart the
information. He must not be assured that my heart is his,
previous to the tender of his own; but he must be convinced
that it has not been given to another; he must be supplied
with space whereon to build a doubt as to the true state of
my affections; he must be prompted to avow himself. The
line of delicate propriety; how hard it is, not to fall short,
and not to overleap it!

This afternoon we shall meet at the temple. We shall not
separate till late. It will be his province to accompany me
home. The airy expanse is without a speck. This breeze is
usually stedfast, and its promise of a bland and cloudless
evening, may be trusted. The moon will rise at eleven, and
at that hour, we shall wind along this bank. Possibly that
hour may decide my fate. If suitable encouragement be
given, Pleyel will reveal his soul to me; and I, ere I reach this
threshold, will be made the happiest of beings. And is this
good to be mine? Add wings to thy speed, sweet evening;
and thou, moon, I charge thee, shroud thy beams at the
moment when my Pleyel whispers love. I would not for the
world, that the burning blushes, and the mounting raptures
of that moment, should be visible.

But what encouragement is wanting? I must be regardful
of insurmountable limits. Yet when minds are imbued with
a genuine sympathy, are not words and looks superfluous?
Are not motion and touch sufficient to impart feelings such
as mine? Has he not eyed me at moments, when the pressure of his hand has thrown me into tumults, and was it
possible that he mistook the impetuosities of love, for the
eloquence of indignation?

But the hastening evening will decide. Would it were
come! And yet I shudder at its near approach. An interview
that must thus terminate, is surely to be wished for by me;
and yet it is not without its terrors. Would to heaven it were
come and gone!

I feel no reluctance, my friends to be thus explicit. Time

was, when these emotions would be hidden with immeasurable solicitude, from every human eye. Alas! these airy and fleeting impulses of shame are gone. My scruples were preposterous and criminal. They are bred in all hearts, by a perverse and vicious education, and they would still have maintained their place in my heart, had not my portion been set in misery. My errors have taught me thus much wisdom; that those sentiments which we ought not to disclose, it is criminal to harbour.

It was proposed to begin the rehearsal at four o'clock; I counted the minutes as they passed; their flight was at once too rapid and too slow; my sensations were of an excruciating kind; I could taste no food, nor apply to any task, nor enjoy a moment's repose: when the hour arrived, I hastened to my brother's.

Pleyel was not there. He had not yet come. On ordinary occasions, he was eminent for punctuality. He had testified great eagerness to share in the pleasures of this rehearsal. He was to divide the task with my brother, and, in tasks like these, he always engaged with peculiar zeal. His elocution was less sweet than sonorous; and, therefore, better adapted than the mellifluences of his friend, to the outrageous vehemence of this drama.

What could detain him? Perhaps he lingered through forgetfulness. Yet this was incredible. Never had his memory been known to fail upon even more trivial occasions. Not less impossible was it, that the scheme had lost its attractions, and that he staid, because his coming would afford him no gratification. But why should we expect him to adhere to the minute?

An half hour elapsed, but Pleyel was still at a distance. Perhaps he had misunderstood the hour which had been proposed. Perhaps he had conceived that to-morrow, and not to-day, had been selected for this purpose: but no. A review of preceding circumstances demonstrated that such misapprehension was impossible; for he had himself proposed this day, and this hour. This day, his attention would not otherwise be occupied; but to-morrow, an indispensible engagement was foreseen, by which all his time would be engrossed: his detention, therefore, must be owing to some unforeseen and extraordinary event. Our conjectures were vague, tumultuous, and sometimes fearful. His sickness and his death might possibly have detained him.

Tortured with suspense, we sat gazing at each other, and at the path which led from the road. Every horseman that passed was, for a moment, imagined to be him. Hour succeeded hour, and the sun, gradually declining, at length, disappeared. Every signal of his coming proved fallacious, and our hopes were at length dismissed. His absence affected my friends in no insupportable degree. They should be obliged, they said, to defer this undertaking till the morrow; and, perhaps, their impatient curiosity would compel them to dispense entirely with his presence. No doubt, some harmless occurrence had diverted him from his purpose; and they trusted that they should receive a satisfactory account of him in the morning.

It may be supposed that this disappointment affected me in a very different manner. I turned aside my head to conceal my tears. I fled into solitude, to give vent to my reproaches, without interruption or restraint. My heart was ready to burst with indignation and grief. Pleyel was not the only object of my keen but unjust upbraiding. Deeply did I execrate my own folly. Thus fallen into ruins was the gay fabric which I had reared! Thus had my golden vision melted into air!

How fondly did I dream that Pleyel was a lover! If he were, would he have suffered any obstacle to hinder his coming? Blind and infatuated man! I exclaimed. Thou sportest with happiness. The good that is offered thee, thou hast the insolence and folly to refuse. Well, I will henceforth intrust my felicity to no one's keeping but my own.

The first agonies of this disappointment would not allow me to be reasonable or just. Every ground on which I had built the persuasion that Pleyel was not unimpressed in my favor, appeared to vanish. It seemed as if I had been misled into this opinion, by the most palpable illusions.

I made some trifling excuse, and returned, much earlier than I expected, to my own house. I retired early to my chamber, without designing to sleep. I placed myself at a window, and gave the reins to reflection.

The hateful and degrading impulses which had lately controuled me were, in some degree, removed. New dejection succeeded, but was now produced by contemplating my late behaviour. Surely that passion is worthy to be abhorred which obscures our understanding, and urges us to the commission of injustice. What right had I to expect his attendance? Had I not demeaned myself like one indifferent to his happiness, and as having bestowed my regards upon another? His absence might be prompted by the love which I considered his absence as a proof that he wanted. He came not because the sight of me, the spectacle of my coldness or aversion, contributed to his despair. Why should I prolong, by hypocrisy or silence, his misery as well as my own? Why not deal with him explicitly, and assure him of the truth?

You will hardly believe that, in obedience to this suggestion, I rose for the purpose of ordering a light, that I might instantly make this confession in a letter. A second thought shewed me the rashness of this scheme, and I wondered by what infirmity of mind I could be betrayed into a momentary approbation of it. I saw with the utmost clearness that a confession like that would be the most remediless and unpardonable outrage upon the dignity of my sex, and utterly unworthy of that passion which controuled me.

I resumed my seat and my musing. To account for the absence of Pleyel became once more the scope of my conjectures. How many incidents might occur to raise an insuperable impediment in his way? When I was a child, a scheme of pleasure, in which he and his sister were parties, had been, in like manner, frustrated by his absence; but his absence, in that instance, had been occasioned by his falling from a boat into the river, in consequence of which he had run the most imminent hazard of being drowned. Here was a second disappointment endured by the same persons, and produced by his failure. Might it not originate in the same cause? Had he not designed to cross the river that morning to make some necessary purchases in Jersey? He had preconcerted to return to his own house to dinner; but, perhaps, some disaster had befallen him. Experience had taught me the insecurity of a canoe, and that was the only kind of boat which Pleyel used: I was, likewise, actuated by an hereditary dread of water. These circumstances combined to bestow considerable plausibility on this conjecture; but the consternation with which I began to be seized was allayed by reflecting, that if this disaster had happened my brother would have received the speediest information of it. The consolation which this idea imparted was ravished from me by a new thought. This disaster might have happened, and his family not be apprized of it. The first intelligence of his fate may be communicated by the livid corpse which the tide may cast, many days hence, upon the shore.

Thus was I distressed by opposite conjectures: thus was I tormented by phantoms of my own creation. It was not always thus. I cannot ascertain the date when my mind became the victim of this imbecility; perhaps it was coeval with the inroad of a fatal passion; a passion that will never rank me in the number of its eulogists; it was alone sufficient to the extermination of my peace: it was itself a plenteous source of calamity, and needed not the concurrence of other evils to take away the attractions of existence, and dig for me an untimely grave.

The state of my mind naturally introduced a train of reflections upon the dangers and cares which inevitably beset an human being. By no violent transition was I led to ponder on the turbulent life and mysterious end of my father. I cherished, with the utmost veneration, the memory of this man, and every relique connected with his fate was preserved with the most scrupulous care. Among these was to be numbered a manuscript, containing memoirs of his own life. The narrative was by no means recommended by its eloquence; but neither did all its value flow from my relationship to the author. Its stile had an unaffected and picturesque simplicity. The great variety and circumstantial display of the incidents, together with their intrinsic importance, as descriptive of human manners and passions, made it the most useful book in my collection. It was late; but

83

being sensible of no inclination to sleep, I resolved to betake myself to the perusal of it.

To do this it was requisite to procure a light. The girl had long since retired to her chamber: it was therefore proper to wait upon myself. A lamp, and the means of lighting it, were only to be found in the kitchen. Thither I resolved forthwith to repair; but the light was of use merely to enable me to read the book. I knew the shelf and the spot where it stood. Whether I took down the book, or prepared the lamp, in the first place, appeared to be a matter of no moment. The latter was preferred, and, leaving my seat, I approached the closet in which, as I mentioned formerly, my books and papers were deposited.

Suddenly the remembrance of what had lately passed in this closet occurred. Whether midnight was approaching, or had passed, I knew not. I was, as then, alone, and defenceless. The wind was in that direction in which, aided by the deathlike repose of nature, it brought to me the murmur of the water-fall. This was mingled with that solemn and enchanting sound, which a breeze produces among the leaves of pines. The words of that mysterious dialogue, their fearful import, and the wild excess to which I was transported by my terrors, filled my imagination anew. My steps faultered, and I stood a moment to recover myself.

I prevailed on myself at length to move towards the closet. I touched the lock, but my fingers were powerless; I was visited afresh by unconquerable apprehensions. A sort of belief darted into my mind, that some being was concealed within, whose purposes were evil. I began to contend with these fears, when it occurred to me that I might, without impropriety, go for a lamp previously to opening the closet. I receded a few steps; but before I reached my chamber door my thoughts took a new direction. Motion seemed to produce a mechanical influence upon me. I was ashamed of my weakness. Besides, what aid could be afforded me by a lamp?

My fears had pictured to themselves no precise object. It would be difficult to depict, in words, the ingredients and hues of that phantom which haunted me. An hand invisible and of preternatural strength, lifted by human passions, and selecting my life for its aim, were parts of this terrific image. All places were alike accessible to this foe, or if his empire were restricted by local bounds, those bounds were utterly inscrutable by me. But had I not been told by some one in league with this enemy, that every place but the recess in the bank was exempt from danger?

I returned to the closet, and once more put my hand upon the lock. O! may my ears lose their sensibility, ere they be again assailed by a shriek so terrible! Not merely my understanding was subdued by the sound: it acted on my nerves like an edge of steel. It appeared to cut asunder the fibres of my brain, and rack every joint with agony.

The cry, loud and piercing as it was, was nevertheless human. No articulation was ever more distinct. The breath which accompanied it did not fan my hair, yet did every circumstance combine to persuade me that the lips which uttered it touched my very shoulder.

"Hold! Hold!" were the words of this tremendous prohibition, in whose tone the whole soul seemed to be rapt up, and every energy converted into eagerness and terror.

Shuddering, I dashed myself against the wall, and by the same involuntary impulse, turned my face backward to examine the mysterious monitor. The moon-light streamed into each window, and every corner of the room was conspicuous, and yet I beheld nothing!

The interval was too brief to be artificially measured, between the utterance of these words, and my scrutiny directed to the quarter whence they came. Yet if a human being had been there, could he fail to have been visible? Which of my senses was the prey of a fatal illusion? The shock which the sound produced was still felt in every part of my frame. The sound, therefore, could not but be a genuine commotion. But that I had heard it, was not more true than that the being who uttered it was stationed at my right ear; yet my attendant was invisible.

I cannot describe the state of my thoughts at that moment. Surprize had mastered my faculties. My frame shook, and the vital current was congealed. I was conscious only to the vehemence of my sensations. This condition could not be lasting. Like a tide, which suddenly mounts to an overwhelming height, and then gradually subsides, my confusion slowly gave place to order, and my tumults to a calm. I was able to deliberate and move. I resumed my feet, and advanced into the midst of the room. Upward, and behind, and on each side, I threw penetrating glances. I was not satisfied with one examination. He that hitherto refused to be seen, might change his purpose, and on the next survey be clearly distinguishable.

Solitude imposes least restraint upon the fancy. Dark is less fertile of images than the feeble lustre of the moon. I was alone, and the walls were chequered by shadowy forms. As the moon passed behind a cloud and emerged, these shadows seemed to be endowed with life, and to move. The apartment was open to the breeze, and the curtain was occasionally blown from its ordinary position. This motion was not unaccompanied with sound. I failed not to snatch a look, and to listen when this motion and this sound occurred. My belief that my monitor was posted near, was strong, and instantly converted these appearances to tokens of his presence, and yet I could discern nothing.

When my thoughts were at length permitted to revert to the past, the first idea that occurred was the resemblance between the words of the voice which I had just heard, and those which had terminated my dream in the summer-house. There are means by which we are able to distinguish a substance from a shadow, a reality from the phantom of a dream. The pit, my brother beckoning me forward, the seizure of my arm, and the voice behind, were surely imaginary. That these incidents were fashioned in my sleep, is supported by the same indubitable evidence that compels me to believe myself awake at present; yet the words and the voice were the same. Then, by some inexplicable contrivance, I was aware of the danger, while my actions and sensations were those of one wholly unacquainted with it. Now, was it not equally true that my actions and persuasions were at war? Had not the belief, that evil lurked in the closet, gained admittance, and had not my actions betokened an unwarrantable security? To obviate the effects of my infatuation, the same means had been used.

In my dream, he that tempted me to my destruction, was my brother. Death was ambushed in my path. From what evil was I now rescued? What minister or implement of ill was shut up in this recess? Who was it whose suffocating grasp I was to feel, should I dare to enter it? What monstrous conception is this? my brother!

No; protection, and not injury is his province. Strange and terrible chimera! Yet it would not be suddenly dismissed. It was surely no vulgar agency that gave this form to my fears. He to whom all parts of time are equally present, whom no contingency approaches, was the author of that spell which now seized upon me. Life was dear to me. No consideration was present that enjoined me to relinquish it. Sacred duty combined with every spontaneous sentiment to endear to me my being. Should I not shudder when my being was endangered? But what emotion should possess me when the arm lifted against me was Wieland's?

Ideas exist in our minds that can be accounted for by no established laws. Why did I dream that my brother was my foe? Why but because an omen of my fate was ordained to be communicated? Yet what salutary end did it serve? Did it arm me with caution to elude, or fortitude to bear the evils to which I was reserved? My present thoughts were, no doubt, indebted for their hue to the similitude existing between these incidents and those of my dream. Surely it was phrenzy that dictated my deed. That a ruffian was hidden in the closet, was an idea, the genuine tendency of which was to urge me to flight. Such had been the effect formerly produced. Had my mind been simply occupied with this thought at present, no doubt, the same impulse would have been experienced; but now it was my brother whom I was irresistably persuaded to regard as the contriver of that ill of which I had been forewarned. This persuasion did not extenuate my fears or my danger. Why then did I again approach the closet and withdraw the bolt? My resolution was instantly conceived, and executed without faultering.

The door was formed of light materials. The lock, of

simple structure, easily forewent its hold. It opened into the room, and commonly moved upon its hinges, after being unfastened, without any effort of mine. This effort, however, was bestowed upon the present occasion. It was my purpose to open it with quickness, but the exertion which I made was ineffectual. It refused to open.

At another time, this circumstance would not have looked with a face of mystery. I should have supposed some casual obstruction, and repeated my efforts to surmount it. But now my mind was accessible to no conjecture but one. The door was hindered from opening by human force. Surely, here was new cause for affright. This was confirmation proper to decide my conduct. Now was all ground of hesitation taken away. What could be supposed but that I deserted the chamber and the house? that I at least endeavoured no longer to withdraw the door?

Have I not said that my actions were dictated by phrenzy? My reason had forborne, for a time, to suggest or to sway my resolves. I reiterated my endeavours. I exerted all my force to overcome the obstacle, but in vain. The strength that was exerted to keep it shut, was superior to mine.

A casual observer might, perhaps, applaud the audaciousness of this conduct. Whence, but from an habitual defiance of danger, could my perseverance arise? I have already assigned, as distinctly as I am able, the cause of it. The frantic conception that my brother was within, that the resistance made to my design was exerted by him, had rooted itself in my mind. You will comprehend the height of this infatuation, when I tell you, that, finding all my exertions vain, I betook myself to exclamations. Surely I was utterly bereft of understanding.

Now had I arrived at the crisis of my fate. "O! hinder not the door to open," I exclaimed, in a tone that had less of fear than of grief in it. "I know you well. Come forth, but harm me not. I beseech you come forth."

I had taken my hand from the lock, and removed to a small distance from the door. I had scarcely uttered these words, when the door swung upon its hinges, and displayed to my view the interior of the closet. Whoever was within, was shrouded in darkness. A few seconds passed without interruption of the silence. I knew not what to expect or to fear. My eyes would not stray from the recess. Presently, a deep sigh was heard. The quarter from which it came heightened the eagerness of my gaze. Some one approached from the farther end. I quickly perceived the outlines of a human figure. Its steps were irresolute and slow. I recoiled as it advanced.

By coming at length within the verge of the room, his form was clearly distinguishable. I had prefigured to myself a very different personage. The face that presented itself was the last that I should desire to meet at an hour, and in a place like this. My wonder was stifled by my fears. Assassins had lurked in this recess. Some divine voice warned me of danger, that at this moment awaited me. I had spurned the intimation, and challenged my adversary.

I recalled the mysterious countenance and dubious character of Carwin. What motive but atrocious ones could guide his steps hither? I was alone. My habit suited the hour, and the place, and the warmth of the season. All succour was remote. He had placed himself between me and the door. My frame shook with the vehemence of my apprehensions.

Yet I was not wholly lost to myself: I vigilantly marked his demeanour. His looks were grave, but not without perturbation. What species of inquietude it betrayed, the light was not strong enough to enable me to discover. He stood still; but his eyes wandered from one object to another. When these powerful organs were fixed upon me, I shrunk into myself. At length, he broke silence. Earnestness, and not embarrassment, was in his tone. He advanced close to me while he spoke.

"What voice was that which lately addressed you?"

He paused for an answer; but observing my trepidation, he resumed, with undiminished solemnity: "Be not terrified. Whoever he was, he hast done you an important service. I need not ask you if it were the voice of a companion. That sound was beyond the compass of human organs. The knowledge that enabled him to tell you who was in the closet, was obtained by incomprehensible means.

"You knew that Carwin was there. Were you not apprized of his intents? The same power could impart the one as well as the other. Yet, knowing these, you persisted. Audacious girl! but, perhaps, you confided in his guardianship. Your confidence was just. With succour like this at hand you may safely defy me.

"He is my eternal foe; the baffler of my best concerted schemes. Twice have you been saved by his accursed interposition. But for him I should long ere now have borne away the spoils of your honor."

He looked at me with greater stedfastness than before. I became every moment more anxious for my safety. It was with difficulty I stammered out an entreaty that he would instantly depart, or suffer me to do so. He paid no regard to my request, but proceeded in a more impassioned manner.

"What is it you fear? Have I not told you, you are safe? Has not one in whom you more reasonably place trust assured you of it? Even if I execute my purpose, what injury is done? Your prejudices will call it by that name, but it merits it not.

"I was impelled by a sentiment that does you honor; a sentiment, that would sanctify my deed; but, whatever it be, you are safe. Be this chimera still worshipped; I will do nothing to pollute it." Here he stopped.

The accents and gestures of this man left me drained of all courage. Surely, on no other occasion should I have been thus pusillanimous. My state I regarded as a hopeless one. I was wholly at the mercy of this being. Whichever way I turned my eyes, I saw no avenue by which I might escape. The resources of my personal strength, my ingenuity, and my eloquence, I estimated at nothing. The dignity of virtue, and the force of truth, I had been accustomed to celebrate; and had frequently vaunted of the conquests which I should make with their assistance.

I used to suppose that certain evils could never befall a being in possession of a sound mind; that true virtue supplies us with energy which vice can never resist; that it was always in our power to obstruct, by his own death, the designs of an enemy who aimed at less than our life. How was it that a sentiment like despair had now invaded me, and that I trusted to the protection of chance, or to the pity of my persecutor?

His words imparted some notion of the injury which he had meditated. He talked of obstacles that had risen in his way. He had relinquished his design. These sources supplied me with slender consolation. There was no security but in his absence. When I looked at myself, when I reflected on the hour and the place, I was overpowered by horror and dejection.

He was silent, museful, and inattentive to my situation, yet made no motion to depart. I was silent in my turn. What could I say? I was confident that reason in this contest would be impotent. I must owe my safety to his own suggestions. Whatever purpose brought him hither, he had changed it. Why then did he remain? His resolutions might fluctuate, and the pause of a few minutes restore to him his first resolutions.

Yet was not this the man whom we had treated with unwearied kindness? Whose society was endeared to us by his intellectual elevation and accomplishments? Who had a thousand times expatiated on the usefulness and beauty of virtue? Why should such a one be dreaded? If I could have forgotten the circumstances in which our interview had taken place, I might have treated his words as jests. Presently, he resumed:

"Fear me not: the space that severs us is small, and all visible succour is distant. You believe yourself completely in my power; that you stand upon the brink of ruin. Such are your groundless fears. I cannot lift a finger to hurt you. Easier it would be to stop the moon in her course than to injure you. The power that protects you would crumble my sinews, and reduce me to a heap of ashes in a moment, if I were to harbour a thought hostile to your safety.

"Thus are appearances at length solved. Little did I expect that they originated hence. What a portion is assigned to you? Scanned by the eyes of this intelligence, your path will be without pits to swallow, or snares to entangle you. Environed by the arms of this protection, all artifices will be frustrated, and all malice repelled."

Here succeeded a new pause. I was still observant of every gesture and look. The tranquil solemnity that had lately possessed his countenance gave way to a new expression. All now was trepidation and anxiety.

"I must be gone," said he in a faltering accent. "Why do I linger here? I will not ask your forgiveness. I see that your terrors are invincible. Your pardon will be extorted by fear, and not dictated by compassion. I must fly from you forever. He that could plot against your honor, must expect from you and your friends persecution and death. I must doom myself to endless exile."

Saying this, he hastily left the room. I listened while he descended the stairs, and, unbolting the outer door, went forth. I did not follow him with my eyes, as the moon-light would have enabled me to do. Relieved by his absence, and exhausted by the conflict of my fears, I threw myself on a chair, and resigned myself to those bewildering ideas which incidents like these could not fail to produce.

CHAPTER X

ORDER could not readily be introduced into my thoughts. The voice still rung in my ears. Every accent that was uttered by Carwin was fresh in my remembrance. His unwelcome approach, the recognition of his person, his hasty departure, produced a complex impression on my mind which no words can delineate. I strove to give a slower motion to my thoughts, and to regulate a confusion which became painful; but my efforts were nugatory. I covered my eyes with my hand, and sat, I know not how long, without power to arrange or utter my conceptions.

I had remained for hours, as I believed, in absolute solitude. No thought of personal danger had molested my tranquillity. I had made no preparation for defence. What was it that suggested the design of perusing my father's manuscript? If, instead of this, I had retired to bed, and to sleep, to what fate might I not have been reserved? The ruffian, who must almost have suppressed his breathings to screen himself from discovery, would have noticed this signal, and I should have awakened only to perish with affright, and to abhor myself. Could I have remained unconscious of my danger? Could I have tranquilly slept in the midst of so deadly a snare?

And who was he that threatened to destroy me? By what means could he hide himself in this closet? Surely he is gifted with supernatural power. Such is the enemy of whose attempts I was forewarned. Daily I had seen him and conversed with him. Nothing could be discerned through the impenetrable veil of his duplicity. When busied in conjectures, as to the author of the evil that was threatened, my mind did not light, for a moment, upon his image. Yet has he not avowed himself my enemy? Why should he be here if he had not meditated evil?

He confesses that this has been his second attempt. What was the scene of his former conspiracy? Was it not he whose whispers betrayed him? Am I deceived; or was there not a faint resemblance between the voice of this man and that which talked of grasping my throat, and extinguishing my life in a moment? Then he had a colleague in his crime; now he is alone. Then death was the scope of his thoughts; now an injury unspeakably more dreadful. How thankful should I be to the power that has interposed to save me!

That power is invisible. It is subject to the cognizance of one of my senses. What are the means that will inform me of what nature it is? He has set himself to counterwork the machinations of this man, who had menaced destruction to all that is dear to me, and whose cunning had surmounted every human impediment. There was none to rescue me from his grasp. My rashness even hastened the completion of his scheme, and precluded him from the benefits of deliberation. I had robbed him of the power to repent and forbear. Had I been apprized of the danger, I should have regarded my conduct as the means of rendering my escape from it impossible. Such, likewise, seem to have been the fears of my invisible protector. Else why that startling intreaty to refrain from opening the closet? By what inexplicable infatuation was I compelled to proceed?

Yet my conduct was wise. Carwin, unable to comprehend my folly, ascribed my behaviour to my knowledge. He conceived himself previously detected, and such detection being possible to flow only from *my* heavenly friend, and *his* enemy, his fears acquired additional strength.

He is apprized of the nature and intentions of this being. Perhaps he is a human agent. Yet, on that supposition his atchievements are incredible. Why should I be selected as the object of his care; or, if a mere mortal, should I not recognize some one, whom, benefits imparted and received had prompted to love me? What were the limits and duration of his guardianship? Was the genius of my birth entrusted by divine benignity with this province? Are human faculties adequate to receive stronger proofs of the existence of unfettered and beneficent intelligences than I have received?

But who was this man's coadjutor? The voice that acknowledged an alliance in treachery with Carwin warned me to avoid the summer-house. He assured me that there only my safety was endangered. His assurance, as it now appears, was fallacious. Was there not deceit in his admonition? Was his compact really annulled? Some purpose was, perhaps, to be accomplished by preventing my future visits to that spot. Why was I enjoined silence to others, on the subject of this admonition, unless it were for some unauthorized and guilty purpose?

No one but myself was accustomed to visit it. Backward, it was hidden from distant view by the rock, and in front, it was screened from all examination, by creeping plants, and the branches of cedars. What recess could be more propitious to secrecy? The spirit which haunted it formerly was pure and rapturous. It was a fane sacred to the memory of infantile days, and to blissful imaginations of the future! What a gloomy reverse had succeeded since the ominous arrival of this stranger! Now, perhaps, it is the scene of his meditations. Purposes fraught with horror, that shun the light, and contemplate the pollution of innocence, are here engendered, and fostered, and reared to maturity.

Such were the ideas that, during the night, were tumultuously revolved by me. I reviewed every conversation in which Carwin had borne a part. I studied to discover the true inferences deducible from his deportment and words with regard to his former adventures and actual views. I pondered on the comments which he made on the relation which I had given of the closet dialogue. No new ideas suggested themselves in the course of this review. My expectation had, from the first, been disappointed on the small degree of surprize which this narrative excited in him.

He never explicitly declared his opinion as to the nature of those voices, or decided whether they were real or visionary. He recommended no measures of caution or prevention.

But what measures were now to be taken? Was the danger which threatened me at an end? Had I nothing more to fear? I was lonely, and without means of defence. I could not calculate the motives and regulate the footsteps of this person. What certainty was there, that he would not re-assume his purposes, and swiftly return to the execution of them?

This idea covered me once more with dismay. How deeply did I regret the solitude in which I was placed, and how ardently did I desire the return of day! But neither of these inconveniencies were susceptible of remedy. At first, it occurred to me to summon my servant, and make her spend the night in my chamber; but the inefficacy of this expedient to enhance my safety was easily seen. Once I resolved to leave the house, and retire to my brother's, but was deterred by reflecting on the unseasonableness of the hour, on the alarm which my arrival, and the account which I should be obliged to give, might occasion, and on the danger to which I might expose myself in the way thither. I began, likewise, to consider Carwin's return to molest me as exceedingly improbable. He had relinquished, of his own accord, his design, and departed without compulsion.

Surely, said I, there is omnipotence in the cause that changed the views of a man like Carwin. The divinity that shielded me from his attempts will take suitable care of my future safety. Thus to yield to my fears is to deserve that they should be realized.

Scarcely had I uttered these words, when my attention was startled by the sound of footsteps. They denoted some one stepping into the piazza in front of my house. My new-born confidence was extinguished in a moment. Carwin, I thought, had repented his departure, and was hastily returning. The possibility that his return was prompted by intentions consistent with my safety, found no place in my mind. Images of violation and murder assailed me anew, and the terrors which succeeded almost incapacitated me from taking any measures for my defence. It was an impulse of which I was scarcely conscious, that made me fasten the lock and draw the bolts of my chamber door. Having done this, I threw myself on a seat; for I trembled to a degree which disabled me from standing, and my soul was so perfectly absorbed in the act of listening, that almost the vital motions were stopped.

The door below creaked on its hinges. It was not again thrust to, but appeared to remain open. Footsteps entered, traversed the entry, and began to mount the stairs. How I detested the folly of not pursuing the man when he withdrew, and bolting after him the outer door! Might he not conceive this omission to be a proof that my angel had deserted me, and be thereby fortified in guilt?

Every step on the stairs, which brought him nearer to my chamber, added vigor to my desperation. The evil with which I was menaced was to be at any rate eluded. How little did I preconceive the conduct which, in an exigence like this, I should be prone to adopt. You will suppose that deliberation and despair would have suggested the same course of action, and that I should have, unhesitatingly, resorted to the best means of personal defence within my power. A penknife lay open upon my table. I remembered that it was there, and seized it. For what purpose you will scarcely inquire. It will be immediately supposed that I meant it for my last refuge, and that if all other means should fail, I should plunge it into the heart of my ravisher.

I have lost all faith in the stedfastness of human resolves. It was thus that in periods of calm I had determined to act. No cowardice had been held by me in greater abhorrence than that which prompted an injured female to destroy, not her injurer ere the injury was perpetrated, but herself when it was without remedy. Yet now this penknife appeared to me of no other use than to baffle my assailant, and prevent the crime by destroying myself. To deliberate at such a time was impossible; but among the tumultuous suggestions of the moment, I do not recollect that it once occurred to me to use it as an instrument of direct defence.

The steps had now reached the second floor. Every footfall accelerated the completion, without augmenting the certainty of evil. The consciousness that the door was fast, now that nothing but that was interposed between me and danger, was a source of some consolation. I cast my eye towards the window. This, likewise, was a new suggestion. If the door should give way, it was my sudden resolution to throw myself from the window. Its height from the ground, which was covered beneath by a brick pavement, would insure my destruction; but I thought not of that.

When opposite to my door the footsteps ceased. Was he listening whether my fears were allayed, and my caution were asleep? Did he hope to take me by surprize? Yet, if so, why did he allow so many noisy signals to betray his approach? Presently the steps were again heard to approach the door. An hand was laid upon the lock, and the latch pulled back. Did he imagine it possible that I should fail to secure the door? A slight effort was made to push it open, as if all bolts being withdrawn, a slight effort only was required.

I no sooner perceived this, than I moved swiftly towards the window. Carwin's frame might be said to be all muscle. His strength and activity had appeared, in various instances, to be prodigious. A slight exertion of his force would demolish the door. Would not that exertion be made? Too surely it would; but, at the same moment that this obstacle should yield, and he should enter the apartment, my determination was formed to leap from the window. My senses were still bound to this object. I gazed at the door in momentary expectation that the assault would be made. The pause continued. The person without was irresolute and motionless.

Suddenly, it occurred to me that Carwin might conceive me to have fled. That I had not betaken myself to flight was, indeed, the least probable of all conclusions. In this persuasion he must have been confirmed on finding the lower door unfastened, and the chamber door locked. Was it not wise to foster this persuasion? Should I maintain deep silence, this, in addition to other circumstances, might encourage the belief, and he would once more depart. Every new reflection added plausibility to this reasoning. It was presently more strongly enforced, when I noticed footsteps withdrawing from the door. The blood once more flowed back to my heart, and a dawn of exultation began to rise: but my joy was short lived. Instead of descending the stairs, he passed to the door of the opposite chamber, opened it, and having entered, shut it after him with a violence that shook the house.

How was I to interpret this circumstance? For what end could he have entered this chamber? Did the violence with which he closed the door testify the depth of his vexation? This room was usually occupied by Pleyel. Was Carwin aware of his absence on this night? Could he be suspected of a design so sordid as pillage? If this were his view there were no means in my power to frustrate it. It behoved me to seize the first opportunity to escape; but if my escape were supposed by my enemy to have been already effected, no asylum was more secure than the present. How could my passage from the house be accomplished without noises that might incite him to pursue me?

Utterly at a loss to account for his going into Pleyel's chamber, I waited in instant expectation of hearing him come forth. All, however, was profoundly still. I listened in vain for a considerable period, to catch the sound of the door when it should again be opened. There was no other avenue by which he could escape, but a door which led into the girl's chamber. Would any evil from this quarter befall the girl?

Hence arose a new train of apprehensions. They merely added to the turbulence and agony of my reflections. Whatever evil impended over her, I had no power to avert it. Seclusion and silence were the only means of saving myself from the perils of this fatal night. What solemn vows did I put up, that if I should once more behold the light of day, I would never trust myself again within the threshold of this dwelling!

Minute lingered after minute, but no token was given that Carwin had returned to the passage. What, I again asked, could detain him in this room? Was it possible that he had returned, and glided, unperceived, away? I was speedily aware of the difficulty that attended an enterprize like this; and yet, as if by that means I were capable of gaining any information on that head, I cast anxious looks from the window.

The object that first attracted my attention was an human figure standing on the edge of the bank. Perhaps my penetration was assisted by my hopes. Be that as it will, the figure of Carwin was clearly distinguishable. From the obscurity of my station, it was impossible that I should be discerned by him, and yet he scarcely suffered me to catch a glimpse of him. He turned and went down the steep, which, in this part, was not difficult to be scaled.

My conjecture then had been right. Carwin has softly opened the door, descended the stairs, and issued forth. That I should not have overheard his steps, was only less incredible than that my eyes had deceived me. But what was now to be done? The house was at length delivered from this detested inmate. By one avenue might he again re-enter. Was it not wise to bar the lower door? Perhaps he had gone out by the kitchen door. For this end, he must have passed through Judith's chamber. These entrances being closed and bolted, as great security was gained as was compatible with my lonely condition.

The propriety of these measures was too manifest not to make me struggle successfully with my fears. Yet I opened my own door with the utmost caution, and descended as if I were afraid that Carwin had been still immured in Pleyel's chamber. The outer door was a-jar. I shut, with trembling eagerness, and drew every bolt that appended to it. I then passed with light and less cautious steps through the parlour, but was surprized to discover that the kitchen door was secure. I was compelled to acquiesce in the first conjecture that Carwin had escaped through the entry.

My heart was now somewhat eased of the load of apprehension. I returned once more to my chamber, the door of which I was careful to lock. It was no time to think of repose. The moon-light began already to fade before the light of the day. The approach of morning was betokened by the usual signals. I mused upon the events of this night, and determined to take up my abode henceforth at my brother's. Whether I should inform him of what had happened was a question which seemed to demand some consideration. My safety unquestionably required that I should abandon my present habitation.

As my thoughts began to flow with fewer impediments, the image of Pleyel, and the dubiousness of his condition, again recurred to me. I again ran over the possible causes of his absence on the preceding day. My mind was attuned to melancholy. I dwelt, with an obstinacy for which I could not account, on the idea of his death. I painted to myself his struggles with the billows, and his last appearance. I imagined myself a midnight wanderer on the shore, and to have stumbled on his corpse, which the tide had cast up. These dreary images affected me even to tears. I endeavoured not to restrain them. They imparted a relief which I had not anticipated. The more copiously they flowed, the more did my general sensations appear to subside into calm, and a certain restlessness give way to repose.

Perhaps, relieved by this effusion, the slumber so much wanted might have stolen on my senses, had there been no new cause of alarm.

CHAPTER XI

I WAS aroused from this stupor by sounds that evidently arose in the next chamber. Was it possible that I had been mistaken in the figure which I had seen on the bank? or had Carwin, by some inscrutable means, penetrated once more into this chamber? The opposite door opened; footsteps came forth, and the person, advancing to mine, knocked.

So unexpected an incident robbed me of all presence of mind, and, starting up, I involuntarily exclaimed, "Who is there?" An answer was immediately given. The voice, to my inexpressible astonishment, was Pleyel's.

"It is I. Have you risen? If you have not, make haste; I want three minutes conversation with you in the parlour—I will wait for you there." Saying this he retired from the door.

Should I confide in the testimony of my ears? If that were true, it was Pleyel that had been hitherto immured in the opposite chamber: he whom my rueful fancy had depicted in so many ruinous and ghastly shapes: he whose footsteps had been listened to with such inquietude! What is man, that knowledge is so sparingly conferred upon him! that his heart should be wrung with distress, and his frame be exanimated with fear, though his safety be encompassed with impregnable walls! What are the bounds of human imbecility! He that warned me of the presence of my foe refused the intimation by which so many racking fears would have been precluded.

Yet who would have imagined the arrival of Pleyel at such an hour? His tone was desponding and anxious. Why this unseasonable summons? and why this hasty departure? Some tidings he, perhaps, bears of mysterious and unwelcome import.

My impatience would not allow me to consume much time in deliberation: I hastened down. Pleyel I found standing at a window, with eyes cast down as in meditation, and arms folded on his breast. Every line in his countenance was pregnant with sorrow. To this was added a certain wanness and air of fatigue. The last time I had seen him appearances had been the reverse of these. I was startled at the change. The first impulse was to question him as to the cause. This impulse was supplanted by some degree of confusion, flowing from a consciousness that love had too large, and, as it might prove, a perceptible share in creating this impulse. I was silent.

Presently he raised his eyes and fixed them upon me. I read in them an anguish altogether ineffable. Never had I witnessed a like demeanour in Pleyel. Never, indeed, had I observed an human countenance in which grief was more legibly inscribed. He seemed struggling for utterance; but his struggles being fruitless, he shook his head and turned away from me.

My impatience would not allow me to be longer silent: "What," said I, "for heaven's sake, my friend, what is the matter?"

He started at the sound of my voice. His looks, for a moment, became convulsed with an emotion very different from grief. His accents were broken with rage.

"The matter—O wretch!—thus exquisitely fashioned— on whom nature seemed to have exhausted all her graces; with charms so awful and so pure! how art thou fallen! From what height fallen! A ruin so complete—so unheard of!"

His words were again choaked by emotion. Grief and pity were again mingled in his features. He resumed, in a tone half suffocated by sobs:

"But why should I upbraid thee? Could I restore to thee

103

what thou has lost; efface this cursed stain; snatch thee from the jaws of this fiend; I would do it. Yet what will avail my efforts? I have not arms with which to contend with so consummate, so frightful a depravity.

"Evidence less than this would only have excited resentment and scorn. The wretch who should have breathed a suspicion injurious to thy honor, would have been regarded without anger; not hatred or envy could have prompted him; it would merely be an argument of madness. That my eyes, that my ears, should bear witness to thy fall! By no other way could detestible conviction be imparted.

"Why do I summon thee to this conference? Why expose myself to thy derision? Here admonition and entreaty are vain. Thou knowest him already, for a murderer and thief. I had thought to have been the first to disclose to thee his infamy; to have warned thee of the pit to which thou art hastening; but thy eyes are open in vain. O foul and insupportable disgrace!

"There is but one path. I know you will disappear together. In thy ruin, how will the felicity and honor of multitudes be involved! But it must come. This scene shall not be blotted by his presence. No doubt thou wilt shortly see thy detested paramour. This scene will be again polluted by a midnight assignation. Inform him of his danger; tell him that his crimes are known; let him fly far and instantly from this spot, if he desires to avoid the fate which menaced him in Ireland.

"And wilt thou not stay behind?—But shame upon my weakness. I know not what I would say.—I have done what I purposed. To stay longer, to expostulate, to beseech, to enumerate the consequences of thy act—what end can it serve but to blazon thy infamy and embitter our woes? And yet, O think, think ere it be too late, on the distresses which thy flight will entail upon us; on the base, grovelling, and atrocious character of the wretch to whom thou hast sold thy honor. But what is this? Is not thy effrontery impenetrable, and thy heart thoroughly cankered? O most specious, and most profligate of women!"

Saying this, he rushed out of the house. I saw him in a few

moments hurrying along the path which led to my brother's. I had no power to prevent his going, or to recall, or to follow him. The accents I had heard were calculated to confound and bewilder. I looked around me to assure myself that the scene was real. I moved that I might banish the doubt that I was awake. Such enormous imputations from the mouth of Pleyel! To be stigmatized with the names of wanton and profligate! To be charged with the sacrifice of honor! with midnight meetings with a wretch known to be a murderer and thief! with an intention to fly in his company!

What I had heard was surely the dictate of phrenzy, or it was built upon some fatal, some incomprehensible mistake. After the horrors of the night, after undergoing perils so imminent from this man, to be summoned to an interview like this; to find Pleyel fraught with a belief that, instead of having chosen death as a refuge from the violence of this man, I had hugged his baseness to my heart, had sacrificed for him my purity, my spotless name, my friendships, and my fortune! that even madness could engender accusations like these was not to be believed.

What evidence could possibly suggest conceptions so wild? After the unlooked-for interview with Carwin in my chamber, he retired. Could Pleyel have observed his exit? It was not long after that Pleyel himself entered. Did he build on this incident, his odious conclusions? Could the long series of my actions and sentiments grant me no exemption from suspicions so foul? Was it not more rational to infer that Carwin's designs had been illicit; that my life had been endangered by the fury of one whom, by some means, he had discovered to be an assassin and robber; that my honor had been assailed, not by blandishments, but by violence?

He has judged me without hearing. He has drawn from dubious appearances, conclusions the most improbable and unjust. He has loaded me with all outrageous epithets. He has ranked me with prostitutes and thieves. I cannot pardon thee, Pleyel, for this injustice. Thy understanding must be hurt. If it be not, if thy conduct was sober and deliberate, I can never forgive an outrage so unmanly, and so gross.

These thoughts gradually gave place to others. Pleyel was possessed by some momentary phrenzy: appearances had led him into palpable errors. Whence could his sagacity have contracted this blindness? Was it not love? Previously assured of my affection for Carwin, distracted with grief and jealousy, and impelled hither at that late hour by some unknown instigation, his imagination transformed shadows into monsters, and plunged him into these deplorable errors.

This idea was not unattended with consolation. My soul was divided between indignation at his injustice, and delight on account of the source from which I conceived it to spring. For a long time they would allow admission to no other thoughts. Surprize is an emotion that enfeebles, not invigorates. All my meditations were accompanied with wonder. I rambled with vagueness, or clung to one image with an obstinacy which sufficiently testified the maddening influence of late transactions.

Gradually I proceeded to reflect upon the consequences of Pleyel's mistake, and on the measures I should take to guard myself against future injury from Carwin. Should I suffer this mistake to be detected by time? When his passion should subside, would he not perceive the flagrancy of his injustice, and hasten to atone for it? Did it not become my character to testify resentment for language and treatment so opprobrious? Wrapt up in the consciousness of innocence, and confiding in the influence of time and reflection to confute so groundless a charge, it was my province to be passive and silent.

As to the violences meditated by Carwin, and the means of eluding them, the path to be taken by me was obvious. I resolved to tell the tale to my brother, and regulate myself by his advice. For this end, when the morning was somewhat advanced, I took the way to his house. My sister was engaged in her customary occupations. As soon as I appeared, she remarked a change in my looks. I was not willing to alarm her by the information which I had to communicate. Her health was in that condition which rendered a disastrous tale particularly unsuitable. I forbore a direct answer to her inquiries, and inquired, in my turn, for Wieland.

"Why," said she, "I suspect something mysterious and unpleasant has happened this morning. Scarcely had we risen when Pleyel dropped among us. What could have prompted him to make us so early and so unseasonable a visit I cannot tell. To judge from the disorder of his dress, and his countenance, something of an extraordinary nature has occurred. He permitted me merely to know that he had slept none, nor even undressed, during the past night. He took your brother to walk with him. Some topic must have deeply engaged them, for Wieland did not return till the breakfast hour was passed, and returned alone. His disturbance was excessive; but he would not listen to my importunities, or tell me what had happened. I gathered from hints which he let fall, that your situation was, in some way, the cause: yet he assured me that you were at your own house, alive, in good health, and in perfect safety. He scarcely ate a morsel, and immediately after breakfast went out again. He would not inform me whither he was going, but mentioned that he probably might not return before night."

I was equally astonished and alarmed by this information. Pleyel had told his tale to my brother, and had, by a plausible and exaggerated picture, instilled into him unfavorable thoughts of me. Yet would not the more correct judgment of Wieland perceive and expose the fallacy of his conclusions? Perhaps his uneasiness might arise from some insight into the character of Carwin, and from apprehensions for my safety. The appearances by which Pleyel had been misled, might induce him likewise to believe that I entertained an indiscreet, though not dishonorable affection for Carwin. Such were the conjectures rapidly formed. I was inexpressibly anxious to change them into certainty. For this end an interview with my brother was desirable. He was gone, no one knew whither, and was not expected speedily to return. I had no clue by which to trace his footsteps.

My anxieties could not be concealed from my sister. They

107

heightened her solicitude to be acquainted with the cause. There were many reasons persuading me to silence: at least, till I had seen my brother, it would be an act of inexcusable temerity to unfold what had lately passed. No other expedient for eluding her importunities occurred to me, but that of returning to my own house. I recollected my determination to become a tenant of this roof. I mentioned it to her. She joyfully acceded to this proposal, and suffered me, with less reluctance, to depart, when I told her that it was with a view to collect and send to my new dwelling what articles would be immediately useful to me.

Once more I returned to the house which had been the scene of so much turbulence and danger. I was at no great distance from it when I observed my brother coming out. On seeing me he stopped, and after ascertaining, as it seemed, which way I was going, he returned into the house before me. I sincerely rejoiced at this event, and I hastened to set things, if possible, on their right footing.

His brow was by no means expressive of those vehement emotions with which Pleyel had been agitated. I drew a favorable omen from this circumstance. Without delay I began the conversation.

"I have been to look for you," said I, "but was told by Catharine that Pleyel had engaged you on some important and disagreeable affair. Before his interview with you he spent a few minutes with me. These minutes he employed in upbraiding me for crimes and intentions with which I am by no means chargeable. I believe him to have taken up his opinions on very insufficient grounds. His behaviour was in the highest degree precipitate and unjust, and, until I receive some atonement, I shall treat him, in my turn, with that contempt which he justly merits: meanwhile I am fearful that he has prejudiced my brother against me. That is an evil which I most anxiously deprecate, and which I shall indeed exert myself to remove. Has he made me the subject of this morning's conversation?"

My brother's countenance testified no surprize at my address. The benignity of his looks were no wise diminished.

"It is true," said he, "your conduct was the subject of our discourse. I am your friend, as well as your brother. There is no human being whom I love with more tenderness, and whose welfare is nearer my heart. Judge then with what emotions I listened to Pleyel's story. I expect and desire you to vindicate yourself from aspersions so foul, if vindication be possible."

The tone with which he uttered the last words affected me deeply. "If vindication be possible!" repeated I. "From what you know, do you deem a formal vindication necessary? Can you harbour for a moment the belief of my guilt?"

He shook his head with an air of acute anguish. "I have struggled," said he, "to dismiss that belief. You speak before a judge who will profit by any pretence to acquit you: who is ready to question his own senses when they plead against you."

These words incited a new set of thoughts in my mind. I began to suspect that Pleyel had built his accusations on some foundation unknown to me. "I may be a stranger to the grounds of your belief. Pleyel loaded me with indecent and virulent invectives, but he withheld from me the facts that generated his suspicions. Events took place last night of which some of the circumstances were of an ambiguous nature. I conceived that these might possibly have fallen under his cognizance, and that, viewed through the mists of prejudice and passion, they supplied a pretence for his conduct, but believed that your more unbiassed judgment would estimate them at their just value. Perhaps his tale has been different from what I suspect it to be. Listen then to my narrative. If there be any thing in his story inconsistent with mine, his story is false."

I then proceeded to a circumstantial relation of the incidents of the last night. Wieland listened with deep attention. Having finished, "This," continued I, "is the truth; you see in what circumstances an interview took place between Carwin and me. He remained for hours in my closet, and for some minutes in my chamber. He departed without haste or interruption. If Pleyel marked him as he left the house, and it is not impossible that he did, inferences injurious to my character might suggest themselves to him. In admitting them, he gave proofs of less discernment and less candor than I once ascribed to him."

"His proofs," said Wieland, after a considerable pause, "are different. That he should be deceived, is not possible. That he himself is not the deceiver, could not be believed, if his testimony were not inconsistent with yours; but the doubts which I entertained are now removed. Your tale, some parts of it, is marvellous; the voice which exclaimed against your rashness in approaching the closet, your persisting notwithstanding that prohibition, your belief that I was the ruffian, and your subsequent conduct, are believed by me, because I have known you from childhood, because a thousand instances have attested your veracity, and because nothing less than my own hearing and vision would convince me, in opposition to her own assertions, that my sister had fallen into wickedness like this."

I threw my arms around him, and bathed his cheek with my tears. "That," said I, "is spoken like my brother. But what are the proofs?"

He replied—"Pleyel informed me that, in going to your house, his attention was attracted by two voices. The persons speaking sat beneath the bank out of sight. These persons, judging by their voices, were Carwin and you. I will not repeat the dialogue. If my sister was the female, Pleyel was justified in concluding you to be, indeed, one of the most profligate of women. Hence, his accusations of you, and his efforts to obtain my concurrence to a plan by which an eternal separation should be brought about between my sister and this man."

I made Wieland repeat this recital. Here, indeed, was a tale to fill me with terrible foreboding. I had vainly thought that my safety could be sufficiently secured by doors and bars, but this is a foe from whose grasp no power of divinity can save me! His artifices will ever lay my fame and happiness at his mercy. How shall I counterwork his plots, or detect his coadjutor? He has taught some vile and abandoned female to mimic my voice. Pleyel's ears were the witnesses of my dishonor. This is the midnight assignation to which he alluded. Thus is the silence he maintained when attempting to open the door of my chamber, accounted for. He supposed me absent, and meant, perhaps, had my apartment been accessible, to leave in it some accusing memorial.

Pleyel was no longer equally culpable. The sincerity of his anguish, the depth of his despair, I remembered with some tendencies to gratitude. Yet was he not precipitate? Was the conjecture that my part was played by some mimic so utterly untenable? Instances of this faculty are common. The wickedness of Carwin must, in his opinion, have been adequate to such contrivances, and yet the supposition of my guilt was adopted in preference to that.

But how was this error to be unveiled? What but my own assertion had I to throw in the balance against it? Would this be permitted to outweigh the testimony of his senses? I had no witnesses to prove my existence in another place. The real events of that night are marvellous. Few, to whom they should be related, would scruple to discredit them. Pleyel is sceptical in a transcendant degree. I cannot summon Carwin to my bar, and make him the attestor of my innocence, and the accuser of himself.

My brother saw and comprehended my distress. He was unacquainted, however, with the full extent of it. He knew not by how many motives I was incited to retrieve the good opinion of Pleyel. He endeavored to console me. Some new event, he said, would occur to disentangle the maze. He did not question the influence of my eloquence, if I thought proper to exert it. Why not seek an interview with Pleyel, and exact from him a minute relation, in which something may be met with serving to destroy the probability of the whole?

I caught, with eagerness, at this hope; but my alacrity was damped by new reflections. Should I, perfect in this respect, and unblemished as I was, thrust myself, uncalled, into his presence, and make my felicity depend upon his arbitrary verdict?

"If you chuse to seek an interview," continued Wieland,

"you must make haste, for Pleyel informed me of his intention to set out this evening or to-morrow on a long journey."

No intelligence was less expected or less welcome than this. I had thrown myself in a window seat; but now, starting on my feet, I exclaimed, "Good heavens! what is it you say? a journey? whither? when?"

"I cannot say whither. It is a sudden resolution I believe. I did not hear of it till this morning. He promises to write to me as soon as he is settled."

I needed no further information as to the cause and issue of this journey. The scheme of happiness to which he had devoted his thoughts was blasted by the discovery of last night. My preference of another, and my unworthiness to be any longer the object of his adoration, were evinced by the same act and in the same moment. The thought of utter desertion, a desertion originating in such a cause, was the prelude to distraction. That Pleyel should abandon me forever, because I was blind to his excellence, because I coveted pollution, and wedded infamy, when, on the contrary, my heart was the shrine of all purity, and beat only for his sake, was a destiny which, as long as my life was in my own hands, I would by no means consent to endure.

I remembered that this evil was still preventable; that this fatal journey it was still in my power to procrastinate, or, perhaps, to occasion it to be laid aside. There were no impediments to a visit: I only dreaded lest the interview should be too long delayed. My brother befriended my impatience, and readily consented to furnish me with a chaise and servant to attend me. My purpose was to go immediately to Pleyel's farm, where his engagements usually detained him during the day.

CHAPTER XII

MY way lay through the city. I had scarcely entered it when I was seized with a general sensation of sickness. Every object grew dim and swam before my sight. It was with difficulty I prevented myself from sinking to the bottom of the carriage. I ordered myself to be carried to Mrs. Baynton's, in hope that an interval of repose would invigorate and refresh me. My distracted thoughts would allow me but little rest. Growing somewhat better in the afternoon, I resumed my journey.

My contemplations were limited to a few objects. I regarded my success, in the purpose which I had in view, as considerably doubtful. I depended, in some degree, on the suggestions of the moment, and on the materials which Pleyel himself should furnish me. When I reflected on the nature of the accusation, I burned with disdain. Would not truth, and the consciousness of innocence, render me triumphant? Should I not cast from me, with irresistible force, such atrocious imputations?

What an entire and mournful change has been effected in a few hours! The gulf that separates man from insects is not wider than that which severs the polluted from the chaste among women. Yesterday and to-day I am the same. There is a degree of depravity to which it is impossible for me to sink; yet, in the apprehension of another, my ancient and intimate associate, the perpetual witness of my actions, and partaker of my thoughts, I had ceased to be the same. My integrity was tarnished and withered in his eyes. I was the colleague of a murderer, and the paramour of a thief!

His opinion was not destitute of evidence: yet what proofs could reasonably avail to establish an opinion like this? If the sentiments corresponded not with the voice that was heard, the evidence was deficient; but this want of correspondence would have been supposed by me if I had been the auditor and Pleyel the criminal. But mimicry might still more plausibly have been employed to explain the scene. Alas! it is the fate of Clara Wieland to fall into the hands of a precipitate and inexorable judge.

But what, O man of mischief! is the tendency of thy thoughts? Frustrated in thy first design, thou wilt not forego the immolation of thy victim. To exterminate my reputation was all that remained to thee, and this my guardian has permitted. To dispossess Pleyel of this prejudice may be impossible; but if that be effected, it cannot be supposed that thy wiles are exhausted; thy cunning will discover innumerable avenues to the accomplishment of thy malignant purpose.

Why should I enter the lists against thee? Would to heaven I could disarm thy vengeance by my deprecations! When I think of all the resources with which nature and education have supplied thee; that thy form is a combination of steely fibres and organs of exquisite ductility and boundless compass, actuated by an intelligence gifted with infinite endowments, and comprehending all knowledge, I perceive that my doom is fixed. What obstacle will be able to divert thy zeal or repel thy efforts? That being who has hitherto protected me has borne testimony to the formidableness of thy attempts, since nothing less than supernatural interference could check thy career.

Musing on these thoughts, I arrived, towards the close of the day, at Pleyel's house. A month before, I had traversed the same path; but how different were my sensations! Now I was seeking the presence of one who regarded me as the most degenerate of human kind. I was to plead the cause of my innocence, against witnesses the most explicit and unerring, of those which support the fabric of human knowledge. The nearer I approached the crisis, the more did my confidence decay. When the chaise stopped at the door, my strength refused to support me, and I threw myself into the arms of an ancient female domestic. I had not courage to inquire whether her master was at home. I was tormented with fears that the projected journey was already undertaken. These fears were removed, by her asking me whether she should call her young master, who had just gone into his own room. I was somewhat revived by this intelligence, and resolved immediately to seek him there.

In my confusion of mind, I neglected to knock at the door, but entered his apartment without previous notice. This abruptness was altogether involuntary. Absorbed in reflections of such unspeakable moment, I had no leisure to heed the niceties of punctilio. I discovered him standing with his back towards the entrance. A small trunk, with its lid raised, was before him, in which it seemed as if he had been busy in packing his clothes. The moment of my entrance, he was employed in gazing at something which he held in his hand.

I imagined that I fully comprehended this scene. The image which he held before him, and by which his attention was so deeply engaged, I doubted not to be my own. These preparations for his journey, the cause to which it was to be imputed, the hopelessness of success in the undertaking on which I had entered, rushed at once upon my feelings, and dissolved me into a flood of tears.

Startled by this sound, he dropped the lid of the trunk and turned. The solemn sadness that previously overspread his countenance, gave sudden way to an attitude and look of the most vehement astonishment. Perceiving me unable to uphold myself, he stepped towards me without speaking, and supported me by his arm. The kindness of this action called forth a new effusion from my eyes. Weeping was a solace to which, at that time, I had not grown familiar, and which, therefore, was peculiarly delicious. Indignation was no longer to be read in the features of my friend. They were pregnant with a mixture of wonder and pity. Their expression was easily interpreted. This visit, and these tears, were tokens of my penitence. The wretch whom he had stigmatized as incurably and obdurately wicked, now shewed herself susceptible of remorse, and had come to confess her guilt.

This persuasion had no tendency to comfort me. It only shewed me, with new evidence, the difficulty of the task which I had assigned myself. We were mutually silent. I had less power and less inclination than ever to speak. I extricated myself from his hold, and threw myself on a sofa. He placed himself by my side, and appeared to wait with impatience and anxiety for some beginning of the conversation. What could I say? If my mind had suggested any thing suitable to the occasion, my utterance was suffocated by tears.

Frequently he attempted to speak, but seemed deterred by some degree of uncertainty as to the true nature of the scene. At length, in faltering accents he spoke:

"My friend! would to heaven I were still permitted to call you by that name. The image that I once adored existed only in my fancy; but though I cannot hope to see it realized, you may not be totally insensible to the horrors of that gulf into which you are about to plunge. What heart is forever exempt from the goadings of compunction and the influx of laudable propensities?

"I thought you accomplished and wise beyond the rest of women. Not a sentiment you uttered, not a look you assumed, that were not, in my apprehension, fraught with the sublimities of rectitude and the illuminations of genius. Deceit has some bounds. Your education could not be without influence. A vigorous understanding cannot be utterly devoid of virtue; but you could not counterfeit the powers of invention and reasoning. I was rash in my invectives. I will not, but with life, relinquish all hopes of you. I will shut out every proof that would tell me that your heart is incurably diseased.

"You come to restore me once more to happiness; to convince me that you have torn her mask from vice, and feel nothing but abhorrence for the part you have hitherto acted."

At these words my equanimity forsook me. For a moment

116

I forgot the evidence from which Pleyel's opinions were derived, the benevolence of his remonstrances, and the grief which his accents bespoke; I was filled with indignation and horror at charges so black; I shrunk back and darted at him a look of disdain and anger. My passion supplied me with words.

"What detestable infatuation was it that led me hither! Why do I patiently endure these horrible insults! My offences exist only in your own distempered imagination: you are leagued with the traitor who assailed my life: you have vowed the destruction of my peace and honor. I deserve infamy for listening to calumnies so base!"

These words were heard by Pleyel without visible resentment. His countenance relapsed into its former gloom; but he did not even look at me. The ideas which had given place to my angry emotions returned, and once more melted me into tears. "O!" I exclaimed, in a voice broken by sobs, "what a task is mine! Compelled to hearken to charges which I feel to be false, but which I know to be believed by him that utters them; believed too not without evidence, which, though fallacious, is not unplausible.

"I came hither not to confess, but to vindicate. I know the source of your opinions. Wieland has informed me on what your suspicions are built. These suspicions are fostered by you as certainties; the tenor of my life, of all my conversations and letters, affords me no security; every sentiment that my tongue and my pen have uttered, bear testimony to the rectitude of my mind; but this testimony is rejected. I am condemned as brutally profligate: I am classed with the stupidly and sordidly wicked.

"And where are the proofs that must justify so foul and so improbable an accusation? You have overheard a midnight conference. Voices have saluted your ear, in which you imagine yourself to have recognized mine, and that of a detected villain. The sentiments expressed were not allowed to outweigh the casual or concerted resemblance of voice. Sentiments the reverse of all those whose influence my former life had attested, denoting a mind polluted by grovelling vices, and entering into compact with that of a thief and a murderer. The nature of these sentiments did not enable you to detect the cheat, did not suggest to you the possibility that my voice had been counterfeited by another.

"You were precipitate and prone to condemn. Instead of rushing on the impostors, and comparing the evidence of sight with that of hearing, you stood aloof, or you fled. My innocence would not now have stood in need of vindication, if this conduct had been pursued. That you did not pursue it, your present thoughts incontestibly prove. Yet this conduct might surely have been expected from Pleyel. That he would not hastily impute the blackest of crimes, that he would not couple my name with infamy, and cover me with ruin for inadequate or slight reasons, might reasonably have been expected." The sobs which convulsed my bosom would not suffer me to proceed.

Pleyel was for a moment affected. He looked at me with some expression of doubt; but this quickly gave place to a mournful solemnity. He fixed his eyes on the floor as in reverie, and spoke:

"Two hours hence I am gone. Shall I carry away with me the sorrow that is now my guest? or shall that sorrow be accumulated tenfold? What is she that is now before me? Shall every hour supply me with new proofs of a wickedness beyond example? Already I deem her the most abandoned and detestable of human creatures. Her coming and her tears imparted a gleam of hope, but that gleam has vanished."

He now fixed his eyes upon me, and every muscle in his face trembled. His tone was hollow and terrible—"Thou knowest that I was a witness of your interview, yet thou comest hither to upbraid me for injustice! Thou canst look me in the face and say that I am deceived!—An inscrutable providence has fashioned thee for some end. Thou wilt live, no doubt, to fulfil the purposes of thy maker, if he repent not of his workmanship, and send not his vengeance to exterminate thee, ere the measure of thy days be full. Surely nothing in the shape of man can vie with thee!

"But I thought I had stifled this fury. I am not constituted thy judge. My office is to pity and amend, and not to punish and revile. I deemed myself exempt from all tempestuous passions. I had almost persuaded myself to weep over thy fall; but I am frail as dust, and mutable as water; I am calm, I am compassionate only in thy absence.—Make this house, this room, thy abode as long as thou wilt, but forgive me if I prefer solitude for the short time during which I shall stay." Saying this, he motioned as if to leave the apartment.

The stormy passions of this man affected me by sympathy. I ceased to weep. I was motionless and speechless with agony. I sat with my hands clasped, mutely gazing after him as he withdrew. I desired to detain him, but was unable to make any effort for that purpose, till he had passed out of the room. I then uttered an involuntary and piercing cry—"Pleyel! Art thou gone? Gone forever?"

At this summons he hastily returned. He beheld me wild, pale, gasping for breath, and my head already sinking on my bosom. A painful dizziness seized me, and I fainted away.

When I recovered, I found myself stretched on a bed in the outer apartment, and Pleyel, with two female servants, standing beside it. All the fury and scorn which the countenance of the former lately expressed, had now disappeared, and was succeeded by the most tender anxiety. As soon as he perceived that my senses were returned to me, he clasped his hands, and exclaimed, "God be thanked! you are once more alive. I had almost despaired of your recovery. I fear I have been precipitate and unjust. My senses must have been the victims of some inexplicable and momentary phrenzy. Forgive me, I beseech you, forgive my reproaches. I would purchase conviction of your purity, at the price of my existence here and hereafter."

He once more, in a tone of the most fervent tenderness, besought me to be composed, and then left me to the care of the women.

CHAPTER XIII

ERE was wrought a surprizing change in my friend. What was it that had shaken conviction so firm? Had any thing occurred during my fit, adequate to produce so total an alteration? My attendants informed me that he had not left my apartment; that the unusual duration of my fit, and the failure, for a time, of all the means used for my recovery, had filled him with grief and dismay. Did he regard the effect which his reproaches had produced as a proof of my sincerity?

In this state of mind, I little regarded my languors of body. I rose and requested an interview with him before my departure, on which I was resolved, notwithstanding his earnest solicitation to spend the night at his house. He complied with my request. The tenderness which he had lately betrayed, had now disappeared, and he once more relapsed into a chilling solemnity.

I told him that I was preparing to return to my brother's; that I had come hither to vindicate my innocence from the foul aspersions which he had cast upon it. My pride had not taken refuge in silence or distance. I had not relied upon time, or the suggestions of his cooler thoughts, to confute his charges. Conscious as I was that I was perfectly guiltless, and entertaining some value for his good opinion, I could not prevail upon myself to believe that my efforts to make my innocence manifest, would be fruitless. Adverse appearances might be numerous and specious, but they were unquestionably false. I was willing to believe him sincere, that he made no charges which he himself did not believe; but these charges were destitute of truth. The grounds of his opinion were fallacious; and I desired an opportunity of detecting their fallacy. I entreated him to be explicit, and to give me a detail of what he had heard, and what he had seen.

At these words, my companion's countenance grew darker. He appeared to be struggling with his rage. He opened his lips to speak, but his accents died away ere they were formed. This conflict lasted for some minutes, but his fortitude was finally successful. He spoke as follows:

"I would fain put an end to this hateful scene: what I shall say, will be breath idly and unprofitably consumed. The clearest narrative will add nothing to your present knowledge. You are acquainted with the grounds of my opinion, and yet you avow yourself innocent: Why then should I rehearse these grounds? You are apprized of the character of Carwin: Why then should I enumerate the discoveries which I have made respecting him? Yet, since it is your request; since, considering the limitedness of human faculties, some error may possibly lurk in those appearances which I have witnessed, I will briefly relate what I know.

"Need I dwell upon the impressions which your conversation and deportment originally made upon me? We parted in childhood; but our intercourse, by letter, was copious and uninterrupted. How fondly did I anticipate a meeting with one whom her letters had previously taught me to consider as the first of women, and how fully realized were the expectations that I had formed!

"Here, said I, is a being, after whom sages may model their transcendent intelligence, and painters, their ideal beauty. Here is exemplified, that union between intellect and form, which has hitherto existed only in the conceptions of the poet. I have watched your eyes; my attention has hung upon your lips. I have questioned whether the enchantments of your voice were more conspicuous in the intricacies of melody, or the emphasis of rhetoric. I have marked the transitions of your discourse, the felicities of your expression, your refined argumentation, and glowing imagery; and been forced to acknowledge, that all delights were meagre and contemptible, compared with those connected with the audience and sight of you. I have contemplated your principles, and been astonished at the solidity of their foundation, and the perfection of their structure. I have traced you to your home. I have viewed you in relation to your servants, to your family, to your neighbours, and to the world. I have seen by what skilful arrangements you facilitate the performance of the most arduous and complicated duties; what daily accessions of strength your judicious discipline bestowed upon your memory; what correctness and abundance of knowledge was daily experienced by your unwearied application to books, and to writing. If she that possesses so much in the bloom of youth, will go on accumulating her stores, what, said I, is the picture she will display at a mature age?

"You know not the accuracy of my observation. I was desirous that others should profit by an example so rare. I therefore noted down, in writing, every particular of your conduct. I was anxious to benefit by an opportunity so seldom afforded us. I laboured not to omit the slightest shade, or the most petty line in your portrait. Here there was no other task incumbent on me but to copy; there was no need to exaggerate or overlook, in order to produce a more unexceptionable pattern. Here was a combination of harmonies and graces, incapable of diminution or accession without injury to its completeness.

"I found no end and no bounds to my task. No display of a scene like this could be chargeable with redundancy or superfluity. Even the colour of a shoe, the knot of a ribband, or your attitude in plucking a rose, were of moment to be recorded. Even the arrangements of your breakfast-table and your toilet have been amply displayed.

"I know that mankind are more easily enticed to virtue by example than by precept. I know that the absoluteness of a model, when supplied by invention, diminishes its salutary influence, since it is useless, we think, to strive after that which we know to be beyond our reach. But the picture which I drew was not a phantom; as a model, it was devoid of imperfection; and to aspire to that height which had been really attained, was by no means unreasonable. I had another and more interesting object in view. One existed who claimed all my tenderness. Here, in all its parts, was a model worthy of assiduous study, and indefatigable imitation. I called upon her, as she wished to secure and enhance my esteem, to mould her thoughts, her words, her countenance, her actions, by this pattern.

"The task was exuberant of pleasure, and I was deeply engaged in it, when an imp of mischief was let loose in the form of Carwin. I admired his powers and accomplishments. I did not wonder that they were admired by you. On the rectitude of your judgment, however, I relied to keep this admiration within discreet and scrupulous bounds. I assured myself, that the strangeness of his deportment, and the obscurity of his life, would teach you caution. Of all errors, my knowledge of your character informed me that this was least likely to befall you.

"You were powerfully affected by his first appearance; you were bewitched by his countenance and his tones; your description was ardent and pathetic: I listened to you with some emotions of surprize. The portrait you drew in his absence, and the intensity with which you mused upon it, were new and unexpected incidents. They bespoke a sensibility somewhat too vivid; but from which, while subjected to the guidance of an understanding like yours, there was nothing to dread.

"A more direct intercourse took place between you. I need not apologize for the solicitude which I entertained for your safety. He that gifted me with perception of excellence, compelled me to love it. In the midst of danger and pain, my contemplations have ever been cheered by your image. Every object in competition with you, was worthless and trivial. No price was too great by which your safety could be purchased. For that end, the sacrifice of ease, of health, and even of life, would cheerfully have been made by me. What wonder then, that I scrutinized the sentiments and deportment of this man with ceaseless vigilance; that I watched your words and your looks when he was present;

and that I extracted cause for the deepest inquietudes, from every token which you gave of having put your happiness into this man's keeping?

"I was cautious in deciding. I recalled the various conversations in which the topics of love and marriage had been discussed. As a woman, young, beautiful, and independent, it behoved you to have fortified your mind with just principles on this subject. Your principles were eminently just. Had not their rectitude and their firmness been attested by your treatment of that specious seducer Dashwood? These principles, I was prone to believe, exempted you from danger in this new state of things. I was not the last to pay my homage to the unrivalled capacity, insinuation, and eloquence of this man. I have disguised, but could never stifle the conviction, that his eyes and voice had a witchcraft in them, which rendered him truly formidable: but I reflected on the ambiguous expression of his countenance—an ambiguity which you were the first to remark; on the cloud which obscured his character; and on the suspicious nature of that concealment which he studied; and concluded you to be safe. I denied the obvious construction to appearances. I referred your conduct to some principle which had not been hitherto disclosed, but which was reconcileable with those already known.

"I was not suffered to remain long in this suspence. One evening, you may recollect, I came to your house, where it was my purpose, as usual, to lodge, somewhat earlier than ordinary. I spied a light in your chamber as I approached from the outside, and on inquiring of Judith, was informed that you were writing. As your kinsman and friend, and fellow-lodger, I thought I had a right to be familiar. You were in your chamber, but your employment and the time were such as to make it no infraction of decorum to follow you thither. The spirit of mischievous gaiety possessed me. I proceeded on tiptoe. You did not perceive my entrance; and I advanced softly till I was able to overlook your shoulder.

"I had gone thus far in error, and had no power to recede. How cautiously should we guard against the first

inroads of temptation! I knew that to pry into your papers
was criminal; but I reflected that no sentiment of yours was
of a nature which made it your interest to conceal it. You
wrote much more than you permitted your friends to peruse. My curiosity was strong, and I had only to throw a
glance upon the paper, to secure its gratification. I should
never have deliberately committed an act like this. The
slightest obstacle would have repelled me; but my eye
glanced almost spontaneously upon the paper. I caught
only parts of sentences; but my eyes comprehended more at
a glance, because the characters were short-hand. I lighted
on the words *summer-house, midnight,* and made out a passage which spoke of the propriety and of the effects to be
expected from *another* interview. All this passed in less than
a moment. I then checked myself, and made myself known
to you, by a tap upon your shoulder.

"I could pardon and account for some trifling alarm; but
your trepidation and blushes were excessive. You hurried
the paper out of sight, and seemed too anxious to discover
whether I knew the contents to allow yourself to make any
inquiries. I wondered at these appearances of consternation, but did not reason on them until I had retired. When
alone, these incidents suggested themselves to my reflections anew.

"To what scene, or what interview, I asked, did you
allude? Your disappearance on a former evening, my tracing you to the recess in the bank, your silence on my first
and second call, your vague answers and invincible embarrassment, when you, at length, ascended the hill, I recollected with new surprize. Could this be the summer-house
alluded to? A certain timidity and consciousness had generally attended you, when this incident and this recess had
been the subjects of conversation. Nay, I imagined that the
last time that adventure was mentioned, which happened in
the presence of Carwin, the countenance of the latter betrayed some emotion. Could the interview have been with
him?

"This was an idea calculated to rouse every faculty to
contemplation. An interview at that hour, in this darksome

retreat, with a man of this mysterious but formidable character; a clandestine interview, and one which you afterwards endeavoured with so much solicitude to conceal! It was a fearful and portentous occurrence. I could not measure his power, or fathom his designs. Had he rifled from you the secret of your love, and reconciled you to concealment and nocturnal meetings? I scarcely ever spent a night of more inquietude.

"I knew not how to act. The ascertainment of this man's character and views seemed to be, in the first place, necessary. Had he openly preferred his suit to you, we should have been impowered to make direct inquiries; but since he had chosen this obscure path, it seemed reasonable to infer that his character was exceptionable. It, at least, subjected us to the necessity of resorting to other means of information. Yet the improbability that you should commit a deed of such rashness, made me reflect anew upon the insufficiency of those grounds on which my suspicions had been built, and almost to condemn myself for harbouring them.

"Though it was mere conjecture that the interview spoken of had taken place with Carwin, yet two ideas occurred to involve me in the most painful doubts. This man's reasonings might be so specious, and his artifices so profound, that, aided by the passion which you had conceived for him, he had finally succeeded; or his situation might be such as to justify the secrecy which you maintained. In neither case did my wildest reveries suggest to me, that your honor had been forfeited.

"I could not talk with you on this subject. If the imputation was false, its atrociousness would have justly drawn upon me your resentment, and I must have explained by what facts it had been suggested. If it were true, no benefit would follow from the mention of it. You had chosen to conceal it for some reasons, and whether these reasons were true or false, it was proper to discover and remove them in the first place. Finally, I acquiesced in the least painful supposition, trammelled as it was with perplexities, that Carwin was upright, and that, if the reasons of your silence were known, they would be found to be just.

CHAPTER XIV

"THREE days have elapsed since this occurrence. I have been haunted by perpetual inquietude. To bring myself to regard Carwin without terror, and to acquiesce in the belief of your safety, was impossible. Yet to put an end to my doubts, seemed to be impracticable. If some light could be reflected on the actual situation of this man, a direct path would present itself. If he were, contrary to the tenor of his conversation, cunning and malignant, to apprize you of this, would be to place you in security. If he were merely unfortunate and innocent, most readily would I espouse his cause; and if his intentions were upright with regard to you, most eagerly would I sanctify your choice by my approbation.

"It would be vain to call upon Carwin for an avowal of his deeds. It was better to know nothing, than to be deceived by an artful tale. What he was unwilling to communicate, and this unwillingness had been repeatedly manifested, could never be extorted from him. Importunity might be appeased, or imposture effected by fallacious representations. To the rest of the world he was unknown. I had often made him the subject of discourse; but a glimpse of his figure in the street was the sum of their knowledge who knew most. None had ever seen him before, and received as new, the information which my intercourse with him in Valencia, and my present intercourse, enabled me to give.

"Wieland was your brother. If he had really made you the object of his courtship, was not a brother authorized to interfere and demand from him the confession of his views? Yet what were the grounds on which I had reared this supposition? Would they justify a measure like this? Surely not.

"In the course of my restless meditations, it occurred to me, at length, that my duty required me to speak to you, to confess the indecorum of which I had been guilty, and to state the reflections to which it had led me. I was prompted by no mean or selfish views. The heart within my breast was not more precious than your safety: most cheerfully would I have interposed my life between you and danger. Would you cherish resentment at my conduct? When acquainted with the motive which produced it, it would not only exempt me from censure, but entitle me to gratitude.

"Yesterday had been selected for the rehearsal of the newly-imported tragedy. I promised to be present. The state of my thoughts but little qualified me for a performer or auditor in such a scene; but I reflected that, after it was finished, I should return home with you, and should then enjoy an opportunity of discoursing with you fully on this topic. My resolution was not formed without a remnant of doubt, as to its propriety. When I left this house to perform the visit I had promised, my mind was full of apprehension and despondency. The dubiousness of the event of our conversation, fear that my interference was too late to secure your peace, and the uncertainty, to which hope gave birth, whether I had not erred in believing you devoted to this man, or, at least, in imagining that he had obtained your consent to midnight conferences, distracted me with contradictory opinions, and repugnant emotions.

"I can assign no reason for calling at Mrs. Baynton's. I had seen her in the morning, and knew her to be well. The concerted hour had nearly arrived, and yet I turned up the street which leads to her house, and dismounted at her door. I entered the parlour and threw myself in a chair. I saw and inquired for no one. My whole frame was overpowered by dreary and comfortless sensations. One idea possessed me wholly; the inexpressible importance of unveiling the designs and character of Carwin, and the utter improbability that this ever would be effected. Some instinct induced me to lay my hand upon a newspaper. I had perused all the general intelligence it contained in the morning, and at the same spot. The act was rather mechanical than voluntary.

"I threw a languid glance at the first column that presented itself. The first words which I read, began with the offer of a reward of three hundred guineas for the apprehension of a convict under sentence of death, who had escaped from Newgate prison in Dublin. Good heaven! how every fibre of my frame tingled when I proceeded to read that the name of the criminal was Francis Carwin!

"The descriptions of his person and address were minute. His stature, hair, complexion, the extraordinary position and arrangement of his features, his aukward and disproportionate form, his gesture and gait, corresponded perfectly with those of our mysterious visitant. He had been found guilty in two indictments. One for the murder of the Lady Jane Conway, and the other for a robbery committed on the person of the honorable Mr. Ludloe.

"I repeatedly perused this passage. The ideas which flowed in upon my mind, affected me like an instant transition from death to life. The purpose dearest to my heart was thus effected, at a time and by means the least of all others within the scope of my foresight. But what purpose? Carwin was detected. Acts of the blackest and most sordid guilt had been committed by him. Here was evidence which imparted to my understanding the most luminous certainty. The name, visage, and deportment, were the same. Between the time of his escape, and his appearance among us, there was a sufficient agreement. Such was the man with whom I suspected you to maintain a clandestine correspondence. Should I not haste to snatch you from the talons of this vulture? Should I see you rushing to the verge of a dizzy precipice, and not stretch forth a hand to pull you back? I had no need to deliberate. I thrust the paper in my pocket, and resolved to obtain an immediate conference with you. For a time, no other image made its way to my understanding. At length, it occurred to me, that though

129

the information I possessed was, in one sense, sufficient, yet if more could be obtained, more was desirable. This passage was copied from a British paper; part of it only, perhaps, was transcribed. The printer was in possession of the original.

"Towards his house I immediately turned my horse's head. He produced the paper, but I found nothing more than had already been seen. While busy in perusing it, the printer stood by my side. He noticed the object of which I was in search. 'Aye,' said he, 'that is a strange affair. I should never have met with it, had not Mr. Hallet sent to me the paper, with a particular request to republish that advertisement.'

"Mr. Hallet! What reasons could he have for making this request? Had the paper sent to him been accompanied by any information respecting the convict? Had he personal or extraordinary reasons for desiring its republication? This was to be known only in one way. I speeded to his house. In answer to my interrogations, he told me that Ludloe had formerly been in America, and that during his residence in this city, considerable intercourse had taken place between them. Hence a confidence arose, which has since been kept alive by occasional letters. He had lately received a letter from him, enclosing the newspaper from which this extract had been made. He put it into my hands, and pointed out the passages which related to Carwin.

"Ludloe confirms the facts of his conviction and escape; and adds, that he had reason to believe him to have embarked for America. He describes him in general terms, as the most incomprehensible and formidable among men; as engaged in schemes, reasonably suspected to be, in the highest degree, criminal, but such as no human intelligence is able to unravel: that his ends are pursued by means which leave it in doubt whether he be not in league with some infernal spirit: that his crimes have hitherto been perpetrated with the aid of some unknown but desperate accomplices: that he wages a perpetual war against the happiness of mankind, and sets his engines of destruction at work against every object that presents itself.

130

"This is the substance of the letter. Hallet expressed some surprize at the curiosity which was manifested by me on this occasion. I was too much absorbed by the ideas suggested by this letter, to pay attention to his remarks. I shuddered with the apprehension of the evil to which our indiscreet familiarity with this man had probably exposed us. I burnt with impatience to see you, and to do what in me lay to avert the calamity which threatened us. It was already five o'clock. Night was hastening, and there was no time to be lost. On leaving Mr. Hallet's house, who should meet me in the street, but Bertrand, the servant whom I left in Germany. His appearance and accoutrements bespoke him to have just alighted from a toilsome and long journey. I was not wholly without expectation of seeing him about this time, but no one was then more distant from my thoughts. You know what reasons I have for anxiety respecting scenes with which this man was conversant. Carwin was for a moment forgotten. In answer to my vehement inquiries, Bertrand produced a copious packet. I shall not at present mention its contents, nor the measures which they obliged me to adopt. I bestowed a brief perusal on these papers, and having given some directions to Bertrand, resumed my purpose with regard to you. My horse I was obliged to resign to my servant, he being charged with a commission that required speed. The clock had struck ten, and Mettingen was five miles distant. I was to journey thither on foot. These circumstances only added to my expedition.

"As I passed swiftly along, I reviewed all the incidents accompanying the appearance and deportment of that man among us. Late events have been inexplicable and mysterious beyond any of which I have either read or heard. These events were coeval with Carwin's introduction. I am unable to explain their origin and mutual dependance; but I do not, on that account, believe them to have a supernatural original. Is not this man the agent? Some of them seem to be propitious; but what should I think of those threats of assassination with which you were lately alarmed? Bloodshed is the trade, and horror is the element of this man. The process by which the sympathies of nature are extinguished in our hearts, by which evil is made our good, and by which we are made susceptible of no activity but in the infliction, and no joy but in the spectacle of woes, is an obvious process. As to an alliance with evil geniuses, the power and the malice of dæmons have been a thousand times exemplified in human beings. There are no devils but those which are begotten upon selfishness, and reared by cunning.

"Now, indeed, the scene was changed. It was not his secret poniard that I dreaded. It was only the success of his efforts to make you a confederate in your own destruction, to make your will the instrument by which he might bereave you of liberty and honor.

"I took, as usual, the path through your brother's ground. I ranged with celerity and silence along the bank. I approached the fence, which divides Wieland's estate from yours. The recess in the bank being near this line, it being necessary for me to pass near it, my mind being tainted with inveterate suspicions concerning you; suspicions which were indebted for their strength to incidents connected with this spot; what wonder that it seized upon my thoughts!

"I leaped on the fence; but before I descended on the opposite side, I paused to survey the scene. Leaves dropping with dew, and glistening in the moon's rays, with no moving object to molest the deep repose, filled me with security and hope. I left the station at length, and tended forward. You were probably at rest. How should I communicate without alarming you, the intelligence of my arrival? An immediate interview was to be procured. I could not bear to think that a minute should be lost by remissness or hesitation. Should I knock at the door? or should I stand under your chamber windows, which I perceived to be open, and awaken you by my calls?

"These reflections employed me, as I passed opposite to the summer-house. I had scarcely gone by, when my ear caught a sound unusual at this time and place. It was almost too faint and too transient to allow me a distinct perception of it. I stopped to listen; presently it was heard again, and now it was somewhat in a louder key. It was laughter; and unquestionably produced by a female voice. That voice was familiar to my senses. It was yours.

"Whence it came, I was at first at a loss to conjecture; but this uncertainty vanished when it was heard the third time. I threw back my eyes towards the recess. Every other organ and limb was useless to me. I did not reason on the subject. I did not, in a direct manner, draw my conclusions from the hour, the place, the hilarity which this sound betokened, and the circumstance of having a companion, which it no less incontestably proved. In an instant, as it were, my heart was invaded with cold, and the pulses of life at a stand.

"Why should I go further? Why should I return? Should I not hurry to a distance from a sound, which, though formerly so sweet and delectable, was now more hideous than the shrieks of owls?

"I had no time to yield to this impulse. The thought of approaching and listening occurred to me. I had no doubt of which I was conscious. Yet my certainty was capable of increase. I was likewise stimulated by a sentiment that partook of rage. I was governed by an half-formed and tempestuous resolution to break in upon your interview, and strike you dead with my upbraiding.

"I approached with the utmost caution. When I reached the edge of the bank immediately above the summer-house, I thought I heard voices from below, as busy in conversation. The steps in the rock are clear of bushy impediments. They allowed me to descend into a cavity beside the building without being detected. Thus to lie in wait could only be justified by the momentousness of the occasion."

Here Pleyel paused in his narrative, and fixed his eyes upon me. Situated as I was, my horror and astonishment at this tale gave way to compassion for the anguish which the countenance of my friend betrayed. I reflected on his force of understanding. I reflected on the powers of my enemy. I could easily divine the substance of the conversation that was overheard. Carwin had constructed his plot in a manner suited to the characters of those whom he had selected for his victims. I saw that the convictions of Pleyel were immutable. I forbore to struggle against the storm, because I saw that all struggles would be fruitless. I was calm; but my calmness was the torpor of despair, and not the tranquillity of fortitude. It was calmness invincible by any thing that his grief and his fury could suggest to Pleyel. He resumed—

"Woman! wilt thou hear me further? Shall I go on to repeat the conversation? Is it shame that makes thee tongue-tied? Shall I go on? or art thou satisfied with what has been already said?"

I bowed my head. "Go on," said I. "I make not this request in the hope of undeceiving you. I shall no longer contend with my own weakness. The storm is let loose, and I shall peaceably submit to be driven by its fury. But go on. This conference will end only with affording me a clearer foresight of my destiny; but that will be some satisfaction, and I will not part without it."

Why, on hearing these words, did Pleyel hesitate? Did some unlooked-for doubt insinuate itself into his mind? Was his belief suddenly shaken by my looks, or my words, or by some newly recollected circumstance? Whencesoever it arose, it could not endure the test of deliberation. In a few minutes the flame of resentment was again lighted up in his bosom. He proceeded with his accustomed vehemence—

"I hate myself for this folly. I can find no apology for this tale. Yet I am irresistibly impelled to relate it. She that hears me is apprized of every particular. I have only to repeat to her her own words. She will listen with a tranquil air, and the spectacle of her obduracy will drive me to some desperate act. Why then should I persist! yet persist I must."

Again he paused. "No," said he, "it is impossible to repeat your avowals of love, your appeals to former confessions of your tenderness, to former deeds of dishonor, to the circumstances of the first interview that took place between you. It was on that night when I traced you to this recess. Thither had he enticed you, and there had you ratified an unhallowed compact by admitting him—

"Great God! Thou witnessedst the agonies that tore my bosom at that moment! Thou witnessedst my efforts to repel the testimony of my ears! It was in vain that you dwelt

134

upon the confusion which my unlooked-for summons excited in you; the tardiness with which a suitable excuse occurred to you; your resentment that my impertinent intrusion had put an end to that charming interview: A disappointment for which you endeavoured to compensate yourself, by the frequency and duration of subsequent meetings.

"In vain you dwelt upon incidents of which you only could be conscious; incidents that occurred on occasions on which none beside your own family were witnesses. In vain was your discourse characterized by peculiarities inimitable of sentiment and language. My conviction was effected only by an accumulation of the same tokens. I yielded not but to evidence which took away the power to withhold my faith.

"My sight was of no use to me. Beneath so thick an umbrage, the darkness was intense. Hearing was the only avenue to information, which the circumstances allowed to be open. I was couched within three feet of you. Why should I approach nearer? I could not contend with your betrayer. What could be the purpose of a contest? You stood in no need of a protector. What could I do, but retire from the spot overwhelmed with confusion and dismay? I sought my chamber, and endeavoured to regain my composure. The door of the house, which I found open, your subsequent entrance, closing, and fastening it and going into your chamber, which had been thus long deserted, were only confirmations of the truth.

"Why should I paint the tempestuous fluctuation of my thoughts between grief and revenge, between rage and despair? Why should I repeat my vows of eternal implacability and persecution, and the speedy recantation of these vows?

"I have said enough. You have dismissed me from a place in your esteem. What I think, and what I feel, is of no importance in your eyes. May the duty which I owe myself enable me to forget your existence. In a few minutes I go hence. Be the maker of your fortune, and may adversity instruct you in that wisdom, which education was unable to impart to you."

These were the last words which Pleyel uttered. He left the room, and my new emotions enabled me to witness his departure without any apparent loss of composure. As I sat alone, I ruminated on these incidents. Nothing was more evident than that I had taken an eternal leave of happiness. Life was a worthless thing, separate from that good which had now been wrested from me; yet the sentiment that now possessed me had no tendency to palsy my exertions, and overbear my strength. I noticed that the light was declining, and perceived the propriety of leaving this house. I placed myself again in the chaise, and returned slowly towards the city.

CHAPTER XV

BEFORE I reached the city it was dusk. It was my purpose to spend the night at Mettingen. I was not solicitous, as long as I was attended by a faithful servant, to be there at an early hour. My exhausted strength required me to take some refreshment. With this view, and in order to pay respect to one whose affection for me was truly maternal, I stopped at Mrs. Baynton's. She was absent from home; but I had scarcely entered the house when one of her domestics presented me a letter. I opened and read as follows:

"To Clara Wieland,

"What shall I say to extenuate the misconduct of last night? It is my duty to repair it to the utmost of my power, but the only way in which it can be repaired, you will not, I fear, be prevailed on to adopt. It is by granting me an interview, at your own house, at eleven o'clock this night. I have no means of removing any fears that you may entertain of my designs, but my simple and solemn declarations. These, after what has passed between us, you may deem unworthy of confidence. I cannot help it. My folly and rashness has left me no other resource. I will be at your door by that hour. If you chuse to admit me to a conference, provided that conference has no witnesses, I will disclose to you particulars, the knowledge of which is of the utmost importance to your happiness. Farewell.

CARWIN."

What a letter was this! A man known to be an assassin and robber; one capable of plotting against my life and my fame; detected lurking in my chamber, and avowing designs the most flagitious and dreadful, now solicits me to grant him a midnight interview! To admit him alone into my presence! Could he make this request with the expectation of my compliance? What had he seen in me, that could justify him in admitting so wild a belief? Yet this request is preferred with the utmost gravity. It is not unaccompanied by an appearance of uncommon earnestness. Had the misconduct to which he alludes been a slight incivility, and the interview requested to take place in the midst of my friends, there would have been no extravagance in the tenor of this letter; but, as it was, the writer had surely been bereft of his reason.

I perused this epistle frequently. The request it contained might be called audacious or stupid, if it had been made by a different person; but from Carwin, who could not be unaware of the effect which it must naturally produce, and of the manner in which it would unavoidably be treated, it was perfectly inexplicable. He must have counted on the success of some plot, in order to extort my assent. None of those motives by which I am usually governed would ever have persuaded me to meet any one of his sex, at the time and place which he had prescribed. Much less would I consent to a meeting with a man, tainted with the most detestable crimes, and by whose arts my own safety had been so imminently endangered, and my happiness irretrievably destroyed. I shuddered at the idea that such a meeting was possible. I felt some reluctance to approach a spot which he still visited and haunted.

Such were the ideas which first suggested themselves on the perusal of the letter. Meanwhile, I resumed my journey. My thoughts still dwelt upon the same topic. Gradually from ruminating on this epistle, I reverted to my interview with Pleyel. I recalled the particulars of the dialogue to which he had been an auditor. My heart sunk anew on viewing the inextricable complexity of this deception, and the inauspicious concurrence of events, which tended to

138

confirm him in his error. When he approached my chamber door, my terror kept me mute. He put his ear, perhaps, to the crevice, but it caught the sound of nothing human. Had I called, or made any token that denoted some one to be within, words would have ensued; and as omnipresence was impossible, this discovery, and the artless narrative of what had just passed, would have saved me from his murderous invectives. He went into his chamber, and after some interval, I stole across the entry and down the stairs, with inaudible steps. Having secured the outer doors, I returned with less circumspection. He heard me not when I descended; but my returning steps were easily distinguished. Now, he thought, was the guilty interview at an end. In what other way was it possible for him to construe these signals?

How fallacious and precipitate was my decision! Carwin's plot owed its success to a coincidence of events scarcely credible. The balance was swayed from its equipoise by a hair. Had I even begun the conversation with an account of what befel me in my chamber, my previous interview with Wieland would have taught him to suspect me of imposture; yet, if I were discoursing with this ruffian, when Pleyel touched the lock of my chamber door, and when he shut his own door with so much violence, how, he might ask, should I be able to relate these incidents? Perhaps he had withheld the knowledge of these circumstances from my brother, from whom, therefore, I could not obtain it, so that my innocence would have thus been irresistibly demonstrated.

The first impulse which flowed from these ideas was to return upon my steps, and demand once more an interview; but he was gone: his parting declarations were remembered.

Pleyel, I exclaimed, thou art gone for ever! Are thy mistakes beyond the reach of detection? Am I helpless in the midst of this snare? The plotter is at hand. He even speaks in the style of penitence. He solicits an interview which he promises shall end in the disclosure of something momentous to my happiness. What can he say which will avail to turn aside this evil? But why should his remorse be feigned?

I have done him no injury. His wickedness is fertile only of despair; and the billows of remorse will some time overbear him. Why may not this event have already taken place? Why should I refuse to see him?

This idea was present, as it were, for a moment. I suddenly recoiled from it, confounded at that frenzy which could give even momentary harbour to such a scheme; yet presently it returned. At length I even conceived it to deserve deliberation. I questioned whether it was not proper to admit, at a lonely spot, in a sacred hour, this man of tremendous and inscrutable attributes, this performer of horrid deeds, and whose presence was predicted to call down unheard-of and unutterable horrors.

What was it that swayed me? I felt myself divested of the power to will contrary to the motives that determined me to seek his presence. My mind seemed to be split into separate parts, and these parts to have entered into furious and implacable contention. These tumults gradually subsided. The reasons why I should confide in that interposition which had hitherto defended me; in those tokens of compunction which this letter contained; in the efficacy of this interview to restore its spotlessness to my character, and banish all illusions from the mind of my friend, continually acquired new evidence and new strength.

What should I fear in his presence? This was unlike an artifice intended to betray me into his hands. If it were an artifice, what purpose would it serve? The freedom of my mind was untouched, and that freedom would defy the assaults of blandishments or magic. Force was I not able to repel. On the former occasion my courage, it is true, had failed at the imminent approach of danger; but then I had not enjoyed opportunities of deliberation; I had foreseen nothing; I was sunk into imbecility by my previous thoughts; I had been the victim of recent disappointments and anticipated ills: Witness my infatuation in opening the closet in opposition to divine injunctions.

Now, perhaps, my courage was the offspring of a no less erring principle. Pleyel was for ever lost to me. I strove in vain to assume his person, and suppress my resentment; I strove in vain to believe in the assuaging influence of time, to look forward to the birth-day of new hopes, and the re-exaltation of that luminary, of whose effulgencies I had so long and so liberally partaken.

What had I to suffer worse than was already inflicted?

Was not Carwin my foe? I owed my untimely fate to his treason. Instead of flying from his presence, ought I not to devote all my faculties to the gaining of an interview, and compel him to repair the ills of which he has been the author? Why should I suppose him impregnable to argument? Have I not reason on my side, and the power of imparting conviction? Cannot he be made to see the justice of unravelling the maze in which Pleyel is bewildered?

He may, at least, be accessible to fear. Has he nothing to fear from the rage of an injured woman? But suppose him inaccessible to such inducements; suppose him to persist in all his flagitious purposes; are not the means of defence and resistance in my power?

In the progress of such thoughts, was the resolution at last formed. I hoped that the interview was sought by him for a laudable end; but, be that as it would, I trusted that, by energy of reasoning or of action, I should render it auspicious, or, at least, harmless.

Such a determination must unavoidably fluctuate. The poet's chaos was no unapt emblem of the state of my mind. A torment was awakened in my bosom, which I foresaw would end only when this interview was past, and its consequences fully experienced. Hence my impatience for the arrival of the hour which had been prescribed by Carwin.

Meanwhile, my meditations were tumultuously active. New impediments to the execution of the scheme were speedily suggested. I had apprized Catharine of my intention to spend this and many future nights with her. Her husband was informed of this arrangement, and had zealously approved it. Eleven o'clock exceeded their hour of retiring. What excuse should I form for changing my plan? Should I shew this letter to Wieland, and submit myself to his direction? But I knew in what way he would decide. He would fervently dissuade me from going. Nay, would he not do more? He was apprized of the offences of Carwin, and of the reward offered for his apprehension. Would he not seize this opportunity of executing justice on a criminal?

This idea was new. I was plunged once more into doubt. Did not equity enjoin me thus to facilitate his arrest? No. I disdained the office of betrayer. Carwin was unapprized of his danger, and his intentions were possibly beneficent. Should I station guards about the house, and make an act, intended perhaps for my benefit, instrumental to his own destruction? Wieland might be justified in thus employing the knowledge which I should impart, but I, by imparting it, should pollute myself with more hateful crimes than those undeservedly imputed to me. This scheme, therefore, I unhesitatingly rejected. The views with which I should return to my own house, it would therefore be necessary to conceal. Yet some pretext must be invented. I had never been initiated into the trade of lying. Yet what but falsehood was a deliberate suppression of the truth? To deceive by silence or by words is the same.

Yet what would a lie avail me? What pretext would justify this change in my plan? Would it not tend to confirm the imputations of Pleyel? That I should voluntarily return to an house in which honor and life had so lately been endangered, could be explained in no way favorable to my integrity.

These reflections, if they did not change, at least suspended my decision. In this state of uncertainty I alighted at the *Hut*. We gave this name to the house tenanted by the farmer and his servants, and which was situated on the verge of my brother's ground, and at a considerable distance from the mansion. The path to the mansion was planted by a double row of walnuts. Along this path I proceeded alone. I entered the parlour, in which was a light just expiring in the socket. There was no one in the room. I perceived by the clock that stood against the wall, that it was near eleven. The lateness of the hour startled me. What had become of the family? They were usually retired an hour before this; but the unextinguished taper, and the un-

142

barred door were indications that they had not retired. I again returned to the hall, and passed from one room to another, but still encountered not a human being.

I imagined that, perhaps, the lapse of a few minutes would explain these appearances. Meanwhile I reflected that the preconcerted hour had arrived. Carwin was perhaps waiting my approach. Should I immediately retire to my own house, no one would be apprized of my proceeding. Nay, the interview might pass, and I be enabled to return in half an hour. Hence no necessity would arise for dissimulation.

I was so far influenced by these views that I rose to execute this design; but again the unusual condition of the house occurred to me, and some vague solicitude as to the condition of the family. I was nearly certain that my brother had not retired; but by what motives he could be induced to desert his house thus unseasonably, I could by no means divine. Louisa Conway, at least, was at home, and had, probably, retired to her chamber; perhaps she was able to impart the information I wanted.

I went to her chamber, and found her asleep. She was delighted and surprized at my arrival, and told me with how much impatience and anxiety my brother and his wife had waited my coming. They were fearful that some mishap had befallen me, and had remained up longer than the usual period. Notwithstanding the lateness of the hour, Catharine would not resign the hope of seeing me. Louisa said she had left them both in the parlour, and she knew of no cause for their absence.

As yet I was not without solicitude on account of their personal safety. I was far from being perfectly at ease on that head, but entertained no distinct conception of the danger that impended over them. Perhaps to beguile the moments of my long protracted stay, they had gone to walk upon the bank. The atmosphere, though illuminated only by the star-light, was remarkably serene. Meanwhile the desireableness of an interview with Carwin again returned, and I finally resolved to seek it.

143

I passed with doubting and hasty steps along the path. My dwelling, seen at a distance, was gloomy and desolate. It had no inhabitant, for my servant, in consequence of my new arrangement, had gone to Mettingen. The temerity of this attempt began to shew itself in more vivid colours to my understanding. Whoever has pointed steel is not without arms; yet what must have been the state of my mind when I could meditate, without shuddering, on the use of a murderous weapon, and believe myself secure merely because I was capable of being made so by the death of another? Yet this was not my state. I felt as if I was rushing into deadly toils, without the power of pausing or receding.

CHAPTER XVI

A S soon as I arrived in sight of the front of the house, my attention was excited by a light from the window of my own chamber. No appearance could be less explicable. A meeting was expected with Carwin, but that he pre-occupied my chamber, and had supplied himself with light, was not to be believed. What motive could influence him to adopt this conduct? Could I proceed until this was explained? Perhaps, if I should proceed to a distance in front, some one would be visible. A sidelong but feeble beam from the window, fell upon the piny copse which skirted the bank. As I eyed it, it suddenly became mutable, and after flitting to and fro, for a short time, it vanished. I turned my eye again toward the window, and perceived that the light was still there; but the change which I had noticed was occasioned by a change in the position of the lamp or candle within. Hence, that some person was there was an unavoidable inference.

I paused to deliberate on the propriety of advancing. Might I not advance cautiously, and, therefore, without danger? Might I not knock at the door, or call, and be apprized of the nature of my visitant before I entered? I approached and listened at the door, but could hear nothing. I knocked at first timidly, but afterwards with loudness. My signals were unnoticed. I stepped back and looked, but the light was no longer discernible. Was it suddenly extinguished by a human agent? What purpose but concealment was intended? Why was the illumination produced, to be thus suddenly brought to an end? And why, since some one was there, had silence been observed?

These were questions, the solution of which may be readily supposed to be entangled with danger. Would not this danger, when measured by a woman's fears, expand into gigantic dimensions? Menaces of death; the stunning exertions of a warning voice; the known and unknown attributes of Carwin; our recent interview in this chamber; the pre-appointment of a meeting at this place and hour, all thronged into my memory. What was to be done?

Courage is no definite or stedfast principle. Let that man who shall purpose to assign motives to the actions of another, blush at his folly and forbear. Not more presumptuous would it be to attempt the classification of all nature, and the scanning of supreme intelligence. I gazed for a minute at the window, and fixed my eyes, for a second minute, on the ground. I drew forth from my pocket, and opened, a penknife. This, said I, be my safe-guard and avenger. The assailant shall perish, or myself shall fall.

I had locked up the house in the morning, but had the key of the kitchen door in my pocket. I, therefore, determined to gain access behind. Thither I hastened, unlocked and entered. All was lonely, darksome, and waste. Familiar as I was with every part of my dwelling, I easily found my way to a closet, drew forth a taper, a flint, tinder, and steel, and, in a moment, as it were, gave myself the guidance and protection of light.

What purpose did I meditate? Should I explore my way to my chamber, and confront the being who had dared to intrude into this recess, and had laboured for concealment? By putting out the light did he seek to hide himself, or mean only to circumvent my incautious steps? Yet was it not more probable that he desired my absence by thus encouraging the supposition that the house was unoccupied? I would see this man in spite of all impediments; ere I died, I would see his face, and summon him to penitence and retribution; no matter at what cost an interview was purchased. Reputation and life might be wrested from me by another, but my rectitude and honor were in my own keeping, and were safe.

146

I proceeded to the foot of the stairs. At such a crisis my thoughts may be supposed at no liberty to range; yet vague images rushed into my mind, of the mysterious interposition which had been experienced on the last night. My case, at present, was not dissimilar; and, if my angel were not weary of fruitless exertions to save, might not a new warning be expected? Who could say whether his silence were ascribable to the absence of danger, or to his own absence?

In this state of mind, no wonder that a shivering cold crept through my veins; that my pause was prolonged; and, that a fearful glance was thrown backward.

Alas! my heart droops, and my fingers are enervated; my ideas are vivid, but my language is faint; now know I what it is to entertain incommunicable sentiments. The chain of subsequent incidents is drawn through my mind, and being linked with those which forewent, by turns rouse up agonies and sink me into hopelessness.

Yet I will persist to the end. My narrative may be invaded by inaccuracy and confusion; but if I live no longer, I will, at least, live to complete it. What but ambiguities, abruptnesses, and dark transitions, can be expected from the historian who is, at the same time, the sufferer of these disasters?

I have said that I cast a look behind. Some object was expected to be seen, or why should I have gazed in that direction? Two senses were at once assailed. The same piercing exclamation of *"hold! hold!"* was uttered within the same distance of my ear. This it was that I heard. The airy undulation, and the shock given to my nerves, were real. Whether the spectacle which I beheld existed in my fancy or without, might be doubted.

I had not closed the door of the apartment I had just left. The stair-case, at the foot of which I stood, was eight or ten feet from the door, and attached to the wall through which the door led. My view, therefore, was sidelong, and took in no part of the room.

Through this aperture was an head thrust and drawn back with so much swiftness, that the immediate conviction was, that thus much of a form, ordinarily invisible, had been unshrowded. The face was turned towards me. Every muscle was tense; the forehead and brows were drawn into vehement expression; the lips were stretched as in the act of shrieking; and the eyes emitted sparks, which, no doubt, if I had been unattended by a light, would have illuminated like the corruscations of a meteor. The sound and the vision were present, and departed together at the same instant; but the cry was blown into my ear, while the face was many paces distant.

This face was well suited to a being whose performances exceeded the standard of humanity, and yet its features were akin to those I had before seen. The image of Carwin was blended in a thousand ways with the stream of my thoughts. This visage was, perhaps, pourtrayed by my fancy. If so, it will excite no surprize that some of his lineaments were now discovered. Yet affinities were few and unconspicuous, and were lost amidst the blaze of opposite qualities.

What conclusion could I form? Be the face human or not, the intimation was imparted from above. Experience had evinced the benignity of that being who gave it. Once he had interposed to shield me from harm, and subsequent events demonstrated the usefulness of that interposition. Now was I again warned to forbear. I was hurrying to the verge of the same gulf, and the same power was exerted to recall my steps. Was it possible for me not to obey? Was I capable of holding on in the same perilous career? Yes. Even of this I was capable!

The intimation was imperfect: it gave no form to my danger, and prescribed no limits to my caution. I had formerly neglected it, and yet escaped. Might I not trust to the same issue? This idea might possess, though imperceptibly, some influence. I persisted; but it was not merely on this account. I cannot delineate the motives that led me on. I now speak as if no remnant of doubt existed in my mind as to the supernal origin of these sounds; but this is owing to the imperfection of my language, for I only mean that the belief was more permanent, and visited more frequently my sober meditations than its opposite. The immediate effects served only to undermine the foundations of my judgment and precipitate my resolutions.

148

I must either advance or return. I chose the former, and began to ascend the stairs. The silence underwent no second interruption. My chamber door was closed, but unlocked, and, aided by vehement efforts of my courage, I opened and looked in.

No hideous or uncommon object was discernible. The danger, indeed, might easily have lurked out of sight, have sprung upon me as I entered, and have rent me with his iron talons; but I was blind to this fate, and advanced, though cautiously, into the room.

Still every thing wore its accustomed aspect. Neither lamp nor candle was to be found. Now, for the first time, suspicions were suggested as to the nature of the light which I had seen. Was it possible to have been the companion of that supernatural visage; a meteorous refulgence producible at the will of him to whom that visage belonged, and partaking of the nature of that which accompanied my father's death?

The closet was near, and I remembered the complicated horrors of which it had been productive. Here, perhaps, was inclosed the source of my peril, and the gratification of my curiosity. Should I adventure once more to explore its recesses? This was a resolution not easily formed. I was suspended in thought: when glancing my eye on a table, I perceived a written paper. Carwin's hand was instantly recognized, and snatching up the paper, I read as follows:—

"There was folly in expecting your compliance with my invitation. Judge how I was disappointed in finding another in your place. I have waited, but to wait any longer would be perilous. I shall still seek an interview, but it must be at a different time and place: meanwhile, I will write this—How will you bear—How inexplicable will be this transaction!—An event so unexpected—a sight so horrible!"

Such was this abrupt and unsatisfactory script. The ink was yet moist, the hand was that of Carwin. Hence it was to be inferred that he had this moment left the apartment, or was still in it. I looked back, on the sudden expectation of seeing him behind me.

What other did he mean? What transaction had taken place adverse to my expectations? What sight was about to be exhibited? I looked around me once more, but saw nothing which indicated strangeness. Again I remembered the closet, and was resolved to seek in that the solution of these mysteries. Here, perhaps, was inclosed the scene destined to awaken my horrors and baffle my foresight.

I have already said, that the entrance into this closet was beside my bed, which, on two sides, was closely shrouded by curtains. On that side nearest the closet, the curtain was raised. As I passed along I cast my eye thither. I started, and looked again. I bore a light in my hand, and brought it nearer my eyes, in order to dispel any illusive mists that might have hovered before them. Once more I fixed my eyes upon the bed, in hope that this more stedfast scrutiny would annihilate the object which before seemed to be there.

This then was the sight which Carwin had predicted! This was the event which my understanding was to find inexplicable! This was the fate which had been reserved for me, but which, by some untoward chance, had befallen on another!

I had not been terrified by empty menaces. Violation and death awaited my entrance into this chamber. Some inscrutable chance had led *her* hither before me, and the merciless fangs of which I was designed to be the prey, had mistaken their victim, and had fixed themselves in *her* heart. But where was my safety? Was the mischief exhausted or flown? The steps of the assassin had just been here; they could not be far off; in a moment he would rush into my presence, and I should perish under the same polluting and suffocating grasp!

My frame shook, and my knees were unable to support me. I gazed alternately at the closet door and at the door of my room. At one of these avenues would enter the exterminator of my honor and my life. I was prepared for defence; but now that danger was imminent, my means of defence, and my power to use them were gone. I was not qualified, by education and experience, to encounter perils

150

like these: or, perhaps, I was powerless because I was again assaulted by surprize, and had not fortified my mind by foresight and previous reflection against a scene like this.

Fears for my own safety again yielded place to reflections on the scene before me. I fixed my eyes upon her countenance. My sister's well-known and beloved features could not be concealed by convulsion or lividness. What direful illusion led thee hither? Bereft of thee, what hold on happiness remains to thy offspring and thy spouse? To lose thee by a common fate would have been sufficiently hard; but thus suddenly to perish—to become the prey of this ghastly death! How will a spectacle like this be endured by Wieland? To die beneath his grasp would not satisfy thy enemy. This was mercy to the evils which he previously made thee suffer! After these evils death was a boon which thou besoughtest him to grant. He entertained no enmity against thee: I was the object of his treason; but by some tremendous mistake his fury was misplaced. But how camest thou hither? and where was Wieland in thy hour of distress?

I approached the corpse: I lifted the still flexible hand, and kissed the lips which were breathless. Her flowing drapery was discomposed. I restored it to order, and seating myself on the bed, again fixed stedfast eyes upon her countenance. I cannot distinctly recollect the ruminations of that moment. I saw confusedly, but forcibly, that every hope was extinguished with the life of *Catharine*. All happiness and dignity must henceforth be banished from the house and name of Wieland: all that remained was to linger out in agonies a short existence; and leave to the world a monument of blasted hopes and changeable fortune. Pleyel was already lost to me; yet, while Catharine lived life was not a detestable possession: but now, severed from the companion of my infancy, the partaker of all my thoughts, my cares, and my wishes, I was like one set afloat upon a stormy sea, and hanging his safety upon a plank; night was closing upon him, and an unexpected surge had torn him from his hold and overwhelmed him forever.

CHAPTER XVII

I HAD no inclination nor power to move from this spot. For more than an hour, my faculties and limbs seemed to be deprived of all activity. The door below creaked on its hinges, and steps ascended the stairs. My wandering and confused thoughts were instantly recalled by these sounds, and dropping the curtain of the bed, I moved to a part of the room where any one who entered should be visible; such are the vibrations of sentiment, that notwithstanding the seeming fulfilment of my fears, and increase of my danger, I was conscious, on this occasion, to no turbulence but that of curiosity.

At length he entered the apartment, and I recognized my brother. It was the same Wieland whom I had ever seen. Yet his features were pervaded by a new expression. I supposed him unacquainted with the fate of his wife, and his appearance confirmed this persuasion. A brow expanding into exultation I had hitherto never seen in him, yet such a brow did he now wear. Not only was he unapprized of the disaster that had happened, but some joyous occurrence had betided. What a reverse was preparing to annihilate his transitory bliss! No husband ever doated more fondly, for no wife ever claimed so boundless a devotion. I was not uncertain as to the effects to flow from the discovery of her fate. I confided not at all in the efforts of his reason or his piety. There were few evils which his modes of thinking would not disarm of their sting; but here, all opiates to grief, and all compellers of patience were vain. This specta-

152

cle would be unavoidably followed by the outrages of desperation, and a rushing to death.

For the present, I neglected to ask myself what motive brought him hither. I was only fearful of the effects to flow from the sight of the dead. Yet could it be long concealed from him? Some time and speedily he would obtain this knowledge. No stratagems could considerably or usefully prolong his ignorance. All that could be sought was to take away the abruptness of the change, and shut out the confusion of despair, and the inroads of madness: but I knew my brother, and knew that all exertions to console him would be fruitless.

What could I say? I was mute, and poured forth those tears on his account, which my own unhappiness had been unable to extort. In the midst of my tears, I was not unobservant of his motions. These were of a nature to rouse some other sentiment than grief, or, at least, to mix with it a portion of astonishment.

His countenance suddenly became troubled. His hands were clasped with a force that left the print of his nails in his flesh. His eyes were fixed on my feet. His brain seemed to swell beyond its continent. He did not cease to breathe, but his breath was stifled into groans. I had never witnessed the hurricane of human passions. My element had, till lately, been all sunshine and calm. I was unconversant with the altitudes and energies of sentiment, and was transfixed with inexplicable horror by the symptoms which I now beheld.

After a silence and a conflict which I could not interpret, he lifted his eyes to heaven, and in broken accents exclaimed, "This is too much! Any victim but this, and thy will be done. Have I not sufficiently attested my faith and my obedience? She that is gone, they that have perished, were linked with my soul by ties which only thy command would have broken; but here is sanctity and excellence surpassing human. This workmanship is thine, and it cannot be thy will to heap it into ruins."

Here suddenly unclasping his hands, he struck one of them against his forehead, and continued—"Wretch! who

153

made thee quicksighted in the councils of thy Maker? Deliverance from mortal fetters is awarded to this being, and thou art the minister of this decree."

So saying, Wieland advanced towards me. His words and his motions were without meaning, except on one supposition. The death of Catharine was already known to him, and that knowledge, as might have been suspected, had destroyed his reason. I had feared nothing less; but now that I beheld the extinction of a mind the most luminous and penetrating that ever dignified the human form, my sensations were fraught with new and insupportable anguish.

I had not time to reflect in what way my own safety would be affected by this revolution, or what I had to dread from the wild conceptions of a mad-man. He advanced towards me. Some hollow noises were wafted by the breeze. Confused clamours were succeeded by many feet traversing the grass, and then crowding into the piazza.

These sounds suspended my brother's purpose, and he stood to listen. The signals multiplied and grew louder; perceiving this, he turned from me, and hurried out of my sight. All about me was pregnant with motives to astonishment. My sister's corpse, Wieland's frantic demeanour, and, at length, this crowd of visitants so little accorded with my foresight, that my mental progress was stopped. The impulse had ceased which was accustomed to give motion and order to my thoughts.

Footsteps thronged upon the stairs, and presently many faces shewed themselves within the door of my apartment. These looks were full of alarm and watchfulness. They pryed into corners as if in search of some fugitive; next their gaze was fixed upon me, and betokened all the vehemence of terror and pity. For a time I questioned whether these were not shapes and faces like that which I had seen at the bottom of the stairs, creatures of my fancy or airy existences.

My eye wandered from one to another, till at length it fell on a countenance which I well knew. It was that of Mr. Hallet. This man was a distant kinsman of my mother,

154

venerable for his age, his uprightness, and sagacity. He had long discharged the functions of a magistrate and good citizen. If any terrors remained, his presence was sufficient to dispel them.

He approached, took my hand with a compassionate air, and said in a low voice, "Where, my dear Clara, are your brother and sister?" I made no answer, but pointed to the bed. His attendants drew aside the curtain, and while their eyes glared with horror at the spectacle which they beheld, those of Mr. Hallet overflowed with tears.

After considerable pause, he once more turned to me. "My dear girl, this sight is not for you. Can you confide in my care, and that of Mrs. Baynton's? We will see performed all that circumstances require."

I made strenuous opposition to this request. I insisted on remaining near her till she were interred. His remonstrances, however, and my own feelings, shewed me the propriety of a temporary dereliction. Louisa stood in need of a comforter, and my brother's children of a nurse. My unhappy brother was himself an object of solicitude and care. At length, I consented to relinquish the corpse, and go to my brother's, whose house, I said, would need a mistress, and his children a parent.

During this discourse, my venerable friend struggled with his tears, but my last intimation called them forth with fresh violence. Meanwhile, his attendants stood round in mournful silence, gazing on me and at each other. I repeated my resolution, and rose to execute it; but he took my hand to detain me. His countenance betrayed irresolution and reluctance. I requested him to state the reason of his opposition to this measure. I entreated him to be explicit. I told him that my brother had just been there, and that I knew his condition. This misfortune had driven him to madness, and his offspring must not want a protector. If he chose, I would resign Wieland to his care; but his innocent and helpless babes stood in instant need of nurse and mother, and these offices I would by no means allow another to perform while I had life.

Every word that I uttered seemed to augment his perplexity and distress. At last he said, "I think, Clara, I have entitled myself to some regard from you. You have professed your willingness to oblige me. Now I call upon you to confer upon me the highest obligation in your power. Permit Mrs. Baynton to have the management of your brother's house for two or three days; then it shall be yours to act in it as you please. No matter what are my motives in making this request: perhaps I think your age, your sex, or the distress which this disaster must occasion, incapacitates you for the office. Surely you have no doubt of Mrs. Baynton's tenderness or discretion."

New ideas now rushed into my mind. I fixed my eyes stedfastly on Mr. Hallet. "Are they well?" said I. "Is Louisa well? Are Benjamin, and William, and Constantine, and Little Clara, are they safe? Tell me truly, I beseech you!"

"They are well," he replied; "they are perfectly safe."

"Fear no effeminate weakness in me: I can bear to hear the truth. Tell me truly, are they well?"

He again assured me that they were well.

"What then," resumed I, "do you fear? Is it possible for any calamity to disqualify me for performing my duty to these helpless innocents? I am willing to divide the care of them with Mrs. Baynton; I shall be grateful for her sympathy and aid; but what should I be to desert them at an hour like this!"

I will cut short this distressful dialogue. I still persisted in my purpose, and he still persisted in his opposition. This excited my suspicions anew; but these were removed by solemn declarations of their safety. I could not explain this conduct in my friend; but at length consented to go to the city, provided I should see them for a few minutes at present, and should return on the morrow.

Even this arrangement was objected to. At length he told me they were removed to the city. Why were they removed, I asked, and whither? My importunities would not now be eluded. My suspicions were roused, and no evasion or artifice was sufficient to allay them. Many of the audience began to give vent to their emotions in tears. Mr. Hallet himself seemed as if the conflict were too hard to be longer

156

sustained. Something whispered to my heart that havoc had been wider than I now witnessed. I suspected this conceal-ment to arise from apprehensions of the effects which a knowledge of the truth would produce in me. I once more entreated him to inform me truly of their state. To enforce my entreaties, I put on an air of insensibility. "I can guess," said I, "what has happened—They are indeed beyond the reach of injury, for they are dead! Is it not so?" My voice faltered in spite of my courageous efforts.

"Yes," said he, "they are dead! Dead by the same fate, and by the same hand, with their mother!"

"Dead!" replied I; "what, all?"

"All!" replied he: "he spared *not one!*"

Allow me, my friends, to close my eyes upon the after-scene. Why should I protract a tale which I already begin to feel is too long? Over this scene at least let me pass lightly. Here, indeed, my narrative would be imperfect. All was tempestuous commotion in my heart and in my brain. I have no memory for ought but unconscious transitions and rueful sights. I was ingenious and indefatigable in the in-vention of torments. I would not dispense with any specta-cle adapted to exasperate my grief. Each pale and mangled form I crushed to my bosom. Louisa, whom I loved with so ineffable a passion, was denied to me at first, but my obsti-nacy conquered their reluctance.

They led the way into a darkened hall. A lamp pendant from the ceiling was uncovered, and they pointed to a table. The assassin had defrauded me of my last and miserable consolation. I sought not in her visage, for the tinge of the morning, and the lustre of heaven. These had vanished with life; but I hoped for liberty to print a last kiss upon her lips. This was denied me; for such had been the merciless blow that destroyed her, that *not a lineament remained!*

I was carried hence to the city. Mrs. Hallet was my com-panion and my nurse. Why should I dwell upon the rage of fever, and the effusions of delirium? Carwin was the phan-tom that pursued my dreams, the giant oppressor under whose arm I was for ever on the point of being crushed. Strenuous muscles were required to hinder my flight, and hearts of steel to withstand the eloquence of my fears. In vain I called upon them to look upward, to mark his sparkling rage and scowling contempt. All I sought was to fly from the stroke that was lifted. Then I heaped upon my guards the most vehement reproaches, or betook myself to wailings on the haplessness of my condition.

This malady, at length, declined, and my weeping friends began to look for my restoration. Slowly, and with intermitted beams, memory revisited me. The scenes that I had witnessed were revived, became the theme of deliberation and deduction, and called forth the effusions of more rational sorrow.

CHAPTER XVIII

I HAD imperfectly recovered my strength, when I was informed of the arrival of my mother's brother, Thomas Cambridge. Ten years since, he went to Europe, and was a surgeon in the British forces in Germany during the whole of the late war. After its conclusion, some connection that he had formed with an Irish officer, made him retire into Ireland. Intercourse had been punctually maintained by letters with his sister's children, and hopes were given that he would shortly return to his native country, and pass his old age in our society. He was now in an evil hour arrived.

I desired an interview with him for numerous and urgent reasons. With the first returns of my understanding I had anxiously sought information of the fate of my brother. During the course of my disease I had never seen him; and vague and unsatisfactory answers were returned to all my inquiries. I had vehemently interrogated Mrs. Hallet and her husband, and solicited an interview with this unfortunate man; but they mysteriously insinuated that his reason was still unsettled, and that his circumstances rendered an interview impossible. Their reserve on the particulars of this destruction, and the author of it, was equally invincible.

For some time, finding all my efforts fruitless, I had desisted from direct inquiries and solicitations, determined, as soon as my strength was sufficiently renewed, to pursue other means of dispelling my uncertainty. In this state of things my uncle's arrival and intention to visit me were announced. I almost shuddered to behold the face of this man. When I reflected on the disasters that had befallen us, I was half unwilling to witness that dejection and grief which would be disclosed in his countenance. But I believed that all transactions had been thoroughly disclosed to him, and confided in my importunity to extort from him the knowledge that I sought.

I had no doubt as to the person of our enemy; but the motives that urged him to perpetrate these horrors, the means that he used, and his present condition, were totally unknown. It was reasonable to expect some information on this head, from my uncle. I therefore waited his coming with impatience. At length, in the dusk of the evening, and in my solitary chamber, this meeting took place.

This man was our nearest relation, and had ever treated us with the affection of a parent. Our meeting, therefore, could not be without overflowing tenderness and gloomy joy. He rather encouraged than restrained the tears that I poured out in his arms, and took upon himself the task of comforter. Allusions to recent disasters could not be long omitted. One topic facilitated the admission of another. At length, I mentioned and deplored the ignorance in which I had been kept respecting my brother's destiny, and the circumstances of our misfortunes. I entreated him to tell me what was Wieland's condition, and what progress had been made in detecting or punishing the author of this unheard-of devastation.

"The author!" said he; "Do you know the author?"

"Alas!" I answered, "I am too well acquainted with him. The story of the grounds of my suspicions would be painful and too long. I am not apprized of the extent of your present knowledge. There are none but Wieland, Pleyel, and myself, who are able to relate certain facts."

"Spare yourself the pain," said he. "All that Wieland and Pleyel can communicate, I know already. If any thing of moment has fallen within your own exclusive knowledge, and the relation be not too arduous for your present strength, I confess I am desirous of hearing it. Perhaps you allude to one by the name of Carwin. I will anticipate your

160

curiosity by saying, that since these disasters, no one has seen or heard of him. His agency is, therefore, a mystery still unsolved."

I readily complied with his request, and related as distinctly as I could, though in general terms, the events transacted in the summer-house and my chamber. He listened without apparent surprize to the tale of Pleyel's errors and suspicions, and with augmented seriousness, to my narrative of the warnings and inexplicable vision, and the letter found upon the table. I waited for his comments.

"You gather from this," said he, "that Carwin is the author of all this misery."

"Is it not," answered I, "an unavoidable inference? But what know you respecting it? Was it possible to execute this mischief without witness or coadjutor? I beseech you to relate to me, when and why Mr. Hallet was summoned to the scene, and by whom this disaster was first suspected or discovered. Surely, suspicion must have fallen upon some one, and pursuit was made."

My uncle rose from his seat, and traversed the floor with hasty steps. His eyes were fixed upon the ground, and he seemed buried in perplexity. At length he paused, and said with an emphatic tone, "It is true; the instrument is known. Carwin may have plotted, but the execution was another's. That other is found, and his deed is ascertained."

"Good heaven!" I exclaimed, "what say you? Was not Carwin the assassin? Could any hand but his have carried into act this dreadful purpose?"

"Have I not said," returned he, "that the performance was another's? Carwin, perhaps, or heaven, or insanity, prompted the murderer; but Carwin is unknown. The actual performer has, long since, been called to judgment and convicted, and is, at this moment, at the bottom of a dungeon loaded with chains."

I lifted my hands and eyes. "Who then is this assassin? By what means, and whither was he traced? What is the testimony of his guilt?"

"His own, corroborated with that of a servant-maid who spied the murder of the children from a closet where she was concealed. The magistrate returned from your dwelling to your brother's. He was employed in hearing and recording the testimony of the only witness, when the criminal himself, unexpected, unsolicited, unsought, entered the hall, acknowledged his guilt, and rendered himself up to justice.

"He has since been summoned to the bar. The audience was composed of thousands whom rumours of this wonderful event had attracted from the greatest distance. A long and impartial examination was made, and the prisoner was called upon for his defence. In compliance with this call he delivered an ample relation of his motives and actions." There he stopped.

I besought him to say who this criminal was, and what the instigations that compelled him. My uncle was silent. I urged this inquiry with new force. I reverted to my own knowledge, and sought in this some basis to conjecture. I ran over the scanty catalogue of the men whom I knew; I lighted on no one who was qualified for ministering to malice like this. Again I resorted to importunity. Had I ever seen the criminal? Was it sheer cruelty, or diabolical revenge that produced this overthrow?

He surveyed me, for a considerable time, and listened to my interrogations in silence. At length he spoke: "Clara, I have known thee by report, and in some degree by observation. Thou art a being of no vulgar sort. Thy friends have hitherto treated thee as a child. They meant well, but, perhaps, they were unacquainted with thy strength. I assure myself that nothing will surpass thy fortitude.

"Thou art anxious to know the destroyer of thy family, his actions, and his motives. Shall I call him to thy presence, and permit him to confess before thee? Shall I make him the narrator of his own tale?"

I started on my feet, and looked round me with fearful glances, as if the murderer was close at hand. "What do you mean?" said I; "put an end, I beseech you, to this suspence."

"Be not alarmed; you will never more behold the face of this criminal, unless he be gifted with supernatural strength, and sever like threads the constraint of links and bolts. I have said that the assassin was arraigned at the bar, and that the trial ended with a summons from the judge to confess or to vindicate his actions. A reply was immediately made with significance of gesture, and a tranquil majesty, which denoted less of humanity than god-head. Judges, advocates and auditors were panic-struck and breathless with attention. One of the hearers faithfully recorded the speech. There it is," continued he, putting a roll of papers in my hand, "you may read it at your leisure."

With these words my uncle left me alone. My curiosity refused me a moment's delay. I opened the papers, and read as follows.

CHAPTER XIX

THEODORE WIELAND, the prisoner at the bar, was now called upon for his defence. He looked around him for some time in silence, and with a mild countenance. At length he spoke:

"It is strange; I am known to my judges and my auditors. Who is there present a stranger to the character of Wieland? who knows him not as an husband—as a father—as a friend? yet here am I arraigned as a criminal. I am charged with diabolical malice; I am accused of the murder of my wife and my children!

"It is true, they were slain by me; they all perished by my hand. The task of vindication is ignoble. What is it that I am called to vindicate? and before whom?

"You know that they are dead, and that they were killed by me. What more would you have? Would you extort from me a statement of my motives? Have you failed to discover them already? You charge me with malice; but your eyes are not shut; your reason is still vigorous; your memory has not forsaken you. You know whom it is that you thus charge. The habits of his life are known to you; his treatment of his wife and his offspring is known to you; the soundness of his integrity, and the unchangeableness of his principles, are familiar to your apprehension; yet you persist in this charge! You lead me hither manacled as a felon; you deem me worthy of a vile and tormenting death!

"Who are they whom I have devoted to death? My wife—the little ones that drew their being from me—that

164

creature who, as she surpassed them in excellence, claimed a larger affection than those whom natural affinities bound to my heart. Think ye that malice could have urged me to this deed? Hide your audacious fronts from the scrutiny of heaven. Take refuge in some cavern unvisited by human eyes. Ye may deplore your wickedness or folly, but ye cannot expiate it.

"Think not that I speak for your sakes. Hug to your hearts this detestable infatuation. Deem me still a murderer, and drag me to untimely death. I make not an effort to dispel your illusion: I utter not a word to cure you of your sanguinary folly: but there are probably some in this assembly who have come from far: for their sakes, whose distance has disabled them from knowing me, I will tell what I have done, and why.

"It is needless to say that God is the object of my supreme passion. I have cherished, in his presence, a single and upright heart. I have thirsted for the knowledge of his will. I have burnt with ardour to approve my faith and my obedience.

"My days have been spent in searching for the revelation of that will; but my days have been mournful, because my search failed. I solicited direction: I turned on every side where glimmerings of light could be discovered. I have not been wholly uninformed; but my knowledge has always stopped short of certainty. Dissatisfaction has insinuated itself into all my thoughts. My purposes have been pure; my wishes indefatigable; but not till lately were these purposes thoroughly accomplished, and these wishes fully gratified.

"I thank thee, my father, for thy bounty; that thou didst not ask a less sacrifice than this; that thou placedst me in a condition to testify my submission to thy will! What have I withheld which it was thy pleasure to exact? Now may I, with dauntless and erect eye, claim my reward, since I have given thee the treasure of my soul.

"I was at my own house: it was late in the evening: my sister had gone to the city, but proposed to return. It was in expectation of her return that my wife and I delayed going to bed beyond the usual hour; the rest of the family, however, were retired.

"My mind was contemplative and calm; not wholly devoid of apprehension on account of my sister's safety. Recent events, not easily explained, had suggested the existence of some danger; but this danger was without a distinct form in our imagination, and scarcely ruffled our tranquillity.

"Time passed, and my sister did not arrive; her house is at some distance from mine, and though her arrangements had been made with a view to residing with us, it was possible that, through forgetfulness, or the occurrence of unforeseen emergencies, she had returned to her own dwelling.

"Hence it was conceived proper that I should ascertain the truth by going thither. I went. On my way my mind was full of those ideas which related to my intellectual condition. In the torrent of fervid conceptions, I lost sight of my purpose. Some times I stood still; some times I wandered from my path, and experienced some difficulty, on recovering from my fit of musing, to regain it.

"The series of my thoughts is easily traced. At first every vein beat with raptures known only to the man whose parental and conjugal love is without limits, and the cup of whose desires, immense as it is, overflows with gratification. I know not why emotions that were perpetual visitants should now have recurred with unusual energy. The transition was not new from sensations of joy to a consciousness of gratitude. The author of my being was likewise the dispenser of every gift with which that being was embellished. The service to which a benefactor like this was entitled, could not be circumscribed. My social sentiments were indebted to their alliance with devotion for all their value. All passions are base, all joys feeble, all energies malignant, which are not drawn from this source.

"For a time, my contemplations soared above earth and its inhabitants. I stretched forth my hands; I lifted my eyes, and exclaimed, O! that I might be admitted to thy presence;

166

that mine were the supreme delight of knowing thy will, and of performing it! The blissful privilege of direct communication with thee, and of listening to the audible enunciation of thy pleasure!

"What task would I not undertake, what privation would I not cheerfully endure, to testify my love of thee? Alas! thou hidest thyself from my view: glimpses only of thy excellence and beauty are afforded me. Would that a momentary emanation from thy glory would visit me! that some unambiguous token of thy presence would salute my senses!

"In this mood, I entered the house of my sister. It was vacant. Scarcely had I regained recollection of the purpose that brought me hither. Thoughts of a different tendency had such absolute possession of my mind, that the relations of time and space were almost obliterated from my understanding. These wanderings, however, were restrained, and I ascended to her chamber.

"I had no light, and might have known by external observation, that the house was without any inhabitant. With this, however, I was not satisfied. I entered the room, and the object of my search not appearing, I prepared to return.

"The darkness required some caution in descending the stair. I stretched my hand to seize the balustrade by which I might regulate my steps. How shall I describe the lustre, which, at that moment, burst upon my vision!

"I was dazzled. My organs were bereaved of their activity. My eye-lids were half-closed, and my hands withdrawn from the balustrade. A nameless fear chilled my veins, and I stood motionless. This irradiation did not retire or lessen. It seemed as if some powerful effulgence covered me like a mantle.

"I opened my eyes and found all about me luminous and glowing. It was the element of heaven that flowed around. Nothing but a fiery stream was at first visible; but, anon, a shrill voice from behind called upon me to attend.

"I turned: It is forbidden to describe what I saw: Words, indeed, would be wanting to the task. The lineaments of that being, whose veil was now lifted, and whose visage beamed upon my sight, no hues of pencil or of language can pourtray.

"As it spoke, the accents thrilled to my heart. 'Thy prayers are heard. In proof of thy faith, render me thy wife. This is the victim I chuse. Call her hither, and here let her fall.'—The sound, and visage, and light vanished at once.

"What demand was this? The blood of Catharine was to be shed! My wife was to perish by my hand! I sought opportunity to attest my virtue. Little did I expect that a proof like this would have been demanded.

" 'My wife!' I exclaimed: 'O God! substitute some other victim. Make me not the butcher of my wife. My own blood is cheap. This will I pour out before thee with a willing heart; but spare, I beseech thee, this precious life, or commission some other than her husband to perform the bloody deed.'

"In vain. The conditions were prescribed; the decree had gone forth, and nothing remained but to execute it. I rushed out of the house and across the intermediate fields, and stopped not till I entered my own parlour.

"My wife had remained here during my absence, in anxious expectation of my return with some tidings of her sister. I had none to communicate. For a time, I was breathless with my speed: This, and the tremors that shook my frame, and the wildness of my looks, alarmed her. She immediately suspected some disaster to have happened to her friend, and her own speech was as much overpowered by emotion as mine.

"She was silent, but her looks manifested her impatience to hear what I had to communicate. I spoke, but with so much precipitation as scarcely to be understood; catching her, at the same time, by the arm, and forcibly pulling her from her seat.

" 'Come along with me: fly: waste not a moment: time will be lost, and the deed will be omitted. Tarry not; question not; but fly with me!'

"This deportment added afresh to her alarms. Her eyes pursued mine, and she said, 'What is the matter? For God's

168

sake what is the matter? Where would you have me go?'

"My eyes were fixed upon her countenance while she spoke. I thought upon her virtues; I viewed her as the mother of my babes; as my wife: I recalled the purpose for which I thus urged her attendance. My heart faltered, and I saw that I must rouse to this work all my faculties. The danger of the least delay was imminent.

"I looked away from her, and again exerting my force, drew her towards the door—'You must go with me—indeed you must.'

"In her fright she half-resisted my efforts, and again exclaimed, 'Good heaven! what is it you mean? Where go? What has happened? Have you found Clara?'

" 'Follow me, and you will see,' I answered, still urging her reluctant steps forward.

" 'What phrenzy has seized you? Something must needs have happened. Is she sick? Have you found her?'

" 'Come and see. Follow me, and know for yourself.'

"Still she expostulated and besought me to explain this mysterious behaviour. I could not trust myself to answer her; to look at her; but grasping her arm, I drew her after me. She hesitated, rather through confusion of mind than from unwillingness to accompany me. This confusion gradually abated, and she moved forward, but with irresolute footsteps, and continual exclamations of wonder and terror. Her interrogations of what was the matter? and whither was I going? were ceaseless and vehement.

"It was the scope of my efforts not to think; to keep up a conflict and uproar in my mind in which all order and distinctness should be lost; to escape from the sensations produced by her voice. I was, therefore, silent. I strove to abridge this interval by my haste, and to waste all my attention in furious gesticulations.

"In this state of mind we reached my sister's door. She looked at the windows and saw that all was desolate—'Why come we here? There is no body here. I will not go in.'

"Still I was dumb; but opening the door, I drew her into the entry. This was the allotted scene: here she was to fall. I let go her hand, and pressing my palms against my

169

forehead, made one mighty effort to work up my soul to the deed.

"In vain; it would not be; my courage was appalled; my arms nerveless: I muttered prayers that my strength might be aided from above. They availed nothing.

"Horror diffused itself over me. This conviction of my cowardice, my rebellion, fastened upon me, and I stood rigid and cold as marble. From this state I was somewhat relieved by my wife's voice, who renewed her supplications to be told why we came hither, and what was the fate of my sister.

"What could I answer? My words were broken and inarticulate. Her fears naturally acquired force from the observation of these symptoms; but these fears were misplaced. The only inference she deduced from my conduct was, that some terrible mishap had befallen Clara.

"She wrung her hands, and exclaimed in an agony, 'O tell me, where is she? What has become of her? Is she sick? Dead? Is she in her chamber? O let me go thither and know the worst!'

"This proposal set my thoughts once more in motion. Perhaps what my rebellious heart refused to perform here, I might obtain strength enough to execute elsewhere.

" 'Come then,' said I, 'let us go.'

" 'I will, but not in the dark. We must first procure a light.'

" 'Fly then and procure it; but I charge you, linger not. I will await for your return.'

"While she was gone, I strode along the entry. The fellness of a gloomy hurricane but faintly resembled the discord that reigned in my mind. To omit this sacrifice must not be; yet my sinews had refused to perform it. No alternative was offered. To rebel against the mandate was impossible; but obedience would render me the executioner of my wife. My will was strong, but my limbs refused their office.

"She returned with a light; I led the way to the chamber; she looked round her; she lifted the curtain of the bed; she saw nothing.

"At length, she fixed inquiring eyes upon me. The light now enabled her to discover in my visage what darkness had

170

hitherto concealed. Her cares were now transferred from my sister to myself, and she said in a tremulous voice, 'Wieland! you are not well: What ails you? Can I do nothing for you?'

"That accents and looks so winning should disarm me of my resolution, was to be expected. My thoughts were thrown anew into anarchy. I spread my hand before my eyes that I might not see her, and answered only by groans. She took my other hand between her's, and pressing it to her heart, spoke with that voice which had ever swayed my will, and wafted away sorrow.

"'My friend! my soul's friend! tell me thy cause of grief. Do I not merit to partake with thee in thy cares? Am I not thy wife?'

"This was too much. I broke from her embrace, and retired to a corner of the room. In this pause, courage was once more infused into me. I resolved to execute my duty. She followed me, and renewed her passionate entreaties to know the cause of my distress.

"I raised my head and regarded her with stedfast looks. I muttered something about death, and the injunctions of my duty. At these words she shrunk back, and looked at me with a new expression of anguish. After a pause, she clasped her hands, and exclaimed—

"'O Wieland! Wieland! God grant that I am mistaken; but surely something is wrong. I see it: it is too plain: thou art undone—lost to me and to thyself.' At the same time she gazed on my features with intensest anxiety, in hope that different symptoms would take place. I replied to her with vehemence—

"'Undone! No; my duty is known, and I thank my God that my cowardice is now vanquished, and I have power to fulfil it. Catharine! I pity the weakness of thy nature: I pity thee, but must not spare. Thy life is claimed from my hands: thou must die!'

"Fear was now added to her grief. 'What mean you? Why talk you of death? Bethink yourself, Wieland: bethink yourself, and this fit will pass. O why came I hither! Why did you drag me hither?'

171

" 'I brought thee hither to fulfil a divine command. I am appointed thy destroyer, and destroy thee I must.' Saying this I seized her wrists. She shrieked aloud, and endeavoured to free herself from my grasp; but her efforts were vain.

" 'Surely, surely Wieland, thou dost not mean it. Am I not thy wife? and wouldst thou kill me? Thou wilt not; and yet—I see—thou art Wieland no longer! A fury resistless and horrible possesses thee—Spare me—spare—help —help——'

"Till her breath was stopped she shrieked for help—for mercy. When she could speak no longer, her gestures, her looks appealed to my compassion. My accursed hand was irresolute and tremulous. I meant thy death to be sudden, thy struggles to be brief. Alas! my heart was infirm; my resolves mutable. Thrice I slackened my grasp, and life kept its hold, though in the midst of pangs. Her eye-balls started from their sockets. Grimness and distortion took place of all that used to bewitch me into transport, and subdue me into reverence.

"I was commissioned to kill thee, but not to torment thee with the foresight of thy death; not to multiply thy fears, and prolong thy agonies. Haggard, and pale, and lifeless, at length thou ceasedst to contend with thy destiny.

"This was a moment of triumph. Thus had I successfully subdued the stubbornness of human passions: the victim which had been demanded was given: the deed was done past recal.

"I lifted the corpse in my arms and laid it on the bed. I gazed upon it with delight. Such was the elation of my thoughts, that I even broke into laughter. I clapped my hands and exclaimed, 'It is done! My sacred duty is fulfilled! To that I have sacrificed, O my God! thy last and best gift, my wife!'

"For a while I thus soared above frailty. I imagined I had set myself forever beyond the reach of selfishness; but my imaginations were false. This rapture quickly subsided. I looked again at my wife. My joyous ebullitions vanished, and I asked myself who it was whom I saw? Methought it

172

could not be Catharine. It could not be the woman who had lodged for years in my heart; who had slept, nightly, in my bosom; who had borne in her womb, who had fostered at her breast, the beings who called me father; whom I had watched with delight, and cherished with a fondness ever new and perpetually growing: it could not be the same.

"Where was her bloom! These deadly and blood-suffused orbs but ill resemble the azure and exstatic tenderness of her eyes. The lucid stream that meandered over that bosom, the glow of love that was wont to sit upon that cheek, are much unlike these livid stains and this hideous deformity. Alas! these were the traces of agony; the gripe of the assassin had been here!

"I will not dwell upon my lapse into desperate and outrageous sorrow. The breath of heaven that sustained me was withdrawn, and I sunk into *mere man*. I leaped from the floor: I dashed my head against the wall: I uttered screams of horror: I panted after torment and pain. Eternal fire, and the bickerings of hell, compared with what I felt, were music and a bed of roses.

"I thank my God that this degeneracy was transient, that he deigned once more to raise me aloft. I thought upon what I had done as a sacrifice to duty, and *was calm*. My wife was dead; but I reflected, that though this source of human consolation was closed, yet others were still open. If the transports of an husband were no more, the feelings of a father had still scope for exercise. When remembrance of their mother should excite too keen a pang, I would look upon them, and *be comforted*.

"While I revolved these ideas, new warmth flowed in upon my heart—I was wrong. These feelings were the growth of selfishness. Of this I was not aware, and to dispel the mist that obscured my perceptions, a new effulgence and a new mandate were necessary.

"From these thoughts I was recalled by a ray that was shot into the room. A voice spake like that which I had before heard—'Thou hast done well; but all is not done—the sacrifice is incomplete—thy children must be offered—they must perish with their mother!—'"

173

CHAPTER XX

WILL you wonder that I read no farther? Will you not rather be astonished that I read thus far? What power supported me through such a task I know not. Perhaps the doubt from which I could not disengage my mind, that the scene here depicted was a dream, contributed to my perseverance. In vain the solemn introduction of my uncle, his appeals to my fortitude, and allusions to something monstrous in the events he was about to disclose; in vain the distressful perplexity, the mysterious silence and ambiguous answers of my attendants, especially when the condition of my brother was the theme of my inquiries, were remembered. I recalled the interview with Wieland in my chamber, his preternatural tranquillity succeeded by bursts of passion and menacing actions. All these coincided with the tenor of this paper.

Catharine and her children, and Louisa were dead. The act that destroyed them was, in the highest degree, inhuman. It was worthy of savages trained to murder, and exulting in agonies.

Who was the performer of the deed? Wieland! My brother! The husband and the father! That man of gentle virtues and invincible benignity! placable and mild—an idolator of peace! Surely, said I, it is a dream. For many days have I been vexed with frenzy. Its dominion is still felt; but new forms are called up to diversify and augment my torments.

The paper dropped from my hand, and my eyes followed

it. I shrunk back, as if to avoid some petrifying influence that approached me. My tongue was mute; all the functions of nature were at a stand, and I sunk upon the floor lifeless.

The noise of my fall, as I afterwards heard, alarmed my uncle, who was in a lower apartment, and whose apprehensions had detained him. He hastened to my chamber, and administered the assistance which my condition required. When I opened my eyes I beheld him before me. His skill as a reasoner as well as a physician, was exerted to obviate the injurious effects of this disclosure; but he had wrongly estimated the strength of my body or of my mind. This new shock brought me once more to the brink of the grave, and my malady was much more difficult to subdue than at first.

I will not dwell upon the long train of dreary sensations, and the hideous confusion of my understanding. Time slowly restored its customary firmness to my frame, and order to my thoughts. The images impressed upon my mind by this fatal paper were somewhat effaced by my malady. They were obscure and disjointed like the parts of a dream. I was desirous of freeing my imagination from this chaos. For this end I questioned my uncle, who was my constant companion. He was intimidated by the issue of his first experiment, and took pains to elude or discourage my inquiry. My impetuosity some times compelled him to have resort to misrepresentations and untruths.

Time effected that end, perhaps, in a more beneficial manner. In the course of my meditations the recollections of the past gradually became more distinct. I revolved them, however, in silence, and being no longer accompanied with surprise, they did not exercise a death-dealing power. I had discontinued the perusal of the paper in the midst of the narrative; but what I read, combined with information elsewhere obtained, threw, perhaps, a sufficient light upon these detestable transactions; yet my curiosity was not inactive. I desired to peruse the remainder.

My eagerness to know the particulars of this tale was mingled and abated by my antipathy to the scene which

175

would be disclosed. Hence I employed no means to effect my purpose. I desired knowledge, and, at the same time, shrunk back from receiving the boon.

One morning, being left alone, I rose from my bed, and went to a drawer where my finer clothing used to be kept. I opened it, and this fatal paper saluted my sight. I snatched it involuntarily, and withdrew to a chair. I debated, for a few minutes, whether I should open and read. Now that my fortitude was put to trial, it failed. I felt myself incapable of deliberately surveying a scene of so much horror. I was prompted to return it to its place, but this resolution gave way, and I determined to peruse some part of it. I turned over the leaves till I came near the conclusion. The narrative of the criminal was finished. The verdict of *guilty* reluctantly pronounced by the jury, and the accused interrogated why sentence of death should not pass. The answer was brief, solemn, and emphatical.

"No. I have nothing to say. My tale has been told. My motives have been truly stated. If my judges are unable to discern the purity of my intentions, or to credit the statement of them, which I have just made; if they see not that my deed was enjoined by heaven; that obedience was the test of perfect virtue, and the extinction of selfishness and error, they must pronounce me a murderer.

"They refuse to credit my tale; they impute my acts to the influence of dæmons; they account me an example of the highest wickedness of which human nature is capable; they doom me to death and infamy. Have I power to escape this evil? If I have, be sure I will exert it. I will not accept evil at their hand, when I am entitled to good; I will suffer only when I cannot elude suffering.

"You say that I am guilty. Impious and rash! thus to usurp the prerogatives of your Maker! to set up your bounded views and halting reason, as the measure of truth!

"Thou, Omnipotent and Holy! Thou knowest that my actions were conformable to thy will. I know not what is crime; what actions are evil in their ultimate and comprehensive tendency or what are good. Thy knowledge, as thy power, is unlimited. I have taken thee for my guide, and

176

cannot err. To the arms of thy protection, I entrust my safety. In the awards of thy justice, I confide for my recompense.

"Come death when it will, I am safe. Let calumny and abhorrence pursue me among men; I shall not be defrauded of my dues. The peace of virtue, and the glory of obedience, will be my portion hereafter."

Here ended the speaker. I withdrew my eyes from the page; but before I had time to reflect on what I had read, Mr. Cambridge entered the room. He quickly perceived how I had been employed, and betrayed some solicitude respecting the condition of my mind.

His fears, however, were superfluous. What I had read, threw me into a state not easily described. Anguish and fury, however, had no part in it. My faculties were chained up in wonder and awe. Just then, I was unable to speak. I looked at my friend with an air of inquisitiveness, and pointed at the roll. He comprehended my inquiry, and answered me with looks of gloomy acquiescence. After some time, my thoughts found their way to my lips.

"Such then were the acts of my brother. Such were his words. For this he was condemned to die: To die upon the gallows! A fate, cruel and unmerited! And is it so?" continued I, struggling for utterance, which this new idea made difficult; "is he—dead!"

"No. He is alive. There could be no doubt as to the cause of these excesses. They originated in sudden madness; but that madness continues, and he is condemned to perpetual imprisonment."

"Madness, say you? Are you sure? Were not these sights, and these sounds, really seen and heard?"

My uncle was surprised at my question. He looked at me with apparent inquietude. "Can you doubt," said he, "that these were illusions? Does heaven, think you, interfere for such ends?"

"O no; I think it not. Heaven cannot stimulate to such unheard-of outrage. The agent was not good, but evil."

"Nay, my dear girl," said my friend, "lay aside these fancies. Neither angel nor devil had any part in this affair."

"You misunderstand me," I answered; "I believe the agency to be external and real, but not supernatural."

"Indeed!" said he, in an accent of surprize. "Whom do you then suppose to be the agent?"

"I know not. All is wildering conjecture. I cannot forget Carwin. I cannot banish the suspicion that he was the setter of these snares. But how can we suppose it to be madness? Did insanity ever before assume this form?"

"Frequently. The illusion, in this case, was more dreadful in its consequences, than any that has come to my knowledge; but, I repeat that similar illusions are not rare. Did you never hear of an instance which occurred in your mother's family?"

"No. I beseech you relate it. My grandfather's death I have understood to have been extraordinary, but I know not in what respect. A brother, to whom he was much attached, died in his youth, and this, as I have heard, influenced, in some remarkable way, the fate of my grandfather; but I am unacquainted with particulars."

"On the death of that brother," resumed my friend, "my father was seized with dejection, which was found to flow from two sources. He not only grieved for the loss of a friend, but entertained the belief that his own death would be inevitably consequent on that of his brother. He waited from day to day in expectation of the stroke which he predicted was speedily to fall upon him. Gradually, however, he recovered his cheerfulness and confidence. He married, and performed his part in the world with spirit and activity. At the end of twenty-one years it happened that he spent the summer with his family at an house which he possessed on the sea coast in Cornwall. It was at no great distance from a cliff which overhung the ocean, and rose into the air to a great height. The summit was level and secure, and easily ascended on the land side. The company frequently repaired hither in clear weather, invited by its pure airs and extensive prospects. One evening in June my father, with his wife and some friends, chanced to be on this spot. Every one was happy, and my father's imagination seemed particularly alive to the grandeur of the scenery.

178

"Suddenly, however, his limbs trembled and his features betrayed alarm. He threw himself into the attitude of one listening. He gazed earnestly in a direction in which nothing was visible to his friends. This lasted for a minute; then turning to his companions, he told them that his brother had just delivered to him a summons, which must be instantly obeyed. He then took an hasty and solemn leave of each person, and, before their surprize would allow them to understand the scene, he rushed to the edge of the cliff, threw himself headlong, and was seen no more.

"In the course of my practice in the German army, many cases, equally remarkable, have occurred. Unquestionably the illusions were maniacal, though the vulgar thought otherwise. They are all reducible to one class,* and are not more difficult of explication and cure than most affections of our frame."

This opinion my uncle endeavoured, by various means, to impress upon me. I listened to his reasonings and illustrations with silent respect. My astonishment was great on finding proofs of an influence of which I had supposed there were no examples; but I was far from accounting for appearances in my uncle's manner. Ideas thronged into my mind which I was unable to disjoin or to regulate. I reflected that this madness, if madness it were, had affected Pleyel and myself as well as Wieland. Pleyel had heard a mysterious voice. I had seen and heard. A form had showed itself to me as well as to Wieland. The disclosure had been made in the same spot. The appearance was equally complete and equally prodigious in both instances. Whatever supposition I should adopt, had I not equal reason to tremble? What was my security against influences equally terrific and equally irresistable?

It would be vain to attempt to describe the state of mind which this idea produced. I wondered at the change which a moment had effected in my brother's condition. Now was I stupified with tenfold wonder in contemplating myself. Was I not likewise transformed from rational and human

*Mania Mutabilis. See Darwin's Zoonomia, vol. ii. Class III. 1. 2. where similar cases are stated.

into a creature of nameless and fearful attributes? Was I not transported to the brink of the same abyss? Ere a new day should come, my hands might be embrued in blood, and my remaining life be consigned to a dungeon and chains.

With moral sensibility like mine, no wonder that this new dread was more insupportable than the anguish I had lately endured. Grief carries its own antidote along with it. When thought becomes merely a vehicle of pain, its progress must be stopped. Death is a cure which nature or ourselves must administer: To this cure I now looked forward with gloomy satisfaction.

My silence could not conceal from my uncle the state of my thoughts. He made unwearied efforts to divert my attention from views so pregnant with danger. His efforts, aided by time, were in some measure successful. Confidence in the strength of my resolution, and in the healthful state of my faculties, was once more revived. I was able to devote my thoughts to my brother's state, and the causes of this disasterous proceeding.

My opinions were the sport of eternal change. Some times I conceived the apparition to be more than human. I had no grounds on which to build a disbelief. I could not deny faith to the evidence of my religion; the testimony of men was loud and unanimous: both these concurred to persuade me that evil spirits existed, and that their energy was frequently exerted in the system of the world.

These ideas connected themselves with the image of Carwin. Where is the proof, said I, that dæmons may not be subjected to the controul of men? This truth may be distorted and debased in the minds of the ignorant. The dogmas of the vulgar, with regard to this subject, are glaringly absurd; but though these may justly be neglected by the wise, we are scarcely justified in totally rejecting the possibility that men may obtain supernatural aid.

The dreams of superstition are worthy of contempt. Witchcraft, its instruments and miracles, the compact ratified by a bloody signature, the apparatus of sulpherous smells and thundering explosions, are monstrous and chimerical. These have no part in the scene over which the

180

genius of Carwin presides. That conscious beings, dissimilar from human, but moral and voluntary agents as we are, some where exist, can scarcely be denied. That their aid may be employed to benign or malignant purposes, cannot be disproved.

Darkness rests upon the designs of this man. The extent of his power is unknown; but is there not evidence that it has been now exerted?

I recurred to my own experience. Here Carwin had actually appeared upon the stage; but this was in a human character. A voice and a form were discovered; but one was apparently exerted, and the other disclosed, not to befriend, but to counteract Carwin's designs. There were tokens of hostility, and not of alliance, between them. Carwin was the miscreant whose projects were resisted by a minister of heaven. How can this be reconciled to the stratagem which ruined my brother? There the agency was at once preternatural and malignant.

The recollection of this fact led my thoughts into a new channel. The malignity of that influence which governed my brother had hitherto been no subject of doubt. His wife and children were destroyed; they had expired in agony and fear; yet was it indisputably certain that their murderer was criminal? He was acquitted at the tribunal of his own conscience; his behaviour at his trial and since, was faithfully reported to me; appearances were uniform; not for a moment did he lay aside the majesty of virtue; he repelled all invectives by appealing to the deity, and to the tenor of his past life; surely there was truth in this appeal: none but a command from heaven could have swayed his will; and nothing but unerring proof of divine approbation could sustain his mind in its present elevation.

CHAPTER XXI

S UCH, for some time, was the course of my meditations. My weakness, and my aversion to be pointed at as an object of surprize or compassion, prevented me from going into public. I studiously avoided the visits of those who came to express their sympathy, or gratify their curiosity. My uncle was my principal companion. Nothing more powerfully tended to console me than his conversation.

With regard to Pleyel, my feelings seemed to have undergone a total revolution. It often happens that one passion supplants another. Late disasters had rent my heart, and now that the wound was in some degree closed, the love which I had cherished for this man seemed likewise to have vanished.

Hitherto, indeed, I had had no cause for despair. I was innocent of that offence which had estranged him from my presence. I might reasonably expect that my innocence would at some time be irresistably demonstrated, and his affection for me be revived with his esteem. Now my aversion to be thought culpable by him continued, but was unattended with the same impatience. I desired the removal of his suspicions, not for the sake of regaining his love, but because I delighted in the veneration of so excellent a man, and because he himself would derive pleasure from conviction of my integrity.

My uncle had early informed me that Pleyel and he had seen each other, since the return of the latter from Europe.

Amidst the topics of their conversation, I discovered that Pleyel had carefully omitted the mention of those events which had drawn upon me so much abhorrence. I could not account for his silence on this subject. Perhaps time or some new discovery had altered or shaken his opinion. Perhaps he was unwilling, though I were guilty, to injure me in the opinion of my venerable kinsman. I understood that he had frequently visited me during my disease, had watched many successive nights by my bedside, and manifested the utmost anxiety on my account.

The journey which he was preparing to take, at the termination of our last interview, the catastrophe of the ensuing night induced him to delay. The motives of this journey I had, till now, totally mistaken. They were explained to me by my uncle, whose tale excited my astonishment without awakening my regret. In a different state of mind, it would have added unspeakably to my distress, but now it was more a source of pleasure than pain. This, perhaps, is not the least extraordinary of the facts contained in this narrative. It will excite less wonder when I add, that my indifference was temporary, and that the lapse of a few days shewed me that my feelings were deadened for a time, rather than finally extinguished.

Theresa de Stolberg was alive. She had conceived the resolution of seeking her lover in America. To conceal her flight, she had caused the report of her death to be propagated. She put herself under the conduct of Bertrand, the faithful servant of Pleyel. The pacquet which the latter received from the hands of his servant, contained the tidings of her safe arrival at Boston, and to meet her there was the purpose of his journey.

This discovery had set this man's character in a new light. I had mistaken the heroism of friendship for the phrenzy of love. He who had gained my affections, may be supposed to have previously entitled himself to my reverence; but the levity which had formerly characterized the behaviour of this man, tended to obscure the greatness of his sentiments. I did not fail to remark, that since this lady was still alive, the voice in the temple which asserted her death, must either have been intended to deceive, or have been itself deceived. The latter supposition was inconsistent with the notion of a spiritual, and the former with that of a benevolent being.

When my disease abated, Pleyel had forborne his visits, and had lately set out upon this journey. This amounted to a proof that my guilt was still believed by him. I was grieved for his errors, but trusted that my vindication would, sooner or later, be made.

Meanwhile, tumultuous thoughts were again set afloat by a proposal made to me by my uncle. He imagined that new airs would restore my languishing constitution, and a varied succession of objects tend to repair the shock which my mind had received. For this end, he proposed to me to take up my abode with him in France or Italy.

At a more prosperous period, this scheme would have pleased for its own sake. Now my heart sickened at the prospect of nature. The world of man was shrouded in misery and blood, and constituted a loathsome spectacle. I willingly closed my eyes in sleep, and regretted that the respite it afforded me was so short. I marked with satisfaction the progress of decay in my frame, and consented to live, merely in the hope that the course of nature would speedily relieve me from the burthen. Nevertheless, as he persisted in his scheme, I concurred in it merely because he was entitled to my gratitude, and because my refusal gave him pain.

No sooner was he informed of my consent, than he told me I must make immediate preparation to embark, as the ship in which he had engaged a passage would be ready to depart in three days. This expedition was unexpected. There was an impatience in his manner when he urged the necessity of dispatch that excited my surprize. When I questioned him as to the cause of this haste, he generally stated reasons which, at that time, I could not deny to be plausible; but which, on the review, appeared insufficient. I suspected that the true motives were concealed, and believed that these motives had some connection with my brother's destiny.

I now recollected that the information respecting Wieland which had, from time to time, been imparted to me, was always accompanied with airs of reserve and mysteriousness. What had appeared sufficiently explicit at the time it was uttered, I now remembered to have been faltering and ambiguous. I was resolved to remove my doubts, by visiting the unfortunate man in his dungeon.

Heretofore the idea of this visit had occurred to me; but the horrors of his dwelling-place, his wild yet placid physiognomy, his neglected locks, the fetters which constrained his limbs, terrible as they were in description, how could I endure to behold!

Now, however, that I was preparing to take an everlasting farewell of my country, now that an ocean was henceforth to separate me from him, how could I part without an interview? I would examine his situation with my own eyes. I would know whether the representations which had been made to me were true. Perhaps the sight of the sister whom he was wont to love with a passion more than fraternal, might have an auspicious influence on his malady.

Having formed this resolution, I waited to communicate it to Mr. Cambridge. I was aware that, without his concurrence, I could not hope to carry it into execution; and could discover no objection to which it was liable. If I had not been deceived as to his condition, no inconvenience could arise from this proceeding. His consent, therefore, would be the test of his sincerity.

I seized this opportunity to state my wishes on this head. My suspicions were confirmed by the manner in which my request affected him. After some pause, in which his countenance betrayed every mark of perplexity, he said to me, "Why would you pay this visit? What useful purpose can it serve?"

"We are preparing," said I, "to leave the country forever: What kind of being should I be to leave behind me a brother in calamity without even a parting interview? Indulge me for three minutes in the sight of him. My heart will be much easier after I have looked at him, and shed a few tears in his presence."

"I believe otherwise. The sight of him would only aug-

185

ment your distress, without contributing, in any degree, to his benefit."

"I know not that," returned I. "Surely the sympathy of his sister, proofs that her tenderness is as lively as ever, must be a source of satisfaction to him. At present he must regard all mankind as his enemies and calumniators. His sister he, probably, conceives to partake in the general infatuation, and to join in the cry of abhorrence that is raised against him. To be undeceived in this respect, to be assured that, however I may impute his conduct to delusion, I still retain all my former affection for his person, and veneration for the purity of his motives, cannot but afford him pleasure. When he hears that I have left the country, without even the ceremonious attention of a visit, what will he think of me? His magnanimity may hinder him from repining, but he will surely consider my behaviour as savage and unfeeling. Indeed, dear Sir, I must pay this visit. To embark with you without paying it, will be impossible. It may be of no service to him, but will enable me to acquit myself of what I cannot but esteem a duty. Besides," continued I, "if it be a mere fit of insanity that has seized him, may not my presence chance to have a salutary influence? The mere sight of me, it is not impossible, may rectify his perceptions."

"Ay," said my uncle, with some eagerness; "it is by no means impossible that your interview may have that effect; and for that reason, beyond all others, would I dissuade you from it."

I expressed my surprize at this declaration. "Is it not to be desired that an error so fatal as this should be rectified?"

"I wonder at your question. Reflect on the consequences of this error. Has he not destroyed the wife whom he loved, the children whom he idolized? What is it that enables him to bear the remembrance, but the belief that he acted as his duty enjoined? Would you rashly bereave him of this belief? Would you restore him to himself, and convince him that he was instigated to this dreadful outrage by a perversion of his organs, or a delusion from hell?

"Now his visions are joyous and elate. He conceives himself to have reached a loftier degree of virtue, than any other human being. The merit of his sacrifice is only enhanced in the eyes of superior beings, by the detestation that pursues him here, and the sufferings to which he is condemned. The belief that even his sister has deserted him, and gone over to his enemies, adds to his sublimity of feelings, and his confidence in divine approbation and future recompense.

"Let him be undeceived in this respect, and what floods of despair and of horror will overwhelm him! Instead of glowing approbation and serene hope, will he not hate and torture himself? Self-violence, or a phrenzy far more savage and destructive than this, may be expected to succeed. I beseech you, therefore, to relinquish this scheme. If you calmly reflect upon it, you will discover that your duty lies in carefully shunning him."

Mr. Cambridge's reasonings suggested views to my understanding, that had not hitherto occurred. I could not but admit their validity, but they shewed, in a new light, the depth of that misfortune in which my brother was plunged. I was silent and irresolute.

Presently, I considered, that whether Wieland was a maniac, a faithful servant of his God, the victim of hellish illusions, or the dupe of human imposture, was by no means certain. In this state of my mind it became me to be silent during the visit that I projected. This visit should be brief: I should be satisfied merely to snatch a look at him. Admitting that a change in his opinions were not to be desired, there was no danger, from the conduct which I should pursue, that this change should be wrought.

But I could not conquer my uncle's aversion to this scheme. Yet I persisted, and he found that to make me voluntarily relinquish it, it was necessary to be more explicit than he had hitherto been. He took both my hands, and anxiously examining my countenance as he spoke, "Clara," said he, "this visit must not be paid. We must hasten with the utmost expedition from this shore. It is folly to conceal the truth from you, and, since it is only by disclosing the truth that you can be prevailed upon to lay aside this project, the truth shall be told.

"O my dear girl!" continued he with increasing energy in his accent, "your brother's phrenzy is, indeed, stupendous and frightful. The soul that formerly actuated his frame has disappeared. The same form remains; but the wise and benevolent Wieland is no more. A fury that is rapacious of blood, that lifts his strength almost above that of mortals, that bends all his energies to the destruction of whatever was once dear to him, possesses him wholly.

"You must not enter his dungeon; his eyes will no sooner be fixed upon you, than an exertion of his force will be made. He will shake off his fetters in a moment, and rush upon you. No interposition will then be strong or quick enough to save you.

"The phantom that has urged him to the murder of Catharine and her children is not yet appeased. Your life, and that of Pleyel, are exacted from him by this imaginary being. He is eager to comply with this demand. Twice he has escaped from his prison. The first time, he no sooner found himself at liberty, than he hasted to Pleyel's house. It being midnight, the latter was in bed. Wieland penetrated unobserved to his chamber, and opened his curtain. Happily, Pleyel awoke at the critical moment, and escaped the fury of his kinsman, by leaping from his chamber-window into the court. Happily, he reached the ground without injury. Alarms were given, and after diligent search, your brother was found in a chamber of your house, whither, no doubt, he had sought you.

"His chains, and the watchfulness of his guards, were redoubled; but again, by some miracle, he restored himself to liberty. He was now incautiously apprized of the place of your abode: and had not information of his escape been instantly given, your death would have been added to the number of his atrocious acts.

"You now see the danger of your project. You must not only forbear to visit him, but if you would save him from the crime of embruing his hands in your blood, you must leave the country. There is no hope that his malady will end but with his life, and no precaution will ensure your safety, but that of placing the ocean between you.

"I confess I came over with an intention to reside among you, but these disasters have changed my views. Your own safety and my happiness require that you should accompany me in my return, and I entreat you to give your cheerful concurrence to this measure."

After these representations from my uncle, it was impossible to retain my purpose. I readily consented to seclude myself from Wieland's presence. I likewise acquiesced in the proposal to go to Europe; not that I ever expected to arrive there, but because, since my principles forbad me to assail my own life, change had some tendency to make supportable the few days which disease should spare to me.

What a tale had thus been unfolded! I was hunted to death, not by one whom my misconduct had exasperated, who was conscious of illicit motives, and who sought his end by circumvention and surprize; but by one who deemed himself commissioned for this act by heaven, who regarded this career of horror as the last refinement of virtue, whose implacability was proportioned to the reverence and love which he felt for me, and who was inaccessible to the fear of punishment and ignominy!

In vain should I endeavour to stay his hand by urging the claims of a sister or friend: these were his only reasons for pursuing my destruction. Had I been a stranger to his blood; had I been the most worthless of human kind; my safety had not been endangered.

Surely, said I, my fate is without example. The phrenzy which is charged upon my brother, must belong to myself. My foe is manacled and guarded; but I derive no security from these restraints. I live not in a community of savages; yet, whether I sit or walk, go into crouds, or hide myself in solitude, my life is marked for a prey to inhuman violence; I am in perpetual danger of perishing; of perishing under the grasp of a brother!

I recollected the omens of this destiny; I remembered the gulf to which my brother's invitation had conducted me; I remembered that, when on the brink of danger, the author

189

of my peril was depicted by my fears in his form: Thus realized, were the creatures of prophetic sleep, and of wakeful terror!

These images were unavoidably connected with that of Carwin. In this paroxysm of distress, my attention fastened on him as the grand deceiver; the author of this black conspiracy; the intelligence that governed in this storm.

Some relief is afforded in the midst of suffering, when its author is discovered or imagined; and an object found on which we may pour out our indignation and our vengeance. I ran over the events that had taken place since the origin of our intercourse with him, and reflected on the tenor of that description which was received from Ludloe. Mixed up with notions of supernatural agency, were the vehement suspicions which I entertained, that Carwin was the enemy whose machinations had destroyed us.

I thirsted for knowledge and for vengeance. I regarded my hasty departure with reluctance, since it would remove me from the means by which this knowledge might be obtained, and this vengeance gratified. This departure was to take place in two days. At the end of two days I was to bid an eternal adieu to my native country. Should I not pay a parting visit to the scene of these disasters? Should I not bedew with my tears the graves of my sister and her children? Should I not explore their desolate habitation, and gather from the sight of its walls and furniture food for my eternal melancholy?

This suggestion was succeeded by a secret shuddering. Some disastrous influence appeared to overhang the scene. How many memorials should I meet with serving to recall the images of those I had lost!

I was tempted to relinquish my design, when it occurred to me that I had left among my papers a journal of transactions in short-hand. I was employed in this manuscript on that night when Pleyel's incautious curiosity tempted him to look over my shoulder. I was then recording my adventure in *the recess*, an imperfect sight of which led him into such fatal errors.

I had regulated the disposition of all my property. This

manuscript, however, which contained the most secret transactions of my life, I was desirous of destroying. For this end I must return to my house, and this I immediately determined to do.

I was not willing to expose myself to opposition from my friends, by mentioning my design; I therefore bespoke the use of Mr. Hallet's chaise, under pretence of enjoying an airing, as the day was remarkably bright.

This request was gladly complied with, and I directed the servant to conduct me to Mettingen. I dismissed him at the gate, intending to use, in returning, a carriage belonging to my brother.

CHAPTER XXII

THE inhabitants of the *Hut* received me with a mixture of joy and surprize. Their homely welcome, and their artless sympathy, were grateful to my feelings. In the midst of their inquiries, as to my health, they avoided all allusions to the source of my malady. They were honest creatures, and I loved them well. I participated in the tears which they shed when I mentioned to them my speedy departure for Europe, and promised to acquaint them with my welfare during my long absence.

They expressed great surprize when I informed them of my intention to visit my cottage. Alarm and foreboding overspread their features, and they attempted to dissuade me from visiting an house which they firmly believed to be haunted by a thousand ghastly apparitions.

These apprehensions, however, had no power over my conduct. I took an irregular path which led me to my own house. All was vacant and forlorn. A small enclosure, near which the path led, was the burying-ground belonging to the family. This I was obliged to pass. Once I had intended to enter it, and ponder on the emblems and inscriptions which my uncle had caused to be made on the tombs of Catharine and her children; but now my heart faltered as I approached, and I hastened forward, that distance might conceal it from my view.

When I approached the recess, my heart again sunk. I averted my eyes, and left it behind me as quickly as possible.

192

Silence reigned through my habitation and a darkness, which closed doors and shutters produced. Every object was connected with mine or my brother's history. I passed the entry, mounted the stair, and unlocked the door of my chamber. It was with difficulty that I curbed my fancy and smothered my fears. Slight movements and casual sounds were transformed into beckoning shadows and calling shapes.

I proceeded to the closet. I opened and looked round it with fearfulness. All things were in their accustomed order. I sought and found the manuscript where I was used to deposit it. This being secured, there was nothing to detain me; yet I stood and contemplated awhile the furniture and walls of my chamber. I remembered how long this apartment had been a sweet and tranquil asylum; I compared its former state with its present dreariness, and reflected that I now beheld it for the last time.

Here it was that the incomprehensible behaviour of Carwin was witnessed: this the stage on which that enemy of man shewed himself for a moment unmasked. Here the menaces of murder were wafted to my ear; and here these menaces were executed.

These thoughts had a tendency to take from me my self-command. My feeble limbs refused to support me, and I sunk upon a chair. Incoherent and half-articulate exclamations escaped my lips. The name of Carwin was uttered, and eternal woes, woes like that which his malice had entailed upon us, were heaped upon him. I invoked all-seeing heaven to drag to light and to punish this betrayer, and accused its providence for having thus long delayed the retribution that was due to so enormous a guilt.

I have said that the window shutters were closed. A feeble light, however, found entrance through the crevices. A small window illuminated the closet, and the door being closed, a dim ray streamed through the key-hole. A kind of twilight was thus created, sufficient for the purposes of vision; but, at the same time, involving all minuter objects in obscurity.

This darkness suited the colour of my thoughts. I sick-

193

ened at the remembrance of the past. The prospect of the future excited my loathing. I muttered in a low voice, Why should I live longer? Why should I drag on a miserable being? All, for whom I ought to live, have perished. Am I not myself hunted to death?

At that moment, my despair suddenly became vigorous. My nerves were no longer unstrung. My powers, that had long been deadened, were revived. My bosom swelled with a sudden energy, and the conviction darted through my mind, that to end my torments was, at once, practicable and wise.

I knew how to find way to the recesses of life. I could use a lancet with some skill, and could distinguish between vein and artery. By piercing deep into the latter, I should shun the evils which the future had in store for me, and take refuge from my woes in quiet death.

I started on my feet, for my feebleness was gone, and hasted to the closet. A lancet and other small instruments were preserved in a case which I had deposited here. Inattentive as I was to foreign considerations, my ears were still open to any sound of mysterious import that should occur. I thought I heard a step in the entry. My purpose was suspended, and I cast an eager glance at my chamber door, which was open. No one appeared, unless the shadow which I discerned upon the floor, was the outline of a man. If it were, I was authorized to suspect that some one was posted close to the entrance, who possibly had overheard my exclamations.

My teeth chattered, and a wild confusion took place of my momentary calm. Thus it was when a terrific visage had disclosed itself on a former night. Thus it was when the evil destiny of Wieland assumed the lineaments of something human. What horrid apparition was preparing to blast my sight?

Still I listened and gazed. Not long, for the shadow moved; a foot, unshapely and huge, was thrust forward; a form advanced from its concealment, and stalked into the room. It was Carwin!

While I had breath I shrieked. While I had power over

194

my muscles, I motioned with my hand that he should vanish. My exertions could not last long; I sunk into a fit.

O that this grateful oblivion had lasted for ever! Too quickly I recovered my senses. The power of distinct vision was no sooner restored to me, than this hateful form again presented itself, and I once more relapsed.

A second time, untoward nature recalled me from the sleep of death. I found myself stretched upon the bed. When I had power to look up, I remembered only that I had cause to fear. My distempered fancy fashioned to itself no distinguishable image. I threw a languid glance round me; once more my eyes lighted upon Carwin.

He was seated on the floor, his back rested against the wall, his knees were drawn up, and his face was buried in his hands. That his station was at some distance, that his attitude was not menacing, that his ominous visage was concealed, may account for my now escaping a shock, violent as those which were past. I withdrew my eyes, but was not again deserted by my senses.

On perceiving that I had recovered my sensibility, he lifted his head. This motion attracted my attention. His countenance was mild, but sorrow and astonishment sat upon his features. I averted my eyes and feebly exclaimed—"O! fly—fly far and for ever!—I cannot behold you and live!"

He did not rise upon his feet, but clasped his hands, and said in a tone of deprecation—"I will fly. I am become a fiend, the sight of whom destroys. Yet tell me my offence! You have linked curses with my name; you ascribe to me a malice monstrous and infernal. I look around; all is loneliness and desert! This house and your brother's are solitary and dismantled! You die away at the sight of me! My fear whispers that some deed of horror has been perpetrated; that I am the undesigning cause."

What language was this? Had he not avowed himself a ravisher? Had not this chamber witnessed his atrocious purposes? I besought him with new vehemence to go.

He lifted his eyes—"Great heaven! what have I done? I think I know the extent of my offences. I have acted, but my

195

actions have possibly effected more than I designed. This fear has brought me back from my retreat. I come to repair the evil of which my rashness was the cause, and to prevent more evil. I come to confess my errors."

"Wretch!" I cried when my suffocating emotions would permit me to speak, "the ghosts of my sister and her children, do they not rise to accuse thee? Who was it that blasted the intellects of Wieland? Who was it that urged him to fury, and guided him to murder? Who, but thou and the devil, with whom thou art confederated?"

At these words a new spirit pervaded his countenance. His eyes once more appealed to heaven. "If I have memory, if I have being, I am innocent. I intended no ill; but my folly, indirectly and remotely, may have caused it; but what words are these! Your brother lunatic! His children dead!"

What should I infer from this deportment? Was the ignorance which these words implied real or pretended?—Yet how could I imagine a mere human agency in these events? But if the influence was preternatural or maniacal in my brother's case, they must be equally so in my own. Then I remembered that the voice exerted, was to save me from Carwin's attempts. These ideas tended to abate my abhorrence of this man, and to detect the absurdity of my accusations.

"Alas!" said I, "I have no one to accuse. Leave me to my fate. Fly from a scene stained with cruelty; devoted to despair."

Carwin stood for a time musing and mournful. At length he said, "What has happened? I came to expiate my crimes: let me know them in their full extent. I have horrible forebodings! What has happened?"

I was silent; but recollecting the intimation given by this man when he was detected in my closet, which implied some knowledge of that power which interfered in my favor, I eagerly inquired, "What was that voice which called upon me to hold when I attempted to open the closet? What face was that which I saw at the bottom of the stairs? Answer me truly."

"I came to confess the truth. Your allusions are horrible

196

and strange. Perhaps I have but faint conceptions of the evils which my infatuation has produced; but what remains I will perform. It was *my voice* that you heard! It was *my face* that you saw!"

For a moment I doubted whether my remembrance of events were not confused. How could he be at once stationed at my shoulder and shut up in my closet? How could he stand near me and yet be invisible? But if Carwin's were the thrilling voice and the fiery visage which I had heard and seen, then was he the prompter of my brother, and the author of these dismal outrages.

Once more I averted my eyes and struggled for speech. "Begone! thou man of mischief! Remorseless and implacable miscreant! begone!"

"I will obey," said he in a disconsolate voice; "yet, wretch as I am, am I unworthy to repair the evils that I have committed? I came as a repentant criminal. It is you whom I have injured, and at your bar am I willing to appear, and confess and expiate my crimes. I have deceived you: I have sported with your terrors: I have plotted to destroy your reputation. I come now to remove your errors; to set you beyond the reach of similar fears; to rebuild your fame as far as I am able.

"This is the amount of my guilt, and this the fruit of my remorse. Will you not hear me? Listen to my confession, and then denounce punishment. All I ask is a patient audience."

"What!" I replied, "was not thine the voice that commanded my brother to imbrue his hands in the blood of his children—to strangle that angel of sweetness his wife? Has he not vowed my death, and the death of Pleyel, at thy bidding? Hast thou not made him the butcher of his family; changed him who was the glory of his species into worse than brute; robbed him of reason; and consigned the rest of his days to fetters and stripes?"

Carwin's eyes glared, and his limbs were petrified at this intelligence. No words were requisite to prove him guiltless of these enormities: at the time, however, I was nearly insensible to these exculpatory tokens. He walked to the

197

farther end of the room, and having recovered some degree of composure, he spoke—

"I am not this villain; I have slain no one; I have prompted none to slay; I have handled a tool of wonderful efficacy without malignant intentions, but without caution; ample will be the punishment of my temerity, if my conduct has contributed to this evil." He paused.—

I likewise was silent. I struggled to command myself so far as to listen to the tale which he should tell. Observing this, he continued—

"You are not apprized of the existence of a power which I possess. I know not by what name to call it.* It enables me to mimic exactly the voice of another, and to modify the sound so that it shall appear to come from what quarter, and be uttered at what distance I please.

"I know not that every one possesses this power. Perhaps, though a casual position of my organs in my youth shewed me that I possessed it, it is an art which may be taught to all. Would to God I had died unknowing of the secret! It has produced nothing but degradation and calamity.

"For a time the possession of so potent and stupendous

*Biloquium, or vetrilocution. Sound is varied according to the variations of direction and distance. The art of the ventriloquist consists in modifying his voice according to all these variations, without changing his place. See the work of the Abbe de la Chappelle, in which are accurately recorded the performances of one of these artists, and some ingenious, though unsatisfactory speculations are given on the means by which the effects are produced. This power is, perhaps, given by nature, but is doubtless improvable, if not acquirable, by art. It may, possibly, consist in an unusual flexibility or exertion of the bottom of the tongue and the uvula. That speech is producible by these alone must be granted, since anatomists mention two instances of persons speaking without a tongue. In one case, the organ was originally wanting, but its place was supplied by a small tubercle, and the uvula was perfect. In the other, the tongue was destroyed by disease, but probably a small part of it remained.

This power is difficult to explain, but the fact is undeniable. Experience shews that the human voice can imitate the voice of all men and of all inferior animals. The sound of musical instruments, and even noises from the contact of inanimate substances, have been accurately imitated. The mimicry of animals is notorious; and Dr. Burney (Musical Travels) mentions one who imitated a flute and violin, so as to deceive even his ears.

an endowment elated me with pride. Unfortified by principle, subjected to poverty, stimulated by headlong passions, I made this powerful engine subservient to the supply of my wants, and the gratification of my vanity. I shall not mention how diligently I cultivated this gift, which seemed capable of unlimited improvement; nor detail the various occasions on which it was successfully exerted to lead superstition, conquer avarice, or excite awe.

"I left America, which is my native soil, in my youth. I have been engaged in various scenes of life, in which my peculiar talent has been exercised with more or less success. I was finally betrayed by one who called himself my friend, into acts which cannot be justified, though they are susceptible of apology.

"The perfidy of this man compelled me to withdraw from Europe. I returned to my native country, uncertain whether silence and obscurity would save me from his malice. I resided in the purlieus of the city. I put on the garb and assumed the manners of a clown.

"My chief recreation was walking. My principal haunts were the lawns and gardens of Mettingen. In this delightful region the luxuriances of nature had been chastened by judicious art, and each successive contemplation unfolded new enchantments.

"I was studious of seclusion: I was satiated with the intercourse of mankind, and discretion required me to shun their intercourse. For these reasons I long avoided the observation of your family, and chiefly visited these precincts at night.

"I was never weary of admiring the position and ornaments of *the temple*. Many a night have I passed under its roof, revolving no pleasing meditations. When, in my frequent rambles, I perceived this apartment was occupied, I gave a different direction to my steps. One evening, when a shower had just passed, judging by the silence that no one was within, I ascended to this building. Glancing carelessly round, I perceived an open letter on the pedestal. To read it was doubtless an offence against politeness. Of this offence, however, I was guilty.

199

"Scarcely had I gone half through when I was alarmed by the approach of your brother. To scramble down the cliff on the opposite side was impracticable. I was unprepared to meet a stranger. Besides the aukwardness attending such an interview in these circumstances, concealment was necessary to my safety. A thousand times had I vowed never again to employ the dangerous talent which I possessed; but such was the force of habit and the influence of present convenience, that I used this method of arresting his progress and leading him back to the house, with his errand, whatever it was, unperformed. I had often caught parts, from my station below, of your conversation in this place, and was well acquainted with the voice of your sister.

"Some weeks after this I was again quietly seated in this recess. The lateness of the hour secured me, as I thought, from all interruption. In this, however, I was mistaken, for Wieland and Pleyel, as I judged by their voices, earnest in dispute, ascended the hill.

"I was not sensible that any inconvenience could possibly have flowed from my former exertion; yet it was followed with compunction, because it was a deviation from a path which I had assigned to myself. Now my aversion to this means of escape was enforced by an unauthorized curiosity, and by the knowledge of a bushy hollow on the edge of the hill, where I should be safe from discovery. Into this hollow I thrust myself.

"The propriety of removal to Europe was the question eagerly discussed. Pleyel intimated that his anxiety to go was augmented by the silence of Theresa de Stolberg. The temptation to interfere in this dispute was irresistible. In vain I contended with inveterate habits. I disguised to myself the impropriety of my conduct, by recollecting the benefits which it might produce. Pleyel's proposal was unwise, yet it was enforced with plausible arguments and indefatigable zeal. Your brother might be puzzled and wearied, but could not be convinced. I conceived that to terminate the controversy in favor of the latter was conferring a benefit on all parties. For this end I profited by an opening in the conversation, and assured them of

Catharine's irreconcilable aversion to the scheme, and of the death of the Saxon baroness. The latter event was merely a conjecture, but rendered extremely probable by Pleyel's representations. My purpose, you need not be told, was effected.

"My passion for mystery, and a species of imposture, which I deemed harmless, was thus awakened afresh. This second lapse into error made my recovery more difficult. I cannot convey to you an adequate idea of the kind of gratification which I derived from these exploits; yet I meditated nothing. My views were bounded to the passing moment, and commonly suggested by the momentary exigence.

"I must not conceal any thing. Your principles teach you to abhor a voluptuous temper; but, with whatever reluctance, I acknowledge this temper to be mine. You imagine your servant Judith to be innocent as well as beautiful; but you took her from a family where hypocrisy, as well as licentiousness, was wrought into a system. My attention was captivated by her charms, and her principles were easily seen to be flexible.

"Deem me not capable of the iniquity of seduction. Your servant is not destitute of feminine and virtuous qualities; but she was taught that the best use of her charms consists in the sale of them. My nocturnal visits to Mettingen were now prompted by a double view, and my correspondence with your servant gave me, at all times, access to your house.

"The second night after our interview, so brief and so little foreseen by either of us, some dæmon of mischief seized me. According to my companion's report, your perfections were little less than divine. Her uncouth but copious narratives converted you into an object of worship. She chiefly dwelt upon your courage, because she herself was deficient in that quality. You held apparitions and goblins in contempt. You took no precautions against robbers. You were just as tranquil and secure in this lonely dwelling, as if you were in the midst of a crowd.

"Hence a vague project occurred to me, to put this courage to the test. A woman capable of recollection in danger, of warding off groundless panics, of discerning the true mode of proceeding, and profiting by her best resources, is a prodigy. I was desirous of ascertaining whether you were such an one.

"My expedient was obvious and simple: I was to counterfeit a murderous dialogue; but this was to be so conducted that another, and not yourself, should appear to be the object. I was not aware of the possibility that you should appropriate these menaces to yourself. Had you been still and listened, you would have heard the struggles and prayers of the victim, who would likewise have appeared to be shut up in the closet, and whose voice would have been Judith's. This scene would have been an appeal to your compassion; and the proof of cowardice or courage which I expected from you, would have been your remaining inactive in your bed, or your entering the closet with a view to assist the sufferer. Some instances which Judith related of your fearlessness and promptitude made me adopt the latter supposition with some degree of confidence.

"By the girl's direction I found a ladder, and mounted to your closet window. This is scarcely large enough to admit the head, but it answered my purpose too well.

"I cannot express my confusion and surprize at your abrupt and precipitate flight. I hastily removed the ladder; and, after some pause, curiosity and doubts of your safety induced me to follow you. I found you stretched on the turf before your brother's door, without sense or motion. I felt the deepest regret at this unlooked-for consequence of my scheme. I knew not what to do to procure you relief. The idea of awakening the family naturally presented itself. This emergency was critical, and there was no time to deliberate. It was a sudden thought that occurred. I put my lips to the key-hole, and sounded an alarm which effectually roused the sleepers. My organs were naturally forcible, and had been improved by long and assiduous exercise.

"Long and bitterly did I repent of my scheme. I was somewhat consoled by reflecting that my purpose had not been evil, and renewed my fruitless vows never to attempt such dangerous experiments. For some time I adhered, with laudable forbearance, to this resolution.

"My life has been a life of hardship and exposure. In the summer I prefer to make my bed of the smooth turf, or, at most, the shelter of a summer-house suffices. In all my rambles I never found a spot in which so many picturesque beauties and rural delights were assembled as at Mettingen. No corner of your little domain unites fragrance and secrecy in so perfect a degree as the recess in the bank. The odour of its leaves, the coolness of its shade, and the music of its water-fall, had early attracted my attention. Here my sadness was converted into peaceful melancholy—here my slumbers were sound, and my pleasures enhanced.

"As most free from interruption, I chose this as the scene of my midnight interviews with Judith. One evening, as the sun declined, I was seated here, when I was alarmed by your approach. It was with difficulty that I effected my escape unnoticed by you.

"At the customary hour, I returned to your habitation, and was made acquainted by Judith, with your unusual absence. I half suspected the true cause, and felt uneasiness at the danger there was that I should be deprived of my retreat; or, at least, interrupted in the possession of it. The girl, likewise, informed me, that among your other singularities, it was not uncommon for you to leave your bed, and walk forth for the sake of night-airs and starlight contemplations.

"I desired to prevent this inconvenience. I found you easily swayed by fear. I was influenced, in my choice of means, by the facility and certainty of that to which I had been accustomed. All that I foresaw was, that, in future, this spot would be cautiously shunned by you.

"I entered the recess with the utmost caution, and discovered, by your breathings, in what condition you were. The unexpected interpretation which you placed upon my former proceeding, suggested my conduct on the present occasion. The mode in which heaven is said by the poet, to interfere for the prevention of crimes,* was somewhat analogous to my province, and never failed to occur to me

*—Peeps through the blanket of the dark, and cries
Hold! Hold!—   SHAKESPEARE

203

at seasons like this. It was requisite to break your slumbers, and for this end I uttered the powerful monosyllable, 'hold! hold!' My purpose was not prescribed by duty, yet surely it was far from being atrocious and inexpiable. To effect it, I uttered what was false, but it was well suited to my purpose. Nothing less was intended, than to injure you. Nay, the evil resulting from my former act, was partly removed by assuring you that in all places but this you were safe.

CHAPTER XXIII

"MY morals will appear to you far from rigid, yet my conduct will fall short of your suspicions. I am now to confess actions less excusable, and yet surely they will not entitle me to the name of a desperate or sordid criminal.

"Your house was rendered, by your frequent and long absences, easily accessible to my curiosity. My meeting with Pleyel was the prelude to direct intercourse with you. I had seen much of the world, but your character exhibited a specimen of human powers that was wholly new to me. My intercourse with your servant furnished me with curious details of your domestic management. I was of a different sex: I was not your husband; I was not even your friend; yet my knowledge of you was of that kind, which conjugal intimacies can give, and, in some respects, more accurate. The observation of your domestic was guided by me.

"You will not be surprized that I should sometimes profit by your absence, and adventure to examine with my own eyes, the interior of your chamber. Upright and sincere, you used no watchfulness, and practised no precautions. I scrutinized every thing, and pried every where. Your closet was usually locked, but it was once my fortune to find the key on a bureau. I opened and found new scope for my curiosity in your books. One of these was manuscript, and written in characters which essentially agreed with a shorthand system which I had learned from a Jesuit missionary.

"I cannot justify my conduct, yet my only crime was

curiosity. I perused this volume with eagerness. The intellect which it unveiled, was brighter than my limited and feeble organs could bear. I was naturally inquisitive as to your ideas respecting my deportment, and the mysteries that had lately occurred.

"You know what you have written. You know that in this volume the key to your inmost soul was contained. If I had been a profound and malignant impostor, what plenteous materials were thus furnished me of stratagems and plots!

"The coincidence of your dream in the summer-house with my exclamation, was truly wonderful. The voice which warned you to forbear was, doubtless, mine; but mixed by a common process of the fancy, with the train of visionary incidents.

"I saw in a stronger light than ever, the dangerousness of that instrument which I employed, and renewed my resolutions to abstain from the use of it in future; but I was destined perpetually to violate my resolutions. By some perverse fate, I was led into circumstances in which the exertion of my powers was the sole or the best means of escape.

"On that memorable night on which our last interview took place, I came as usual to Mettingen. I was apprized of your engagement at your brother's, from which you did not expect to return till late. Some incident suggested the design of visiting your chamber. Among your books which I had not examined, might be something tending to illustrate your character, or the history of your family. Some intimation had been dropped by you in discourse, respecting a performance of your father, in which some important transaction in his life was recorded.

"I was desirous of seeing this book; and such was my habitual attachment to mystery, that I preferred the clandestine perusal of it. Such were the motives that induced me to make this attempt. Judith had disappeared, and finding the house unoccupied, I supplied myself with a light, and proceeded to your chamber.

"I found it easy, on experiment, to lock and unlock your closet door without the aid of a key. I shut myself in this

206

recess, and was busily exploring your shelves, when I heard some one enter the room below. I was at a loss who it could be, whether you or your servant. Doubtful, however, as I was, I conceived it prudent to extinguish the light. Scarcely was this done, when some one entered the chamber. The footsteps were easily distinguished to be yours.

"My situation was now full of danger and perplexity. For some time, I cherished the hope that you would leave the room so long as to afford me an opportunity of escaping. As the hours passed, this hope gradually deserted me. It was plain that you had retired for the night.

"I knew not how soon you might find occasion to enter the closet. I was alive to all the horrors of detection, and ruminated without ceasing, on the behaviour which it would be proper, in case of detection, to adopt. I was unable to discover any consistent method of accounting for my being thus immured.

"It occurred to me that I might withdraw you from your chamber for a few minutes, by counterfeiting a voice from without. Some message from your brother might be delivered, requiring your presence at his house. I was deterred from this scheme by reflecting on the resolution I had formed, and on the possible evils that might result from it. Besides, it was not improbable that you would speedily retire to bed, and then, by the exercise of sufficient caution, I might hope to escape unobserved.

"Meanwhile I listened with the deepest anxiety to every motion from without. I discovered nothing which betokened preparation for sleep. Instead of this I heard deep-drawn sighs, and occasionally an half-expressed and mournful ejaculation. Hence I inferred that you were unhappy. The true state of your mind with regard to Pleyel your own pen had disclosed; but I supposed you to be framed of such materials, that, though a momentary sadness might affect you, you were impregnable to any permanent and heartfelt grief. Inquietude for my own safety was, for a moment, suspended by sympathy with your distress.

"To the former consideration I was quickly recalled by a motion of yours which indicated I knew not what. I fostered

207

the persuasion that you would now retire to bed; but presently you approached the closet, and detection seemed to be inevitable. You put your hand upon the lock. I had formed no plan to extricate myself from the dilemma in which the opening of the door would involve me. I felt an irreconcilable aversion to detection. Thus situated, I involuntarily seized the door with a resolution to resist your efforts to open it.

"Suddenly you receded from the door. This deportment was inexplicable, but the relief it afforded me was quickly gone. You returned, and I once more was thrown into perplexity. The expedient that suggested itself was precipitate and inartificial. I exerted my organs and called upon you to *hold*.

"That you should persist in spite of this admonition, was a subject of astonishment. I again resisted your efforts; for the first expedient having failed, I knew not what other to resort to. In this state, how was my astonishment increased when I heard your exclamations!

"It was now plain that you knew me to be within. Further resistance was unavailing and useless. The door opened, and I shrunk backward. Seldom have I felt deeper mortification, and more painful perplexity. I did not consider that the truth would be less injurious than any lie which I could hastily frame. Conscious as I was of a certain degree of guilt, I conceived that you would form the most odious suspicions. The truth would be imperfect, unless I were likewise to explain the mysterious admonition which had been given; but that explanation was of too great moment, and involved too extensive consequences to make me suddenly resolve to give it.

"I was aware that this discovery would associate itself in your mind, with the dialogue formerly heard in this closet. Thence would your suspicions be aggravated, and to escape from these suspicions would be impossible. But the mere truth would be sufficiently opprobrious, and deprive me for ever of your good opinion.

"Thus was I rendered desperate, and my mind rapidly passed to the contemplation of the use that might be made

of previous events. Some good genius would appear to you
to have interposed to save you from injury intended by me.
Why, I said, since I must sink in her opinion, should I not
cherish this belief? Why not personate an enemy, and pretend that celestial interference has frustrated my schemes?
I must fly, but let me leave wonder and fear behind me.
Elucidation of the mystery will always be practicable. I shall
do no injury, but merely talk of evil that was designed, but is
now past.

"Thus I extenuated my conduct to myself, but I scarcely
expect that this will be to you a sufficient explication of the
scene that followed. Those habits which I have imbibed, the
rooted passion which possesses me for scattering around
me amazement and fear, you enjoy no opportunities of
knowing. That a man should wantonly impute to himself
the most flagitious designs, will hardly be credited, even
though you reflect that my reputation was already, by my
own folly, irretrievably ruined; and that it was always in my
power to communicate the truth, and rectify the mistake.

"I left you to ponder on this scene. My mind was full of
rapid and incongruous ideas. Compunction, self-
upbraiding, hopelessness, satisfaction at the view of those
effects likely to flow from my new scheme, misgivings as to
the beneficial result of this scheme, took possession of my
mind, and seemed to struggle for the mastery.

"I had gone too far to recede. I had painted myself to you
as an assassin and ravisher, withheld from guilt only by a
voice from heaven. I had thus reverted into the path of
error, and now, having gone thus far, my progress seemed
to be irrevocable. I said to myself, I must leave these precincts for ever. My acts have blasted my fame in the eyes of
the Wielands. For the sake of creating a mysterious dread, I
have made myself a villain. I may complete this mysterious
plan by some new imposture, but I cannot aggravate my
supposed guilt.

"My resolution was formed, and I was swiftly ruminating
on the means for executing it, when Pleyel appeared in
sight. This incident decided my conduct. It was plain that
Pleyel was a devoted lover, but he was, at the same time, a

209

man of cold resolves and exquisite sagacity. To deceive him would be the sweetest triumph I had ever enjoyed. The deception would be momentary, but it would likewise be complete. That his delusion would so soon be rectified, was a recommendation to my scheme, for I esteemed him too much to desire to entail upon him lasting agonies.

"I had no time to reflect further, for he proceeded, with a quick step, towards the house. I was hurried onward involuntarily and by a mechanical impulse. I followed him as he passed the recess in the bank, and shrowding myself in that spot, I counterfeited sounds which I knew would arrest his steps.

"He stopped, turned, listened, approached, and overheard a dialogue whose purpose was to vanquish his belief in a point where his belief was most difficult to vanquish. I exerted all my powers to imitate your voice, your general sentiments, and your language. Being master, by means of your journal, of your personal history and most secret thoughts, my efforts were the more successful. When I reviewed the tenor of this dialogue, I cannot believe but that Pleyel was deluded. When I think of your character, and of the inferences which this dialogue was intended to suggest, it seems incredible that this delusion should be produced.

"I spared not myself. I called myself murderer, thief, guilty of innumerable perjuries and misdeeds: that you had debased yourself to the level of such an one, no evidence, methought, would suffice to convince him who knew you so thoroughly as Pleyel; and yet the imposture amounted to proof which the most jealous scrutiny would find to be unexceptionable.

"He left his station precipitately and resumed his way to the house. I saw that the detection of his error would be instantaneous, since, not having gone to bed, an immediate interview would take place between you. At first this circumstance was considered with regret; but as time opened my eyes to the possible consequences of this scene, I regarded it with pleasure.

"In a short time the infatuation which had led me thus far

began to subside. The remembrance of former reasonings and transactions was renewed. How often I had repented this kind of exertion; how many evils were produced by it which I had not foreseen; what occasions for the bitterest remorse it had administered, now passed through my mind. The black catalogue of stratagems was now increased. I had inspired you with the most vehement terrors: I had filled your mind with faith in shadows and confidence in dreams: I had depraved the imagination of Pleyel: I had exhibited you to his understanding as devoted to brutal gratifications and consummate in hypocrisy. The evidence which accompanied this delusion would be irresistible to one whose passion had perverted his judgment, whose jealousy with regard to me had already been excited, and who, therefore, would not fail to overrate the force of this evidence. What fatal act of despair or of vengeance might not this error produce?

"With regard to myself, I had acted with a phrenzy that surpassed belief. I had warred against my peace and my fame: I had banished myself from the fellowship of vigorous and pure minds: I was self-expelled from a scene which the munificence of nature had adorned with unrivalled beauties, and from haunts in which all the muses and humanities had taken refuge.

"I was thus torn by conflicting fears and tumultuous regrets. The night passed away in this state of confusion; and next morning in the gazette left at my obscure lodging, I read a description and an offer of reward for the apprehension of my person. I was said to have escaped from an Irish prison, in which I was confined as an offender convicted of enormous and complicated crimes.

"This was the work of an enemy, who, by falsehood and stratagem, had procured my condemnation. I was, indeed, a prisoner, but escaped, by the exertion of my powers, the fate to which I was doomed, but which I did not deserve. I had hoped that the malice of my foe was exhausted; but I now perceived that my precautions had been wise, for that the intervention of an ocean was insufficient for my security.

211

"Let me not dwell on the sensations which this discovery produced. I need not tell by what steps I was induced to seek an interview with you, for the purpose of disclosing the truth, and repairing, as far as possible, the effects of my misconduct. It was unavoidable that this gazette would fall into your hands, and that it would tend to confirm every erroneous impression.

"Having gained this interview, I purposed to seek some retreat in the wilderness, inaccessible to your inquiry and to the malice of my foe, where I might henceforth employ myself in composing a faithful narrative of my actions. I designed it as my vindication from the aspersions that had rested on my character, and as a lesson to mankind on the evils of credulity on the one hand, and of imposture on the other.

"I wrote you a billet, which was left at the house of your friend, and which I knew would, by some means, speedily come to your hands. I entertained a faint hope that my invitation would be complied with. I knew not what use you would make of the opportunity which this proposal afforded you of procuring the seizure of my person; but this fate I was determined to avoid, and I had no doubt but due circumspection, and the exercise of the faculty which I possessed, would enable me to avoid it.

"I lurked, through the day, in the neighbourhood of Mettingen: I approached your habitation at the appointed hour: I entered it in silence, by a trap-door which led into the cellar. This had formerly been bolted on the inside, but Judith had, at an early period in our intercourse, removed this impediment. I ascended to the first floor, but met with no one, nor any thing that indicated the presence of an human being.

"I crept softly up stairs, and at length perceived your chamber door to be opened, and a light to be within. It was of moment to discover by whom this light was accompanied. I was sensible of the inconveniencies to which my being discovered at your chamber door by any one within would subject me; I therefore called out in my own voice, but so modified that it should appear to ascend from the court below, 'Who is in the chamber? Is it Miss Wieland?'

"No answer was returned to this summons. I listened, but no motion could be heard. After a pause I repeated my call, but no less ineffectually.

"I now approached nearer the door, and adventured to look in. A light stood on the table, but nothing human was discernible. I entered cautiously, but all was solitude and stillness.

"I knew not what to conclude. If the house were inhabited, my call would have been noticed; yet some suspicion insinuated itself that silence was studiously kept by persons who intended to surprize me. My approach had been wary, and the silence that ensued my call had likewise preceded it; a circumstance that tended to dissipate my fears.

"At length it occurred to me that Judith might possibly be in her own room. I turned my steps thither; but she was not to be found. I passed into other rooms, and was soon convinced that the house was totally deserted. I returned to your chamber, agitated by vain surmises and opposite conjectures. The appointed hour had passed, and I dismissed the hope of an interview.

"In this state of things I determined to leave a few lines on your toilet, and prosecute my journey to the mountains. Scarcely had I taken the pen when I laid it aside, uncertain in what manner to address you. I rose from the table and walked across the floor. A glance thrown upon the bed acquainted me with a spectacle to which my conceptions of horror had not yet reached.

"In the midst of shuddering and trepidation, the signal of your presence in the court below recalled me to myself. The deed was newly done: I only was in the house: what had lately happened justified any suspicions, however enormous. It was plain that this catastrophe was unknown to you: I thought upon the wild commotion which the discovery would awaken in your breast: I found the confusion of my own thoughts unconquerable, and perceived that the end for which I sought an interview was not now to be accomplished.

"In this state of things it was likewise expedient to conceal my being within. I put out the light and hurried down stairs.

213

To my unspeakable surprize, notwithstanding every motive to fear, you lighted a candle and proceeded to your chamber.

"I retired to that room below from which a door leads into the cellar. This door concealed me from your view as you passed. I thought upon the spectacle which was about to present itself. In an exigence so abrupt and so little foreseen, I was again subjected to the empire of mechanical and habitual impulses. I dreaded the effects which this shocking exhibition, bursting on your unprepared senses, might produce.

"Thus actuated, I stept swiftly to the door, and thrusting my head forward, once more pronounced the mysterious interdiction. At that moment, by some untoward fate, your eyes were cast back, and you saw me in the very act of utterance. I fled through the darksome avenue at which I entered, covered with the shame of this detection.

"With diligence, stimulated by a thousand ineffable emotions, I pursued my intended journey. I have a brother whose farm is situated in the bosom of a fertile desert, near the sources of the Leheigh, and thither I now repaired.

CHAPTER XXIV

"**D**EEPLY did I ruminate on the occurrences that had just passed. Nothing excited my wonder so much as the means by which you discovered my being in the closet. This discovery appeared to be made at the moment when you attempted to open it. How could you have otherwise remained so long in the chamber apparently fearless and tranquil? And yet, having made this discovery, how could you persist in dragging me forth: persist in defiance of an interdiction so emphatical and solemn?

"But your sister's death was an event detestable and ominous. She had been the victim of the most dreadful species of assassination. How, in a state like yours, the murderous intention could be generated, was wholly inconceivable.

"I did not relinquish my design of confessing to you the part which I had sustained in your family, but I was willing to defer it till the task which I had set myself was finished. That being done, I resumed the resolution. The motives to incite me to this continually acquired force. The more I revolved the events happening at Mettingen, the more insupportable and ominous my terrors became. My waking hours and my sleep were vexed by dismal presages and frightful intimations.

"Catharine was dead by violence. Surely my malignant stars had not made me the cause of her death; yet had I not rashly set in motion a machine, over whose progress I had no controul, and which experience had shewn me was infinite in power? Every day might add to the catalogue of horrors of which this was the source, and a seasonable disclosure of the truth might prevent numberless ills.

"Fraught with this conception, I have turned my steps hither. I find your brother's house desolate: the furniture removed, and the walls stained with damps. Your own is in the same situation. Your chamber is dismantled and dark, and you exhibit an image of incurable grief, and of rapid decay.

"I have uttered the truth. This is the extent of my offences. You tell me an horrid tale of Wieland being led to the destruction of his wife and children, by some mysterious agent. You charge me with the guilt of this agency; but I repeat that the amount of my guilt has been truly stated. The perpetrator of Catharine's death was unknown to me till now; nay, it is still unknown to me."

At that moment, the closing of a door in the kitchen was distinctly heard by us. Carwin started and paused. "There is some one coming. I must not be found here by my enemies, and need not, since my purpose is answered."

I had drunk in, with the most vehement attention, every word that he had uttered. I had no breath to interrupt his tale by interrogations or comments. The power that he spoke of was hitherto unknown to me: its existence was incredible; it was susceptible of no direct proof.

He owns that his were the voice and face which I heard and saw. He attempts to give an human explanation of these phantasms; but it is enough that he owns himself to be the agent; his tale is a lie, and his nature devilish. As he deceived me, he likewise deceived my brother, and now do I behold the author of all our calamities!

Such were my thoughts when his pause allowed me to think. I should have bad him begone if the silence had not been interrupted; but now I feared no more for myself; and the milkiness of my nature was curdled into hatred and rancour. Some one was near, and this enemy of God and man might possibly be brought to justice. I reflected not that the preternatural power which he had hitherto exerted, would avail to rescue him from any toils in which his feet might be entangled. Meanwhile, looks, and not words of menace and abhorrence, were all that I could bestow.

He did not depart. He seemed dubious, whether, by passing out of the house, or by remaining somewhat longer where he was, he should most endanger his safety. His confusion increased when steps of one barefoot were heard upon the stairs. He threw anxious glances sometimes at the closet, sometimes at the window, and sometimes at the chamber door, yet he was detained by some inexplicable fascination. He stood as if rooted to the spot.

As to me, my soul was bursting with detestation and revenge. I had no room for surmises and fears respecting him that approached. It was doubtless a human being, and would befriend me so far as to aid me in arresting this offender.

The stranger quickly entered the room. My eyes and the eyes of Carwin were, at the same moment, darted upon him. A second glance was not needed to inform us who he was. His locks were tangled, and fell confusedly over his forehead and ears. His shirt was of coarse stuff, and open at the neck and breast. His coat was once of bright and fine texture, but now torn and tarnished with dust. His feet, his legs, and his arms were bare. His features were the seat of a wild and tranquil solemnity, but his eyes bespoke inquietude and curiosity.

He advanced with firm step, and looking as in search of some one. He saw me and stopped. He bent his sight on the floor, and clenching his hands, appeared suddenly absorbed in meditation. Such were the figure and deportment of Wieland! Such, in his fallen state, were the aspect and guise of my brother!

Carwin did not fail to recognize the visitant. Care for his own safety was apparently swallowed up in the amazement which this spectacle produced. His station was conspicuous, and he could not have escaped the roving glances of Wieland; yet the latter seemed totally unconscious of his presence.

217

Grief at this scene of ruin and blast was at first the only sentiment of which I was conscious. A fearful stillness ensued. At length Wieland, lifting his hands, which were locked in each other, to his breast, exclaimed, "Father! I thank thee. This is thy guidance. Hither thou hast led me, that I might perform thy will: yet let me not err: let me hear again thy messenger!"

He stood for a minute as if listening; but recovering from his attitude, he continued—"It is not needed. Dastardly wretch! thus eternally questioning the behests of thy Maker! weak in resolution! wayward in faith!"

He advanced to me, and, after another pause, resumed: "Poor girl! a dismal fate has set its mark upon thee. Thy life is demanded as a sacrifice. Prepare thee to die. Make not my office difficult by fruitless opposition. Thy prayers might subdue stones; but none but he who enjoined my purpose can shake it."

These words were a sufficient explication of the scene. The nature of his phrenzy, as described by my uncle, was remembered. I who had sought death, was now thrilled with horror because it was near. Death in this form, death from the hand of a brother, was thought upon with undescribable repugnance.

In a state thus verging upon madness, my eye glanced upon Carwin. His astonishment appeared to have struck him motionless and dumb. My life was in danger, and my brother's hand was about to be embrued in my blood. I firmly believed that Carwin's was the instigation. I could rescue me from this abhorred fate; I could dissipate this tremendous illusion; I could save my brother from the perpetration of new horrors, by pointing out the devil who seduced him; to hesitate a moment was to perish. These thoughts gave strength to my limbs, and energy to my accents: I started on my feet.

"O brother! spare me, spare thyself: There is thy betrayer. He counterfeited the voice and face of an angel, for the purpose of destroying thee and me. He has this moment confessed it. He is able to speak where he is not. He is leagued with hell, but will not avow it; yet he confesses that the agency was his."

My brother turned slowly his eyes, and fixed them upon Carwin. Every joint in the frame of the latter trembled. His complexion was paler than a ghost's. His eye dared not meet that of Wieland, but wandered with an air of distraction from one space to another.

"Man," said my brother, in a voice totally unlike that which he had used to me, "what art thou? The charge has been made. Answer it. The visage—the voice—at the bottom of these stairs—at the hour of eleven—To whom did they belong? To thee?"

Twice did Carwin attempt to speak, but his words died away upon his lips. My brother resumed in a tone of greater vehemence—

"Thou falterest; faltering is ominous; say yes or no: one word will suffice; but beware of falsehood. Was it a stratagem of hell to overthrow my family? Wast thou the agent?"

I now saw that the wrath which had been prepared for me was to be heaped upon another. The tale that I heard from him, and his present trepidations, were abundant testimonies of his guilt. But what if Wieland should be undeceived! What if he shall find his acts to have proceeded not from an heavenly prompter, but from human treachery! Will not his rage mount into whirlwind? Will not he tear limb from limb this devoted wretch?

Instinctively I recoiled from this image, but it gave place to another. Carwin may be innocent, but the impetuosity of his judge may misconstrue his answers into a confession of guilt. Wieland knows not that mysterious voices and appearances were likewise witnessed by me. Carwin may be ignorant of those which misled my brother. Thus may his answers unwarily betray himself to ruin.

Such might be the consequences of my frantic precipitation, and these, it was necessary, if possible, to prevent. I attempted to speak, but Wieland, turning suddenly upon me, commanded silence, in a tone furious and terrible. My lips closed, and my tongue refused its office.

"What art thou?" he resumed, addressing himself to Carwin. "Answer me; whose form—whose voice—was it thy contrivance? Answer me."

219

The answer was now given, but confusedly and scarcely articulated. "I meant nothing—I intended no ill—if I understand—if I do not mistake you—it is too true—I did appear—in the entry—did speak. The contrivance was mine, but—"

These words were no sooner uttered, than my brother ceased to wear the same aspect. His eyes were downcast: he was motionless: his respiration became hoarse, like that of a man in the agonies of death. Carwin seemed unable to say more. He might have easily escaped, but the thought which occupied him related to what was horrid and unintelligible in this scene, and not to his own danger.

Presently the faculties of Wieland, which, for a time, were chained up, were seized with restlessness and trembling. He broke silence. The stoutest heart would have been appalled by the tone in which he spoke. He addressed himself to Carwin.

"Why art thou here? Who detains thee? Go and learn better. I will meet thee, but it must be at the bar of thy Maker. There shall I bear witness against thee."

Perceiving that Carwin did not obey, he continued; "Dost thou wish me to complete the catalogue by thy death? Thy life is a worthless thing. Tempt me no more. I am but a man, and thy presence may awaken a fury which may spurn my controul. Begone!"

Carwin, irresolute, striving in vain for utterance, his complexion pallid as death, his knees beating one against another, slowly obeyed the mandate and withdrew.

CHAPTER XXV

A FEW words more and I lay aside the pen for ever. Yet why should I not relinquish it now? All that I have said is preparatory to this scene, and my fingers, tremulous and cold as my heart, refuse any further exertion. This must not be. Let my last energies support me in the finishing of this task. Then will I lay down my head in the lap of death. Hushed will be all my murmurs in the sleep of the grave.

Every sentiment has perished in my bosom. Even friendship is extinct. Your love for me has prompted me to this task; but I would not have complied if it had not been a luxury thus to feast upon my woes. I have justly calculated upon my remnant of strength. When I lay down the pen the taper of life will expire: my existence will terminate with my tale.

Now that I was left alone with Wieland, the perils of my situation presented themselves to my mind. That this paroxysm should terminate in havock and rage it was reasonable to predict. The first suggestion of my fears had been disproved by my experience. Carwin had acknowledged his offences, and yet had escaped. The vengeance which I had harboured had not been admitted by Wieland, and yet the evils which I had endured, compared with those inflicted on my brother, were as nothing. I thirsted for his blood, and was tormented with an insatiable appetite for his destruction; yet my brother was unmoved, and had dismissed him in safety. Surely thou wast more than man, while I am sunk below the beasts.

Did I place a right construction on the conduct of Wieland? Was the error that misled him so easily rectified? Were views so vivid and faith so strenuous thus liable to fading and to change? Was there not reason to doubt the accuracy of my perceptions? With images like these was my mind thronged, till the deportment of my brother called away my attention.

I saw his lips move and his eyes cast up to heaven. Then would he listen and look back, as if in expectation of some one's appearance. Thrice he repeated these gesticulations and this inaudible prayer. Each time the mist of confusion and doubt seemed to grow darker and to settle on his understanding. I guessed at the meaning of these tokens. The words of Carwin had shaken his belief, and he was employed in summoning the messenger who had formerly communed with him, to attest the value of these new doubts. In vain the summons was repeated, for his eye met nothing but vacancy, and not a sound saluted his ear.

He walked to the bed, gazed with eagerness at the pillow which had sustained the head of the breathless Catharine, and then returned to the place where I sat. I had no power to lift my eyes to his face: I was dubious of his purpose: this purpose might aim at my life.

Alas! nothing but subjection to danger, and exposure to temptation, can show us what we are. By this test was I now tried, and found to be cowardly and rash. Men can deliberately untie the thread of life, and of this I had deemed myself capable; yet now that I stood upon the brink of fate, that the knife of the sacrificer was aimed at my heart, I shuddered and betook myself to any means of escape, however monstrous.

Can I bear to think—can I endure to relate the outrage which my heart meditated? Where were my means of safety? Resistance was vain. Not even the energy of despair could set me on a level with that strength which his terrific prompter had bestowed upon Wieland. Terror enables us to perform incredible feats; but terror was not then the state of my mind: where then were my hopes of rescue?

Methinks it is too much. I stand aside, as it were, from myself; I estimate my own deservings; a hatred, immortal

222

and inexorable, is my due. I listen to my own pleas, and find them empty and false: yes, I acknowledge that my guilt surpasses that of all mankind: I confess that the curses of a world, and the frowns of a deity, are inadequate to my demerits. Is there a thing in the world worthy of infinite abhorrence? It is I.

What shall I say! I was menaced, as I thought, with death, and, to elude this evil, my hand was ready to inflict death upon the menacer. In visiting my house, I had made provision against the machinations of Carwin. In a fold of my dress an open penknife was concealed. This I now seized and drew forth. It lurked out of view; but I now see that my state of mind would have rendered the deed inevitable if my brother had lifted his hand. This instrument of my preservation would have been plunged into his heart.

O, insupportable remembrance! hide thee from my view for a time; hide it from me that my heart was black enough to meditate the stabbing of a brother! a brother thus supreme in misery; thus towering in virtue!

He was probably unconscious of my design, but presently drew back. This interval was sufficient to restore me to myself. The madness, the iniquity of that act which I had purposed rushed upon my apprehension. For a moment I was breathless with agony. At the next moment I recovered my strength, and threw the knife with violence on the floor.

The sound awoke my brother from his reverie. He gazed alternately at me and at the weapon. With a movement equally solemn he stooped and took it up. He placed the blade in different positions, scrutinizing it accurately, and maintaining, at the same time, a profound silence.

Again he looked at me, but all that vehemence and loftiness of spirit which had so lately characterized his features, were flown. Fallen muscles, a forehead contracted into folds, eyes dim with unbidden drops, and a ruefulness of aspect which no words can describe, were now visible.

His looks touched into energy the same sympathies in me, and I poured forth a flood of tears. This passion was quickly checked by fear, which had now, no longer my own, but his safety for their object. I watched his deportment in silence. At length he spoke:

"Sister," said he, in an accent mournful and mild, "I have acted poorly my part in this world. What thinkest thou? Shall I not do better in the next?"

I could make no answer. The mildness of his tone astonished and encouraged me. I continued to regard him with wistful and anxious looks.

"I think," resumed he, "I will try. My wife and my babes have gone before. Happy wretches! I have sent you to repose, and ought not to linger behind."

These words had a meaning sufficiently intelligible. I looked at the open knife in his hand and shuddered, but knew not how to prevent the deed which I dreaded. He quickly noticed my fears, and comprehended them. Stretching towards me his hand, with an air of increasing mildness: "Take it," said he: "Fear not for thy own sake, nor for mine. The cup is gone by, and its transient inebriation is succeeded by the soberness of truth.

"Thou angel whom I was wont to worship! fearest thou, my sister, for thy life? Once it was the scope of my labours to destroy thee, but I was prompted to the deed by heaven; such, at least, was my belief. Thinkest thou that thy death was sought to gratify malevolence? No. I am pure from all stain. I believed that my God was my mover!

"Neither thee nor myself have I cause to injure. I have done my duty, and surely there is merit in having sacrificed to that, all that is dear to the heart of man. If a devil has deceived me, he came in the habit of an angel. If I erred, it was not my judgment that deceived me, but my senses. In thy sight, being of beings! I am still pure. Still will I look for my reward in thy justice!"

Did my ears truly report these sounds? If I did not err, my brother was restored to just perceptions. He knew himself to have been betrayed to the murder of his wife and children, to have been the victim of infernal artifice; yet he found consolation in the rectitude of his motives. He was not devoid of sorrow, for this was written on his countenance; but his soul was tranquil and sublime.

Perhaps this was merely a transition of his former madness into a new shape. Perhaps he had not yet awakened to

224

the memory of the horrors which he had perpetrated. Infatuated wretch that I was! To set myself up as a model by which to judge of my heroic brother! My reason taught me that his conclusions were right; but conscious of the impotence of reason over my own conduct; conscious of my cowardly rashness and my criminal despair, I doubted whether any one could be stedfast and wise.

Such was my weakness, that even in the midst of these thoughts, my mind glided into abhorrence of Carwin, and I uttered in a low voice, "O! Carwin! Carwin! What hast thou to answer for!"

My brother immediately noticed the involuntary exclamation: "Clara!" said he, "be thyself. Equity used to be a theme for thy eloquence. Reduce its lessons to practice, and be just to that unfortunate man. The instrument has done its work, and I am satisfied.

"I thank thee, my God, for this last illumination! My enemy is thine also. I deemed him to be man, the man with whom I have often communed; but now thy goodness has unveiled to me his true nature. As the performer of thy behests, he is my friend."

My heart began now to misgive me. His mournful aspect had gradually yielded place to a serene brow. A new soul appeared to actuate his frame, and his eyes to beam with preternatural lustre. These symptoms did not abate, and he continued:

"Clara! I must not leave thee in doubt. I know not what brought about thy interview with the being whom thou callest Carwin. For a time, I was guilty of thy error, and deduced from his incoherent confessions that I had been made the victim of human malice. He left us at my bidding, and I put up a prayer that my doubts should be removed. Thy eyes were shut, and thy ears sealed to the vision that answered my prayer.

"I was indeed deceived. The form thou hast seen was the incarnation of a dæmon. The visage and voice which urged me to the sacrifice of my family, were his. Now he personates a human form: then he was invironed with the lustre of heaven.—

225

"Clara," he continued, advancing closer to me, "thy death must come. This minister is evil, but he from whom his commission was received is God. Submit then with all thy wonted resignation to a decree that cannot be reversed or resisted. Mark the clock. Three minutes are allowed to thee, in which to call up thy fortitude, and prepare thee for thy doom." There he stopped.

Even now, when this scene exists only in memory, when life and all its functions have sunk into torpor, my pulse throbs, and my hairs uprise: my brows are knit, as then; and I gaze around me in distraction. I was unconquerably averse to death; but death, imminent and full of agony as that which was threatened, was nothing. This was not the only or chief inspirer of my fears.

For him, not for myself, was my soul tormented. I might die, and no crime, surpassing the reach of mercy, would pursue me to the presence of my Judge; but my assassin would survive to contemplate his deed, and that assassin was Wieland!

Wings to bear me beyond his reach I had not. I could not vanish with a thought. The door was open, but my murderer was interposed between that and me. Of self-defence I was incapable. The phrenzy that lately prompted me to blood was gone; my state was desperate; my rescue was impossible.

The weight of these accumulated thoughts could not be borne. My sight became confused; my limbs were seized with convulsion; I spoke, but my words were half-formed: —

"Spare me, my brother! Look down, righteous Judge! snatch me from this fate! take away this fury from him, or turn it elsewhere!"

Such was the agony of my thoughts, that I noticed not steps entering my apartment. Supplicating eyes were cast upward, but when my prayer was breathed, I once more wildly gazed at the door. A form met my sight: I shuddered as if the God whom I invoked were present. It was Carwin that again intruded, and who stood before me, erect in attitude, and stedfast in look!

The sight of him awakened new and rapid thoughts. His recent tale was remembered: his magical transitions and mysterious energy of voice: Whether he were infernal, or miraculous, or human, there was no power and no need to decide. Whether the contriver or not of this spell, he was able to unbind it, and to check the fury of my brother. He had ascribed to himself intentions not malignant. Here now was afforded a test of his truth. Let him interpose, as from above; revoke the savage decree which the madness of Wieland has assigned to heaven; and extinguish for ever this passion for blood!

My mind detected at a glance this avenue to safety. The recommendations it possessed thronged as it were together, and made but one impression on my intellect. Remoter effects and collateral dangers I saw not. Perhaps the pause of an instant had sufficed to call them up. The improbability that the influence which governed Wieland was external or human; the tendency of this stratagem to sanction so fatal an error, or substitute a more destructive rage in place of this; the sufficiency of Carwin's mere muscular forces to counteract the efforts, and restrain the fury of Wieland, might, at a second glance, have been discovered; but no second glance was allowed. My first thought hurried me to action, and, fixing my eyes upon Carwin I exclaimed—

"O wretch! once more hast thou come? Let it be to abjure thy malice; to counterwork this hellish stratagem; to turn from me and from my brother, this desolating rage!

"Testify thy innocence or thy remorse: exert the powers which pertain to thee, whatever they be, to turn aside this ruin. Thou art the author of these horrors! What have I done to deserve thus to die? How have I merited this unrelenting persecution? I adjure thee, by that God whose voice thou hast dared to counterfeit, to save my life!

"Wilt thou then go? leave me! Succourless!"

Carwin listened to my intreaties unmoved, and turned from me. He seemed to hesitate a moment: then glided through the door. Rage and despair stifled my utterance. The interval of respite was passed; the pangs reserved for me by Wieland, were not to be endured; my thoughts rushed again into anarchy. Having received the knife from his hand, I held it loosely and without regard; but now it seized again my attention, and I grasped it with force.

He seemed to notice not the entrance or exit of Carwin. My gesture and the murderous weapon appeared to have escaped his notice. His silence was unbroken; his eye, fixed upon the clock for a time, was now withdrawn; fury kindled in every feature; all that was human in his face gave way to an expression supernatural and tremendous. I felt my left arm within his grasp.—

Even now I hesitated to strike. I shrunk from his assault, but in vain.—

Here let me desist. Why should I rescue this event from oblivion? Why should I paint this detestable conflict? Why not terminate at once this series of horrors?—hurry to the verge of the precipice, and cast myself for ever beyond remembrance and beyond hope?

Still I live: with this load upon my breast; with this phantom to pursue my steps; with adders lodged in my bosom, and stinging me to madness: still I consent to live!

Yes, I will rise above the sphere of mortal passions: I will spurn at the cowardly remorse that bids me seek impunity in silence, or comfort in forgetfulness. My nerves shall be new strung to the task. Have I not resolved? I will die. The gulph before me is inevitable and near. I will die, but then only when my tale is at an end.

CHAPTER XXVI

MY right hand, grasping the unseen knife, was still disengaged. It was lifted to strike. All my strength was exhausted, but what was sufficient to the performance of this deed. Already was the energy awakened, and the impulse given, that should bear the fatal steel to his heart, when—Wieland shrunk back: his hand was withdrawn. Breathless with affright and desperation, I stood, freed from his grasp; unassailed; untouched.

Thus long had the power which controuled the scene forborne to interfere; but now his might was irresistible, and Wieland in a moment was disarmed of all his purposes. A voice, louder than human organs could produce, shriller than language can depict, burst from the ceiling, and commanded him—to *hold!*

Trouble and dismay succeeded to the stedfastness that had lately been displayed in the looks of Wieland. His eyes roved from one quarter to another, with an expression of doubt. He seemed to wait for a further intimation.

Carwin's agency was here easily recognized. I had besought him to interpose in my defence. He had flown. I had imagined him deaf to my prayer, and resolute to see me perish: yet he disappeared merely to devise and execute the means of my relief.

Why did he not forbear when this end was accomplished? Why did his misjudging zeal and accursed precipitation overpass that limit? Or meant he thus to crown the scene, and conduct his inscrutable plots to this consummation?

Such ideas were the fruit of subsequent contemplation. This moment was pregnant with fate. I had no power to reason. In the career of my tempestuous thoughts, rent into pieces, as my mind was, by accumulating horrors, Carwin was unseen and unsuspected. I partook of Wieland's credulity, shook with his amazement, and panted with his awe.

Silence took place for a moment; so much as allowed the attention to recover its post. Then new sounds were uttered from above.

"Man of errors! cease to cherish thy delusion: not heaven or hell, but thy senses have misled thee to commit these acts. Shake off thy phrenzy, and ascend into rational and human. Be lunatic no longer."

My brother opened his lips to speak. His tone was terrific and faint. He muttered an appeal to heaven. It was not difficult to comprehend the theme of his inquiries. They implied doubt as to the nature of the impulse that hitherto had guided him, and questioned whether he had acted in consequence of insane perceptions.

To these interrogatories the voice, which now seemed to hover at his shoulder, loudly answered in the affirmative. Then uninterrupted silence ensued.

Fallen from his lofty and heroic station; now finally restored to the perception of truth; weighed to earth by the recollection of his own deeds; consoled no longer by a consciousness of rectitude, for the loss of offspring and wife —a loss for which he was indebted to his own misguided hand; Wieland was transformed at once into the *man of sorrows*!

He reflected not that credit should be as reasonably denied to the last, as to any former intimation; that one might as justly be ascribed to erring or diseased senses as the other. He saw not that this discovery in no degree affected the integrity of his conduct; that his motives had lost none of their claims to the homage of mankind; that the preference of supreme good, and the boundless energy of duty, were undiminished in his bosom.

It is not for me to pursue him through the ghastly changes of his countenance. Words he had none. Now he

230

sat upon the floor, motionless in all his limbs, with his eyes glazed and fixed; a monument of woe.

Anon a spirit of tempestuous but undesigning activity seized him. He rose from his place and strode across the floor, tottering and at random. His eyes were without moisture, and gleamed with the fire that consumed his vitals. The muscles of his face were agitated by convulsion. His lips moved, but no sound escaped him.

That nature should long sustain this conflict was not to be believed. My state was little different from that of my brother. I entered, as it were, into his thought. My heart was visited and rent by his pangs—Oh that thy phrenzy had never been cured! that thy madness, with its blissful visions, would return! or, if that must not be, that thy scene would hasten to a close! that death would cover thee with his oblivion!

What can I wish for thee? Thou who hast vied with the great preacher of thy faith in sanctity of motives, and in elevation above sensual and selfish! Thou whom thy fate has changed into paricide and savage! Can I wish for the continuance of thy being? No.

For a time his movements seemed destitute of purpose. If he walked; if he turned; if his fingers were entwined with each other; if his hands were pressed against opposite sides of his head with a force sufficient to crush it into pieces; it was to tear his mind from self-contemplation; to waste his thoughts on external objects.

Speedily this train was broken. A beam appeared to be darted into his mind, which gave a purpose to his efforts. An avenue to escape presented itself; and now he eagerly gazed about him: when my thoughts became engaged by his demeanour, my fingers were stretched as by a mechanical force, and the knife, no longer heeded or of use, escaped from my grasp, and fell unperceived on the floor. His eye now lighted upon it; he seized it with the quickness of thought.

I shrieked aloud, but it was too late. He plunged it to the hilt in his neck; and his life instantly escaped with the stream that gushed from the wound. He was stretched at my feet; and my hands were sprinkled with his blood as he fell.

Such was thy last deed, my brother! For a spectacle like this was it my fate to be reserved! Thy eyes were closed—thy face ghastly with death—thy arms, and the spot where thou liedest, floated in thy life's blood! These images have not, for a moment, forsaken me. Till I am breathless and cold, they must continue to hover in my sight.

Carwin, as I said, had left the room, but he still lingered in the house. My voice summoned him to my aid; but I scarcely noticed his re-entrance, and now faintly recollect his terrified looks, his broken exclamations, his vehement avowals of innocence, the effusions of his pity for me, and his offers of assistance.

I did not listen—I answered him not—I ceased to up-braid or accuse. His guilt was a point to which I was indif-ferent. Ruffian or devil, black as hell or bright as angels, thenceforth he was nothing to me. I was incapable of spar-ing a look or a thought from the ruin that was spread at my feet.

When he left me, I was scarcely conscious of any variation in the scene. He informed the inhabitants of the *Hut* of what had passed, and they flew to the spot. Careless of his own safety, he hasted to the city to inform my friends of my condition.

My uncle speedily arrived at the house. The body of Wieland was removed from my presence, and they sup-posed that I would follow it; but no, my home is ascer-tained; here I have taken up my rest, and never will I go hence, till, like Wieland, I am borne to my grave.

Importunity was tried in vain: they threatened to remove me by violence—nay, violence was used; but my soul prizes too dearly this little roof to endure to be bereaved of it. Force should not prevail when the hoary locks and sup-plicating tears of my uncle were ineffectual. My repug-nance to move gave birth to ferociousness and phrenzy when force was employed, and they were obliged to consent to my return.

232

They besought me—they remonstrated—they appealed to every duty that connected me with him that made me, and with my fellow-men—in vain. While I live I will not go hence. Have I not fulfilled my destiny?

Why will ye torment me with your reasonings and reproofs? Can ye restore to me the hope of my better days? Can ye give me back Catharine and her babes? Can ye recall to life him who died at my feet?

I will eat—I will drink—I will lie down and rise up at your bidding—all I ask is the choice of my abode. What is there unreasonable in this demand? Shortly will I be at peace. This is the spot which I have chosen in which to breathe my last sigh. Deny me not, I beseech you, so slight a boon.

Talk not to me, O my revered friend! of Carwin. He has told thee his tale, and thou exculpatest him from all direct concern in the fate of Wieland. This scene of havock was produced by an illusion of the senses. Be it so: I care not from what source these disasters have flowed; it suffices that they have swallowed up our hopes and our existence.

What his agency began, his agency conducted to a close. He intended, by the final effort of his power, to rescue me and to banish his illusions from my brother. Such is his tale, concerning the truth of which I care not. Henceforth I foster but one wish—I ask only quick deliverance from life and all the ills that attend it.—

Go wretch! torment me not with thy presence and thy prayers.—Forgive thee? Will that avail thee when thy fateful hour shall arrive? Be thou acquitted at thy own tribunal, and thou needest not fear the verdict of others. If thy guilt be capable of blacker hues, if hitherto thy conscience be without stain, thy crime will be made more flagrant by thus violating my retreat. Take thyself away from my sight if thou wouldest not behold my death!

Thou art gone! murmuring and reluctant! And now my repose is coming—my work is done!

CHAPTER XXVII

[Written three years after the foregoing, and dated at Montpellier.]

I IMAGINED that I had forever laid aside the pen; and that I should take up my abode in this part of the world, was of all events the least probable. My destiny I believed to be accomplished, and I looked forward to a speedy termination of my life with the fullest confidence.

Surely I had reason to be weary of existence, to be impatient of every tie which held me from the grave. I experienced this impatience in its fullest extent. I was not only enamoured of death, but conceived, from the condition of my frame, that to shun it was impossible, even though I had ardently desired it; yet here am I, a thousand leagues from my native soil, in full possession of life and of health, and not destitute of happiness.

Such is man. Time will obliterate the deepest impressions. Grief the most vehement and hopeless, will gradually decay and wear itself out. Arguments may be employed in vain: every moral prescription may be ineffectually tried: remonstrances, however cogent or pathetic, shall have no power over the attention, or shall be repelled with disdain; yet, as day follows day, the turbulence of our emotions shall subside, and our fluctuations be finally succeeded by a calm.

Perhaps, however, the conquest of despair was chiefly owing to an accident which rendered my continuance in my own house impossible. At the conclusion of my long, and, as I then supposed, my last letter to you, I mentioned my resolution to wait for death in the very spot which had been the principal scene of my misfortunes. From this resolution my friends exerted themselves with the utmost zeal and perseverance to make me depart. They justly imagined that to be thus surrounded by memorials of the fate of my family, would tend to foster my disease. A swift succession of new objects, and the exclusion of every thing calculated to remind me of my loss, was the only method of cure.

I refused to listen to their exhortations. Great as my calamity was, to be torn from this asylum was regarded by me as an aggravation of it. By a perverse constitution of mind, he was considered as my greatest enemy who sought to withdraw me from a scene which supplied eternal food to my melancholy, and kept my despair from languishing.

In relating the history of these disasters I derived a similar species of gratification. My uncle earnestly dissuaded me from this task; but his remonstrances were as fruitless on this head as they had been on others. They would have withheld from me the implements of writing; but they quickly perceived that to withstand would be more injurious than to comply with my wishes. Having finished my tale, it seemed as if the scene were closing. A fever lurked in my veins, and my strength was gone. Any exertion, however slight, was attended with difficulty, and, at length, I refused to rise from my bed.

I now see the infatuation and injustice of my conduct in its true colours. I reflect upon the sensations and reasonings of that period with wonder and humiliation. That I should be insensible to the claims and tears of my friends; that I should overlook the suggestions of duty, and fly from that post in which only I could be instrumental to the benefit of others; that the exercise of the social and beneficent affections, the contemplation of nature and the acquisition of wisdom should not be seen to be means of happiness still within my reach, is, at this time, scarcely credible.

It is true that I am now changed; but I have not the consolation to reflect that my change was owing to my fortitude or to my capacity for instruction. Better thoughts grew up in my mind imperceptibly. I cannot but congratulate myself on the change, though, perhaps, it merely argues a fickleness of temper, and a defect of sensibility.

After my narrative was ended I betook myself to my bed, in the full belief that my career in this world was on the point of finishing. My uncle took up his abode with me, and performed for me every office of nurse, physician and friend. One night, after some hours of restlessness and pain, I sunk into deep sleep. Its tranquillity, however, was of no long duration. My fancy became suddenly distempered, and my brain was turned into a theatre of uproar and confusion. It would not be easy to describe the wild and phantastical incongruities that pestered me. My uncle, Wieland, Pleyel and Carwin were successively and momently discerned amidst the storm. Sometimes I was swallowed up by whirlpools, or caught up in the air by half-seen and gigantic forms, and thrown upon pointed rocks, or cast among the billows. Sometimes gleams of light were shot into a dark abyss, on the verge of which I was standing, and enabled me to discover, for a moment, its enormous depth and hideous precipices. Anon, I was transported to some ridge of Ætna, and made a terrified spectator of its fiery torrents and its pillars of smoke.

However strange it may seem, I was conscious, even during my dream, of my real situation. I knew myself to be asleep, and struggled to break the spell, by muscular exertions. These did not avail, and I continued to suffer these abortive creations till a loud voice, at my bed side, and some one shaking me with violence, put an end to my reverie. My eyes were unsealed, and I started from my pillow.

My chamber was filled with smoke, which, though in some degree luminous, would permit me to see nothing, and by which I was nearly suffocated. The crackling of flames, and the deafening clamour of voices without, burst upon my ears. Stunned as I was by this hubbub, scorched with heat, and nearly choaked by the accumulating vapours, I was unable to think or act for my own preservation; I was incapable, indeed, of comprehending my danger.

I was caught up, in an instant, by a pair of sinewy arms, borne to the window, and carried down a ladder which had been placed there. My uncle stood at the bottom and received me. I was not fully aware of my situation till I found myself sheltered in the *Hut*, and surrounded by its inhabitants.

By neglect of the servant, some unextinguished embers had been placed in a barrel in the cellar of the building. The barrel had caught fire; this was communicated to the beams of the lower floor, and thence to the upper part of the structure. It was first discovered by some persons at a distance, who hastened to the spot and alarmed my uncle and the servants. The flames had already made considerable progress, and my condition was overlooked till my escape was rendered nearly impossible.

My danger being known, and a ladder quickly procured, one of the spectators ascended to my chamber, and effected my deliverance in the manner before related.

This incident, disastrous as it may at first seem, had, in reality, a beneficial effect upon my feelings. I was, in some degree, roused from the stupor which had seized my faculties. The monotonous and gloomy series of my thoughts was broken. My habitation was levelled with the ground, and I was obliged to seek a new one. A new train of images, disconnected with the fate of my family, forced itself on my attention, and a belief insensibly sprung up, that tranquillity, if not happiness, was still within my reach. Notwithstanding the shocks which my frame had endured, the anguish of my thoughts no sooner abated than I recovered my health.

I now willingly listened to my uncle's solicitations to be the companion of his voyage. Preparations were easily made, and after a tedious passage, we set our feet on the shore of the ancient world. The memory of the past did not forsake me; but the melancholy which it generated, and the tears with which it filled my eyes, were not unprofitable. My curiosity was revived, and I contemplated, with ardour, the spectacle of living manners and the monuments of past ages.

In proportion as my heart was reinstated in the possession of its ancient tranquillity, the sentiment which I had cherished with regard to Pleyel returned. In a short time he was united to the Saxon woman, and made his residence in the neighbourhood of Boston. I was glad that circumstances would not permit an interview to take place between us. I could not desire their misery; but I reaped no pleasure from reflecting on their happiness. Time, and the exertions of my fortitude, cured me, in some degree, of this folly. I continued to love him, but my passion was disguised to myself; I considered it merely as a more tender species of friendship, and cherished it without compunction.

Through my uncle's exertions a meeting was brought about between Carwin and Pleyel, and explanations took place which restored me at once to the good opinion of the latter. Though separated so widely our correspondence was punctual and frequent, and paved the way for that union which can only end with the death of one of us.

In my letters to him I made no secret of my former sentiments. This was a theme on which I could talk without painful, though not without delicate emotions. That knowledge which I should never have imparted to a lover, I felt little scruple to communicate to a friend.

A year and an half elapsed, when Theresa was snatched from him by death, in the hour in which she gave him the first pledge of their mutual affection. This event was borne by him with his customary fortitude. It induced him, however, to make a change in his plans. He disposed of his property in America, and joined my uncle and me, who had terminated the wanderings of two years at Montpellier, which will henceforth, I believe, be our permanent abode.

If you reflect upon that entire confidence which had subsisted from our infancy between Pleyel and myself; on the passion that I had contracted, and which was merely smothered for a time; and on the esteem which was mutual, you will not, perhaps, be surprized that the renovation of our intercourse should give birth to that union which at present subsists. When the period had elapsed necessary to weaken the remembrance of Theresa, to whom he had been bound by ties more of honor than of love, he tendered his affections to me. I need not add that the tender was eagerly accepted.

Perhaps you are somewhat interested in the fate of Carwin. He saw, when too late, the danger of imposture. So much affected was he by the catastrophe to which he was a witness, that he laid aside all regard to his own safety. He sought my uncle, and confided to him the tale which he had just related to me. He found a more impartial and indulgent auditor in Mr. Cambridge, who imputed to maniacal illusion the conduct of Wieland, though he conceived the previous and unseen agency of Carwin, to have indirectly but powerfully predisposed him to this deplorable perversion of mind.

It was easy for Carwin to elude the persecutions of Ludloe. It was merely requisite to hide himself in a remote district of Pennsylvania. This, when he parted from us, he determined to do. He is now probably engaged in the harmless pursuits of agriculture, and may come to think, without insupportable remorse, on the evils to which his fatal talents have given birth. The innocence and usefulness of his future life may, in some degree, atone for the miseries so rashly or so thoughtlessly inflicted.

More urgent considerations hindered me from mentioning, in the course of my former mournful recital, any particulars respecting the unfortunate father of Louisa Conway. That man surely was reserved to be a monument of capricious fortune. His southern journeys being finished, he returned to Philadelphia. Before he reached the city he left the highway, and alighted at my brother's door. Contrary to his expectation, no one came forth to welcome him, or hail his approach. He attempted to enter the house, but bolted doors, barred windows, and a silence broken only by unanswered calls, shewed him that the mansion was deserted.

He proceeded thence to my habitation, which he found, in like manner, gloomy and tenantless. His surprize may be easily conceived. The rustics who occupied the *Hut* told him an imperfect and incredible tale. He hasted to the city, and extorted from Mrs. Baynton a full disclosure of late disasters.

He was inured to adversity, and recovered, after no long

time, from the shocks produced by this disappointment of his darling scheme. Our intercourse did not terminate with his departure from America. We have since met with him in France, and light has at length been thrown upon the motives which occasioned the disappearance of his wife, in the manner which I formerly related to you.

I have dwelt upon the ardour of their conjugal attachment, and mentioned that no suspicion had ever glanced upon her purity. This, though the belief was long cherished, recent discoveries have shewn to be questionable. No doubt her integrity would have survived to the present moment, if an extraordinary fate had not befallen her.

Major Stuart had been engaged, while in Germany, in a contest of honor with an Aid de Camp of the Marquis of Granby. His adversary had propagated a rumour injurious to his character. A challenge was sent; a meeting ensued; and Stuart wounded and disarmed the calumniator. The offence was atoned for, and his life secured by suitable concessions.

Maxwell, that was his name, shortly after, in consequence of succeeding to a rich inheritance, sold his commission and returned to London. His fortune was speedily augmented by an opulent marriage. Interest was his sole inducement to this marriage, though the lady had been swayed by a credulous affection. The true state of his heart was quickly discovered, and a separation, by mutual consent, took place. The lady withdrew to an estate in a distant county, and Maxwell continued to consume his time and fortune in the dissipation of the capital.

Maxwell, though deceitful and sensual, possessed great force of mind and specious accomplishments. He contrived to mislead the generous mind of Stuart, and to regain the esteem which his misconduct, for a time, had forfeited. He was recommended by her husband to the confidence of Mrs. Stuart. Maxwell was stimulated by revenge, and by a lawless passion, to convert this confidence into a source of guilt.

The education and capacity of this woman, the worth of

her husband, the pledge of their alliance which time had produced, her maturity in age and knowledge of the world—all combined to render this attempt hopeless. Maxwell, however, was not easily discouraged. The most perfect being, he believed, must owe his exemption from vice to the absence of temptation. The impulses of love are so subtile, and the influence of false reasoning, when enforced by eloquence and passion, so unbounded, that no human virtue is secure from degeneracy. All arts being tried, every temptation being summoned to his aid, dissimulation being carried to its utmost bound, Maxwell, at length, nearly accomplished his purpose. The lady's affections were withdrawn from her husband and transferred to him. She could not, as yet, be reconciled to dishonor. All efforts to induce her to elope with him were ineffectual. She permitted herself to love, and to avow her love; but at this limit she stopped, and was immoveable.

Hence this revolution in her sentiments was productive only of despair. Her rectitude of principle preserved her from actual guilt, but could not restore to her her ancient affection, or save her from being the prey of remorseful and impracticable wishes. Her husband's absence produced a state of suspense. This, however, approached to a period, and she received tidings of his intended return. Maxwell, being likewise apprized of this event, and having made a last and unsuccessful effort to conquer her reluctance to accompany him in a journey to Italy, whither he pretended an invincible necessity of going, left her to pursue the measures which despair might suggest. At the same time she received a letter from the wife of Maxwell, unveiling the true character of this man, and revealing facts which the artifices of her seducer had hitherto concealed from her. Mrs. Maxwell had been prompted to this disclosure by a knowledge of her husband's practices, with which his own impetuosity had made her acquainted.

This discovery, joined to the delicacy of her scruples and the anguish of remorse, induced her to abscond. This scheme was adopted in haste, but effected with consummate prudence. She fled, on the eve of her husband's arrival, in the disguise of a boy, and embarked at Falmouth in a packet bound for America.

The history of her disastrous intercourse with Maxwell, the motives inducing her to forsake her country, and the measures she had taken to effect her design, were related to Mrs. Maxwell, in reply to her communication. Between these women an ancient intimacy and considerable similitude of character subsisted. This disclosure was accompanied with solemn injunctions of secrecy, and these injunctions were, for a long time, faithfully observed.

Mrs. Maxwell's abode was situated on the banks of the Wey. Stuart was her kinsman; their youth had been spent together; and Maxwell was in some degree indebted to the man whom he betrayed, for his alliance with this unfortunate lady. Her esteem for the character of Stuart had never been diminished. A meeting between them was occasioned by a tour which the latter had undertaken, in the year after his return from America, to Wales and the western counties. This interview produced pleasure and regret in each. Their own transactions naturally became the topics of their conversation; and the untimely fate of his wife and daughter were related by the guest.

Mrs. Maxwell's regard for her friend, as well as for the safety of her husband, persuaded her to concealment; but the former being dead, and the latter being out of the kingdom, she ventured to produce Mrs. Stuart's letter, and to communicate her own knowledge of the treachery of Maxwell. She had previously extorted from her guest a promise not to pursue any scheme of vengeance; but this promise was made while ignorant of the full extent of Maxwell's depravity, and his passion refused to adhere to it.

At this time my uncle and I resided at Avignon. Among the English resident there, and with whom we maintained a social intercourse, was Maxwell. This man's talents and address rendered him a favorite both with my uncle and myself. He had even tendered me his hand in marriage; but this being refused, he had sought and obtained permission to continue with us the intercourse of friendship. Since a legal marriage was impossible, no doubt, his views were flagitious. Whether he had relinquished these views I was unable to judge.

He was one in a large circle at a villa in the environs, to which I had likewise been invited, when Stuart abruptly entered the apartment. He was recognized with genuine satisfaction by me, and with seeming pleasure by Maxwell. In a short time, some affair of moment being pleaded, which required an immediate and exclusive interview, Maxwell and he withdrew together. Stuart and my uncle had been known to each other in the German army; and the purpose contemplated by the former in this long and hasty journey, was confided to his old friend.

A defiance was given and received, and the banks of a rivulet, about a league from the city, was selected as the scene of this contest. My uncle, having exerted himself in vain to prevent an hostile meeting, consented to attend them as a surgeon.—Next morning, at sun-rise, was the time chosen.

I returned early in the evening to my lodgings. Preliminaries being settled between the combatants, Stuart had consented to spend the evening with us, and did not retire till late. On the way to his hotel he was exposed to no molestation, but just as he stepped within the portico, a swarthy and malignant figure started from behind a column, and plunged a stiletto into his body.

The author of this treason could not certainly be discovered; but the details communicated by Stuart, respecting the history of Maxwell, naturally pointed him out as an object of suspicion. No one expressed more concern, on account of this disaster, than he; and he pretended an ardent zeal to vindicate his character from the aspersions that were cast upon it. Thenceforth, however, I denied myself to his visits; and shortly after he disappeared from this scene.

Few possessed more estimable qualities, and a better title to happiness and the tranquil honors of long life, than the mother and father of Louisa Conway: yet they were cut off in the bloom of their days; and their destiny was thus accomplished by the same hand. Maxwell was the instrument of their destruction, though the instrument was applied to this end in so different a manner.

I leave you to moralize on this tale. That virtue should become the victim of treachery is, no doubt, a mournful consideration; but it will not escape your notice, that the evils of which Carwin and Maxwell were the authors, owed their existence to the errors of the sufferers. All efforts would have been ineffectual to subvert the happiness or shorten the existence of the Stuarts, if their own frailty had not seconded these efforts. If the lady had crushed her disastrous passion in the bud, and driven the seducer from her presence, when the tendency of his artifices was seen; if Stuart had not admitted the spirit of absurd revenge, we should not have had to deplore this catastrophe. If Wieland had framed juster notions of moral duty, and of the divine attributes; or if I had been gifted with ordinary equanimity or foresight, the double-tongued deceiver would have been baffled and repelled.

MEMOIRS OF CARWIN

THE BILOQUIST

MEMOIRS OF CARWIN THE BILOQUIST

I was the second son of a farmer, whose place of residence was a western district of Pennsylvania. My eldest brother seemed fitted by nature for the employment to which he was destined. His wishes never led him astray from the hay-stack and the furrow. His ideas never ranged beyond the sphere of his vision, or suggested the possibility that to-morrow could differ from to-day. He could read and write, because he had no alternative between learning the lesson prescribed to him, and punishment. He was diligent, as long as fear urged him forward, but his exertions ceased with the cessation of this motive. The limits of his acquirements consisted in signing his name, and spelling out a chapter in the bible.

My character was the reverse of his. My thirst of knowledge was augmented in proportion as it was supplied with gratification. The more I heard or read, the more restless and unconquerable my curiosity became. My senses were perpetually alive to novelty, my fancy teemed with visions of the future, and my attention fastened upon every thing mysterious or unknown.

My father intended that my knowledge should keep pace with that of my brother, but conceived that all beyond the mere capacity to write and read was useless or pernicious. He took as much pains to keep me within these limits, as to make the acquisitions of my brother come up to them, but his efforts were not equally successful in both cases. The most vigilant and jealous scrutiny was exerted in vain: Reproaches and blows, painful privations and ignominious penances had no power to slacken my zeal and abate my perseverance. He might enjoin upon me the most laborious tasks, set the envy of my brother to watch me during the performance, make the most diligent search after my books, and destroy them without mercy, when they were found; but he could not outroot my darling propensity. I exerted all my powers to elude his watchfulness. Censures and stripes were sufficiently unpleasing to make me strive to avoid them. To effect this desirable end, I was incessantly employed in the invention of stratagems and the execution of expedients.

My passion was surely not deserving of blame, and I have frequently lamented the hardships to which it subjected me; yet, perhaps, the claims which were made upon my ingenuity and fortitude were not without beneficial effects upon my character.

This contention lasted from the sixth to the fourteenth year of my age. My father's opposition to my schemes was incited by a sincere though unenlightened desire for my happiness. That all his efforts were secretly eluded or obstinately repelled, was a source of the bitterest regret. He has often lamented, with tears, what he called my incorrigible depravity, and encouraged himself to perseverance by the notion of the ruin that would inevitably overtake me if I were allowed to persist in my present career. Perhaps the sufferings which arose to him from the disappointment, were equal to those which he inflicted on me.

In my fourteenth year, events happened which ascertained my future destiny. One evening I had been sent to bring cows from a meadow, some miles distant from my father's mansion. My time was limited, and I was menaced with severe chastisement if, according to my custom, I should stay beyond the period assigned.

For some time these menaces rung in my ears, and I went on my way with speed. I arrived at the meadow, but the cattle had broken the fence and escaped. It was my duty to carry home the earliest tidings of this accident, but the first suggestion was to examine the cause and manner of this escape. The field was bounded by cedar railing. Five of these rails were laid horizontally from post to post. The upper one had been broken in the middle, but the rest had merely been drawn out of the holes on one side, and rested with their ends on the ground. The means which had been used for this end, the reason why one only was broken, and that one the uppermost, how a pair of horns could be so managed as to effect that which the hands of man would have found difficult, supplied a theme of meditation.

Some accident recalled me from this reverie, and reminded me how much time had thus been consumed. I was terrified at the consequences of my delay, and sought with eagerness how they might be obviated. I asked myself if there were not a way back shorter than that by which I had come. The beaten road was rendered circuitous by a precipice that projected into a neighbouring stream, and closed up a passage by which the length of the way would have been diminished one half: at the foot of the cliff the water was of considerable depth, and agitated by an eddy. I could not estimate the danger which I should incur by plunging into it, but I was resolved to make the attempt. I have reason to think, that this experiment, if it had been tried, would have proved fatal, and my father, while he lamented my untimely fate, would have been wholly unconscious that his own unreasonable demands had occasioned it.

I turned my steps towards the spot. To reach the edge of the stream was by no means an easy undertaking, so many abrupt points and gloomy hollows were interposed. I had frequently skirted and penetrated this tract, but had never been so completely entangled in the maze as now: hence I had remained unacquainted with a narrow pass, which, at the distance of an hundred yards from the river, would conduct me, though not without danger and toil, to the opposite side of the ridge.

This glen was now discovered, and this discovery induced me to change my plan. If a passage could be here effected, it would be shorter and safer than that which led through the stream, and its practicability was to be known only by experiment. The path was narrow, steep, and overshadowed by rocks. The sun was nearly set, and the shadow of the cliff above, obscured the passage almost as much as midnight would have done: I was accustomed to despise danger when it presented itself in a sensible form, but, by a defect common in every one's education, goblins and spectres were to me the objects of the most violent apprehensions. These were unavoidably connected with solitude and darkness, and were present to my fears when I entered this gloomy recess.

These terrors are always lessened by calling the attention away to some indifferent object. I now made use of this expedient, and began to amuse myself by hallowing as loud as organs of unusual compass and vigour would enable me. I uttered the words which chanced to occur to me, and repeated in the shrill tones of a Mohock savage . . . "Cow! cow! come home! home!" . . . These notes were of course reverberated from the rocks which on either side towered aloft, but the echo was confused and indistinct.

I continued, for some time, thus to beguile the way, till I reached a space more than commonly abrupt, and which required all my attention. My rude ditty was suspended till I had surmounted this impediment. In a few minutes I was at leisure to renew it. After finishing the strain, I paused. In a few seconds a voice, as I then imagined, uttered the same cry from the point of a rock some hundred feet behind me; the same words, with equal distinctness and deliberation, and in the same tone, appeared to be spoken. I was startled by this incident, and cast a fearful glance behind, to discover by whom it was uttered. The spot where I stood was buried in dusk, but the eminences were still invested with a luminous and vivid twilight. The speaker, however, was concealed from my view.

I had scarcely begun to wonder at this occurrence, when a new occasion for wonder, was afforded me. A few seconds, in like manner, elapsed, when my ditty was again rehearsed, with a no less perfect imitation, in a different quarter. . . . To this quarter I eagerly turned my eyes, but no one was visible. . . . The station, indeed, which this new speaker seemed to occupy, was inaccessible to man or beast.

If I were surprized at this second repetition of my words, judge how much my surprise must have been augmented, when the same calls were a third time repeated, and coming still in a new direction. Five times was this ditty successively resounded, at intervals nearly equal, always from a new quarter, and with little abatement of its original distinctness and force.

A little reflection was sufficient to shew that this was no more than an echo of an extraordinary kind. My terrors were quickly supplanted by delight. The motives to dispatch were forgotten, and I amused myself for an hour, with talking to these cliffs: I placed myself in new positions, and exhausted my lungs and my invention in new clamours.

The pleasures of this new discovery were an ample compensation for the ill treatment which I expected on my return. By some caprice in my father I escaped merely with a few reproaches. I seized the first opportunity of again visiting this recess, and repeating my amusement; time, and incessant repetition, could scarcely lessen its charms or exhaust the variety produced by new tones and new positions.

The hours in which I was most free from interruption and restraint were those of moonlight. My brother and I occupied a small room above the kitchen, disconnected, in some degree, with the rest of the house. It was the rural custom to retire early to bed and to anticipate the rising of the sun. When the moonlight was strong enough to permit me to read, it was my custom to escape from bed, and hie with my book to some neighbouring eminence, where I would remain stretched on the mossy rock, till the sinking or beclouded moon, forbade me to continue my employment. I was indebted for books to a friendly person in the neighbourhood, whose compliance with my solicitations was prompted partly by benevolence and partly by enmity to my father, whom he could not more egregiously offend than by gratifying my perverse and pernicious curiosity.

In leaving my chamber I was obliged to use the utmost caution to avoid rousing my brother, whose temper disposed him to thwart me in the least of my gratifications. My purpose was surely laudable, and yet on leaving the house and returning to it, I was obliged to use the vigilance and circumspection of a thief.

One night I left my bed with this view. I posted first to my vocal glen, and thence scrambling up a neighbouring steep, which overlooked a wide extent of this romantic country, gave myself up to contemplation, and the perusal of Milton's Comus.

My reflections were naturally suggested by the singularity of this echo. To hear my own voice speak at a distance would have been formerly regarded as prodigious. To hear too, that voice, not uttered by another, by whom it might easily be mimicked, but by myself! I cannot now recollect the transition which led me to the notion of sounds, similar to these, but produced by other means than reverberation. Could I not so dispose my organs as to make my voice appear at a distance?

From speculation I proceeded to experiment. The idea of a distant voice, like my own, was intimately present to my fancy. I exerted myself with a most ardent desire, and with something like a persuasion that I should succeed. I started with surprise, for it seemed as if success had crowned my attempts. I repeated the effort, but failed. A certain position of the organs took place on the first attempt, altogether new, unexampled and, as it were, by accident, for I could not attain it on the second experiment.

You will not wonder that I exerted myself with indefatigable zeal to regain what had once, though for so short a space, been in my power. Your own ears have witnessed the success of these efforts. By perpetual exertion I gained it a second time, and now was a diligent observer of the circumstances attending it. Gradually I subjected these finer and more subtle motions to the command of my will. What was at first difficult, by exercise and habit was rendered easy. I learned to accommodate my voice to all the varieties of distance and direction.

It cannot be denied that this faculty is wonderful and rare, but when we consider the possible modifications of muscular motion, how few of these are usually exerted, how imperfectly they are subjected to the will, and yet that the will is capable of being rendered unlimited and absolute, will not our wonder cease?

We have seen men who could hide their tongues so perfectly that even an Anatomist, after the most accurate inspection that a living subject could admit, has affirmed the organ to be wanting, but this was effected by the exertion of muscles unknown and incredible to the greater part of mankind.

The concurrence of teeth, palate and tongue, in the formation of speech should seem to be indispensable, and yet men have spoken distinctly though wanting a tongue, and to whom, therefore, teeth and palate were superfluous. The tribe of motions requisite to this end, are wholly latent and unknown, to those who possess that organ.

I mean not to be more explicit. I have no reason to suppose a peculiar conformation or activity in my own organs, or that the power which I possess may not, with suitable directions and by steady efforts, be obtained by others, but I will do nothing to facilitate the acquisition. It is by far, too liable to perversion for a good man to desire to possess it, or to teach it to another.

There remained but one thing to render this instrument as powerful in my hands as it was capable of being. From my childhood, I was remarkably skilful at imitation. There were few voices whether of men or birds or beasts which I could not imitate with success. To add my ancient, to my newly acquired skill, to talk from a distance, and at the same time, in the accents of another, was the object of my endeavours, and this object, after a certain number of trials, I finally obtained.

In my present situation every thing that denoted intellectual exertion was a crime, and exposed me to invectives if not to stripes. This circumstance induced me to be silent to all others, on the subject of my discovery. But, added to this, was a confused belief, that it might be made, in some way instrumental to my relief from the hardships and restraints of my present condition. For some time I was not aware of the mode in which it might be rendered subservient to this end.

My father's sister was an ancient lady, resident in Philadelphia, the relict of a merchant, whose decease left her the enjoyment of a frugal competence. She was without children, and had often expressed her desire that her nephew Frank, whom she always considered as a sprightly and promising lad, should be put under her care. She offered to be at the expense of my education, and to bequeath to me at her death her slender patrimony.

This arrangement was obstinately rejected by my father, because it was merely fostering and giving scope to propensities, which he considered as hurtful, and because his avarice desired that this inheritance should fall to no one but himself. To me, it was a scheme of ravishing felicity, and to be debarred from it was a source of anguish known to few. I had too much experience of my father's pertinaciousness ever to hope for a change in his views; yet the bliss of living with my aunt, in a new and busy scene, and in the unbounded indulgence of my literary passion, continually occupied my thoughts: for a long time these thoughts were productive only of despondency and tears.

Time only enhanced the desirableness of this scheme; my new faculty would naturally connect itself with these wishes, and the question could not fail to occur whether it might not aid me in the execution of my favourite plan.

A thousand superstitious tales were current in the family. Apparitions had been seen, and voices had been heard, on a multitude of occasions. My father was a confident believer in supernatural tokens. The voice of his wife, who had been many years dead, had been twice heard at midnight whispering at his pillow. I frequently asked myself whether a scheme favourable to my views might not be built upon these foundations. Suppose (thought I) my mother should be made to enjoin upon him compliance with my wishes?

This idea bred in me a temporary consternation. To imitate the voice of the dead, to counterfeit a commission from heaven, bore the aspect of presumption and impiety. It seemed an offence which could not fail to draw after it the

254

vengeance of the deity. My wishes for a time yielded to my fears, but this scheme in proportion as I meditated on it, became more plausible; no other occurred to me so easy and so efficacious. I endeavoured to persuade myself that the end proposed, was, in the highest degree praiseworthy, and that the excellence of my purpose would justify the means employed to attain it.

My resolutions were, for a time, attended with fluctuations and misgivings. These gradually disappeared, and my purpose became firm; I was next to devise the means of effecting my views; this did not demand any tedious deliberation. It was easy to gain access to my father's chamber without notice or detection; cautious footsteps and the suppression of breath would place me, unsuspected and unthought of, by his bed side. The words I should use, and the mode of utterance were not easily settled, but having at length selected these, I made myself by much previous repetition, perfectly familiar with the use of them.

I selected a blustering and inclement night, in which the darkness was augmented by a veil of the blackest clouds. The building we inhabited was slight in its structure, and full of crevices through which the gale found easy way, and whistled in a thousand cadencies. On this night the elemental music was remarkably sonorous, and was mingled not unfrequently with *thunder heard remote.*

I could not divest myself of secret dread. My heart faultered with a consciousness of wrong. Heaven seemed to be present and to disapprove my work; I listened to the thunder and the wind, as to the stern voice of this disapprobation. Big drops stood on my forehead, and my tremors almost incapacitated me from proceeding.

These impediments however I surmounted; I crept up stairs at midnight, and entered my father's chamber. The darkness was intense, and I sought with outstretched hands for his bed. The darkness, added to the trepidation of my thoughts, disabled me from making a right estimate of distances: I was conscious of this, and when I advanced within the room, paused.

I endeavoured to compare the progress I had made with

my knowledge of the room, and governed by the result of this comparison, proceeded cautiously and with hands still outstretched in search of the foot of the bed. At this moment lightning flashed into the room: the brightness of the gleam was dazzling, yet it afforded me an exact knowledge of my situation. I had mistaken my way, and discovered that my knees nearly touched the bedstead, and that my hands at the next step, would have touched my father's cheek. His closed eyes and every line in his countenance, were painted, as it were, for an instant on my sight.

The flash was accompanied with a burst of thunder, whose vehemence was stunning. I always entertained a dread of thunder, and now recoiled, overborne with terror. Never had I witnessed so luminous a gleam and so tremendous a shock, yet my father's slumber appeared not to be disturbed by it.

I stood irresolute and trembling; to prosecute my purpose in this state of mind was impossible. I resolved for the present to relinquish it, and turned with a view of exploring my way out of the chamber. Just then a light seen through the window, caught my eye. It was at first weak but speedily increased; no second thought was necessary to inform me that the barn, situated at a small distance from the house, and newly stored with hay, was in flames, in consequence of being struck by the lightning.

My terror at this spectacle made me careless of all consequences relative to myself. I rushed to the bed and throwing myself on my father, awakened him by loud cries. The family were speedily roused, and were compelled to remain impotent spectators of the devastation. Fortunately the wind blew in a contrary direction, so that our habitation was not injured.

The impression that was made upon me by the incidents of that night is indelible. The wind gradually rose into an hurricane; the largest branches were torn from the trees, and whirled aloft into the air; others were uprooted and laid prostrate on the ground. The barn was a spacious edifice, consisting wholly of wood, and filled with a plenteous harvest. Thus supplied with fuel, and fanned by the wind, the fire raged with incredible fury; meanwhile clouds rolled above, whose blackness was rendered more conspicuous by reflection from the flames; the vast volumes of smoke were dissipated in a moment by the storm, while glowing fragments and cinders were borne to an immense hight, and tossed every where in wild confusion. Ever and anon the sable canopy that hung around us was streaked with lightning, and the peals, by which it was accompanied, were deafning, and with scarcely any intermission.

It was, doubtless, absurd to imagine any connexion between this portentous scene and the purpose that I had meditated, yet a belief of this connexion, though wavering and obscure, lurked in my mind; something more than a coincidence merely casual, appeared to have subsisted between my situation, at my father's bed side, and the flash that darted through the window, and diverted me from my design. It palsied my courage, and strengthened my conviction, that my scheme was criminal.

After some time had elapsed, and tranquility was, in some degree, restored in the family, my father reverted to the circumstances in which I had been discovered on the first alarm of this event. The truth was impossible to be told. I felt the utmost reluctance to be guilty of a falsehood, but by falsehood only could I elude detection. That my guilt was the offspring of a fatal necessity, that the injustice of others gave it birth and made it unavoidable, afforded me slight consolation. Nothing can be more injurous than a lie, but its evil tendency chiefly respects our future conduct. Its direct consequences may be transient and few, but it facilitates a repetition, strengthens temptation, and grows into habit. I pretended some necessity had drawn me from my bed, and that discovering the condition of the barn, I hastened to inform my father.

Some time after this, my father summoned me to his presence. I had been previously guilty of disobedience to his commands, in a matter about which he was usually very scrupulous. My brother had been privy to my offence, and had threatened to be my accuser. On this occasion I expected nothing but arraignment and punishment. Weary

257

of oppression, and hopeless of any change in my father's temper and views, I had formed the resolution of eloping from his house, and of trusting, young as I was, to the caprice of fortune. I was hesitating whether to abscond without the knowledge of the family, or to make my resolutions known to them, and while I avowed my resolution, to adhere to it in spite of opposition and remonstrances, when I received this summons.

I was employed at this time in the field; night was approaching, and I had made no preparation for departure; all the preparation in my power to make, was indeed small; a few clothes made into a bundle, was the sum of my possessions. Time would have little influence in improving my prospects, and I resolved to execute my scheme immediately.

I left my work intending to seek my chamber, and taking what was my own, to disappear forever. I turned a stile that led out of the field into a bye path, when my father appeared before me, advancing in an opposite direction; to avoid him was impossible, and I summoned my fortitude to a conflict with his passion.

As soon as we met, instead of anger and upbraiding, he told me, that he had been reflecting on my aunt's proposal, to take me under her protection, and had concluded that the plan was proper; if I still retained my wishes on that head, he would readily comply with them; and that, if I chose, I might set off for the city next morning, as a neighbour's waggon was preparing to go.

I shall not dwell on the rapture with which this proposal was listened to: it was with difficulty that I persuaded myself that he was in earnest in making it, nor could I divine the reasons, for so sudden and unexpected a change in his maxims. . . . These I afterwards discovered. Some one had instilled into him fears, that my aunt exasperated at his opposition to her request, respecting the unfortunate Frank, would bequeath her property to strangers; to obviate this evil, which his avarice prompted him to regard as much greater than any mischief, that would accrue to me, from the change of my abode, he embraced her proposal.

258

I entered with exultation and triumph on this new scene; my hopes were by no means disappointed. Detested labour was exchanged for luxurious idleness. I was master of my time, and the chuser of my occupations. My kinswoman on discovering that I entertained no relish for the drudgery of colleges, and was contented with the means of intellectual gratification, which I could obtain under her roof, allowed me to pursue my own choice.

Three tranquil years passed away, during which, each day added to my happiness, by adding to my knowledge. My biloquial faculty was not neglected. I improved it by assiduous exercise; I deeply reflected on the use to which it might be applied. I was not destitute of pure intentions; I delighted not in evil; I was incapable of knowingly contributing to another's misery, but the sole or principal end of my endeavours was not the happiness of others.

I was actuated by ambition. I was delighted to possess superior power; I was prone to manifest that superiority, and was satisfied if this were done, without much solicitude concerning consequences. I sported frequently with the apprehensions of my associates, and threw out a bait for their wonder, and supplied them with occasions for the structure of theories. It may not be amiss to enumerate one or two adventures in which I was engaged.

I had taken much pains to improve the sagacity of a favourite Spaniel. It was my purpose, indeed, to ascertain to what degree of improvement the principles of reasoning and imitation could be carried in a dog. There is no doubt that the animal affixes distinct ideas to sounds. What are the possible limits of his vocabulary no one can tell. In conversing with my dog I did not use English words, but selected simple monosyllables. Habit likewise enabled him to comprehend my gestures. If I crossed my hands on my breast he understood the signal and laid down behind me. If I joined my hands and lifted them to my breast, he returned home. If I grasped one arm above the elbow he ran before me. If I lifted my hand to my forehead he trotted composedly behind. By one motion I could make him bark; by another I could reduce him to silence. He would howl in twenty different strains of mournfulness, at my bidding. He would fetch and carry with undeviating faithfulness.

His actions being thus chiefly regulated by gestures, that to a stranger would appear indifferent or casual, it was easy to produce a belief that the animal's knowledge was much greater than in truth, it was.

One day, in a mixed company, the discourse turned upon the unrivaled abilities of *Damon*. Damon had, indeed, acquired in all the circles which I frequented, an extraordinary reputation. Numerous instances of his sagacity were quoted and some of them exhibited on the spot. Much surprise was excited by the readiness with which he appeared to comprehend sentences of considerable abstraction and complexity, though, he in reality, attended to nothing but the movements of hand or fingers with which I accompanied my words. I enhanced the astonishment of some and excited the ridicule of others, by observing that my dog not only understood English when spoken by others, but actually spoke the language himself, with no small degree of precision.

This assertion could not be admitted without proof; proof, therefore, was readily produced. At a known signal, Damon began a low interrupted noise, in which the astonished hearers clearly distinguished English words. A dialogue began between the animal and his master, which was maintained, on the part of the former, with great vivacity and spirit. In this dialogue the dog asserted the dignity of his species and capacity of intellectual improvement. The company separated lost in wonder, but perfectly convinced by the evidence that had been produced.

On a subsequent occasion a select company was assembled at a garden, at a small distance from the city. Discourse glided through a variety of topics, till it lighted at length on the subject of invisible beings. From the speculations of philosophers we proceeded to the creations of the poet. Some maintained the justness of Shakspear's delineations of aerial beings, while others denied it. By no violent transition, Ariel and his songs were introduced, and a lady, celebrated for her musical skill, was solicited to accompany her pedal harp with the song of "Five fathom deep thy father lies.". . . She was known to have set, for her favourite instrument, all the songs of Shakspeare.

My youth made me little more than an auditor on this occasion. I sat apart from the rest of the company, and carefully noted every thing. The track which the conversation had taken, suggested a scheme which was not thoroughly digested when the lady began her enchanting strain.

She ended and the audience were mute with rapture. The pause continued, when a strain was wafted to our ears from another quarter. The spot where we sat was embowered by a vine. The verdant arch was lofty and the area beneath was spacious.

The sound proceeded from above. At first it was faint and scarcely audible; presently it reached a louder key, and every eye was cast up in expectation of beholding a face among the pendant clusters. The strain was easily recognized, for it was no other than that which Ariel is made to sing when finally absolved from the service of the wizard.

> In the Cowslip's bell I lie,
> On the Bat's back I do fly . . .
> After summer merrily, &c.

Their hearts palpitated as they listened: they gazed at each other for a solution of the mystery. At length the strain died away at distance, and an interval of silence was succeeded by an earnest discussion of the cause of this prodigy. One supposition only could be adopted, which was, that the strain was not uttered by human organs. That the songster was stationed on the roof of the arbour, and having finished his melody had risen into the viewless fields of air.

I had been invited to spend a week at this house: this period was nearly expired when I received information that my aunt was suddenly taken sick, and that her life was in imminent danger. I immediately set out on my return to the city, but before my arrival she was dead.

This lady was entitled to my gratitude and esteem; I had received the most essential benefits at her hand. I was not destitute of sensibility, and was deeply affected by this event: I will own, however, that my grief was lessened by reflecting on the consequences of her death, with regard to my own condition. I had been ever taught to consider myself as her heir, and her death, therefore, would free me from certain restraints.

My aunt had a female servant, who had lived with her for twenty years: she was married, but her husband, who was an artizan, lived apart from her: I had no reason to suspect the woman's sincerity and disinterestedness; but my aunt was no sooner consigned to the grave than a will was produced, in which Dorothy was named her sole and universal heir.

It was in vain to urge my expectations and my claims . . . the instrument was legibly and legally drawn up . . . Dorothy was exasperated by my opposition and surmises, and vigorously enforced her title. In a week after the decease of my kinswoman, I was obliged to seek a new dwelling. As all my property consisted in my clothes and my papers, this was easily done.

My condition was now calamitous and forlorn. Confiding in the acquisition of my aunt's patrimony, I had made no other provision for the future; I hated manual labour, or any task of which the object was gain. To be guided in my choice of occupations by any motive but the pleasure which the occupation was qualified to produce, was intolerable to my proud, indolent, and restive temper.

This resource was now cut off; the means of immediate subsistence were denied me: If I had determined to acquire the knowledge of some lucrative art, the acquisition would demand time, and, meanwhile, I was absolutely destitute of support. My father's house was, indeed, open to me, but I preferred to stifle myself with the filth of the kennel, rather than to return to it.

Some plan it was immediately necessary to adopt. The exigence of my affairs, and this reverse of fortune, continually occupied my thoughts; I estranged myself from society and from books, and devoted myself to lonely walks and mournful meditation.

One morning as I ranged along the bank of Schuylkill, I

encountered a person, by name Ludloe, of whom I had some previous knowledge. He was from Ireland; was a man of some rank and apparently rich: I had met with him before, but in mixed companies, where little direct inter-course had taken place between us. Our last meeting was in the arbour where Ariel was so unexpectedly introduced.

Our acquaintance merely justified a transient salutation; but he did not content himself with noticing me as I passed, but joined me in my walk and entered into conversation. It was easy to advert to the occasion on which we had last met, and to the mysterious incident which then occurred. I was solicitous to dive into his thoughts upon this head and put some questions which tended to the point that I wished.

I was somewhat startled when he expressed his belief, that the performer of this mystic strain was one of the company then present, who exerted, for this end, a faculty not commonly possessed. Who this person was he did not venture to guess, and I could not discover, by the tokens which he suffered to appear, that his suspicions glanced at me. He expatiated with great profoundness and fertility of ideas, on the uses to which a faculty like this might be employed. No more powerful engine, he said, could be conceived, by which the ignorant and credulous might be moulded to our purposes; managed by a man of ordinary talents, it would open for him the straightest and surest avenues to wealth and power.

His remarks excited in my mind a new strain of thoughts. I had not hitherto considered the subject in this light, though vague ideas of the importance of this art could not fail to be occasionally suggested: I ventured to inquire into his ideas of the mode, in which an art like this could be employed, so as to effect the purposes he mentioned.

He dealt chiefly in general representations. Men, he said, believed in the existence and energy of invisible powers, and in the duty of discovering and conforming to their will. This will was supposed to be sometimes made known to them through the medium of their senses. A voice coming from a quarter where no attendant form could be seen would, in most cases, be ascribed to supernal agency, and a command imposed on them, in this manner, would be obeyed with religious scrupulousness. Thus men might be imperiously directed in the disposal of their industry, their property, and even of their lives. Men, actuated by a mistaken sense of duty, might, under this influence, be led to the commission of the most flagitious, as well as the most heroic acts: If it were his desire to accumulate wealth, or institute a new sect, he should need no other instrument.

I listened to this kind of discourse with great avidity, and regretted when he thought proper to introduce new topics. He ended by requesting me to visit him, which I eagerly consented to do. When left alone, my imagination was filled with the images suggested by this conversation. The hopelessness of better fortune, which I had lately harboured, now gave place to cheering confidence. Those motives of rectitude which should deter me from this species of imposture, had never been vivid or stable, and were still more weakened by the artifices of which I had already been guilty. The utility or harmlessness of the end, justified, in my eyes, the means.

No event had been more unexpected, by me, than the bequest of my aunt to her servant. The will, under which the latter claimed, was dated prior to my coming to the city. I was not surprised, therefore, that it had once been made, but merely that it had never been cancelled or superseded by a later instrument. My wishes inclined me to suspect the existence of a later will, but I had conceived that, to ascertain its existence, was beyond my power.

Now, however, a different opinion began to be entertained. This woman like those of her sex and class was unlettered and superstitious. Her faith in spells and apparitions, was of the most lively kind. Could not her conscience be awakened by a voice from the grave! Lonely and at midnight, my aunt might be introduced, upbraiding her for her injustice, and commanding her to attone for it by acknowledging the claim of the rightful proprietor.

True it was, that no subsequent will might exist, but this was the fruit of mistake, or of negligence. She probably intended to cancel the old one, but this act might, by her own weakness, or by the artifices of her servant, be delayed till death had put it out of her power. In either case a mandate from the dead could scarcely fail of being obeyed.

I considered this woman as the usurper of my property. Her husband as well as herself, were laborious and covetous; their good fortune had made no change in their mode of living, but they were as frugal and as eager to accumulate as ever. In their hands, money was inert and sterile, or it served to foster their vices. To take it from them would, therefore, be a benefit both to them and to myself; not even an imaginary injury would be inflicted. Restitution, if legally compelled to it, would be reluctant and painful, but if enjoined by Heaven would be voluntary, and the performance of a seeming duty would carry with it, its own reward.

These reasonings, aided by inclination, were sufficient to determine me. I have no doubt but their fallacy would have been detected in the sequel, and my scheme have been productive of nothing but confusion and remorse. From these consequences, however, my fate interposed, as in the former instance, to save me.

Having formed my resolution, many preliminaries to its execution were necessary to be settled. These demanded deliberation and delay; meanwhile I recollected my promise to Ludloe, and paid him a visit. I met a frank and affectionate reception. It would not be easy to paint the delight which I experienced in this man's society. I was at first oppressed with the sense of my own inferiority in age, knowledge and rank. Hence arose numberless reserves and incapacitating diffidences; but these were speedily dissipated by the fascinations of this man's address. His superiority was only rendered, by time, more conspicuous, but this superiority, by appearing never to be present to his own mind, ceased to be uneasy to me. My questions required to be frequently answered, and my mistakes to be rectified; but my keenest scrutiny, could detect in his manner, neither arrogance nor contempt. He seemed to talk merely from the overflow of his ideas, or a benevolent desire of imparting information.

My visits gradually became more frequent. Meanwhile my wants increased, and the necessity of some change in my condition became daily more urgent. This incited my reflections on the scheme which I had formed. The time and place suitable to my design, were not selected without much anxious inquiry and frequent waverings of purpose. These being at length fixed, the interval to elapse, before the carrying of my design into effect, was not without perturbation and suspense. These could not be concealed from my new friend and at length prompted him to inquire into the cause.

It was not possible to communicate the whole truth; but the warmth of his manner inspired me with some degree of ingenuousness. I did not hide from him my former hopes and my present destitute condition. He listened to my tale with no expressions of sympathy, and when I had finished, abruptly inquired, whether I had any objection to a voyage to Europe? I answered in the negative. He then said that he was preparing to depart in a fortnight and advised me to make up my mind to accompany him.

This unexpected proposal gave me pleasure and surprize, but the want of money occurred to me as an insuperable objection. On this being mentioned, Oho! said he, carelessly, that objection is easily removed; I will bear all expenses of your passage myself.

The extraordinary beneficence of this act as well as the air of uncautiousness attending it, made me doubt the sincerity of his offer, and when new declarations removed this doubt, I could not forbear expressing, at once my sense of his generosity and of my own unworthiness.

He replied, that generosity had been expunged from his catalogue as having no meaning or a vicious one. It was the scope of his exertions to be just. This was the sum of human duty, and he that fell short, ran beside, or outstripped justice was a criminal. What he gave me was my due or not my due. If it were my due, I might reasonably demand it from him and it was wicked to withhold it. Merit on one side or gratitude on the other, were contradictory and unintelligible.

266

If I were fully convinced that this benefit was not my due and yet received it, he should hold me in contempt. The rectitude of my principles and conduct would be the measure of his approbation, and no benefit should he ever bestow which the receiver was not entitled to claim, and which it would not be criminal in him to refuse.

These principles were not new from the mouth of Ludloe, but they had, hitherto, been regarded as the fruits of a venturous speculation in my mind. I had never traced them into their practical consequences, and if his conduct on this occasion had not squared with his maxims, I should not have imputed to him inconsistency. I did not ponder on these reasonings at this time: objects of immediate importance engrossed my thoughts.

One obstacle to this measure was removed. When my voyage was performed how should I subsist in my new abode? I concealed not my perplexity and he commented on it in his usual manner. How did I mean to subsist, he asked, in my own country? The means of living would be at least as much within my reach there as here. As to the pressure of immediate and absolute want, he believed I should be exposed to little hazard. With talents such as mine, I must be hunted by a destiny peculiarly malignant, if I could not provide myself with necessaries wherever my lot were cast.

He would make allowances, however, for my diffidence and self-distrust, and would obviate my fears by expressing his own intentions with regard to me. I must be apprized, however, of his true meaning. He laboured to shun all hurtful and vitious things, and therefore carefully abstained from making or confiding in *promises*. It was just to assist me in this voyage, and it would probably be equally just to continue to me similar assistance when it was finished. That indeed was a subject, in a great degree, within my own cognizance. His aid would be proportioned to my wants and to my merits, and I had only to take care that my claims were just, for them to be admitted.

This scheme could not but appear to me eligible. I thirsted after an acquaintance with new scenes; my present situa-

tion could not be changed for a worse; I trusted to the
constancy of Ludloe's friendship; to this at least it was better
to trust than to the success of my imposture on Dorothy,
which was adopted merely as a desperate expedient: finally
I determined to embark with him.

In the course of this voyage my mind was busily employed. There were no other passengers beside ourselves,
so that my own condition and the character of Ludloe,
continually presented themselves to my reflections. It will
be supposed that I was not a vague or indifferent observer.

There were no vicissitudes in the deportment or lapses in
the discourse of my friend. His feelings appeared to preserve an unchangeable tenor, and his thoughts and words
always to flow with the same rapidity. His slumber was
profound and his wakeful hours serene. He was regular
and temperate in all his exercises and gratifications. Hence
were derived his clear perceptions and exuberant health.

His treatment of me, like all his other mental and cor-
poral operations, was modelled by one inflexible standard.
Certain scruples and delicacies were incident to my situation. Of the existence of these he seemed to be unconscious,
and yet nothing escaped him inconsistent with a state of
absolute equality.

I was naturally inquisitive as to his fortune and the collateral circumstances of his condition. My notions of politeness hindered me from making direct inquiries. By indirect
means I could gather nothing but that his state was opulent
and independent, and that he had two sisters whose situation resembled his own.

Though, in conversation, he appeared to be governed by
the utmost candour; no light was let in upon the former
transactions of his life. The purpose of his visit to America I
could merely guess to be the gratification of curiosity.

My future pursuits must be supposed chiefly to occupy
my attention. On this head I was destitute of all stedfast
views. Without profession or habits of industry or sources
of permanent revenue, the world appeared to me an ocean
on which my bark was set afloat, without compass or sail.
The world into which I was about to enter, was untried and

unknown, and though I could consent to profit by the guidance, I was unwilling to rely on the support of others.

This topic, being nearest my heart, I frequently introduced into conversation with my friend; but on this subject he always allowed himself to be led by me, while on all others, he was zealous to point the way. To every scheme that I proposed he was sure to cause objections. All the liberal professions were censured as perverting the understanding, by giving scope to the sordid motive of gain or embuing the mind with erroneous principles. Skill was slowly obtained, and success, though integrity and independence must be given for it, dubious and instable. The mechanical trades were equally obnoxious; they were vitious by contributing to the spurious gratifications of the rich and multiplying the objects of luxury; they were destructive to the intellect and vigour of the artizan; they enervated his frame and brutalized his mind.

When I pointed out to him the necessity of some species of labour, he tacitly admitted that necessity, but refused to direct me in the choice of a pursuit, which though not free from defect should yet have the fewest inconveniences. He dwelt on the fewness of our actual wants, the temptations which attend the possession of wealth, the benefits of seclusion and privacy, and the duty of unfettering our minds from the prejudices which govern the world.

His discourse tended merely to unsettle my views and increase my perplexity. This effect was so uniform that I at length desisted from all allusions to this theme and endeavoured to divert my own reflections from it. When our voyage should be finished, and I should actually tread this new stage, I believed that I should be better qualified to judge of the measures to be taken by me.

At length we reached Belfast. From thence we immediately repaired to Dublin. I was admitted as a member of his family. When I expressed my uncertainty as to the place to which it would be proper for me to repair, he gave me a blunt but cordial invitation to this house. My circumstances allowed me no option and I readily complied. My attention was for a time engrossed by a diversified succession of new objects. Their novelty, however, disappearing left me at liberty to turn my eyes upon myself and my companion, and here my reflections were supplied with abundant food.

His house was spacious and commodious, and furnished with profusion and elegance. A suit of apartments was assigned to me, in which I was permitted to reign uncontrouled, and access was permitted to a well furnished library. My food was furnished in my own room, prepared in the manner which I had previously directed. Occasionally Ludloe would request my company to breakfast, when an hour was usually consumed in earnest or sprightly conversation. At all other times he was invisible, and his apartments being wholly separate from mine, I had no opportunity of discovering in what way his hours were employed.

He defended this mode of living as being most compatible with liberty. He delighted to expatiate on the evils of cohabitation. Men, subjected to the same regimen, compelled to eat and sleep and associate at certain hours, were strangers to all rational independence and liberty. Society would never be exempt from servitude and misery, till those artificial ties which held human beings together under the same roof were dissolved. He endeavoured to regulate his own conduct in pursuance of these principles, and to secure to himself as much freedom as the present regulations of society would permit. The same independence which he claimed for himself he likewise extended to me. The distribution of my own time, the selection of my own occupations and companions should belong to myself.

But these privileges, though while listening to his arguments I could not deny them to be valuable, I would have willingly dispensed with. The solitude in which I lived became daily more painful. I ate and drank, enjoyed clothing and shelter, without the exercise of forethought or industry; I walked and sat, went out and returned for as long and at what seasons I thought proper, yet my condition was a fertile source of discontent.

I felt myself removed to a comfortless and chilling distance from Ludloe. I wanted to share in his occupations and views. With all his ingenuousness of aspect and overflow of thoughts when he allowed me his company, I felt myself painfully bewildered with regard to his genuine condition and sentiments.

He had it in his power to introduce me to society, and without an introduction, it was scarcely possible to gain access to any social circle or domestic fireside. Add to this, my own obscure prospects and dubious situation. Some regular intellectual pursuit would render my state less irksome, but I had hitherto adopted no scheme of this kind.

Time tended, in no degree, to alleviate my dissatisfaction. It increased till the determination became at length formed of opening my thoughts to Ludloe. At the next breakfast interview which took place, I introduced the subject, and expatiated without reserve, on the state of my feelings. I concluded with intreating him to point out some path in which my talents might be rendered useful to himself or to mankind.

After a pause of some minutes, he said, What would you do? You forget the immaturity of your age. If you are qualified to act a part in the theatre of life, step forth; but you are not qualified. You want knowledge, and with this you ought previously to endow yourself. . . . Means, for this end, are within your reach. Why should you waste your time in idleness, and torment yourself with unprofitable wishes? Books are at hand . . . books from which most sciences and languages can be learned. Read, analise, digest; collect facts, and investigate theories: ascertain the dictates of reason, and supply yourself with the inclination and the power to adhere to them. You will not, legally speaking, be a man in less than three years. Let this period be devoted to the acquisition of wisdom. Either stay here, or retire to an house I have on the banks of Killarney, where you will find all the conveniences of study.

I could not but reflect with wonder at this man's treatment of me. I could plead none of the rights of relationship; yet I enjoyed the privileges of a son. He had not imparted to me any scheme, by pursuit of which I might finally compensate him for the expense to which my maintainance and education would subject him. He gave me reason to hope for the continuance of his bounty. He talked and acted as if my fortune were totally disjoined from his; yet was I indebted to him for the morsel which sustained my life. Now it was proposed to withdraw myself to studious leisure, and romantic solitude. All my wants, personal and intellectual, were to be supplied gratuitously and copiously. No means were prescribed by which I might make compensation for all these benefits. In conferring them he seemed to be actuated by no view to his own ultimate advantage. He took no measures to secure my future services.

I suffered these thoughts to escape me, on this occasion, and observed that to make my application successful, or useful, it was necessary to pursue some end. I must look forward to some post which I might hereafter occupy beneficially to myself or others; and for which all the efforts of my mind should be bent to qualify myself.

These hints gave him visible pleasure; and now, for the first time, he deigned to advise me on this head. His scheme, however, was not suddenly produced. The way to it was circuitous and long. It was his business to make every new step appear to be suggested by my own reflections. His own ideas were the seeming result of the moment, and sprung out of the last idea that was uttered. Being hastily taken up, they were, of course, liable to objection. These objections, sometimes occurring to me and sometimes to him, were admitted or contested with the utmost candour. One scheme went through numerous modifications before it was proved to be ineligible, or before it yielded place to a better. It was easy to perceive, that books alone were insufficient to impart knowledge: that man must be examined with our own eyes to make us acquainted with their nature: that ideas collected from observation and reading, must correct and illustrate each other: that the value of all principles, and their truth, lie in their practical effects. Hence, gradually arose, the usefulness of travelling, of inspecting the habits and manners of a nation, and investigating, on the spot, the causes of their happiness and misery. Finally, it was determined that Spain was more suitable than any other, to the views of a judicious traveller.

My language, habits, and religion were mentioned as obstacles to close and extensive views; but these difficulties successively and slowly vanished. Converse with books, and natives of Spain, a steadfast purpose and unwearied diligence would efface all differences between me and a Castilian with respect to speech. Personal habits, were changeable, by the same means. The bars to unbounded intercourse, rising from the religion of Spain being irreconcilably opposite to mine, cost us no little trouble to surmount, and here the skill of Ludloe was eminently displayed.

I had been accustomed to regard as unquestionable, the fallacy of the Romish faith. This persuasion was habitual and the child of prejudice, and was easily shaken by the artifices of this logician. I was first led to bestow a kind of assent on the doctrines of the Roman church; but my convictions were easily subdued by a new species of argumentation, and, in a short time, I reverted to my ancient disbelief, so that if an exterior conformity to the rites of Spain were requisite to the attainment of my purpose, that conformity must be dissembled.

My moral principles had hitherto been vague and unsettled. My circumstances had led me to the frequent practice of insincerity; but my transgressions, as they were slight and transient, did not much excite my previous reflections, or subsequent remorse. My deviations, however, though rendered easy by habit, were by no means sanctioned by my principles. Now an imposture, more profound and deliberate, was projected; and I could not hope to perform well my part, unless steadfastly and thoroughly persuaded of its rectitude.

My friend was the eulogist of sincerity. He delighted to trace its influence on the happiness of mankind; and proved that nothing but the universal practice of this virtue was necessary to the perfection of human society. His doctrine was splendid and beautiful. To detect its imperfections was no easy task; to lay the foundations of virtue in utility, and to limit, by that scale, the operation of general principles: to see that the value of sincerity, like that of every other mode of action, consisted in its tendency to good, and that, therefore the obligation to speak truth was not paramount or intrinsical; that my duty is modelled on a knowledge and foresight of the conduct of others; and that, since men in their actual state, are infirm and deceitful, a just estimate of consequences may sometimes make dissimulation my duty, were truths that did not speedily occur. The discovery, when made, appeared to be a joint work. I saw nothing in Ludloe but proofs of candour, and a judgment incapable of bias.

The means which this man employed to fit me for his purpose, perhaps owed their success to my youth and ignorance. I may have given you exaggerated ideas of his dexterity and address. Of that I am unable to judge. Certain it is, that no time or reflection has abated my astonishment at the profoundness of his schemes, and the perseverance with which they were pursued by him. To detail their progress would expose me to the risk of being tedious, yet none but minute details would sufficiently display his patience and subtlety.

It will suffice to relate, that after a sufficient period of preparation, and arrangements being made for maintaining a copious intercourse with Ludloe, I embarked for Barcelona. A restless curiosity and vigorous application have distinguished my character in every scene. Here was spacious field for the exercise of all my energies. I sought out a preceptor in my new religion. I entered into the hearts of priests and confessors; the *hidalgo* and the peasant, the monk and the prelate, the austere and voluptuous devotee were scrutinized in all their forms.

Man was the chief subject of my study, and the social sphere that in which I principally moved; but I was not inattentive to inanimate nature, nor unmindful of the past. If the scope of virtue were to maintain the body in health, and to furnish its highest enjoyments to every sense, to increase the number, and accuracy, and order of our intellectual stores, no virtue was ever more unblemished than mine. If to act upon our conceptions of right, and to acquit ourselves of all prejudice and selfishness in the formation of our principles, entitle us to the testimony of a good conscience, I might justly claim it.

I shall not pretend to ascertain my rank in the moral scale. Your notions of duty differ widely from mine. If a system of deceit, pursued merely from the love of truth; if voluptuousness, never gratified at the expense of health, may incur censure, I am censurable. This, indeed, was not the limit of my deviations. Deception was often unnecessarily practised, and my biloquial faculty did not lie unemployed. What has happened to yourselves may enable you, in some degree, to judge of the scenes in which my mystical exploits engaged me. In none of them, indeed, were the effects equally disastrous, and they were, for the most part, the result of well digested projects.

To recount these would be an endless task. They were designed as mere specimens of power: to illustrate the influence of superstition: to give sceptics the consolation of certainty: to annihilate the scruples of a tender female, or facilitate my access to the bosoms of courtiers and monks.

The first achievement of this kind took place in the convent of the Escurial. For some time the hospitality of this brotherhood allowed me a cell in that magnificent and gloomy fabric. I was drawn hither chiefly by the treasures of Arabian literature, which are preserved here in the keeping of a learned Maronite, from Lebanon. Standing one evening on the steps of the great altar, this devout friar expatiated on the miraculous evidences of his religion; and, in a moment of enthusiasm, appealed to San Lorenzo, whose martyrdom was displayed before us. No sooner was the appeal made than the saint, obsequious to the summons, whispered his responses from the shrine, and commanded the heretic to tremble and believe. This event was reported to the convent. With whatever reluctance, I could not refuse my testimony to its truth, and its influence on my faith was clearly shewn in my subsequent conduct.

A lady of rank, in Seville, who had been guilty of many unauthorized indulgences, was, at last, awakened to remorse, by a voice from Heaven, which she imagined had commanded her to expiate her sins by an abstinence from all food for thirty days. Her friends found it impossible to outroot this persuasion, or to overcome her resolution even by force. I chanced to be one in a numerous company where she was present. This fatal illusion was mentioned, and an opportunity afforded to the lady of defending her scheme. At a pause in the discourse, a voice was heard from the ceiling, which confirmed the truth of her tale; but, at the same time revoked the command, and, in consideration of her faith, pronounced her absolution. Satisfied with this proof, the auditors dismissed their unbelief, and the lady consented to eat.

In the course of a copious correspondence with Ludloe, the observations I had collected were given. A sentiment, which I can hardly describe, induced me to be silent on all adventures connected with my bivocal projects. On other topics, I wrote fully, and without restraint. I painted, in vivid hues, the scenes with which I was daily conversant, and pursued, fearlessly, every speculation on religion and government that occurred. This spirit was encouraged by Ludloe, who failed not to comment on my narrative, and multiply deductions from my principles.

He taught me to ascribe the evils that infest society to the errors of opinion. The absurd and unequal distribution of power and property gave birth to poverty and riches, and these were the sources of luxury and crimes. These positions were readily admitted; but the remedy for these ills, the means of rectifying these errors were not easily discovered. We have been inclined to impute them to inherent defects in the moral constitution of men: that oppression and tyranny grow up by a sort of natural necessity, and that they will perish only when the human species is extinct. Ludloe laboured to prove that this was, by no means, the case: that man is the creature of circumstances: that he is capable of endless improvement: that his progress has been stopped by the artificial impediment of government: that by the removal of this, the fondest dreams of imagination will be realized.

From detailing and accounting for the evils which exist

under our present institutions, he usually proceeded to delineate some scheme of Utopian felicity, where the empire of reason should supplant that of force; where justice should be universally understood and practised; where the interest of the whole and of the individual should be seen by all to be the same; where the public good should be the scope of all activity; where the tasks of all should be the same, and the means of subsistence equally distributed.

No one could contemplate his pictures without rapture. By their comprehensiveness and amplitude they filled the imagination. I was unwilling to believe that in no region of the world, or at no period could these ideas be realized. It was plain that the nations of Europe were tending to greater depravity, and would be the prey of perpetual vicissitude. All individual attempts at their reformation would be fruitless. He therefore who desired the diffusion of right principles, to make a just system be adopted by a whole community, must pursue some extraordinary method.

In this state of mind I recollected my native country, where a few colonists from Britain had sown the germe of populous and mighty empires. Attended, as they were, into their new abode, by all their prejudices, yet such had been the influence of new circumstances, of consulting for their own happiness, of adopting simple forms of government, and excluding nobles and kings from their system, that they enjoyed a degree of happiness far superior to their parent state.

To conquer the prejudices and change the habits of millions, are impossible. The human mind, exposed to social influences, inflexibly adheres to the direction that is given to it; but for the same reason why men who begin in error will continue, those who commence in truth, may be expected to persist. Habit and example will operate with equal force in both instances.

Let a few, sufficiently enlightened and disinterested, take up their abode in some unvisited region. Let their social scheme be founded in equity, and how small soever their original number may be, their growth into a nation is inevitable. Among other effects of national justice, was to be ranked the swift increase of numbers. Exempt from servile obligations and perverse habits, endowed with property, wisdom, and health, hundreds will expand, with inconceivable rapidity into thousands, and thousands into millions; and a new race, tutored in truth, may, in a few centuries, overflow the habitable world.

Such were the visions of youth! I could not banish them from my mind. I knew them to be crude; but believed that deliberation would bestow upon them solidity and shape. Meanwhile I imparted them to Ludloe.

In answer to the reveries and speculations which I sent to him respecting this subject, Ludloe informed me, that they had led his mind into a new sphere of meditation. He had long and deeply considered in what way he might essentially promote my happiness. He had entertained a faint hope that I would one day be qualified for a station like that to which he himself had been advanced. This post required an elevation and stability of views which human beings seldom reach, and which could be attained by me only by a long series of heroic labours. Hitherto every new stage in my intellectual progress had added vigour to his hopes, and he cherished a stronger belief than formerly that my career would terminate auspiciously. This, however, was necessarily distant. Many preliminaries must first be settled; many arduous accomplishments be first obtained; and my virtue be subjected to severe trials. At present it was not in his power to be more explicit; but if my reflections suggested no better plan, he advised me to settle my affairs in Spain, and return to him immediately. My knowledge of this country would be of the highest use, on the supposition of my ultimately arriving at the honours to which he had alluded; and some of these preparatory measures could be taken only with his assistance, and in his company.

This intimation was eagerly obeyed, and, in a short time, I arrived at Dublin. Meanwhile my mind had copious occupation in commenting on my friend's letter. This scheme, whatever it was, seemed to be suggested by my mention of a plan of colonization, and my preference of that mode of producing extensive and permanent effects on the condition of mankind. It was easy therefore to conjecture that this mode had been pursued under some mysterious modifications and conditions.

It had always excited my wonder that so obvious an expedient had been overlooked. The globe which we inhabit was very imperfectly known. The regions and nations unexplored, it was reasonable to believe, surpassed in extent, and perhaps in populousness, those with which we were familiar. The order of Jesuits had furnished an example of all the errors and excellencies of such a scheme. Their plan was founded on erroneous notions of religion and policy, and they had absurdly chosen a scene* within reach of the injustice and ambition of an European tyrant.

It was wise and easy to profit by their example. Resting on the two props of fidelity and zeal, an association might exist for ages in the heart of Europe, whose influence might be felt, and might be boundless, in some region of the southern hemisphere; and by whom a moral and political structure might be raised, the growth of pure wisdom and totally unlike those fragments of Roman and Gothic barbarism, which cover the face of what are called the civilized nations. The belief now rose in my mind that some such scheme had actually been prosecuted, and that Ludloe was a coadjutor. On this supposition, the caution with which he approached to his point, the arduous probation which a candidate for a part on this stage must undergo, and the rigours of that test by which his fortitude and virtue must be tried, were easily explained. I was too deeply imbued with veneration for the effects of such schemes, and too sanguine in my confidence in the rectitude of Ludloe, to refuse my concurrence in any scheme by which my qualifications might at length be raised to a due point.

Our interview was frank and affectionate. I found him situated just as formerly. His aspect, manners, and deportment were the same. I entered once more on my former mode of life, but our intercourse became more frequent. We constantly breakfasted together, and our conversation was usually prolonged through half the morning.

*Paraguay.

For a time our topics were general. I thought proper to leave to him the introduction of more interesting themes: this, however, he betrayed no inclination to do. His reserve excited some surprise, and I began to suspect that whatever design he had formed with regard to me, had been laid aside. To ascertain this question, I ventured, at length, to recall his attention to the subject of his last letter, and to enquire whether subsequent reflection had made any change in his views.

He said that his views were too momentous to be hastily taken up, or hastily dismissed; the station, my attainment of which depended wholly on myself, was high above vulgar heads, and was to be gained by years of solicitude and labour. This, at least, was true with regard to minds ordinarily constituted; I, perhaps, deserved to be regarded as an exception, and might be able to accomplish in a few months that for which others were obliged to toil during half their lives.

Man, continued he, is the slave of habit. Convince him to-day that his duty leads straight forward: he shall advance, but at every step his belief shall fade; habit will resume its empire, and to-morrow he shall turn back, or betake himself to oblique paths.

We know not our strength till it be tried. Virtue, till confirmed by habit, is a dream. You are a man imbued by errors, and vincible by slight temptations. Deep enquiries must bestow light on your opinions, and the habit of encountering and vanquishing temptation must inspire you with fortitude. Till this be done, you are unqualified for that post, in which you will be invested with divine attributes, and prescribe the condition of a large portion of mankind.

Confide not in the firmness of your principles, or the stedfastness of your integrity. Be always vigilant and fearful. Never think you have enough of knowledge, and let not your caution slumber for a moment, for you know not when danger is near.

I acknowledged the justice of his admonitions, and professed myself willing to undergo any ordeal which reason should prescribe. What, I asked, were the conditions, on the fulfilment of which depended my advancement to the station he alluded to? Was it necessary to conceal from me the nature and obligations of this rank?

These enquiries sunk him more profoundly into meditation than I had ever before witnessed. After a pause, in which some perplexity was visible, he answered:

I scarcely know what to say. As to promises, I claim them not from you. We are now arrived at a point, in which it is necessary to look around with caution, and that consequences should be fully known. A number of persons are leagued together for an end of some moment. To make yourself one of these is submitted to your choice. Among the conditions of their alliance are mutual fidelity and secrecy.

Their existence depends upon this: their existence is known only to themselves. This secrecy must be obtained by all the means which are possible. When I have said thus much, I have informed you, in some degree, of their existence, but you are still ignorant of the purpose contemplated by this association, and of all the members, except myself. So far no dangerous disclosure is yet made: but this degree of concealment is not sufficient. Thus much is made known to you, because it is unavoidable. The individuals which compose this fraternity are not immortal, and the vacancies occasioned by death must be supplied from among the living. The candidate must be instructed and prepared, and they are always at liberty to recede. Their reason must approve the obligations and duties of their station, or they are unfit for it. If they recede, one duty is still incumbent upon them: they must observe an inviolable silence. To this they are not held by any promise. They must weigh consequences, and freely decide; but they must not fail to number among these consequences their own death.

Their death will not be prompted by vengeance. The executioner will say, he that has once revealed the tale is likely to reveal it a second time; and, to prevent this, the betrayer must die. Nor is this the only consequence: to prevent the further revelation, he, to whom the secret was imparted, must likewise perish. He must not console himself with the belief that his trespass will be unknown. The knowledge cannot, by human means, be withheld from this fraternity. Rare, indeed, will it be that his purpose to disclose is not discovered before it can be effected, and the disclosure prevented by his death.

Be well aware of your condition. What I now, or may hereafter mention, mention not again. Admit not even a doubt as to the propriety of hiding it from all the world. There are eyes who will discern this doubt amidst the closest folds of your heart, and your life will instantly be sacrificed.

At present be the subject dismissed. Reflect deeply on the duty which you have already incurred. Think upon your strength of mind, and be careful not to lay yourself under impracticable obligations. It will always be in your power to recede. Even after you are solemnly enrolled a member, you may consult the dictates of your own understanding, and relinquish your post; but while you live, the obligation to be silent will perpetually attend you.

We seek not the misery or death of any one, but we are swayed by an immutable calculation. Death is to be abhorred, but the life of the betrayer is productive of more evil than his death: his death, therefore, we chuse, and our means are instantaneous and unerring.

I love you. The first impulse of my love is to dissuade you from seeking to know more. Your mind will be full of ideas; your hands will be perpetually busy to a purpose into which no human creature, beyond the verge of your brotherhood, must pry. Believe me, who have made the experiment, that compared with this task, the task of inviolable secrecy, all others are easy. To be dumb will not suffice; never to know any remission in your zeal or your watchfulness will not suffice. If the sagacity of others detect your occupations, however strenuously you may labour for concealment, your doom is ratified, as well as that of the wretch whose evil destiny led him to pursue you.

Yet if your fidelity fail not, great will be your recompence. For all your toils and self-devotion, ample will be the retribution. Hitherto you have been wrapt in darkness and storm; then will you be exalted to a pure and unruffled element. It is only for a time that temptation will environ you, and your path will be toilsome. In a few years you will be permitted to withdraw to a land of sages, and the remainder of your life will glide away in the enjoyments of beneficence and wisdom.

Think deeply on what I have said. Investigate your own motives and opinions, and prepare to submit them to the test of numerous hazards and experiments.

Here my friend passed to a new topic. I was desirous of reverting to this subject, and obtaining further information concerning it, but he assiduously repelled all my attempts, and insisted on my bestowing deep and impartial attention on what had already been disclosed. I was not slow to comply with his directions. My mind refused to admit any other theme of contemplation than this.

As yet I had no glimpse of the nature of this fraternity. I was permitted to form conjectures, and previous incidents bestowed but one form upon my thoughts. In reviewing the sentiments and deportment of Ludloe, my belief continually acquired new strength. I even recollected hints and ambiguous allusions in his discourse, which were easily solved, on the supposition of the existence of a new model of society, in some unsuspected corner of the world.

I did not fully perceive the necessity of secrecy; but this necessity perhaps would be rendered apparent, when I should come to know the connection that subsisted between Europe and this imaginary colony. But what was to be done? I was willing to abide by these conditions. My understanding might not approve of all the ends proposed by this fraternity, and I had liberty to withdraw from it, or to refuse to ally myself with them. That the obligation of secrecy should still remain, was unquestionably reasonable.

It appeared to be the plan of Ludloe rather to damp than to stimulate my zeal. He discouraged all attempts to renew the subject in conversation. He dwelt upon the arduousness of the office to which I aspired, the temptations to violate my duty with which I should be continually beset, the inevitable death with which the slightest breach of my engagements would be followed, and the long apprenticeship which it would be necessary for me to serve, before I should be fitted to enter into this conclave.

Sometimes my courage was depressed by these representations. . . . My zeal, however, was sure to revive; and at length Ludloe declared himself willing to assist me in the accomplishment of my wishes. For this end, it was necessary, he said, that I should be informed of a second obligation, which every candidate must assume. Before any one could be deemed qualified, he must be thoroughly known to his associates. For this end, he must determine to disclose every fact in his history, and every secret of his heart. I must begin with making these confessions, with regard to my past life, to Ludloe, and must continue to communicate, at stated seasons, every new thought, and every new occurrence, to him. This confidence was to be absolutely limitless: no exceptions were to be admitted, and no reserves to be practised; and the same penalty attended the infraction of this rule as of the former. Means would be employed, by which the slightest deviation, in either case, would be detected, and the deathful consequence would follow with instant and inevitable expedition. If secrecy were difficult to practise, sincerity, in that degree in which it was here demanded, was a task infinitely more arduous, and a period of new deliberation was necessary before I should decide. I was at liberty to pause: nay, the longer was the period of deliberation which I took, the better; but, when I had once entered this path, it was not in my power to recede. After having solemnly avowed my resolution to be thus sincere in my confession, any particle of reserve or duplicity would cost me my life.

This indeed was a subject to be deeply thought upon. Hitherto I had been guilty of concealment with regard to my friend. I had entered into no formal compact, but had been conscious to a kind of tacit obligation to hide no important transaction of my life from him. This conscious-ness was the source of continual anxiety. I had exerted, on numerous occasions, my bivocal faculty, but, in my inter-course with Ludloe, had suffered not the slightest intima-tion to escape me with regard to it. This reserve was not easily explained. It was, in a great degree, the product of habit; but I likewise considered that the efficacy of this instrument depended upon its existence being unknown. To confide the secret to one, was to put an end to my privilege: how widely the knowledge would thenceforth be diffused, I had no power to foresee.

Each day multiplied the impediments to confidence. Shame hindered me from acknowledging my past reserves. Ludloe, from the nature of our intercourse, would certainly account my reserve, in this respect, unjustifiable, and to excite his indignation or contempt was an unpleasing undertaking. Now, if I should resolve to persist in my new path, this reserve must be dismissed: I must make him master of a secret which was precious to me beyond all others; by acquainting him with past concealments, I must risk incurring his suspicion and his anger. These reflections were productive of considerable embarrassment.

There was, indeed, an avenue by which to escape these difficulties, if it did not, at the same time, plunge me into greater. My confessions might, in other respects, be unbounded, but my reserves, in this particular, might be continued. Yet should I not expose myself to formidable perils? Would my secret be for ever unsuspected and undiscovered?

When I considered the nature of this faculty, the impossibility of going farther than suspicion, since the agent could be known only by his own confession, and even this confession would not be believed by the greater part of mankind, I was tempted to conceal it.

In most cases, if I had asserted the possession of this power, I should be treated as a liar; it would be considered as an absurd and audacious expedient to free myself from the suspicion of having entered into compact with a dæmon, or of being myself an emissary of the grand foe. Here, however, there was no reason to dread a similar imputation, since Ludloe had denied the preternatural pretensions of these airy sounds.

My conduct on this occasion was nowise influenced by the belief of any inherent sanctity in truth. Ludloe had taught me to model myself in this respect entirely with a view to immediate consequences. If my genuine interest, on the whole, was promoted by veracity, it was proper to adhere to it; but, if the result of my investigation were opposite, truth was to be sacrificed without scruple.

Meanwhile, in a point of so much moment, I was not hasty to determine. My delay seemed to be, by no means, unacceptable to Ludloe, who applauded my discretion, and warned me to be circumspect. My attention was chiefly absorbed by considerations connected with this subject, and little regard was paid to any foreign occupation or amusement.

One evening, after a day spent in my closet, I sought recreation by walking forth. My mind was chiefly occupied by the review of incidents which happened in Spain. I turned my face towards the fields, and recovered not from my reverie, till I had proceeded some miles on the road to Meath. The night had considerably advanced, and the darkness was rendered intense, by the setting of the moon. Being somewhat weary, as well as undetermined in what manner next to proceed, I seated myself on a grassy bank beside the road. The spot which I had chosen was aloof from passengers, and shrowded in the deepest obscurity.

Some time elapsed, when my attention was excited by the slow approach of an equipage. I presently discovered a coach and six horses, but unattended, except by coachman and postillion, and with no light to guide them on their way. Scarcely had they passed the spot where I rested, when some one leaped from beneath the hedge, and seized the head of the fore-horses. Another called upon the coachman to stop, and threatened him with instant death if he disobeyed. A third drew open the coach-door, and ordered those within to deliver their purses. A shriek of terror showed me that a lady was within, who eagerly consented to preserve her life by the loss of her money.

To walk unarmed in the neighbourhood of Dublin, especially at night, has always been accounted dangerous. I had about me the usual instruments of defence. I was desirous of rescuing this person from the danger which surrounded her, but was somewhat at a loss how to effect my purpose.

My single strength was insufficient to contend with three ruffians. After a moment's debate, an expedient was suggested, which I hastened to execute.

Time had not been allowed for the ruffian who stood beside the carriage to receive the plunder, when several voices, loud, clamorous, and eager, were heard in the quarter whence the traveller had come. By trampling with quickness, it was easy to imitate the sound of many feet. The robbers were alarmed, and one called upon another to attend. The sounds increased, and, at the next moment, they betook themselves to flight, but not till a pistol was discharged. Whether it was aimed at the lady in the carriage, or at the coachman, I was not permitted to discover, for the report affrighted the horses, and they set off at full speed.

I could not hope to overtake them: I knew not whither the robbers had fled, and whether, by proceeding, I might not fall into their hands. . . . These considerations induced me to resume my feet, and retire from the scene as expeditiously as possible. I regained my own habitation without injury.

I have said that I occupied separate apartments from those of Ludloe. To these there were means of access without disturbing the family. I hasted to my chamber, but was considerably surprized to find, on entering my apartment, Ludloe seated at a table, with a lamp before him.

My momentary confusion was greater than his. On discovering who it was, he assumed his accustomed looks, and explained appearances, by saying, that he wished to converse with me on a subject of importance, and had therefore sought me at this secret hour, in my own chamber. Contrary to his expectation, I was absent. Conceiving it possible that I might shortly return, he had waited till now. He took no further notice of my absence, nor manifested any desire to know the cause of it, but proceeded to mention the subject which had brought him hither. These were his words.

You have nothing which the laws permit you to call your own. Justice entitles you to the supply of your physical wants, from those who are able to supply them; but there are few who will acknowledge your claim, or spare an atom of their superfluity to appease your cravings. That which they will not spontaneously give, it is not right to wrest from them by violence. What then is to be done?

Property is necessary to your own subsistence. It is useful, by enabling you to supply the wants of others. To give food, and clothing, and shelter, is to give life, to annihilate temptation, to unshackle virtue, and propagate felicity. How shall property be gained?

You may set your understanding or your hands at work. You may weave stockings, or write poems, and exchange them for money; but these are tardy and meagre schemes. The means are disproportioned to the end, and I will not suffer you to pursue them. My justice will supply your wants.

But dependance on the justice of others is a precarious condition. To be the object is a less ennobling state than to be the bestower of benefit. Doubtless you desire to be vested with competence and riches, and to hold them by virtue of the law, and not at the will of a benefactor. . . . He paused as if waiting for my assent to his positions. I readily expressed my concurrence, and my desire to pursue any means compatible with honesty. He resumed.

There are various means, besides labour, violence, or fraud. It is right to select the easiest within your reach. It happens that the easiest is at hand. A revenue of some thousands a year, a stately mansion in the city, and another in Kildare, old and faithful domestics, and magnificent furniture, are good things. Will you have them?

A gift like that, replied I, will be attended by momentous conditions. I cannot decide upon its value, until I know these conditions.

The sole condition is your consent to receive them. Not even the airy obligation of gratitude will be created by acceptance. On the contrary, by accepting them, you will confer the highest benefit upon another.

I do not comprehend you. Something surely must be given in return.

288

Nothing. It may seem strange that, in accepting the absolute controul of so much property, you subject yourself to no conditions; that no claims of gratitude or service will accrue; but the wonder is greater still. The law equitably enough fetters the gift with no restraints, with respect to you that receive it; but not so with regard to the unhappy being who bestows it. That being must part, not only with property but liberty. In accepting the property, you must consent to enjoy the services of the present possessor. They cannot be disjoined.

Of the true nature and extent of the gift, you should be fully apprized. Be aware, therefore, that, together with this property, you will receive absolute power over the liberty and person of the being who now possesses it. That being must become your domestic slave; be governed, in every particular, by your caprice.

Happily for you, though fully invested with this power, the degree and mode in which it will be exercised will depend upon yourself. . . . You may either totally forbear the exercise, or employ it only for the benefit of your slave. However injurious, therefore, this authority may be to the subject of it, it will, in some sense, only enhance the value of the gift to you.

The attachment and obedience of this being will be chiefly evident in one thing. Its duty will consist in conforming, in every instance, to your will. All the powers of this being are to be devoted to your happiness; but there is one relation between you, which enables you to confer, while exacting, pleasure. . . . This relation is *sexual.* Your slave is a woman; and the bond, which transfers her property and person to you, is . . . *marriage.*

My knowledge of Ludloe, his principles, and reasonings, ought to have precluded that surprise which I experienced at the conclusion of his discourse. I knew that he regarded the present institution of marriage as a contract of servitude, and the terms of it unequal and unjust. When my surprise had subsided, my thoughts turned upon the nature of his scheme. After a pause of reflection, I answered:

Both law and custom have connected obligations with

marriage, which, though heaviest on the female, are not light upon the male. Their weight and extent are not immutable and uniform; they are modified by various incidents, and especially by the mental and personal qualities of the lady.

I am not sure that I should willingly accept the property and person of a woman decrepid with age, and enslaved by perverse habits and evil passions: whereas youth, beauty, and tenderness would be worth accepting, even for their own sake, and disconnected with fortune.

As to altar vows, I believe they will not make me swerve from equity. I shall exact neither service nor affection from my spouse. The value of these and, indeed, not only the value, but the very existence of the latter depends upon its spontaneity. A promise to love tends rather to loosen than strengthen the tie.

As to myself, the age of illusion is past. I shall not wed, till I find one whose moral and physical constitution will make personal fidelity easy. I shall judge without mistiness or passion, and habit will come in aid of an enlightened and deliberate choice.

I shall not be fastidious in my choice. I do not expect, and scarcely desire, much intellectual similitude between me and my wife. Our opinions and pursuits cannot be in common. While women are formed by their education, and their education continues in its present state, tender hearts and misguided understandings are all that we can hope to meet with.

What are the character, age, and person of the woman to whom you allude? and what prospect of success would attend my exertions to obtain her favour?

I have told you she is rich. She is a widow, and owes her riches to the liberality of her husband, who was a trader of great opulence, and who died while on a mercantile adventure to Spain. He was not unknown to you. Your letters from Spain often spoke of him. In short, she is the widow of Bennington, whom you met at Barcelona. She is still in the prime of life; is not without many feminine attractions; has an ardent and credulent temper; and is particularly given to devotion. This temper it would be easy to regulate according to your pleasure and your interest, and I now submit to you the expediency of an alliance with her.

I am a kinsman, and regarded by her with uncommon deference; and my commendations, therefore, will be of great service to you, and shall be given.

I will deal ingenuously with you. It is proper you should be fully acquainted with the grounds of this proposal. The benefits of rank, and property, and independence, which I have already mentioned as likely to accrue to you from this marriage, are solid and valuable benefits; but these are not the sole advantages, and to benefit you, in these respects, is not my whole view.

No. My treatment of you henceforth will be regulated by one principle. I regard you only as one undergoing a probation or apprenticeship; as subjected to trials of your sincerity and fortitude. The marriage I now propose to you is desirable, because it will make you independent of me. Your poverty might create an unsuitable bias in favour of proposals, one of whose effects would be to set you beyond fortune's reach. That bias will cease, when you cease to be poor and dependent.

Love is the strongest of all human delusions. That fortitude, which is not subdued by the tenderness and blandishments of woman, may be trusted; but no fortitude, which has not undergone that test, will be trusted by us.

This woman is a charming enthusiast. She will never marry but him whom she passionately loves. Her power over the heart that loves her will scarcely have limits. The means of prying into your transactions, of suspecting and sifting your thoughts, which her constant society with you, while sleeping and waking, her zeal and watchfulness for your welfare, and her curiosity, adroitness, and penetration will afford her, are evident. Your danger, therefore, will be imminent. Your fortitude will be obliged to have recourse, not to flight, but to vigilance. Your eye must never close.

Alas! what human magnanimity can stand this test! How can I persuade myself that you will not fail? I waver between hope and fear. Many, it is true, have fallen, and dragged with them the author of their ruin, but some have soared above even these perils and temptations, with their fiery energies unimpaired, and great has been, as great ought to be, their recompence.

But you are doubtless aware of your danger. I need not repeat the consequences of betraying your trust, the rigour of those who will judge your fault, the unerring and unbounded scrutiny to which your actions, the most secret and indifferent, will be subjected.

Your conduct, however, will be voluntary. At your own option be it, to see or not to see this woman. Circumspection, deliberation, forethought, are your sacred duties and highest interest.

Ludloe's remarks on the seductive and bewitching powers of women, on the difficulty of keeping a secret which they wish to know, and to gain which they employ the soft artillery of tears and prayers, and blandishments and menaces, are familiar to all men, but they had little weight with me, because they were unsupported by my own experience. I had never had any intellectual or sentimental connection with the sex. My meditations and pursuits had all led a different way, and a bias had gradually been given to my feelings, very unfavourable to the refinements of love. I acknowledge, with shame and regret, that I was accustomed to regard the physical and sensual consequences of the sexual relation as realities, and every thing intellectual, disinterested, and heroic, which enthusiasts connect with it, as idle dreams. Besides, said I, I am yet a stranger to the secret, on the preservation of which so much stress is laid, and it will be optional with me to receive it or not. If, in the progress of my acquaintance with Mrs. Benington, I should perceive any extraordinary danger in the gift, cannot I refuse, or at least delay to comply with any new conditions from Ludloe? Will not his candour and his affection for me rather commend than disapprove my diffidence? In fine, I resolved to see this lady.

She was, it seems, the widow of Benington, whom I knew in Spain. This man was an English merchant settled at Barcelona, to whom I had been commended by Ludloe's letters, and through whom my pecuniary supplies were furnished. . . . Much intercourse and some degree of intimacy had taken place between us, and I had gained a pretty accurate knowledge of his character. I had been informed, through different channels, that his wife was much his superior in rank, that she possessed great wealth in her own right, and that some disagreement of temper or views occasioned their separation. She had married him for love, and still doated on him: the occasions for separation having arisen, it seems, not on her side but on his. As his habits of reflection were nowise friendly to religion, and as hers, according to Ludloe, were of the opposite kind, it is possible that some jarring had arisen between them from this source. Indeed, from some casual and broken hints of Benington, especially in the latter part of his life, I had long since gathered this conjecture. . . . Something, thought I, may be derived from my acquaintance with her husband favourable to my views.

I anxiously waited for an opportunity of acquainting Ludloe with my resolution. On the day of our last conversation, he had made a short excursion from town, intending to return the same evening, but had continued absent for several days. As soon as he came back, I hastened to acquaint him with my wishes.

Have you well considered this matter, said he. Be assured it is of no trivial import. The moment at which you enter the presence of this woman will decide your future destiny. Even putting out of view the subject of our late conversations, the light in which you shall appear to her will greatly influence your happiness, since, though you cannot fail to love her, it is quite uncertain what return she may think proper to make. Much, doubtless, will depend on your own perseverance and address, but you will have many, perhaps insuperable, obstacles to encounter on several accounts, and especially in her attachment to the memory of her late husband. As to her devout temper, this is nearly allied to a warm imagination in some other respects, and will operate much more in favour of an ardent and artful lover, than against him.

293

I still expressed my willingness to try my fortune with her.

Well, said he, I anticipated your consent to my proposal, and the visit I have just made was to her. I thought it best to pave the way, by informing her that I had met with one for whom she had desired me to look out. You must know that her father was one of these singular men who set a value upon things exactly in proportion to the difficulty of obtaining or comprehending them. His passion was for antiques, and his favourite pursuit during a long life was monuments in brass, marble, and parchment, of the remotest antiquity. He was wholly indifferent to the character or conduct of our present sovereign and his ministers, but was extremely solicitous about the name and exploits of a king of Ireland that lived two or three centuries before the flood. He felt no curiosity to know who was the father of his wife's child, but would travel a thousand miles, and consume months, in investigating which son of Noah it was that first landed on the coast of Munster. He would give a hundred guineas from the mint for a piece of old decayed copper no bigger than his nail, provided it had aukward characters upon it, too much defaced to be read. The whole stock of a great bookseller was, in his eyes, a cheap exchange for a shred of parchment, containing half a homily written by St. Patrick. He would have gratefully given all his patrimonial domains to one who should inform him what pendragon or druid it was who set up the first stone on Salisbury plain.

This spirit, as you may readily suppose, being seconded by great wealth and long life, contributed to form a very large collection of venerable lumber, which, though beyond all price to the collector himself, is of no value to his heiress but so far as it is marketable. She designs to bring the whole to auction, but for this purpose a catalogue and description are necessary. Her father trusted to a faithful memory, and to vague and scarcely legible memorandums, and has left a very arduous task to any one who shall be named to the office. It occurred to me, that the best means of promoting your views was to recommend you to this office.

You are not entirely without the antiquarian frenzy your-

294

self. The employment, therefore, will be somewhat agree-
able to you for its own sake. It will entitle you to become an
inmate of the same house, and thus establish an incessant
intercourse between you, and the nature of the business is
such, that you may perform it in what time, and with what
degree of diligence and accuracy you please.

I ventured to insinuate that, to a woman of rank and
family, the character of a hireling was by no means a
favourable recommendation.

He answered, that he proposed, by the account he should
give of me, to obviate every scruple of that nature. Though
my father was no better than a farmer, it is not absolutely
certain but that my remoter ancestors had princely blood in
their veins: but as long as proofs of my low extraction did
not impertinently intrude themselves, my silence, or, at
most, equivocal surmises, seasonably made use of, might
secure me from all inconveniences on the score of birth. He
should represent me, and I was such, as his friend, favourite, and equal, and my passion for antiquities should be my
principal inducement to undertake this office, though my
poverty would make no objection to a reasonable pecuniary
recompense.

Having expressed my acquiescence in his measures, he
thus proceeded: My visit was made to my kinswoman, for
the purpose, as I just now told you, of paving your way into
her family; but, on my arrival at her house, I found nothing
but disorder and alarm. Mrs. Benington, it seems, on returning from a longer ride than customary, last Thursday
evening, was attacked by robbers. Her attendants related an
imperfect tale of somebody advancing at the critical moment to her rescue. It seems, however, they did more harm
than good; for the horses took to flight and overturned the
carriage, in consequence of which Mrs. Benington was se-
verely bruised. She has kept her bed ever since, and a fever
was likely to ensue, which has only left her out of danger
to-day.

As the adventure before related, in which I had so much
concern, occurred at the time mentioned by Ludloe, and as
all other circumstances were alike, I could not doubt that

the person whom the exertion of my mysterious powers had relieved was Mrs. Benington: but what an ill-omened interference was mine! The robbers would probably have been satisfied with the few guineas in her purse, and, on receiving these, would have left her to prosecute her journey in peace and security, but, by absurdly offering a succour, which could only operate upon the fears of her assailants, I endangered her life, first by the desperate discharge of a pistol, and next by the fright of the horses. . . . My anxiety, which would have been less if I had not been, in some degree, myself the author of the evil, was nearly removed by Ludloe's proceeding to assure me that all danger was at an end, and that he left the lady in the road to perfect health. He had seized the earliest opportunity of acquainting her with the purpose of his visit, and had brought back with him her cheerful acceptance of my services. The next week was appointed for my introduction.

With such an object in view, I had little leisure to attend to any indifferent object. My thoughts were continually bent upon the expected introduction, and my impatience and curiosity drew strength, not merely from the character of Mrs. Benington, but from the nature of my new employment. Ludloe had truly observed, that I was infected with somewhat of this antiquarian mania myself, and I now remembered that Benington had frequently alluded to this collection in possession of his wife. My curiosity had then been more than once excited by his representations, and I had formed a vague resolution of making myself acquainted with this lady and her learned treasure, should I ever return to Ireland. . . . Other incidents had driven this matter from my mind.

Meanwhile, affairs between Ludloe and myself remained stationary. Our conferences, which were regular and daily, related to general topics, and though his instructions were adapted to promote my improvement in the most useful branches of knowledge, they never afforded a glimpse towards that quarter where my curiosity was most active.

The next week now arrived, but Ludloe informed me that the state of Mrs. Benington's health required a short excursion into the country, and that he himself proposed to bear her company. The journey was to last about a fort-night, after which I might prepare myself for an introduction to her.

This was a very unexpected and disagreeable trial to my patience. The interval of solitude that now succeeded would have passed rapidly and pleasantly enough, if an event of so much moment were not in suspense. Books, of which I was passionately fond, would have afforded me delightful and incessant occupation, and Ludloe, by way of reconciling me to unavoidable delays, had given me access to a little closet, in which his rarer and more valuable books were kept.

All my amusements, both by inclination and necessity, were centered in myself and at home. Ludloe appeared to have no visitants, and though frequently abroad, or at least secluded from me, had never proposed my introduction to any of his friends, except Mrs. Benington. My obligations to him were already too great to allow me to lay claim to new favours and indulgences, nor, indeed, was my disposition such as to make society needful to my happiness. My character had been, in some degree, modelled by the faculty which I possessed. This deriving all its supposed value from impenetrable secrecy, and Ludloe's admonitions tending powerfully to impress me with the necessity of wariness and circumspection in my general intercourse with mankind, I had gradually fallen into sedate, reserved, mysterious, and unsociable habits. My heart wanted not a friend.

In this temper of mind, I set myself to examine the novelties which Ludloe's private book-cases contained. 'Twill be strange, thought I, if his favourite volumes do not show some marks of my friend's character. To know a man's favourite or most constant studies cannot fail of letting in some little light upon his secret thoughts, and though he would not have given me the reading of these books, if he had thought them capable of unveiling more of his concerns than he wished, yet possibly my ingenuity may go one step farther than he dreams of. You shall judge whether I was right in my conjectures.

The books which composed this little library were chiefly the voyages and travels of the missionaries of the sixteenth and seventeenth centuries. Added to these were some works upon political economy and legislation. Those writers who have amused themselves with reducing their ideas to practice, and drawing imaginary pictures of nations or republics, whose manners or government came up to their standard of excellence, were, all of whom I had ever heard, and some I had never heard of before, to be found in this collection. A translation of Aristotle's republic, the political romances of sir Thomas Moore, Harrington, and Hume, appeared to have been much read, and Ludloe had not been sparing of his marginal comments. In these writers he appeared to find nothing but error and absurdity; and his notes were introduced for no other end than to point out groundless principles and false conclusions. . . . The style of these remarks was already familiar to me. I saw nothing new in them, or different from the strain of those speculations with which Ludloe was accustomed to indulge himself in conversation with me.

After having turned over the leaves of the printed volumes, I at length lighted on a small book of maps, from which, of course, I could reasonably expect no information, on that point about which I was most curious. It was an atlas, in which the maps had been drawn by the pen. None of them contained any thing remarkable, so far as I, who was indeed a smatterer in geography, was able to perceive, till I came to the end, when I noticed a map, whose prototype I was wholly unacquainted with. It was drawn on a pretty large scale, representing two islands, which bore some faint resemblance, in their relative proportions at least, to Great Britain and Ireland. In shape they were widely different, but as to size there was no scale by which to measure them. From the great number of subdivisions, and from signs, which apparently represented towns and cities, I was allowed to infer, that the country was at least as extensive as the British isles. This map was apparently unfinished, for it had no names inscribed upon it.

I have just said, my geographical knowledge was imperfect. Though I had not enough to draw the outlines of any country by memory, I had still sufficient to recognize what I had before seen, and to discover that none of the larger islands in our globe resembled the one before me. Having such and so strong motives to curiosity, you may easily imagine my sensations on surveying this map. Suspecting, as I did, that many of Ludloe's intimations alluded to a country well known to him, though unknown to others, I was, of course, inclined to suppose that this country was now before me.

In search of some clue to this mystery, I carefully inspected the other maps in this collection. In a map of the eastern hemisphere I soon observed the outlines of islands, which, though on a scale greatly diminished, were plainly similar to that of the land above described.

It is well known that the people of Europe are strangers to very nearly one half of the surface of the globe*. From the south pole up to the equator, it is only the small space occupied by southern Africa and by South America with which we are acquainted. There is a vast extent, sufficient to receive a continent as large as North America, which our ignorance has filled only with water. In Ludloe's maps nothing was still to be seen, in these regions, but water, except in that spot where the transverse parallels of the southern tropic and the 150th degree east longitude intersect each other. On this spot were Ludloe's islands placed, though without any name or inscription whatever.

I needed not to be told that this spot had never been explored by any European voyager, who had published his adventures. What authority had Ludloe for fixing a habitable land in this spot? and why did he give us nothing but the courses of shores and rivers, and the scite of towns and villages, without a name?

As soon as Ludloe had set out upon his proposed journey of a fortnight, I unlocked his closet, and continued rum-

---

*The reader must be reminded that the incidents of this narrative are supposed to have taken place before the voyages of Bougainville and Cook.

maging among these books and maps till night. By that time I had turned over every book and almost every leaf in this small collection, and did not open the closet again till near the end of that period. Meanwhile I had many reflections upon this remarkable circumstance. Could Ludloe have intended that I should see this atlas? It was the only book that could be styled a manuscript on these shelves, and it was placed beneath several others, in a situation far from being obvious and forward to the eye or the hand. Was it an oversight in him to leave it in my way, or could he have intended to lead my curiosity and knowledge a little farther onward by this accidental disclosure? In either case how was I to regulate my future deportment toward him? Was I to speak and act as if this atlas had escaped my attention or not? I had already, after my first examination of it, placed the volume exactly where I found it. On every supposition I thought this was the safest way, and unlocked the closet a second time, to see that all was precisely in the original order. . . . How was I dismayed and confounded on inspecting the shelves to perceive that the atlas was gone. This was a theft, which, from the closet being under lock and key, and the key always in my own pocket, and which, from the very nature of the thing stolen, could not be imputed to any of the domestics. After a few moments a suspicion occurred, which was soon changed into certainty by applying to the housekeeper, who told me that Ludloe had returned, apparently in much haste, the evening of the day on which he had set out upon his journey, and just after I had left the house, that he had gone into the room where this closet of books was, and, after a few minutes' stay, came out again and went away. She told me also, that he had made general enquiries after me, to which she had answered, that she had not seen me during the day, and supposed that I had spent the whole of it abroad. From this account it was plain, that Ludloe had returned for no other purpose but to remove this book out of my reach. But if he had a double key to this door, what should hinder his having access, by the same means, to every other locked up place in the house?

This suggestion made me start with terror. Of so obvious

a means for possessing a knowledge of every thing under his roof, I had never been till this moment aware. Such is the infatuation which lays our most secret thoughts open to the world's scrutiny. We are frequently in most danger when we deem ourselves most safe, and our fortress is taken sometimes through a point, whose weakness nothing, it should seem, but the blindest stupidity could overlook.

My terrors, indeed, quickly subsided when I came to recollect that there was nothing in any closet or cabinet of mine which could possibly throw light upon subjects which I desired to keep in the dark. The more carefully I inspected my own drawers, and the more I reflected on the character of Ludloe, as I had known it, the less reason did there appear in my suspicions; but I drew a lesson of caution from this circumstance, which contributed to my future safety.

From this incident I could not but infer Ludloe's unwillingness to let me so far into his geographical secret, as well as the certainty of that suspicion, which had very early been suggested to my thoughts, that Ludloe's plans of civilization had been carried into practice in some unvisited corner of the world. It was strange, however, that he should betray himself by such an inadvertency. One who talked so confidently of his own powers, to unveil any secret of mine, and, at the same time, to conceal his own transactions, had surely committed an unpardonable error in leaving this important document in my way. My reverence, indeed, for Ludloe was such, that I sometimes entertained the notion that this seeming oversight was, in truth, a regular contrivance to supply me with a knowledge, of which, when I came maturely to reflect, it was impossible for me to make any ill use. There is no use in relating what would not be believed; and should I publish to the world the existence of islands in the space allotted by Ludloe's maps to these *incognitae*, what would the world answer? That whether the space described was sea or land was of no importance. That the moral and political condition of its inhabitants was the only topic worthy of rational curiosity. Since I had gained no information upon this point; since I had nothing to disclose but vain

301

and fantastic surmises; I might as well be ignorant of every thing. Thus, from secretly condemning Ludloe's imprudence, I gradually passed to admiration of his policy. This discovery had no other effect than to stimulate my curiosity; to keep up my zeal to prosecute the journey I had commenced under his auspices.

I had hitherto formed a resolution to stop where I was in Ludloe's confidence: to wait till the success should be ascertained of my projects with respect to Mrs. Benington, before I made any new advance in the perilous and mysterious road into which he had led my steps. But, before this tedious fortnight had elapsed, I was grown extremely impatient for an interview, and had nearly resolved to undertake whatever obligation he should lay upon me.

This obligation was indeed a heavy one, since it included the confession of my vocal powers. In itself the confession was little. To possess this faculty was neither laudable nor culpable, nor had it been exercised in a way which I should be very much ashamed to acknowledge. It had led me into many insincerities and artifices, which, though not justifiable by any creed, was entitled to some excuse, on the score of youthful ardour and temerity. The true difficulty in the way of these confessions was the not having made them already. Ludloe had long been entitled to this confidence, and, though the existence of this power was venial or wholly innocent, the obstinate concealment of it was a different matter, and would certainly expose me to suspicion and rebuke. But what was the alternative? To conceal it. To incur those dreadful punishments awarded against treason in this particular. Ludloe's menaces still rung in my ears, and appalled my heart. How should I be able to shun them? By concealing from every one what I concealed from him? How was my concealment of such a faculty to be suspected or proved? Unless I betrayed myself, who could betray me?

In this state of mind, I resolved to confess myself to Ludloe in the way that he required, reserving only the secret of this faculty. Awful, indeed, said I, is the crisis of my fate. If Ludloe's declarations are true, a horrid catastrophe awaits me: but as fast as my resolutions were shaken, they were confirmed anew by the recollection—Who can betray me but myself? If I deny, who is there can prove? Suspicion can never light upon the truth. If it does, it can never be converted into certainty. Even my own lips cannot confirm it, since who will believe my testimony?

By such illusions was I fortified in my desperate resolution. Ludloe returned at the time appointed. He informed me that Mrs. Benington expected me next morning. She was ready to depart for her country residence, where she proposed to spend the ensuing summer, and would carry me along with her. In consequence of this arrangement, he said, many months would elapse before he should see me again. You will indeed, continued he, be pretty much shut up from all society. Your books and your new friend will be your chief, if not only companions. Her life is not a social one, because she has formed extravagant notions of the importance of lonely worship and devout solitude. Much of her time will be spent in meditation upon pious books in her closet. Some of it in long solitary rides in her coach, for the sake of exercise. Little will remain for eating and sleeping, so that unless you can prevail upon her to violate her ordinary rules for your sake, you will be left pretty much to yourself. You will have the more time to reflect upon what has hitherto been the theme of our conversations. You can come to town when you want to see me. I shall generally be found in these apartments.

In the present state of my mind, though impatient to see Mrs. Benington, I was still more impatient to remove the veil between Ludloe and myself. After some pause, I ventured to enquire if there was any impediment to my advancement in the road he had already pointed out to my curiosity and ambition.

He replied, with great solemnity, that I was already acquainted with the next step to be taken in this road. If I was prepared to make him my confessor, as to the past, the present, and the future, *without exception or condition*, but what arose from defect of memory, he was willing to receive my confession.

I declared myself ready to do so.

I need not, he returned, remind you of the consequences of concealment or deceit. I have already dwelt upon these consequences. As to the past, you have already told me, perhaps, all that is of any moment to know. It is in relation to the future that caution will be chiefly necessary. Hitherto your actions have been nearly indifferent to the ends of your future existence. Confessions of the past are required, because they are an earnest of the future character and conduct. Have you then—but this is too abrupt. Take an hour to reflect and deliberate. Go by yourself; take yourself to severe task, and make up your mind with a full, entire, and unfailing resolution; for the moment in which you assume this new obligation will make you a new being. Perdition or felicity will hang upon that moment.

This conversation was late in the evening. After I had consented to postpone this subject, we parted, he telling me that he would leave his chamber door open, and as soon as my mind was made up I might come to him.

I retired accordingly to my apartment, and spent the prescribed hour in anxious and irresolute reflections. They were no other than had hitherto occurred, but they oc- curred with more force than ever. Some fatal obstinacy, however, got possession of me, and I persisted in the resolu- tion of concealing *one thing*. We become fondly attached to objects and pursuits, frequently for no conceivable reason but the pain and trouble they cost us. In proportion to the danger in which they involve us do we cherish them. Our darling potion is the poison that scorches our vitals.

After some time, I went to Ludloe's apartment. I found him solemn, and yet benign, at my entrance. After intimat- ing my compliance with the terms prescribed, which I did, in spite of all my labour for composure, with accents half faultering, he proceeded to put various questions to me, relative to my early history.

I knew there was no other mode of accomplishing the end in view, but by putting all that was related in the form of answers to questions; and when meditating on the charac- ter of Ludloe, I experienced excessive uneasiness as to the consummate art and penetration which his questions would manifest. Conscious of a purpose to conceal, my fancy invested my friend with the robe of a judicial inquisitor, all whose questions should aim at extracting the truth, and entrapping the liar.

In this respect, however, I was wholly disappointed. All his inquiries were general and obvious.—They betokened curiosity, but not suspicion; yet there were moments when I saw, or fancied I saw, some dissatisfaction betrayed in his features; and when I arrived at that period of my story which terminated with my departure, as his companion, for Europe, his pauses were, I thought, a little longer and more museful than I liked. At this period, our first conference ended. After a talk, which had commenced at a late hour, and had continued many hours, it was time to sleep, and it was agreed that next morning the conference should be renewed.

On retiring to my pillow, and reviewing all the circumstances of this interview, my mind was filled with apprehension and disquiet. I seemed to recollect a thousand things, which showed that Ludloe was not fully satisfied with my part in this interview. A strange and nameless mixture of wrath and of pity appeared, on recollection, in the glances which, from time to time, he cast upon me. Some emotion played upon his features, in which, as my fears conceived, there was a tincture of resentment and ferocity. In vain I called my usual sophistries to my aid. In vain I pondered on the inscrutable nature of my peculiar faculty. In vain I endeavoured to persuade myself, that, by telling the truth, instead of entitling myself to Ludloe's approbation, I should only excite his anger, by what he could not but deem an attempt to impose upon his belief an incredible tale of impossible events. I had never heard or read of any instance of this faculty. I supposed the case to be absolutely singular, and I should be no more entitled to credit in proclaiming it, than if I should maintain that a certain billet of wood possessed the faculty of articulate speech. It was now, however, too late to retract. I had been guilty of a solemn and deliberate concealment. I was now in the path in which there was no turning back, and I must go forward.

The return of day's encouraging beams in some degree quieted my nocturnal terrors, and I went, at the appointed hour, to Ludloe's presence. I found him with a much more cheerful aspect than I expected, and began to chide myself, in secret, for the folly of my late apprehensions.

After a little pause, he reminded me, that he was only one among many, engaged in a great and arduous design. As each of us, continued he, is mortal, each of us must, in time, yield his post to another.—Each of us is ambitious to provide himself a successor, to have his place filled by one selected and instructed by himself. All our personal feelings and affections are by no means intended to be swallowed up by a passion for the general interest; when they can be kept alive and be brought into play, in subordination and subservience to the *great end,* they are cherished as useful, and revered as laudable; and whatever austerity and rigour you may impute to my character, there are few more susceptible of personal regards than I am.

You cannot know, till *you* are what *I* am, what deep, what all-absorbing interest I have in the success of my tutorship on this occasion. Most joyfully would I embrace a thousand deaths, rather than that you should prove a recreant. The consequences of any failure in your integrity will, it is true, be fatal to yourself: but there are some minds, of a generous texture, who are more impatient under ills they have inflicted upon others, than of those they have brought upon themselves; who had rather perish, themselves, in infamy, than bring infamy or death upon a benefactor.

Perhaps of such noble materials is your mind composed. If I had not thought so, you would never have been an object of my regard, and therefore, in the motives that shall impel you to fidelity, sincerity, and perseverance, some regard to my happiness and welfare will, no doubt, have place.

And yet I exact nothing from you on this score. If your own safety be insufficient to controul you, you are not fit for us. There is, indeed, abundant need of all possible inducements to make you faithful. The task of concealing nothing from me must be easy. That of concealing every thing from others must be the only arduous one. The *first* you can hardly fail of performing, when the exigence requires it, for what motive can you possibly have to practice evasion or disguise with me? You have surely committed no crime; you have neither robbed, nor murdered, nor betrayed. If you have, there is no room for the fear of punishment or the terror of disgrace to step in, and make you hide your guilt from me. You cannot dread any further disclosure, because I can have no interest in your ruin or your shame: and what evil could ensue the confession of the foulest murder, even before a bench of magistrates, more dreadful than that which will inevitably follow the practice of the least concealment to me, or the least undue disclosure to others?

You cannot easily conceive the emphatical solemnity with which this was spoken. Had he fixed piercing eyes on me while he spoke; had I perceived him watching my looks, and labouring to penetrate my secret thoughts, I should doubtless have been ruined: but he fixed his eyes upon the floor, and no gesture or look indicated the smallest suspicion of my conduct. After some pause, he continued, in a more pathetic tone, while his whole frame seemed to partake of his mental agitation.

I am greatly at a loss by what means to impress you with a full conviction of the truth of what I have just said. Endless are the sophistries by which we seduce ourselves into perilous and doubtful paths. What we do not see, we disbelieve, or we heed not. The sword may descend upon our infatuated head from above, but we who are, meanwhile, busily inspecting the ground at our feet, or gazing at the scene around us, are not aware or apprehensive of its irresistible coming. In this case, it must not be seen before it is felt, or before that time comes when the danger of incurring it is over. I cannot withdraw the veil, and disclose to your view the exterminating angel. All must be vacant and blank, and the danger that stands armed with death at your elbow must continue to be totally invisible, till that moment when its vengeance is provoked or unprovokable. I will do my part to encourage you in good, or intimidate you from evil. I am anxious to set before you all the motives which are

307

fitted to influence your conduct; but how shall I work on
your convictions?

Here another pause ensued, which I had not courage
enough to interrupt. He presently resumed.

Perhaps you recollect a visit which you paid, on Christ-
mas day, in the year——, to the cathedral church at Toledo.
Do you remember?

A moment's reflection recalled to my mind all the incidents of that day. I had good reason to remember them. I
felt no small trepidation when Ludloe referred me to that
day, for, at the moment, I was doubtful whether there had
not been some bivocal agency exerted on that occasion.
Luckily, however, it was almost the only similar occasion in
which it had been wholly silent.

I answered in the affirmative: I remember them perfectly.

And yet, said Ludloe, with a smile that seemed intended
to disarm this declaration of some of its terrors, I suspect
your recollection is not as exact as mine, nor, indeed, your
knowledge as extensive. You met there, for the first time, a
female, whose nominal uncle, but real father, a dean of that
ancient church, resided in a blue stone house, the third
from the west angle of the square of St. Jago.

All this was exactly true.

This female, continued he, fell in love with you. Her
passion made her deaf to all the dictates of modesty and
duty, and she gave you sufficient intimations, in subsequent
interviews at the same place, of this passion; which, she
being fair and enticing, you were not slow in comprehending and returning. As not only the safety of your intercourse, but even of both your lives, depended on being
shielded even from suspicion, the utmost wariness and
caution was observed in all your proceedings. Tell me
whether you succeeded in your efforts to this end.

I replied, that, at the time, I had no doubt but I had.

And yet, said he, drawing something from his pocket,
and putting it into my hand, there is the slip of paper, with
the preconcerted emblem inscribed upon it, which the in-

308

fatuated girl dropped in your sight, one evening, in the left aisle of that church. That paper you imagined you afterwards burnt in your chamber lamp. In pursuance of this token, you deferred your intended visit, and next day the lady was accidentally drowned, in passing a river. Here ended your connexion with her, and with her was buried, as you thought, all memory of this transaction.

I leave you to draw your own inference from this disclosure. Meditate upon it when alone. Recal all the incidents of that drama, and labour to conceive the means by which my sagacity has been able to reach events that took place so far off, and under so deep a covering. If you cannot penetrate these means, learn to reverence my assertions, that I cannot be deceived; and let sincerity be henceforth the rule of your conduct towards me, not merely because it is right, but because concealment is impossible.

We will stop here. There is no haste required of us. Yesterday's discourse will suffice for to-day, and for many days to come. Let what has already taken place be the subject of profound and mature reflection. Review, once more, the incidents of your early life, previous to your introduction to me, and, at our next conference, prepare to supply all those deficiences occasioned by negligence, forgetfulness, or design on our first. There must be some. There must be many. The whole truth can only be disclosed after numerous and repeated conversations. These must take place at considerable intervals, and when *all* is told, then shall you be ready to encounter the final ordeal, and load yourself with heavy and terrific sanctions.

I shall be the proper judge of the completeness of your confession.—Knowing previously, and by unerring means, your whole history, I shall be able to detect all that is deficient, as well as all that is redundant. Your confessions have hitherto adhered to the truth, but deficient they are, and they must be, for who, at a single trial, can detail the secrets of his life? whose recollection can fully serve him at an instant's notice? who can free himself, by a single effort, from the dominion of fear and shame? We expect no miracles of fortitude and purity from our disciples. It is our discipline, our wariness, our laborious preparation that creates the excellence we have among us. We find it not ready made.

I counsel you to join Mrs. Bennington without delay. You may see me when and as often as you please. When it is proper to renew the present topic, it shall be renewed. Till then we will be silent.—Here Ludloe left me alone, but not to indifference or vacuity. Indeed I was overwhelmed with the reflections that arose from this conversation. So, said I, I am still saved, if I have wisdom enough to use the opportunity, from the consequences of past concealments. By a distinction which I had wholly overlooked, but which could not be missed by the sagacity and equity of Ludloe, I have praise for telling the truth, and an excuse for withholding some of the truth. It was, indeed, a praise to which I was entitled, for I have made no *additions* to the tale of my early adventures. I had no motive to exaggerate or dress out in false colours. What I sought to conceal, I was careful to exclude entirely, that a lame or defective narrative might awaken no suspicions.

The allusion to incidents at Toledo confounded and bewildered all my thoughts. I still held the paper he had given me. So far as memory could be trusted, it was the same which, an hour after I had received it, I burnt, as I conceived, with my own hands. How Ludloe came into possession of this paper; how he was apprised of incidents, to which only the female mentioned and myself were privy, which she had too good reason to hide from all the world, and which I had taken infinite pains to bury in oblivion, I vainly endeavoured to conjecture.

HISTORICAL ESSAY

I

The recent small-scale revival of Charles Brockden Brown focuses attention on an early American novelist who long awaited "the slow Justice of his countrymen."[1] He bids fair to stay revived, a mysterious and powerful figure in the early annals of our literature.

Brown was a nursling of the eighteenth century—but an uneasy one. Born in 1771, he came to maturity at a time, the early national period, which teemed with conflicting forces. For Brown it was the best of times and the worst of times. Literature as a career beckoned, but with what real encouragement in a provincial society without professional know-how, and in any case with little approval from England, still the mother-country in matters cultural? A democracy of sorts there was, but what did it offer beyond the *assumption* of equality? Perfectibility and Utopianism were in the air, but it was air only recently purged of the reek and din of two revolutions and premonitory of turmoil to come. Little streams of idealism there were, but there remained the nagging thought that possibly John Calvin and his *Institutes* were right: maybe men *were* conditioned by innate depravity. Maybe they weren't the free "children of God" at all but merely responding mechanisms, what Brown himself termed "nothing more than a congeries of fiddle-strings."[2] You could form Utopian visions of beatitude and euphoria to be established on distant islands, but man at home didn't seem to match up with such grandiose conceptions. The economic and political stability of the nation was

[1] George Lippard, "The Heart-Broken," *The Nineteenth Century*, 1 (Jan. 1848), 26.

[2] "The Man at Home," No. VI, *Weekly Magazine*, 1 (10 March 1798), 167.

311

uncertain. An effort could be made to develop trade, but how could you be sure that the hoped-for prosperity (including that of the Brown Family— dependent on merchant shipping) would not be sabotaged by a wrong-headed, head-strong, embargo-mad Jefferson? As a Quaker you could love peace; but what price amity and altruism in a world that spawned the likes of Bourbon monarchs, Robespierres, Napoleons—as well as the arrogant British, vanquished in one war but now lawlessly pecking away at our shipping? You could for a time join with William Godwin, Tom Paine, and others, in fulminating against feudal remnants of wealth and caste in Europe, especially England. Yet if you were, like Brown, less interested in the "natural rights" of man than in man's natural capacities, would radical programs designed to smash the old regime really satisfy you? All such programs could end only in violence or anarchy, both detestable to Brown. He might well have wondered whether the era into which he had been born was really an "Age of Enlightenment."

Nor were there prognostications for happiness in private life, especially for a young man like Brockden Brown—a sensitive, fastidious person endowed with little physical vitality, prone to pulmonary weakness, and with more than a hint of neurosis in his psychological make-up. With few worldly goods; with a talent of untested proportions; ambitious but prone to self-depreciation;[3] "sociable" but not a good mixer; romantically inclined towards girls but frequently inept in action; theoretically against kings and privilege and in favor of equality but with an instinctive patrician scorn for the uncouth, unwashed mob; given to Utopian dreams but no hand at pragmatic procedure; fond of a family solicitous for his welfare but restive under its mild yoke—Brown found the world too disturbing a place for one of his irresolute, Hamlet-like nature to cope with.

Faced with paradoxes he could not resolve, fears he could not banish, Brown finally became a writer. In authorship too he would be beset by manifold problems, but in the very process of struggling with them he achieved a degree of positive satisfaction.

[3] With the unreasoning self-distrust common to the neurotic temperament he once wrote—and this before commencing *Wieland:* "I am sometimes apt to think that few human beings have drunk so deeply of the Cup of self-abhorrence as I have. There is no misery equal to that which flows from this source. I have been for some years in the full fruition of it." Brown to William Dunlap, 1 January 1798 (ALS, PHi; photocopy OKentU.).

His conflicts did not vanish, but it can only be believed that in some obscure way the warring forces within him generated the power that would finally bring him a measure of success. The eighteenth century was a disturbing milieu, but Brown finally learned to work within it, and to such good purpose that he became the one early American novelist that the twentieth century seems eager to recover and retain. And it begins to appear that his *Wieland,* flawed though it is, possesses enough weight to argue against its easy removal from its position as a minor monument on the threshold of our national literature.

Brown's early years in Philadelphia were devoid of spectacular incident. He was the next to the youngest son in a family of five brothers and one sister. His father was a kindly man who respected things literary but thought the idea of letters as a career unwise. His mother apparently had a certain antipathy toward his spending money on "books."[4] The boy early evidenced a studious and brooding nature. Rather than play outdoor games with his contemporaries, he seems to have enjoyed reading by himself.[5] Enamored of architecture and cartography at an early age, he studied maps and practiced drawing them, an activity adumbrating his later interest in far-away Utopian communities such as those envisaged by Carwin's friend Ludloe. After the conclusion of his formal studies under historian Robert Proud in a Friends' school—where the Bible was read in both Greek and Latin—he carried on self-directed studies with unremitted zeal. He wrote his first poetry at the age of fifteen; began the study of law at seventeen; became a "published author" at eighteen, when his essays entitled "The Rhapsodist" appeared in the *Columbian Magazine* (of Philadelphia) from August to November 1789. His youth was not a happy period. He became oppressed by the "rubbish of the law" into which he had been urged by the family. He ridiculed picayune legal distinctions, and he could not bear the thought of becoming "indiscriminately the defender of right or wrong."[6] Probably too his parents were distressed by Brown's

---

[4] Robert Hemenway cites a passage to this effect in Brown's father's transcription of his son's diary. "The Novels of Charles Brockden Brown: A Critical Study," Diss. Kent State 1966, p. 360.

[5] There is perhaps a degree of self-portraiture in Brown's later use of fictional characters given to bookish habits: Wieland, Mr. Dudley, Arthur Mervyn, Edgar Huntly, and Henry Colden.

[6] William Dunlap, *The Life of Charles Brockden Brown* (Philadelphia: James P. Parke, 1815), I, 41. Hereafter referred to as *Life.*

increasing proneness to deistic views and his harsh attack on the
"pernicious" influence of Christian doctrine, and they interfered
with his gestures toward marriage with non-Quaker young
women. His friendship with a group of thoughtful young men
finally became an offset to his loneliness, and toward one of them
he seems to have had (probably unrecognized) homosexual
impulses.[7] With all of them he enjoyed discussions of literature
and science at meetings of their Belles Lettres Club. Nevertheless
Brown's underlying tendency toward depression brought him to
the point of meditating suicide. Ultimately he learned enough law
to be of use in an advisory capacity to his father and older
brothers who conducted the family hardware business, services
for which in effect he was probably allowed a token salary. Yet he
had been hurt by the pressures brought to bear on him, and there
developed a kind of cold-war between Brown and the family. No
open rupture occurred, but he gradually withdrew into himself,
and at last he quietly vanished from the domicile, severing most of
his family ties.[8]

Happily he soon made a new set of friends, many of them older
than himself. These new friends, who became useful to him as,
more and more, letters seemed a likely choice of profession for
Brown, included fellow-members of the New York Friendly
Club: Elihu Hubbard Smith, a physician and the editor of
American Poems (1793), lawyer William Johnson, and dramatist
William Dunlap, Brown's future biographer. Some of the happiest months of his life ensued, though soon darkened by the
tragic death of Smith at the age of twenty-eight in the yellow fever
epidemic of 1798. By now Brown had written several amorphous

[7] Disturbed at Joseph Bringhurst's construing something he had written in a letter as reproof, Brown melodramatically protests how dear
Bringhurst is to him. He would sooner die than offend a friend to whom
he would utter the "tenderest appelations" [sic]. Brown to Bringhurst, 5
May 1792 (letter, transcribed by Daniel Edwards Kennedy in his
"Charles Brockden Brown: His Life and Works," pp. 510-514).
Kennedy's unpublished MS—referred to hereafter as Kennedy—is in
the Kent State Brown Collection. For a description of the Kennedy MS
see Robert Hemenway, "Daniel Edwards Kennedy's Manuscript Biography of Charles Brockden Brown," *Serif,* 3 (Dec. 1966), 16-18.

[8] Nevertheless he continued to accept assistance in connection with his
writing from his father and from his brother James. James it was who saw
the first part of *Arthur Mervyn* through the press—and possibly *Edgar
Huntly* as well. See Brown to James Brown, 15 February 1799 and April
1800 (*Life,* II, 97-100).

speculative narratives, mostly uncompleted, involving highly improbable characters and visionary Utopian myths, among them "Carsol." In 1798 he published Parts I and II of his first major production, *Alcuin; a Dialogue,* a formal discussion of women's rights and morality (including sexual morality).[9] His novels followed in startlingly quick succession: *Wieland* (1798), *Ormond* (1799), *Arthur Mervyn* (1799-1800), *Edgar Huntly* (1799), *Clara Howard* (1801), *Jane Talbot* (1801). By this time, fiction having proved unpromising as a source of livelihood, Brown had turned to periodical work, editing magazines, reviewing books, writing translations, and engaging in miscellaneous journalistic ventures. As Dunlap observed, Brown's aim of becoming "exclusively an author" had been a considerable "novelty" in a land where "no one had relied solely upon the support of his talents as a writer" for his livelihood (*Life,* II, 12). In 1804 Brown married a young lady of the Quaker persuasion. His death, from tuberculosis, occurred in 1810, many of his hopes extinguished but the foundation of his modest fame securely established.

II

Wieland is the most original of Brown's novels and, on first encounter, the least "literary." It does not exhibit "sophistication" so much as simplicity and power. Yet Brown had an acquaintance with a broad diversity of writers. No detailed record of his reading is available, but it seems clear from scattered references (many of them in his letters) that he was an eclectic rather than a systematic or a comprehensive reader. There is no sign that his studies were steadily centered in the standard Hebraic and Hellenic sources of culture. Toward the Greek and Roman classics, as

[9] *Alcuin,* the name by which this work is most familiarly known, is the title it bore as pamphlet. Unbeknownst to Brown, who was publishing it serially in the *Weekly Magazine* (in Philadelphia) as "The Rights of Women," Smith had already prepared his MS copy of the dialogue—given him by Brown in the preceding year (1797)—for pamphlet publication with Swords in New York. Dunlap published Parts III and IV after Brown's death in his *Life* of Brown (I, 75-105). Parts III and IV were finished at about the time that I and II were going to press, but one reason why they may have been withheld is that IV contained the controversial issues of comparative equality for women in marriage and the problem of their freedom to obtain divorces.

toward so many things, he was ambivalent. He was much drawn toward Cicero, man and author, whom he used in *Wieland* as a special interest of Theodore's and whom he portrayed as a lonely, heroic figure in a narrative fragment, "The Death of Cicero" (published in some issues of the first edition of *Edgar Huntly* to fill out Volume III). During his early years the epic form attracted him—so much so that he contemplated writing a triad of epics on American themes. Nevertheless he had but limited interest in classical writers some of whom, he believed, were too much given to celebrating lewdness (Horace) and drunkenness (Anacreon). Several (Homer, Virgil) he complained of for devoting too much attention to "monstrous fables . . . brutal men and sanguinary deities" and the "propagation of . . . national delusions."[10]

Among early British writers, he admired Chaucer, Sir Thomas More, Spenser. There is evidence that even before he wrote *Wieland* he was saturated in and deeply impressed by Shakespeare and Milton. Shakespeare's plays—especially *Macbeth, Othello*, and *Antony and Cleopatra*—are frequently recalled by quotations, echoes, and adaptations.[11] Shakespeare's antic moods find almost no correlative in the works of the sober-minded Brown (that is, save for an occasional quote like that from *The Tempest* in "Carwin"—p. 261), but his tragedies were a major recourse and support. In Milton, one of his favorite authors from boyhood, he found the grandeur and magnitude and the "moral sublimity" which he so much valued.[12]

---

[10] Review of Southey's "Joan of Arc," *Monthly Magazine*, 1 (June 1799), 226.

[11] In *Wieland* (p. 203) a footnote by Brown acknowledges his debt to *Macbeth*, a play evidently much in his mind. (All references to *Wieland* and "Carwin" are of course to the accompanying texts.) Clara's uncle's warning to her—"The phantom that has urged him to the murder of Catharine and her children is not yet appeased" (p. 188)—suggestively resembles a line in *Macbeth:* "This murderous shaft that's shot/Hath not yet lighted" (II.iii.147f.). See also *Wieland*, Chapter 17 (p. 157), for a patent echo of Macduff's response to news of the death of his children. Brown was probably also inspired by *Othello*. The tragic dimensions of the scene in which Wieland takes the life of Catharine are achieved partly by evoking the example of Shakespeare. The mode of Catharine's death, like that of Desdemona, is by strangling; and Wieland, like Othello, wishes to avoid causing her needless sufferings: "I would not have thee linger in thy pain" (*Othello*, V.ii.87; cf. *Wieland*, p. 172).

[12] In *Wieland* he even uses Milton to help him establish the key of doom

Among eighteenth-century British writers, Richardson was a favorite—for his epistolary technique, his harassed heroines, his indispensable prototypal villain Lovelace, and his embodiment of "moral perfection" in *Sir Charles Grandison*. Pope's prosody and diction seem to have monitored Brown in moments when he thought he could become a good poet. Johnson's *Rasselas,* as well as More's *Utopia,* helped to fix his thoughts on the theme of ideal societies. The popular Gothic romance finally attracted him only superficially: he was not really interested, he said, in stories devoted to "murders, ghosts, clanking chains, dead bodies, skeletons, old castles, and damp dungeons."[13]

He had some acquaintance with German writers (Schiller's *Der Geisterseher* was a possible minor source for *Wieland*),[14] and as a youth at least he was well versed in French literature of the eighteenth century, especially the "revolutionary" encyclopedists Diderot, D'Alembert, and Voltaire. A more enduring interest was Rousseau's tale of sentiment and pathos, *La Nouvelle Héloise*. Brown gradually veered toward a belief that hope for the amelioration of mankind lay not so much in political action as in a "return to nature" and the cultivation of benevolence: "rights" seemed finally less important than right feeling. American novelists he makes little of, even failing to extol the one writer of his period who might conceivably vie with Brown for the distinction of being the most important early American novelist, namely, Hugh Henry Brackenridge.

Brown was an original novelist, but he was not an original thinker. He formed no subtle theory of the origin or the essential nature of art. The mediocre poetry he wrote in early youth was largely of Popeian derivation, and his informally articulated aesthetics may be assumed to have coincided with those of the neo-classical age. Indeed, he was so steeped in "methodized" poetry of the era that when the *Lyrical Ballads* appeared—in the

when at the very beginning of the story he has Clara use the phrase "this dreadful eminence" to define her situation, a phrase that echoes Milton's use of "that bad eminence" at the beginning of the great consultation in Hell in *Paradise Lost*. The more conventional type of "atmospheric" use of Milton also occurs, as with Carwin's giving himself up to the "contemplation" of "Comus" (p. 252).

[13] "On the Cause of the Popularity of Novels," *Literary Magazine*, 7 (June 1807), 412.

[14] Harry Warfel has suggested Cajetan Tschink's novel of the same

same year as *Wieland* — they kindled no excitement in his breast. His conception of the novel was essentially simple: a good "story" with moral implications. Excitement there must be: the writer's aim should be to "excite and baffle curiosity, without shocking belief."[15] For the most part the writer should find his material in the "new and untrodden" field of his own country, and "adapt his fiction to all that is genuine and peculiar in the scene before him," relying not on books but on "nature."[16]

As the first group of his books did not sell, it appeared to Brown that he had perhaps erred in too vigorously attempting to "suspend every soul in curiosity" by resorting to too high an incidence of sensational material. Accordingly, he announced his intention (in 1800—looking back upon *Huntly*) of relying less on the use of the "prodigious" and the "singular" and trying to reach his public by stressing materials of greater recognition value for his readers. Instead of "out-of-nature" experiences, he planned to use "moral causes" and the "daily incidents" of ordinary life.[17]

Whatever the fate of his novels, however, Brown never swerved from the conviction that a central purpose of the novelist must be moral truth. He once referred to himself as a "story-telling moralist" (Warfel, p. 5). Despite poor sales he never lost faith in the novel as a literary form. He seems (for once) to have been disingenuous when in 1803 he in effect tried to dissociate himself from his novel-writing past by saying in the prospectus for a magazine he was founding: "I should enjoy a larger share of my own respect, at the present moment, if nothing had ever flowed from my pen, the production of which could be traced to me."[18] Clearly this was in large part propaganda designed to allay the suspicions which many people still credited: was a novel-writer a suitable person to preside over a magazine designed for the whole family? Indeed only a year later he was defending the novel against the charge that novel-reading was bound to "unfit us for

name (translated as *The Victim of Magical Delusion*) as a source. *Charles Brockden Brown: American Gothic Novelist* (Gainesville: Univ. of Florida Press, 1949), p. 110. Tschink's *Victim* appeared serially in the *New York Weekly Magazine* from 2 Dec. 1795 to 12 April 1797.

[15] Brown to James Brown, 15 February 1799 (*Life*, II, 97).
[16] [Prospectus for *Sky-Walk*] *Weekly Magazine*, 1 (17 March 1798), 202.
[17] Brown to James Brown, April 1800 (*Life*, II, 100).
[18] "The Editors' Address to the Public," *Literary Magazine*, 1 (Oct. 1803), 4.

solid and useful reading."[19] In his own work he steadfastly aimed to illuminate the "moral constitution" of man.

Whatever his critical theory, Brown in actual practice was an obsessive writer, a prolific writer, and a speedy producer. It has been justly asserted that writing for him was a "mental necessity," an employment "just as necessary to [his] mind as sustenance to [his] frame."[20] He was in fact able to concentrate on composition even during the harrowing yellow fever epidemic of 1798, working "cheerfully" on three of his novels (one of them *Wieland*) "in spite of the groans of the dying and the rumbling of hearses" (*Life*, II, 96). In the act of writing, a species of mild trance seems to have possessed him, and ideas flowed through him "irresistibly" (Bernard, p. 252). His output during a short life-time was enormous, his nonfiction being perhaps five or six times as much in volume as his novels. With five novels "in a state of progression" at the same time (*Life*, II, 16), his actual production must have been quite rapid. He did not wish to recollect in tranquility but to be excited by the immediate act of creation. "In proportion as I gain power over words, shall I lose dominion over sentiments"—the narrator of the opening part of *Edgar Huntly* could have been speaking for Brown when he wrote these words.[21] Speed might sometimes be the destroyer of his coherence, but it was surely the preserver of his inspiration.

III

The novel for which Charles Brockden Brown is best remembered, *Wieland*, was written and published in 1798, when Brown was twenty-seven years old. The actual writing seems to have been accomplished in about six months. However, Brown may well have begun thinking about the major action of his novel—Wieland's destruction of his family—two years earlier; for the "Account of a Murder Committed by Mr. J[ames] Y[ates] upon His Family . . ." (which is likely the "authentic case" Brown

[19] "A Student's Diary," *Literary Magazine*, 1 (March 1804), 405.
[20] John Bernard, *Retrospections of America, 1797-1811* (New York: Harper & Brothers, 1887), p. 254.
[21] *Edgar Huntly; or, Memoirs of a Sleep-Walker* (Philadelphia: H. Maxwell, 1799), I, 4.

refers to in his "Advertisement" to *Wieland*) had appeared in
1796. Further evidence that *Wieland* had the advantage of
Brown's having ruminated about its development exists in an
"Outline" discovered in a Commonplace Book (No. 14) amid the
large body of materials relating to the Brown family in the manu-
script collection of the Historical Society of Pennsylvania.[22] The
"Outline" is in handwriting slightly different from that of
Brown's letters of the period but is almost unquestionably his.
Although it is undated, it seems sensible to assume that the
"Outline" antedates the actual writing of the novel. Since Brown
seems to have been toying with the idea of having his hero destroy
his wife, children, ward, and sister—events suggested by the
Yates "Account"—the "Outline" may well have been written after
August 1796, when the "Account" appeared in the *Philadelphia
Minerva*. It consists of jottings somewhat fragmentary in nature, a
sketch really rather than a coherent synopsis. As the synopsis is
divided into "Acts," Brown may have originally been thinking
about a plan for dramatization. The narrative embodied in it,
though different in some aspects, contains most of the ground-
work for the novel. Perhaps the most striking addition Brown
made is the elder Wieland's death by spontaneous combustion in
the summer-house; in the "Outline" he merely "died 1749."
Carwin's vivid physical appearance is not provided for, but many
of his ventriloquistic activities match those in the novel, and it is
suggested that he may use his skill in this category for "sport."
The still-vexed question of whether the voice that "commanded"
Wieland to slay his wife was Carwin's or a voice conjured up out of
Wieland's disordered psyche was no question when Brown wrote
the "Outline": Carwin did *not* give the final command. An important variation between "Outline" and novel is that whereas in the
latter the "divine command" is received in Clara's bedroom, in the
"Outline" the scene occurs in the summer-house. Brown was
apparently willing to exchange whatever symbolic effect was conceived in the "Outline" for the greater dramatic impact achieved
in the novel. The secondary Conway-Stuart-Maxwell narrative,
which in the novel constitutes its worst blemish, is present in the
"Outline"; but it would appear that the original plan called for

[22] For a full description of the "Outline" see Robert Hemenway,
"Novels of Charles Brockden Brown," pp. 72-74. A transcription of the
"Outline" is given in an appendix below.

further (and presumably more satisfactory) treatment. Ludloe, prominent in "Carwin," seems also to have been designed for a more extended role.

Whatever the length of time that *Wieland* lay incubating in Brown's mind, his actual production of manuscript seems likely to have begun early in 1798. Toward the end of March, he confided that—as Dunlap relates—he was "assiduously writing Novels & in love."[23] One of these "novels" must certainly have been *Wieland,* but the first specific notation that composition of *Wieland* really *was* underway occurs in Dunlap's diary entry for 12 April 1798, in which he says that Brown had read to him "the beginning of a Novel . . . he calls . . . Wieland or the Transformation" (Dunlap, *Diary,* I, 242). Brown had been living mainly at Philadelphia, but on 3 July he went to New York, bringing with him this, the "not completed," "second novel" he had started. (The unpublished *Sky-Walk,* which was also in MS and being read by his friends, had been his first.) Continuing to work on his novel, Brown lived at the home of William Dunlap for a little over a week; constant companions were his lawyer friend, William Johnson, and the Hartford Wit, Dr. Elihu Hubbard Smith. Brown went to live with the latter when Dunlap left town for several days, and on 23 July, he delivered the "greater part" of *Wieland* to Thomas and James Swords, printers for his publisher, Hocquet Caritat.[24] The author received fifty dollars for his work and was to receive "the rest" of his money upon delivery of "the remaining sheets" (ibid.). Brown—who was also writing installments of *Arthur Mervyn,* for the *Weekly Magazine,* during part of this time—was meanwhile under pressure to keep up with a zealous printer who was giving him proof (the first gathering of twelve pages) two days after copy had been received and was to keep it coming at intervals of from one to four days. On 4 September, in a letter to Dunlap (who had retreated to Perth Amboy), Brown wrote that he had "revised the last sheet of

[23] *Diary of William Dunlap (1766-1839)* (New York: The New York Historical Society, 1930), I, 236. (Hereafter Dunlap, *Diary.*) Dunlap had seen a letter from Brown to Smith, received 28 March 1798. David Lee Clark's suggestion that *Wieland* may possibly have been begun in February is merely a guess. *Charles Brockden Brown: Pioneer Voice of America* (Durham, N.C.: Duke Univ. Press, 1952), p. 162.

[24] "Memoirs of Elihu Hubbard Smith" (MS Diary, CtY), II, 331f. Hereafter Smith, "Memoirs."

Wieland" (Dunlap, *Diary*, I, 335). The book came out on 14
September; thus, in less than two months publication had been
accomplished. Caritat advertised it for sale at a dollar "handsomely bound."[25]

From the time of Brown's July 3rd arrival in New York, he had
periodically read portions of the book to his friends Dunlap,
Smith, and Johnson, and they had commented on it and corrected some proofs for him (Dunlap, *Diary*, I, 317; Smith
"Memoirs," II, 348, et passim). Smith records on 25 July, two days
after the "greater part" had gone to the printer, that he had had
"a very long conversation" with Brown "chiefly on a suitable
catastrophe to his tale." The next day there was talk of "proposed
alterations" suggested to Brown by his friends. About ten days
later Smith writes of having read Brown's "conclusion," and Dunlap mentions having read Brown's "additions" to the novel. A
month after this, on 5 September, Brown alludes to "some ten or
twelve" pages that were added since Dunlap last saw the novel (6
August); at this stage these would presumably have been a new
conclusion (Dunlap,*Diary*, I, 317, 323, 335; Smith, "Memoirs," II,
333, 339).

There is, of course, no way of reconstructing what was specifically done or redone in the light of these suggestions, but the
statement about a "suitable catastrophe" would, from the context,
have to imply finding an appropriately compensatory resolution
to the novel, given the madness loosed in this pastoral world by
the hero's having slaughtered his family. (Intimations of some
such "destroying" had after all been present in Brown's "Outline"
for the story; hence the problem was how to wind up the novel
with respect to what had gone before.)[26] "Additions" also doubt-

[25] For more details on the printing of *Wieland,* see the Textual Essay
below. Caritat's advertisement had been received by the semi-weekly
New York *Spectator* on 15 September 1798, and it appeared in the 26
September issue of the paper (p.[2], col. 4). In the following year, Caritat
was still advertising *Wieland*—for sale at a dollar "neatly bound"—on
the last leaf of the first edition of *Ormond*.

[26] In surmising that "catastrophe" refers to the murders
themselves—in Chapter 16—Joseph Katz takes "catastrophe" altogether
too literally. He ignores the fact that, with the "greater part" of the book
already in the printer's hands, Brown was surely well beyond that chapter when the question of a suitable catastrophe (i.e., denouement) was
being considered. "Analytical Bibliography and Literary History: The
Writing and Printing of *Wieland," Proof,* 1 (1971), 12.

less refer to the concluding part of the book—possibly to the catastrophe worked out in Chapter 26, where Carwin ventrilo-quistically insinuates the crucial doubt into Wieland's mind ("Man of errors! cease to cherish thy delusion: not heaven or hell, but thy senses have misled thee to commit these acts"—p. 230), which thus prepares the way for Wieland's suicide. It seems very likely that the last "ten or twelve" page addition was the ill-fated last chapter (27), in which after burning down Clara's house and tying up loose ends regarding herself and Pleyel and Carwin, Brown has Clara ramble on about the Stuart-Maxwell imbroglio, for the ostensible reason that it too needs to be wrapped up. As if himself aware of how little relevance any of this had, Brown jams Maxwell's "evils" in with Carwin's to point the concluding moral. The oft-cited inadequacy of the Stuart-Maxwell material—initially broached in Chapter 4 regarding Louisa Conway and then forgotten—is not criticized in any now-known remarks of Brown's friends. Dunlap at least may not have seen Chapter 27 in time to advise changes (*Diary,* I, 335). In any case, having nowhere to take the already concluded action of his main plot after devoting seven pages to the wrap-up, Brown—for whatever reason—apparently decided he wanted to fill out the otherwise short last chapter and dipped back into his subplot to do so.

IV

The three most prominent motifs of *Wieland* from the point of view of "reader-interest" are: (1) a murder of his family commit-ted by a man under a religious delusion; (2) a death ascribed to spontaneous combustion; and (3) the use of ventriloquism. The circumstances of the murder were fairly well known. In 1796 there appeared within a month of each other two separate print-ings of an account of a multiple murder, originating in a de-lusion, that had occurred near Tomhanick—presently Tom-hannock—New York, in December 1781. One of these was in the *New York Weekly Magazine* of 20 and 27 July; the other (probably the one read by Brown) in the *Philadelphia Minerva* of 20 and 27 August. Brown's mention in his "Advertisement" of an "authentic case, remarkably similar to that of Wieland" which "most readers will probably recollect" clearly points toward the material in these accounts as Brown's source for the principal motif of his story. The resemblances are close: James Yates, the central figure in the Tomhanick case, and Wieland are both imbued with a conviction that they have a divine injunction to kill their families—a wife and four children in each case. Neither man, when arraigned, evinces the least sign of remorse for his acts. Both also set about attacking their sisters—unsuccessfully; both escape more than once from their places of confinement; and both are retaken and tried.[27]

The death of the elder Wieland by spontaneous combustion is a much greater challenge to the reader's credulity. Almost all discussions of the possibility of the spontaneous combustion of the human body are finally noncommittal: it is easier to accept the combustion than the spontaneous nature of its origin. Even in cases where the supposed victim was a fat person known to have been addicted to the heavy drinking of hard spirits, the reports are far from convincing. In a footnote to *Wieland* (p. 19n.) Brown partially identifies his source for the death of the old man, referring the reader to cases reported in Italian and French journals. Probably his model for the scene was the death of one Don G. Maria Bertholi as reported first in the *Literary Magazine and British Review* of 1790 and reprinted in the *American Museum* for April 1792.[28] Parallel circumstances between the deaths of Bertholi and old Wieland leave little doubt about Brown's source, especially

[27] In a footnote to *Wieland* (p. 179n.) Brown also cites as a source for his version of Theodore's malady the "Mania Mutabilis" described by Erasmus Darwin in *Zoonomia*. J. C. Hendrickson has identified the "J—Y—" of the "Account" as James Yates: "A Note on *Wieland*," *American Literature*, 8 (Nov. 1936), 305-306. Appropriate for the situation in *Wieland* is Darwin's suggestion that this "mutable madness" is marked by hallucination and what we would call schizophrenia: ". . . patients are liable to mistake . . . imaginations for realities. . . ." The "most frequent cause" of the disorder "arises from the pain of some imaginary or mistaken idea; which may be termed hallucinatio maniacalis." Among cases of auditory hallucination, he cites that of a woman who "imagined that she heard a voice say to her one day, as she was at her toilet, 'Repent, or you will be damned.'" *Zoonomia; or, the Laws of Organic Life* (London: J. Johnson, 1796), II, 356-358.

[28] "Letter respecting an Italian priest, killed by an electric commotion, the cause of which resided in his own body," *American Museum*, 11 (April 1792), 146-149. The account was taken from "an extract of a letter from mr. Joseph Battaglia," a surgeon, as given in "one of the journals of Florence." Brown had expressed considerable interest in Sir Richard Joseph Sulivan's *A View of Nature* . . . (London: T. Beckett, 1794) in which there appeared an account of an electrified man at Rouen who

the blow on the right arm and the hearing of the explosion. That spontaneous combustion could be a very popular narrative device was later exemplified by Marryat, Dickens, and Melville. In Brown's story, however, far more than mere "entertainment" or Gothic shivers was the end sought by the author; the strange mode of the death of his father—was it decreed by Heaven?—helped to unsettle the precariously poised reason of Theodore.

The third principal "popular" device used by Brown in *Wieland,* ventriloquism, is finally involved with the mental crisis which brings about the end of Theodore Wieland and his immediate family. Carwin's complicity in the matter, to whatever degree it existed, would seem to fall short of the intentionally criminal. Indeed, in his "Outline" for the novel Brown sets down one fragmentary notation of the possibility of Carwin's using his ventriloquistic skills for the sake of "surprize" and to "sport with credulity." Entertainment has in fact always been one of the chief uses of ventriloquism through the ages to the present time.

Because of its apparently successful violation of a natural law, ventriloquism has fascinated humanity for centuries, evidence of its ancient use existing in Egyptian and Hebraic archaeology. It was far from an unknown practice in Brown's time; and in 1798 it had become the subject of two articles in James Watters' popular *Weekly Magazine,* to which Brown was then a contributor. Brown could have gotten some of his background material on ventriloquism from an *Encyclopedia: or, a Dictionary of the Arts, Sciences and Miscellaneous Literature* published at Philadelphia in 1798. He himself, however, acknowledged aid from *Le Ventriloque ou L'Engastrimythe* by M. de la Chapelle (*Wieland* p. 198n.), issued in two volumes in London and Paris in 1772.

This extremely rare book constitutes a comprehensive study covering the origin, technique, uses, and abuses of ventriloquism with copious examples, which, the author assures the reader, "ont

looked as if he were on fire (II, 54). There is no specific intimation that Brown had this reference in mind with respect to the elder Wieland, but the very fact that he knew of the electrified man and did not see fit to cite him seems to suggest that the interest in self-combustion was not thought to be an entirely strange subject. Brown to Joseph Bringhurst, 20 July 1796 (letter transcribed by Kennedy, pp. 740-744). Pattee discusses the substance of Brown's footnote reference to Merille's article "Sur un effet singulier de la combustion." "Introduction," *Wieland* (New York: Harcourt Brace, 1926), pp. xxixf.

été vérifiées dans leurs sources mêmes."[29] One of the examples involves deception, partly by means of a voice heard outdoors and in effect produced "from above" by a practitioner of the art who used the threat of damnation in quest of a bride and money. In another, comic in effect, a whole community is persuaded to make belated religious "reparation" to one of their number at the time in purgatory. In this case the voice seems to come from the ceiling or high vault of the church, and it is the conjecture of Daniel E. Kennedy that this bit of deception may have provided Brown with a model for his scene in the summer-house in which Wieland hears a voice (pp. 929A-1). Chapelle, evidently a worldly-wise person with a vein of skepticism as well as a Carwin-like penchant for tales of roguery, is aware that the arts of deception are as old as the race and that in a hard world a certain amount of deception has been, and perhaps must be, practiced by men "pour conserver leur éxistence" but that abuses set in when basic need gives way to greed for the superfluous (I, xif.). And he is fain to point out apropos of voices "from above" that "la voix du Ciel n'est presque jamais que la voix d'un Scélérat ou d'un Filou" (II, 481). It is also at least possible, as Kennedy suggests, that in these words Brown may have found one of the cues for his complex portrait of Carwin (p. 930). *Le Ventriloque* also contains an episode involving the supposed unfaithfulness of a lover (the operator in this case being a 73-year-old woman [I, 162–165]), which could have inspired the scene in which Carwin deludes Pleyel. Besides concrete material that could be adapted to his purposes, Brown might well have been interested in the philosophical stance of Chapelle; germane to the motivation of Wieland, for example, is Chapelle's prefatory remark that he wishes to help clear up some of "les vues fausses" which, he says, are "bien plus que les vraies, l'Apanage de l'Humanité," among them illusion and superstition (I, xxi).

In addition, of course, to any more or less documented cases of ventriloquistically-originated "voices," Brown could have drawn

[29] "Prospectus," *Le Ventriloque* . . . (London: De L'Etanville, 1772), I, xxii. In his note on *"Biloquium,* or ventrilocution"—in Chapter 22—Brown says Chapelle (whose name he erroneously spells "Chappelle") gave "some ingenious, though unsatisfactory speculations . . . on the means by which the effects [of ventriloquism] are produced" (*Wieland*, p. 198n.).

upon a background of "heavenly" voices in classical and Scrip-
tural stories coming down through the ages, including the voice
heard by Abraham.

V

It is possible to "derive" *Wieland* in part from Brown's reading
or "explain" it on the basis of his literary theory. Yet any true work
of art transcends its specifiable sources. Finally, no amount of
explanation—no citing of books, historical background, family
papers, documents of whatever sort—can prepare the reader
fully to understand the special phenomenon which is Brockden
Brown's *Wieland*. It does not even closely resemble the other
novels of Brown. Despite its oblique affinity with recognized
literary genres of the day—the Gothic, the Richardsonian, the
novel of purpose, etc.—it is a work sui generis. Every reader of
Wieland senses the presence of another "source," which is the
unique psyche or personality of the author. There are qualities,
depths, in *Wieland* that speak eloquently, if not clearly, of the
turbulence of the mind of the lonely author. Whether defensibly
or not, critics are bound to read an author's thoughts and mental
states in "writings" of his that are not avowedly autobiographical.
Moving in Brown's troubled psyche were shreds of universal
elements at least as old as the Greek myths and the earliest
recorded writers—Oedipus, Orestes, and the almost legendary
Sappho—merging with private and largely suppressed tokens of
conflict in his own life: in relationship to family, religion, sex,
profession. The book came partly out of his external experience
(including reading), but it must also have been derived in part
from his unconscious—richly operative in Clara's introspective
sensibility—and indeed from the collective unconscious itself. It
is full of projections of wishes unrealized, aggressions thwarted,
symptoms of guilt unexpiated. At times *Wieland* seems more like
an exposure of the author's unconscious than a reasoned attempt
to communicate with the reader logically. To understand and
assess accurately these internal factors is impossible, but their
force is felt in the pressures they create for author and reader.
Partial escape from the pressures for Brown came through the
exercise of his art.

Escape for the reader—to whom Brown has transferred much of the pressure—is not easy. Once the narrative is well begun, there is no exit for the reader from the inferno that engulfs the Wieland family. In Brown's novels, particularly *Wieland,* a special relationship exists between author and reader. The reader is constantly aware of being under tensions. If, on his own showing, Brown wrote his books (partly no doubt as unconscious self-therapy) under a species of compulsion, he seems to have set about making sure that the reader would experience a similar compulsion. Brown does not wish to *share* with the reader so much as to *dominate* or take possession of him. He, like Poe, is extremely jealous of the reader's attention; and, like Poe, he prevails partly by a species of spell or enchantment established through his sometimes incantatory style. What he wishes to convey is not so much idea as mood or in Henry James's phrase, "atmosphere of mind." To this end he imperiously demands total response. And, in *Wieland* at least, he gets it: reading Brown is an act of surrender. And while under this spell most readers (Shelley was among them) do not worry about "defects" in the story. They have been through a memorable, sometimes terrifying, experience.

And yet story there is—and a good one. Not only does it have power but, leaving out of account the ill-born Conway-Stuart-Maxwell plot, it has unity and order. Most of the time it has pace and proportion as well. A relatively short book, it is felt to be precisely the right length: packed with horror and unrelieved by humor, it could scarcely be endured longer. It also has a fair measure of economy in execution. In retrospect the reader feels that the right amount of space (two chapters) has been devoted to the period up to and including the demise of the elder Wieland. The problem of the mounting malaise and final psychosis of Theodore is also given the optimum amount of attention, with the climax coming, suitably, at about three-fifths of the way through the novel. The conclusion to the story (newly added by Brown at the end of his period of composition) though marred by unwise emphasis on the secondary plot, none the less provides a kind of catharsis and returns the story to Clara, who, of all the characters, has suffered longest. It is as if some cosmic, cataclysmic storm had moved through the fragile world of the Wielands, leaving almost complete wreckage in its wake, with only Clara surviving to tell of it and, as well as she can, recover from those terrors which had almost totally destroyed her physically and psychologically.

For example, when Clara sees the corpse of Catharine on the bed, she is shocked to consider: "How will a spectacle like this be endured by Wieland?" not knowing that it was Wieland who had perpetrated the horror. This is one of the most poignant moments in the book: the reader must now wonder how the revelation of who killed Catharine will be "endured" by Clara. The dramatic irony is sustained, and increased, a page or two later when Wieland comes: "I supposed him unacquainted with the fate of his wife, and his appearance confirmed this persuasion." How much more must Clara now bear? The irony is deepened when, aware that it would be impossible to "prolong his ignorance" of the facts, Clara realizes the only thing in effect to do is to break the news without "abruptness," so that Wieland will not be affected by it to the point of "madness." Theodore, now evincing in his countenance such a "hurricane" of passion as Clara has never witnessed, soon makes it obvious that it was he himself who, having been admitted to "the councils of [his] Maker," had been the author of this terrible deed. Thereupon it behooves Clara to seek a strategy whereby to escape further extensions of the "decree" being executed by her demented brother; but even this must be deferred, for again by intuitive skill on Brown's part, the episode is interrupted by Mr. Hallet's arrival. A further area of anguish is opened by her instinctive guess (prompted by Mr. Hallet's evasive manner) regarding the children. Just as Ross in talking to Macduff tells him that his children are well, so Mr. Hallet assures Clara: "They are well . . . they are perfectly safe." Ultimately the irony vanishes, leaving Clara broken by the actual news of the death of the children. Now, numbed by almost unendurable grief, she can only, like Macduff, ask: "Dead! . . . what, all?" No manual of Scottish rhetoric or rubric of Aristotle could have taught Brown how to make more out of the grisly material in this ironic sequence than he did (pp. 151–157). He may not always have known how to *plan* narrative sequences, but he had an almost instinctive knowledge of how to seize opportunities that lay in his path.

It is one of the many signs of the ambivalence of Brockden Brown's mind that readers of *Wieland* are unable to make up their minds as to who is the central character in the novel. Brown himself in his "Advertisement" to the reader refers to Carwin as the "principal person" of the novel—a distinction Carwin may well be entitled to, considering his taxing role in the action. Certainly he is a catalyst. As a character, however, Carwin is a sack of inconsistencies and contradictions that never can be reconciled with each other. On his arrival at Clara's home she finds him irresistibly attractive, sleazy clothes, "awkward" gait, and all. With his pointed face he is perhaps not conventionally handsome, but in some indefinable way he fascinates her. When he arrives, as a wayfaring stranger, and asks for a cup of cold water "for charity's sweet sake," he has the air of a Christ-like figure in an ancient parable. Clara weeps. Largely, one guesses, it is his voice that accounts for the magnetism he exerts. At all events Clara is instantly transformed to the status of a psychological thrall—much after the manner of a female bird reduced to will-lessness by the plumage of a male bird—and she sits for hours contemplating the sketch she had immediately made of him. Carwin is a danger to Clara philosophically also, for the exercise of his gift for ventriloquism brings to her sensory experiences that do not square with the empirical data on which she customarily relies; she is forced to reckon with unsettling ideas of an occult world which could imperil her stability as a disciple of "reason."[30] To Clara, Carwin is at first a charming, persuasive, but formidable figure.

On the other hand, as time goes on, Carwin is sometimes seen to be a slack, seedy, unsavory, skulking vagrant-adventurer, with a (perhaps symbolic) tetter on his chin, who pursues no respectable agenda in the story. He makes love to a girl of a low threshold of purity. His assumed Faustian search for knowledge withers away and is replaced by a low-grade itch for spying on people and enjoying their discomfiture. He is also a liar: he submits that his "only crime [is] curiosity," and yet he plays havoc with the innocent Pleyel's peace of mind for no good reason, and he looked forward to the result as the "sweetest triumph I had ever enjoyed" (pp. 205f., 210). On the other hand he may really have started his

---

[30] For a discussion of this aspect of Clara's experience, see Donald Ringe, *Charles Brockden Brown* (New York: Twayne Publishers, 1966), pp. 37-38, et passim.

program of ventriloquistic experiments partly for the fun of it; and it seems finally impossible to ascribe to him the character of criminal. Although the text is ambiguous, it is almost certain that he did not issue the fatal command to Wieland.[31] Most important of all, for *Wieland,* is the fact that Carwin provides a "popular" type of interest in a book heavy with philosophical overtones. The general reader was bound to be interested in ventriloquism, a little-understood phenomenon, based on a confusion of the senses of sight and sound, vested with a faint aura of "science," and, as Brown said, "approach[ing] . . . the nature of miracles." Constantly in and out of the action as he was, Carwin may have been overexposed by Brown (as Theodore was perhaps under-exposed) but fictionally he pays his way handsomely.

All the major characters in *Wieland* are sooner or later psychologically disturbed. There is no raisonneur in this novel; no character in whom one can find a norm by which to measure the behavior of the others. Even Pleyel, the gay, the urbane, the "reasonable" Pleyel, is too readily brought to harbor suspicions regarding the chastity of Clara. Clara herself, as both participant in the action and the narrator of the whole story, is a highly mixed character. With Wieland blood in her, she may be expected to be vulnerable to nervous disturbance. There was moreover a case of delusion followed by suicide on her mother's side (pp. 178f.). Yet her sad but cool prologue to the story betokens a degree at least of underlying stability which is confirmed at the end, when, after having been exposed to almost ineffable terrors, she is able to bring the story to a calm conclusion.

As a Gothic heroine she is subjected to most of the standard ploys. As an "intellectual woman" she is capable of discussing contemporary theories of psychology: can ideas exist in the mind independently of sensory experience? As a person basically emotional she is prone to confusion and self-doubt under stress: "My opinions," she says, "were the sport of eternal change" (p. 180). As a lover she is erratic. Inevitably she invites Freudian interpre-

---

[31] Convincing evidence comes from Clara, who often appears to be the author's spokesman, when after she sees how "petrified" Carwin looks upon hearing from her the full catalogue of horror visited upon the Wieland family, she adds: "No words were requisite to prove him guilt-less of these enormities" (p. 197). See also pp. 219 and 239.

tations of some of her behavior. Her almost instantaneous psychological surrender to Carwin on his arrival at Mettingen is abnormal, as is her prolonged attentiveness to her sketch of him, a symptom of abnormality used later by Poe in his story "Berenice." It seems likely, especially from her dream in which she sees that it is her brother who is trying to urge her into the abyss, that she is possessed by latent incestuous longings for him. The brother is also inclined to love Clara "with a passion more than fraternal" (p. 185).[32] Clara is a distrait and confused person. How disturbed she was is suggested in the uniquely terrifying nightmare she experiences at the climax of her troubles. It is starkly recorded by Brown. Except for brief glimpses of Wieland, Pleyel, and Carwin, she is left completely alone, "rolled round in earth's diurnal course," with the four elements—earth, air, fire, water—added to only by indications of light and dark, height and depth:

> Sometimes I was swallowed up by whirlpools, or caught up in the air by half-seen and gigantic forms, and thrown upon pointed rocks, or cast among the billows. Sometimes gleams of light were shot into a dark abyss, on the verge of which I was standing, and enabled me to discover, for a moment, its enormous depth and hideous precipices. Anon, I was transported to some ridge of Ætna, and made a terrified spectator of its fiery torrents and its pillars of smoke (p. 236).

Considering how much Clara is called upon to endure, one does not wonder at her "alibi" for the incoherence of her story: "My narrative may be invaded by inaccuracy and confusion.... What but ambiguities, abruptnesses, and dark transitions, can be expected from the historian who is, at the same time, the sufferer of these disasters?" (p. 147).

[32] Chapter 9. It would seem to be an anomaly that Brown, an almost prudish person by most tokens, should have made so much comment, in his publications, on sexual freedom and sexual aberrations, including, in *Stephen Calvert,* a reference to a relationship between man and wife in which the husband exhibits "propensities . . . that have not a name which [the wife] can utter" (*Life,* II, 400). For comment on Brown's "obsession with the destructive aspects of the brother-sister relationship," see Leslie Fiedler, *Love and Death in the American Novel* (New York: World Publishing Co., 1962), pp. 135-136.

VI

Not only in her apology for incoherence does Clara seem to have been a "voice" for her author but also elsewhere in the book, notably in the memorable words set down in the second and third paragraphs of the opening chapter:

> My state is not destitute of tranquillity. The sentiment that dictates my feelings is not hope. Futurity has no power over my thoughts. To all that is to come I am perfectly indifferent. With regard to myself, I have nothing more to fear. Fate has done its worst. Henceforth, I am callous to misfortune.
>
> I address no supplication to the Deity. The power that governs the course of human affairs has chosen his path. The decree that ascertained the condition of my life, admits of no recal. No doubt it squares with the maxims of eternal equity. That is neither to be questioned nor denied by me. It suffices that the past is exempt from mutation. The storm that tore up our happiness, and changed into dreariness and desert the blooming scene of our existence, is lulled into grim repose; but not until the victim was transfixed and mangled; till every obstacle was dissipated by its rage; till every remnant of good was wrested from our grasp and exterminated (pp. 5–6).

These words, in their expression as impressive as any in the entire novel, outline a mode of thinking that belongs to Brown, and they establish a tone for the entire narrative. In effect they suggest the real "moral" underlying *Wieland*. The religio-philosophical rationale of *Wieland* is essentially a deistic one modified by "fate." It is apparent in the eloquent words of Clara's opening remarks that she has come finally to a detached realization that human actions cannot be reconciled with the tenets of either reason or religion. She counts not on religion but on time to relieve her condition: "Time will obliterate the deepest impressions. Grief the most vehement and hopeless, will gradually decay and wear itself out" (p. 234).

To many readers the opening of the book must have seemed a cheerless one. True, the very first paragraph carries standard moral counsel: shun the practice of deception and labor to acquire "discipline." These admonitions carry truth (and truth for Brown) but not the whole truth. They coexist with Brown's more

333

sober thoughts, which here have a tone of sad stoicism. The assent to what is designed by decree of fate—"No doubt it squares with the maxims of eternal equity"—is delivered with a quiet but devastating irony that suggests how close at times Brown came to pessimism. There is here, however, the further suggestion that one *must* accept, *must* endure: Brown was no nihilist. Philosophical austerity is relaxed, moreover, in the following paragraph, in which Clara is permitted a plaintive human query as to why or how she deserved to be placed on this "dreadful eminence." Once, at the height of her agony, she does appeal to the "righteous Judge." Nevertheless this story is a tragedy. From beginning to end, a sense of doom hovers over it which is little relieved by the perfunctory (and essentially untrue) moralizing provided by Clara on the final page of the novel. In *Wieland* the moral and the action are really identical with each other: no interpretation is needful. There is no easy reconciliation here, no redemption, no invocation of a Savior, no final salvation, no compensation in "another world." This is not a pitiless book, but it is a comfortless one. In tone it frequently resembles Hawthorne's *The Scarlet Letter*.

Clearly, the clue to the undeniable power and the unforgettable quality of *Wieland* lies not in its "purpose" or its characterization or popular story devices (ventriloquism, etc.) but in its tone and delivery. Although the story is laid in mid-eighteenth century Pennsylvania, its precise chronology and geography become finally almost irrelevant. *Wieland* has the depth and resonance of ancient tragedy, or a legend crudely wrought in stone. In its way it seems as dateless as Ozymandias. The story does not give the impression of having been fabricated but discovered—as if it were not written or even reported by Brown but had always existed—or had been come upon in some fragment of old parchment or scroll. Its almost anonymous mode of presentation supports this feeling. Despite an occasional Latinized sentence or stylistic tag that recalls Brown's early initiation in Augustan idiom, its language is for the most part simple, professionally naïve, in many ways comparable to a primitive style in painting. Mostly Brown eschews gaudy diction and elaborate metaphor. (One is surprised, in "Carwin," to come upon the phrase "the soft artillery of tears and prayers" [p. 292].) He wishes his discourse to be practical rather than ornamented. Capable of writing in a flowing style, he often prefers shorter sentences, mistakenly referred to by many critics as "staccato," which deliver power in bolts of energy coming from no one can say where. There is in the book an air of detachment, of remoteness. Brown does not seem to be present as author, or interpreter, still less as consoler, and the reader is left alone to make what he can of the phantasmagoric pageantry that moves before his eyes.

But the book is all the reader needs. Just as *Wieland* seems to be of ageless origin, it also has an air of permanence. It possesses a certain "hardness" (a quality in writing to which T. S. Eliot referred, in a discussion of Hawthorne, as one of the signs of high art)[33] and weight. Its surface is hard and its center is solid. If the book does not possess text-book coherence, it possesses cohesion: at such high temperatures were its materials compacted and molded by the author. It has what Poe regarded as essential to the artist, namely, "binding force." It also finally impresses the reader by its unity—nothing in excess, nothing needful omitted or (except for the decrees of fate) unexplained. There are no matters to ponder after the story has ended, no ethical arguments to engage in. Brown has told all that he could. Unity and economy are also secured by the fact that all the materials have been completely used (omitting the subplot); there has been complete combustion of materials assembled, as there was to be in another famous story of the extinction of a family, Poe's "The Fall of the House of Usher." Nothing remains of the Wieland family except for the wraith-like Clara, granted survival so that she may be the teller of the tale.

VII

Exactly when Brown determined to make Carwin the subject of a self-contained study cannot be known, but some time before 8 August 1798, he had written a part of what ultimately became "Memoirs of Carwin the Biloquist." On that date Elihu Hubbard Smith entered in his diary: "Read Brown's 'Carwin,' as far as he has written it" ("Memoirs," II, 340). During the next few weeks Brown made additions to the narrative—likewise read by Smith—but on 4 September he wrote to Dunlap of having set

[33] What Eliot saw in Hawthorne was "the firmness, the true coldness, the hard coldness of the genuine artist." F. O. Matthiessen, *American Renaissance* (New York: Oxford Univ. Press, 1941), p. 157.

aside the project: "I have written something of the history of Carwin which I will send. I have desisted for the present from the prosecution of this plan . . ." (Dunlap, *Diary,* I, 335).[34] "Carwin" was not published until Brown placed it in his *Literary Magazine, and American Register.* It ran for a total of ten installments appearing in the numbers for November and December 1803, January to July inclusive (omitting June) 1804, and then in February and March 1805. For the gap between July 1804 and February 1805 Brown felt obliged to give some explanation in the February issue:

> The writer of the Memoirs of Carwin was influenced to discontinue the publication of that work from a persuasion that the narrative was of too grave and argumentative a cast to be generally amusing. He has, however, received so many and such urgent intreaties to resume the story that he should not be justified in suppressing it any longer. Hereafter it will be continued with regularity.[35]

"Carwin" was not, however, "continued with regularity" and indeed was not resumed at all following the March number. Actually Brown had run out of material some time before. To his brother-in-law John Blair Linn he had written on 4 July 1804: "The manuscript of Carwin is exhausted, and it was impossible to piece the thread and continue it in due season for that number [the omitted June number]" (*Life,* II, 111). Nevertheless he apparently did manage to "piece together" *some* further Carwin materials; and the inference must be that what appeared of the work in the July 1804 issue and the February and March 1805 issues of the *Literary Magazine* represents a fresh extension of the narrative begun in the summer of 1798.[36]

[34] The reason Brown gave for desisting was that he was becoming involved with "Stephen Calvert." Smith records—also on September 4—having "read the pages of Brown's continuation to his 'Carwin,' [and] of his new-begun 'Stephen Calvert' . . ." ("Memoirs," II, 354).

[35] "Notes from the Editor," *Literary Magazine,* 3 (Feb. 1805), 160.

[36] With the May installment Brown must have put in print all that he had written of "Carwin" to that time; if he had had more on hand, it is scarcely likely that, as editor, he would have allowed his own story to have been crowded out of the next issue by other matter. He did manage the July installment in spite of having had to do just about the whole of the June and July numbers out of his own head; and he did of course clearly

The first reprinting of "Carwin" was posthumous—with minor changes—in Dunlap's *Life* (II, 200–263). Seven years after Dunlap's reprint, "Carwin" received a new printing in a three-volume collection of Brown's writings published by Henry Colburn at London in 1822: *Carwin the Biloquist and Other American Tales and Pieces,* the other units being "Stephen Calvert," "Jessica," and "The Scribbler." In Colburn's edition more numerous changes were made and the story was divided into five chapters. After this 1822 printing there were no editions of "Carwin" until the appearance of F. L. Pattee's in 1926.

There remain a number of "unknowns" regarding the composition and purpose of "Carwin." It is clear, however, that Brown intended it as a sequel or an interpolated addition to *Wieland.* In any event, it probably should not—as has been suggested—be read as a prologue (Clark, p. 170).

The comparative unavailability of the text of "Carwin" in bound-volume form accounts in part for the fact that until recently little has been written about the work. Actually, although it suffers from dispersion and incompleteness, as well as a number of Brown's customary gaffes (a reference to "Aristotle's" *Republic,* for one), it is potentially a good story, and Carwin, as character, has the curiosity—and ingenuity—of a Bildungsroman hero. First—with reference to story—the primary Ludloe-Carwin relationship yields mystery and strong suspense: Ludloe delays the full disclosure of his plans for Carwin, and Carwin nurses the secret of his ventriloquistic skill (despite having been darkly warned to be candid) while Ludloe's suspicions regarding his new pupil mount rapidly. Secondly, narrative excitement of a good old-fashioned (almost picaresque) sort is promised, and, in

signal his intention to go on with the account after July by ending that installment with the sentence, "You shall judge whether I was right in my conjectures" (p. 297). With respect to the July installment's having been freshly written, one notes that it contains some filling-in and an attempt to step up the pace of action, which is characteristic of a resumption after the previous material has been looked over and added to—as with Ludloe's proposing that Carwin consider a marriage to Mrs. Benington, his suggesting how a relationship with her may be set up, the recall of Carwin's having met her in Spain and the incident of his having saved her from robbers, and his being left alone in Ludloe's library at the end—where he may come upon forbidden manuscripts—as he awaits word that Mrs. Benington is well enough to receive him.

places, partly achieved: early in the narrative there is the scene of Carwin's attempt to prey on his father's superstitious nature by "whispering at his pillow" in his dead mother's voice, only to be foiled by the barn's being set aflame by lightning; and later on Carwin gets involved in an assault by robbers and makes a thrilling "save" of Mrs. Benington, the intended victim. (Other exciting matter, such as allegations of "enormous and complicated crimes," of stealing, even murder, and of his having escaped from an Irish prison had already been associated with him in *Wieland.*) Thirdly, an appeal to the philosophical interest of the reader is provided by (1) subtle probing of the theme of moral responsibility and (2) talk of "a scheme of Utopian felicity, where the empire of reason should supplant that of force" to be established on an unknown island in the Pacific by highminded but ruthless-when-necessary members of a secret society (strongly suggestive of the subversive Illuminati).[37] In addition there is intrigue and sex-interest: although specific detail is not forthcoming, it may be assumed that Carwin's self-confessed "voluptuousness" (p. 275) betokens sexual intimacies whether in Spain or elsewhere.

In such a short narrative as "Carwin" the characters have scarcely enough time to establish themselves significantly. Ludloe, however, is a striking portrait. He is learned, brilliant, wealthy, masterful in deportment, worldly-wise, and pretty much conscienceless—just the sort of person to fascinate the young colonial, Carwin, lately dug up from the fastnesses of frontier Pennsylvania. "It would not be easy," says Carwin, "to paint the delight which I experienced in this man's society" (p. 265). Between Ludloe and Carwin there is built a relationship of patron to protege as similar to that between Falkland and Caleb Williams in Godwin's novel as any relationship in Brown except possibly the Welbeck-Mervyn relationship. Ambiguity sets in here also, for the lad by degrees senses something conceivably sinister in the behavior of his patron. Much interest attaches also to Carwin himself, a different person, at least in the beginning, from the somewhat objectionable character already encountered in *Wieland.* He is morally less repugnant here—and indeed he possesses a certain charm in his emergence from the innocence and

[37] See Lillie Deming Loshe, *The Early American Novel* (New York: Columbia Univ. Press, 1907), pp. 41-43.

wonder of boyhood. Later he proves his attraction as a potential lover. As time goes on, he begins to acquire a facility in snooping and in "dissimulation"—though it could be argued that such defensive measures are only natural when one is conscious of being manipulated for vague but possibly malign purposes, an excuse which Carwin did not have in Mettingen, where he was generously and candidly received. On the whole Carwin comes off well in these Memoirs and one feels that Brown is well disposed toward him, possibly intent on adjusting the mottled image he had given him in *Wieland*. Here Carwin's ventriloquistic gift causes confusion and embarrassment but no disaster; and so far from being guilty of the murder for which he is sought, he is seen in the altruistic role of rescuing Mrs. Benington from criminals.

Haste and inattention by Brown probably account for the apparent contradictions and considerable obscurity that exist in the "Carwin"–*Wieland* narrative. Characteristically Brown fails to provide a consistent point of view and a definite time-scheme. Carwin is once referred to as "an Englishman by birth" (p. 69) and twice as a "native" American (pp. 199, 277). The hypothesis of his being English, however, reaches the reader through Clara's speculations, which are themselves based on Pleyel's admittedly imperfect knowledge of Carwin and his movements during Carwin's three-year sojourn in Spain. His American birth is vouched for by Carwin himself at a time when he has no motive for concealing facts (p. 277). Never fully brought into focus is the detailed record of Carwin's actions in Spain. Nor is the reader of *Wieland* and "Carwin" ever fully apprised of the supposedly exciting action (which, according to newspaper report, led to his conviction and incarceration for murder and robbery) during the approximately three-year interval between his return to Ireland (p. 278) and the beginning of his adventures in Mettingen.[38]

---

[38] Dates for the action overall are never clearly fixed. However, the central events of the novel may well be assigned to the mid 1760's—perhaps 1766, at least not much later than that. This date accords with allusions to several historical events. (1) In his "Advertisement" to *Wieland*, Brown states that the "events" of his novel "took place between the conclusion of the French and the beginning of the revolutionary war." The one ended in 1763 and the other began in 1776. (2) In "Carwin" he says "the incidents of this narrative are supposed to have taken place before the voyages of Bougainville and Cook" (p.

Incomplete as it is, "Carwin" commands the respect of the reader by reason of its well-ordered prose, which has a certain classic repose, especially in the opening chapter detailing the boyhood experiences of Carwin. The boy's relationships with his family, especially his hallucination-prone father, who distrusts all knowledge except the most niggardly minimum needed for daily living, and his aunt, who withholds expected largesse, are treated in a relaxed but vivid manner suggesting the opening of a popular Bildungsroman. Unfortunately the leisurely, controlled account of Carwin's Lehrejahren is destined to be interrupted by inherently exciting but poorly-marshalled fictional elements which finally bring his history to a chaotic and bewildering end, with the Ludloe-Carwin relationship still unresolved. The "sequel" obviously is itself in need of a sequel.

VIII

Not long after the publication of *Wieland,* Brown reported with mixed surprise and pride: "I find to be the writer of Wieland and Ormond is a greater recommendation than I ever imagined it would be" (*Life,* II, 99). It was a mood of self-congratulation not destined for long duration: so far as we know there was not a new edition of *Wieland* in Brown's life-time (see p. 349). Nevertheless the register of encomia bestowed on *Wieland* during the 170 odd years since its first appearance in 1798 has been substantial enough to have given its author (could he have known of his accumulating renown) considerable satisfaction. The record has been one marked not by steadiness but by spurt and decline, sometimes decline to the point of apparent extinction. Yet *Wieland* has proved to be a novel of extraordinary tenacity. In general it has been held in high esteem for three virtues of great importance to a writer seeking permanent fame: (1) its overall originality, (2) the "unforgettable" images found in its pages, and

299n.). Those of the former took place between 1766 and 1769, those of the latter between 1768 and 1779. (3) In "Carwin" critical reference is made to the Jesuit colonization experiments in Paraguay; they "had furnished an example of all the errors and excellencies of such a [Utopian] scheme" (p. 279). The Jesuits were expelled in 1767; in the preceding year the reasons for their impending failure would have been a relevant topic of discussion.

(3) its philosophical and/or psychological weight. It has had some twenty editions or re-issues in the nineteenth century, and has had four in the twentieth century. Four of its appearances were in collected editions printed, respectively, in 1827, 1857, 1859, and 1887. There have been an uncounted but probably not very large number of translations into foreign languages.

The record of response to *Wieland* begins about two months after its publication. The review of *Wieland* that appeared in the New York *Spectator* for 10 November 1798 is of consequence mainly because it is the first review of the first novel published by Brown. Evidently the work of a junior or amateur writer, it reveals an imperfect knowledge of the book—referring to Wieland's having murdered "friends" as well as family—and little insight into Wieland's illness: to the reviewer he is a brute and "worse than savage." Perhaps prophetically the reviewer makes much of the role of Carwin, a character he must both admire and detest. In the novel he finds enough "excellencies and beauties" to make him think it absurd for readers to spend their time on "imported *trash* of other countries" when they might be exhibiting their "patriotism" by supporting American art.[39]

Brown was shrewd enough to perceive that whatever might be said on behalf of his book in the press would not of itself ensure a lasting success. He was aware that "the utmost that any American can look for, in his native country, is to be re-imbursed" for his work, and, he added, "the salelibility [sic] of [his own] works will much depend upon their popularity in England."[40] The first reception he was accorded there was not reassuring, however, for the early notices proved to be "almost all unfavorable."[41] One of the more severe reviewers of the 1811 edition denounced *Wieland* as "most improbable and horrid."[42] But the 1811 London

[39] "Wieland; or The Transformation," New York *Spectator*, 10 Nov. 1798, p. [4], cols. 2-3.

[40] Brown to James Brown, April 1800 (*Life*, II, 100).

[41] William B. Cairns, *British Criticism of American Writings, 1783-1815*, Univ. of Wisconsin Studies in Lang. and Lit., No. 1 (Madison: Univ. of Wisconsin Press, 1918), pp. 91, 92.

[42] The denunciation, a one-sentence "review" in the *Gentleman's Magazine* (81 [April 1811], 364), is counterbalanced by the lengthy and laudatory review in the *Critical Review: Wieland* "possesses strong and powerful claims to attention" (22 [Feb. 1811], 144-163). In general, however, Brown's novels were not very well received in England. *Ormond*, for example, was said to contain "much disgusting and perni-

edition which seems to have been little noticed at home may
nevertheless have helped Brown a little in England. For by 1815
Shelley had read Brown, to his intense pleasure and profit. On
the testimony of Thomas Love Peacock, Brown's novels were
among the books "which took the deepest root in his mind . . . and
nothing so blended itself with the structure of his interior mind as
the creations of Brown."[43] On the lighter side, Shelley was en-
chanted by the summer-house in *Wieland:* everyone, he thought,
should have one! Mary Shelley must also have read *Wieland* at
about this time, for her *Frankenstein,* which was almost surely
influenced by *Wieland,* appeared in 1818.[44] Still another Romantic poet was impressed by *Wieland:* Keats, who having been urged
by Hazlitt to read Brown, testified that to him *Wieland* was a "very
powerful" book.[45] A different kind of response came from the
novelist Scott, who deplored the fact that Brown's "wonderful
powers" had not been expended on a more "wholesome" species
of writing.[46] Novelist William Godwin, however, an early influence on Brown, proved to be also an admirer of his quondam
pupil, referring to him in the preface to *Mandeville* (1817) as "a
person certainly of distinguished genius," and claiming *Wieland*

cious nonsense" (*Anti-Jacobin Review,* 6 [Aug. 1800], 451). Also strongly
condemnatory of *Wieland* were the reviews in the *Lady's Monthly Museum*
(9[Dec. 1810], 338-339) and the *Monthly Review* (64 [Jan. 1811], 96). The
review in the *British Critic and Quarterly Theological Review* was mixed to
lukewarm (37 [Jan. 1811], 70). For a brief summation of early British
reviews of Brown's novels, see William S. Ward, "Charles Brockden
Brown, His Contemporary British Reviewers, and Two Minor Bibliographical Problems," *PBSA,* 65 (Fourth Quarter, 1971), 401, n. 5. Looking back in praise (in 1820), one critic supposed that the reason for
Brown's poor reception in England was that his books had the ill fortune
"to issue from one of the common reservoirs of sentimental trash
[William Lane's Minerva Press], and, consequently . . . to share in the
general contempt attached to those poor productions . . ." "On the
Writings of Charles Brown, the American Novelist," *New Monthly
Magazine and Universal Register,* 14 (Dec. 1820), 609.

[43] *Peacock's Memoirs of Shelley with Shelley's Letters to Peacock,* ed. H. F. B.
Brett-Smith (London: Henry Frowde, 1909), pp. 36-37.

[44] F. C. Prescott, *"Wieland* and *Frankenstein,"American Literature,* 2 (May
1930), 172-173.

[45] *The Letters of John Keats,* ed. Maurice Buxton Forman, 2nd ed.
(London: Oxford Univ. Press, 1935), p. 390.

[46] S. G. Goodrich, *Recollections of a Lifetime* . . . (New York: Miller,
Orton and Co.: 1857), II, 203.

as the source which first led him "to look with . . . favour upon [his] subject" of a "sleep-walking principal personage."[47]

In America too *Wieland* was slowly acquiring credit, perhaps surprisingly, after its relatively poor success in the decade and a half following its birth. In 1819 E. T. Channing, in a long review of Dunlap's *Life,* refers to Brown in mixed but generally favorable terms, testifying, like so many readers to come, to Brown's peculiar power over the reader: "[n]o reader," he thought, "would leave Wieland unfinished" and he ascribes to it a quality of "terrible" "fascination."[48] In a similar eulogy appearing the next year another critic joins the chant of the somehow-captivated readers of *Wieland* avowing that "[t]here are scenes in Wieland which he that has read them . . . once, can never forget."[49] It was perhaps a compliment to Brown that he was even mentioned in William H. Gardiner's now famous review of Cooper's *The Spy.* Of *Edgar Huntly* and *Wieland,* Gardiner says that both books are in his opinion insufficiently "American." Yet, with a shrewd insight, he testifies also to one of the sources of Brown's psychological power in both novels: "So far from exhibiting any thing of our native character and manners, [the] agents are not beings of this world" but "dark monsters of the imagination, which the will of the master may conjure up with an equal horror in the shadows of an American forest, or amidst the gloom of long galleries and vaulted aisles."[50] The publication of Dunlap's biography of Brown in London by Colburn in 1822 naturally drew comments from the British press, by now alerted to Brown's power. Most of the notices were general and favorable—finally too favorable in the opinion of John Neal, the eccentric American novelist and critic.[51] Nevertheless the power of Brown—"undeniably, the most original writer, that America has produced"—Neal could never wholly escape, and in 1824 he came out with the shrewdly

[47] *Mandeville: A Tale of the Seventeenth Century in England* (Edinburgh: Archibald Constable and Co., 1817), I, x, ix.

[48] "The Life of Charles Brockden Brown . . ." *North American Review,* 9 (June 1819), 64.

[49] "On the Writings of Charles Brockden Brown and Washington Irving," *Blackwood's Edinburgh Magazine,* 6 (Feb. 1820), 555.

[50] *North American Review,* 15 (July 1822), 281.

[51] John Neal, *American Writers: A Series of Papers Contributed to Blackwood's Magazine (1824-1825),* ed. Fred Lewis Pattee (Durham, N.C.: Duke Univ. Press, 1937), p. 61.

perceptive comment: "Nobody ever remembered the words of Charles Brockden Brown; nobody ever thought of the arrangement; yet nobody ever forgot what they conveyed."[52]

Despite scattered encomia through the early years of the century, Brown's reputation was greatly in need of the new growth it attained after the first of his collected editions was brought out at Boston in 1827 by the enterprising publisher S. G. Goodrich (Peter Parley). Nor could Brown have hoped for a more discerning report than the long review by R. H. Dana in *The United States Review and Literary Gazette* for August 1827. What deeply impressed Dana was Brown's management of characters who "live, and act, and perish, as if they were the slaves of supernatural powers." He was impressed too by the frightening impersonality, the objectivity, of his books, especially *Wieland:* "Brown's fatal power is unsparing, and never stops; his griefs and sufferings are not of that kind which draws tears and softens the heart; it wears out the heart and takes away the strength of our spirits, so that we lie helpless under it."[53] At about the same time, *Wieland* was accorded an accolade from the most celebrated American novelist of the period, namely, James Fenimore Cooper, who, after having some years before made game of portions of *Edgar Huntly,* now (in 1828) made handsome restitution:

> I remember to have read one of his books (Wieland) when a boy, and I take it to be a never-failing evidence of genius, that, amid a thousand similar pictures which have succeeded, the images it has left, still stand distinct and prominent in my recollection.[54]

The 1840's were a decade rich in promise for the permanence of *Wieland's* modest fame. In this period four reprints of *Wieland* appeared. Edgar Allan Poe, who was a kind of literary cousin

---

[52] Ibid., pp. 68, 57.

[53] "The novels of Charles Brockden Brown . . . ," 2 (Aug. 1827), p. 324. Other reviews of the edition include those in the *Boston Lyceum* for June 1827, and in the *American Quarterly Review* of December 1830, the latter citing *Wieland* as a story "wonderfully original" and written with "terrible intensity" (8, 322).

[54] *Notions of the Americans; Picked Up by a Travelling Bachelor* (1828; facsimile rpt. New York: Frederick Ungar Publishing Co., 1963), II, 111. Cooper had commented on *Edgar Huntly* in his original preface (1821) to *The Spy.*

once removed of Brown's and who was certainly influenced by him,[55] bracketed Brown and Hawthorne as among the best writers of fiction in America.[56] Among other literary kin of Brown was surely Hawthorne himself, who was an admirer of *Arthur Mervyn* and *Wieland*. That Brown, now fifty years before the public, was moving into a new phase of his reputation is suggested by the phrasing of Hawthorne's eulogy in *Mosses from an Old Manse* (1846): "no American writer enjoys a more classic reputation on this side of the water."[57] In 1843 one of the most popular writers of the time, George Lippard, dedicated his *Quaker City* to Brown. It was Whittier, however, who in 1848 paid Brown one of the most glowing compliments of all. Deeply moved by *Wieland,* he commented on the scene in which Wieland slays his wife and children:

> In the entire range of English literature there is no more thrilling passage than that which describes the execution of this [scene]. . . . The masters of the old Greek tragedy have scarcely exceeded the sublime horror of this scene from the American novelist.

Whittier added that Brown's "merits have not yet been sufficiently acknowledged."[58]

Yet the times seemed unpropitious for any general enlargement of the fame of *Wieland.* By the middle of the century, what with the proliferation of profitable American authors, as well as the popularity of European novelists—Dickens, Thackeray, Bulwer-Lytton, Hugo, and Dumas—the struggle for existence of any one novel was difficult indeed. In the second half of the century *Wieland* seems to have slipped into a new category, becoming an object of interest to historians, antiquarians, connoisseurs of curiosa, and makers of encyclopedias, who wrote of it in

---

[55] See "Edgar Allan Poe," *Edinburgh Review*, 107 (April 1858), 419-426, and Boyd Carter, "Poe's Debt to Charles Brockden Brown," *Prairie Schooner*, 27 (Summer 1953), 190-196.

[56] *Complete Works of Edgar Allan Poe*, ed. James A. Harrison (New York: Fred DeFau and Co., 1902), XVI, 41. For the mention of Brown by Poe, see ibid., vols. X-XI and XII-XIII.

[57] "P's Correspondence," *Mosses from an Old Manse* (Philadelphia: David McKay, 1891), p. 367.

[58] *The Prose Works of John Greenleaf Whittier,* (Boston and New York: Houghton, Mifflin and Co.: 1889), III, 393, 392.

autumnal, indulgent tones: here was a part of our national literary heritage, minor to be sure, but distinctly worth preservation. Even so, there was an elaborate edition of Brown's collected works published in 1857 by Polock (at Philadelphia) followed, in 1859 by a Lippincott "edition" which was really another issue of the Polock with an additional title-page and different binding.[59] There followed McKay's Philadelphia edition of Brown's novels in 1887;[60] an edition of *Wieland* (and *Arthur Mervyn*) in 1889 by McKay, to be used as units in an "American Classics Series"; and three undated reprints toward the end of the century, two of them appearing probably in 1892.[61] Little excitement appears to have been generated by these re-issues.

In the twentieth century *Wieland* continued its by-then largely underground existence until 1926, when Fred Lewis Pattee's edition signaled the miniature revival of *Wieland* (and to some extent Brown) in the mid-twentieth century. Pattee's edition (Harcourt Brace's "American Authors Series," reprinted by Hafner in 1958) has errors in the text, but it is provided with an introduction which outlines a basis of the new evaluation of *Wieland*. Occasional articles, retrospective in tone, referring to it as a strange but real part of our literary past continued to appear, and historians (largely professors) of American literature have duly "treated" Brown in their surveys. From the time of Pattee's edition, *Wieland* itself was more and more used as required reading, and doctoral candidates began choosing Brown as a subject for their dissertations. This movement provided a basis for new appraisals of Brown. His Gothic aspect of course proved an entering gambit for the new attention accorded the book, but gradually, as subtler tones became more observable in American literature generally—what with the post-Freudian "Age of Anxiety" and the advent of the existential novel—students and professors alike looked more closely at *Wieland* as a work densely packed with data employable in studies of abnormal psychology: the novel of terror became merged with the modern psychological

[59] Sydney J. Krause and Jane Nieset, "A Census of the Works of Charles Brockden Brown," *Serif*, 3 (Dec. 1966), 50, n. 14.

[60] There have appeared two reprints of this edition—with its scores of readings divergent from the original *Wieland*—one by the Kennikat Press (Port Washington, New York, 1963) and another by Burt Franklin (New York, 1970).

[61] "Census," *Serif*, 3, 33.

346

novel. Brown, often listed as dead, a casualty of sheer time, now became a generator of new insights. Dorothy Scarborough's largely unnoticed reference to Brown in her article on "Super-naturalism in Modern English Fiction" in 1918 was proving to have been prophetic:

> We must go back, it seems, to Charles Brockden Brown in our search for the veritable forerunner of the new psychic fiction as practiced by the adherents and disciples of the psycho-analytic school.

It was Miss Scarborough's opinion that "in studies of the morbid mentality he has few equals." She adds of *Wieland:*

> Such a tragedy of dethroned reason is intolerably powerful; the dark labyrinths of insanity, the gloom-haunted passages of the human mind, are more terrible to traverse than the midnight windings of Gothic dungeons.[62]

A major emphasis in contemporary criticism of Brown remains the skill he exhibited in *Wieland* in converting "the shadowy paths, gloomy recesses, and darkened enclosures"—the "external ter-ror" of Gothic romance—into a rich pattern of psychological symbolism.[63]

If a "classic" can be defined as a book written in one age that speaks to another, *Wieland* has attained to something like that status. Despite many critical attempts throughout the years to demolish and inter it, it possesses a good deal of vitality today. But the *Wieland* of the 1970's is not the *Wieland* of 1798. Any book seen with new eyes becomes in effect a new book. *Wieland* does not exist today mainly because of its eighteenth-century "Gothic"

[62] In *Current Opinion*, 64 (April 1918) p. 278. Portions of this article had appeared in Miss Scarborough's *The Supernatural in Modern English Fiction* (New York: G. P. Putnam's Sons, 1917), p. 39.

[63] Donald A. Ringe, "Charles Brockden Brown," in *Major Writers of Early American Literature,* ed. Everett Emerson (Madison: Univ. of Wisconsin Press, 1972), pp. 284-288. As might be expected, Freudians have also been attracted by the psychological upheaval of the major characters in *Wieland.* One critic believes that much of the mischief can be traced to Carwin's Oedipal relationship with his father (in "Carwin") which as it spills over into *Wieland* thrusts him into the role of "rebellious son" in relation to Wieland, "his surrogate father." David Lyttle, "The Case Against Carwin," *Nineteenth Century Fiction,* 26 (Dec. 1971), 257-269.

devices and qualities. Ventriloquism per se is not a thrilling phenomenon to mid-twentieth-century readers. Carwin's purposes and methods may be explained, but the terror with which his presence is associated does not vanish. Clara is more than the traditional beleaguered female Gothic heroine. It is not Clara huddled in a closet of an isolated Pennsylvania house fearing specific injury to her person or her reputation that finally detains the modern reader, but Clara as representative of humanity cowering in a frightening, lonely, ambiguous universe in which man is uncertain of how to cope with the "decrees" of an apparently capricious "Fate"—this is the aspect of Clara's situation that interests readers in today's depressed existential atmosphere. The appallingly cruel murders committed by the protagonist in *Wieland,* though triggered by a religious mania, can be taken in their stride by readers accustomed to the bizarre behavior and "meaningless violence" characteristic of much contemporary American fiction. Modern readers can understand a Clara no longer looking for comfort or salvation from a traditional "God." The chilling objectivity of Brown's narrative mode accords well with the "stark" reporting of today's technicians. Yet there are differences. Beneath the apparent sangfroid of many modern novelists and protagonists one often detects a note of self-pity which is seldom observable in Brown. For Brown the world can appear a harsh place, but he seems to imply that however bleak the fate visited upon individuals, it must be endured with fortitude. And such pity and compassion as he commands is directed not toward himself but toward mankind. Perhaps this helps to give his novel, *Wieland,* a measurable degree of universality.

A.C.

Textual Essay

WIELAND

Wieland was first published on 14 September 1798 by Hocquet Caritat; Thomas and James Swords were the printers. No manuscripts or proofsheets are known to have survived. The first edition (A) collates as follows: $12°: A^2 B-2C^6$ ($ 1, 3 signed, $3 [first leaf of insert] as 2); 152 leaves, pp. [4] 1 2-298 *299-300*. The first leaf contains the title, with copyright notice (verso blank), the second contains the Advertisement, dated September 3, 1798 (verso blank), and the third (p. 1) the head-title and the beginning of the text, which ends on page 298. Pages 299-300 are blank and are missing from some copies.

So far as we know, this was the only edition that appeared in Brown's lifetime, even though an advertisement at the end of the 1803 edition of *Arthur Mervyn* issued by the Minerva Press lists *Wieland,* along with the extant three-volume *Edgar Huntly,* as "just published." Apparently on this evidence Dorothy Blakey, in her book on the Minerva Press, asserts that Lane and Newman published a *Wieland* "probably" in 1802. But she omits it in her chronological list of Minerva publications, and a recent census of leading American and British libraries has failed to uncover a single 1802-1803 *Wieland.* Caritat reportedly took copies of *Wieland, Ormond,* and *Arthur Mervyn* to England in 1800, and for this and other reasons it is likely that the *Wieland* which the Minerva Press planned consisted of the 1798 sheets, probably with a new title-page, if one eventually appeared at all.[1] Whatever

[1] Blakey, *The Minerva Press, 1790–1820* (London: Bibliographical Society, 1935), p. 43 and Appendix I; Krause with Nieset, "A Census of the Works of Charles Brockden Brown," *Serif,* 3 (December 1966), 27–55. Krause's more recent correspondence with the British Museum and National Central Library has again yielded negative results on this ques-

the precise circumstances surrounding the hypothetical 1802-1803 *Wieland,* it seems nearly certain that new authority would no more have been involved in this projected Minerva issue of Brown than in the other Lane-Newman reprints of his works.

In 1811, a year after Brown's death, Henry Colburn brought out the first extant English edition (E1) in three volumes.[2] Colburn also published the second English edition (E2) in three volumes in 1822, at the time he was publishing *Ormond,* the one-volume *Memoirs of Charles Brockden Brown* (a reprint of parts of William Dunlap's two-volume *Life of Charles Brockden Brown,* 1815), and *Carwin, the Biloquist, and Other American Tales* (viz., "Stephen Calvert," "Jessica," and "The Scribbler," all extracted from the 1815 *Life*).[3]

No other editions can make any claim at all to authority, and both of Colburn's require brief consideration only because of the presence in both E1 and E2 of variants not easily attributed to the compositors and because of Colburn's possible connection with

tion. Brown's letter to his brother James, April 1800, mentions that Caritat "has carried a considerable number of Wieland, Ormond and Mervyn" to England (Dunlap, *Life,* II, 100). Since the *Wieland* is advertised at four shillings, Lane no doubt intended to issue a single volume, rather than his usual three, and like the 1800 *Ormond* this probably would have been a re-issue of remaindered sheets of the Swords printing. Thus if some of the Minerva copies were issued and survive undetected, they are conceivably those that lack a title-page, presumably the Minerva cancellans, which would easily be lost. (Cf. the probably similar case of the nonextant Minerva 1821 *Edgar Huntly* reported from advertisements in the *Port Folio* [1821], p. 241, along with the extant 1821 *Arthur Mervyn,* a re-issue of the 1803.) There remains the fact that British critical reviews of *Wieland* at the time are notably nonexistent (see W. S. Ward, "Charles Brockden Brown, His Contemporary British Reviews, and Two Minor Bibliographical Problems," *PBSA,* 65 [1971], 399–402). *Note:* references to works already cited in the Historical Essay appear in short forms here.

[2] Printed by B. Clarke, Well-Street, Cripplegate in 12°, with a dedication to Sheridan by Colburn, the 1811 volumes are notable for their ascription of the novel to 'B. C. Brown'. A reprint of *Wieland* appeared serially in the New York *Ladies' Literary Cabinet* of 1820, with the usual transmissional error.

[3] See p. 313, n. 6, on Dunlap's *Life,* which was, of course, itself a partial reprinting of the biography by Paul Allen, now at PPHi, printed but apparently never published.

members of Brown's circle.[4] Both editions contain the "spontaneous" variation and simple correction normally found in reprints.[5] Moreover, E1 has some variants (e.g., at 3.26, 15.36, 236.32) that are deliberate and noncompositorial, and some others that may be. These changes occur in clusters, most notably at the beginning and end of the novel; they are like those a publisher might make in a desultory manner before sending copy to his printer.[6] One of the alterations (at 244.10-14) vitiates Brown's attempt—however regrettable—to integrate the Conway-Stuart story into the novel, and another (at 6.29) changes diction that is clearly characteristic of Brown.[7] On literary

[4] The possibility is very remote and deserves mention only because of the clear evidence in the texts of editorial alterations from some source. In a copy of the Colburn-Bentley edition of *Edgar Huntly* (1831) in the Standard Novels series, Daniel Edwards Kennedy found an announcement stating that the novels in the series had been "revised . . . by the respective authors" (Kennedy, "Charles Brockden Brown: His Life and Works," p. 2057; see p. 314, n. 7). Colburn was the guest of some unidentified Browns in France in 1824, along with Washington Irving (Kennedy, p. 205B1). This may have been James Brown, American minister to Paris, who was unrelated to Charles Brockden, but there is another, unidentified Brown who could also have been the mysterious associate; see Washington Irving, *Journals and Notebooks, Volume III, 1819–1827*, ed. Walter A. Reichart (Madison: Univ. of Wisconsin Press, 1970), passim. The possibility of Irving's connection with the Brown circle is raised in William Dunlap's *Diary* (II, 437), and further suggested, as Kennedy notes (pp. 205–205A), by the contents of the notice of Dunlap's *Life* of Brown in the *Analectic Magazine* for August 1814. For more on Irving's connections with Colburn and Brown, see *Journals*, 357, 434, and Stanley T. Williams, *The Life of Washington Irving* (New York: Oxford Univ. Press, 1935), I, 41, 390; and on the Colburn-Bentley series, see Michael Sadleir, *XIX Century Fiction* (Berkeley: Univ. of California Press, 1951), II, 93–96, and also Royal A. Gettmann, "Colburn-Bentley and the March of Intellect," *Studies in Bibliography*, 9 (1957), 209–213.

[5] See, for example, E1's 'part' for 'past' (5.26) or E2's 'too' for 'to' (97.10), E1's 'not' for 'not not' (157.29) or E2's 'present' for E1's 'prelent' (8.27), and other variants in the Historical List. This and the points that follow are covered at greater length and in a broader context in Reid, "Brockden Brown in England," *Early American Literature*, 9 (1974), 188–195.

[6] See the Historical List of Substantive Variants, below; often the variants are on facing pages of A. At least one of the changes (the deletion of 'were', 142.35) was made in proof, as inordinate spaces in the line show.

[7] Cf. 'he mortally offended his relations' (6.29) with "but you have mortally offended the Dr."—Brown to Samuel Miller, 16 March 1803 (ALS, NjP, A.M.2534).

351

grounds, then, these and the other deliberate changes of E1 cannot be attributed to Brown;[8] rather, they are more like the alterations in E2, which undoubtedly lack authority.

The variants in E2 are more numerous than in E1, though not different in kind. E2 preserves some of E1's errors (e.g., at 3.26, 5.18, 5.26, 6.29, 26.8, 107.6, 239.36) and was clearly printed from an annotated copy of it. The work on the copy for E2 was more careful than that on E1's. E2 corrected one subtle error ('designed' for 'deigned', 12.35) that had survived during the printing of A and E1, as well as some other, less subtle errors of A's that E1 reproduced (at 28.7, 96.31, 194.3) and some corruptions first introduced in E1 (e.g., at 6.15, 84.9, 96.25, 198.11, 242.29). But beyond these corrections, a number of alterations occurred in E2 for the first time. These appear throughout the novel and resemble, more than E1's, revisions that an author might make to improve his style. Yet, there are three compelling reasons for not attributing them to Brown. First, in quantity and quality the changes are like those in the 1822 "Carwin," which for several reasons (see below, p. 365) cannot be Brown's. Second, E2 was printed from a copy of the posthumous E1 (in which the changes would ordinarily have been incorporated, had they existed), whereas Brown's revisions would have had to be based on A; thus Colburn's reasons for failing to consult A when repairing a blunder in E1 (at 176.31) and for going to the trouble of annotating E1, rather than using a copy of A, are inexplicable, if we assume that he had Brown's revisions.[9] Third, many of the changes such as 'early' for 'ancient' (10.37) are, from a literary standpoint, clearly unlike Brown. Exactly who made the changes in E2—and in the 1822 "Carwin" and *Ormond*—is not known; probably it was one of Colburn's regular employees, rather than Colburn himself or someone from Brown's circle.[10] But, in any

---

[8] Preliminary collations indicate that, by no coincidence, similar changes occur in the 1811 *Ormond*—first issued in England in 1800 without any such changes in the text—which Colburn published along with *Wieland*.

[9] Even had Brown's revisions been undiscovered in 1811, and in manuscript, rather than a copy of A, they would still have been keyed to A; Colburn's labor in annotating E1 (which cost him some trouble) would not have been recompensed by the fact that E1 had already anglicized A (which saved his printer trouble).

[10] For example, Dunlap's *Diary* for the years 1810–1811 and 1821–1822 does not indicate that he took any notice of Colburn's edi-

case, there are compelling reasons for concluding that E2, like E1, has no claim to independent authority, though both may at times have correct readings botched in A.

This leaves A, then, as our only authority for the text of Brown's first novel published in book form. As the extant document closest to Brown's autograph manuscript, it is the copy-text for the present edition. Much of the manuscript for *Wieland* was in the Swordses' hands by 23 July 1798; the rest was delivered intermittently between that time and 3 September (the date of the "Advertisement"). Brown's own awareness that his first drafts needed transcribing and the practice of writing out fair manuscripts followed by his friends William Dunlap and Elihu Hubbard Smith when preparing printer's copy for the Swordses both suggest that Brown would have supplied, and the Swordses expected, relatively fair copy.[11] However, we cannot know exactly how fair the copy was, or that the bits given to the Swordses at various times after 23 July were all uniform in this respect. Yet regardless of how fair the copy was in its various parts, there is convincing evidence in A that the manuscript contained the infelicities of grammar, spelling, and punctuation which are characteristic of Brown's work and which he himself recognized as regrettable results of the haste with which he wrote (see p. xx).

The Swordses printed the first edition, which is textually invariant, by half-sheet imposition, probably work-and-turn, a method which decreased the lag-time between composition and press-work, which therefore served especially well when copy was delivered spasmodically, and which the Swordses apparently frequently followed.[12] The pages in each gathering of the book would have been printed together at one time, beginning with those (pp. 1-12) in gathering B, followed by those in C (pp. 13-24), and so on. Each forme contained approximately 12,120 ems, and

tions of Brown or even of his own *Life* of Brown. Nevertheless, the changes in E2 show considerable attention to the text such as a regular editor and proofreader, rather than the busy Colburn, would have given it. The "improver" might have been Charles Ollier, who also could be the "O.C." that wrote the introduction to the 1831 Colburn-Bentley *Edgar Huntly.*

[11] See Dunlap, *Life,* I, 107; Elihu Hubbard Smith's autograph manuscript diary ("Memoirs of Elihu Hubbard Smith," CtY), I, 221, 326; Dunlap, *Diary,* I, 207–208, 216, 219. See pp. 321–323 on the writing of *Wieland.*

[12] For example, in an affidavit of 22 September 1792, the Swordses

though the schedule for production of *Wieland* is a little uncertain (see immediately below, p. 357), on the average the shop must have set more than one and one-half formes every two days, or about 10,000 ems per day. Since the daily rate for the competent compositor seems to have been some 6000 or 7000 ems, at least two of the "six or eight hands" in the Swordses' shop—and no doubt others, at various times—set *Wieland*. The preliminaries (gathering *A*) were typeset on 3 September (perhaps when Brown delivered copy), as the date on the "Advertisement" and external evidence suggest, and they were the last pages printed—probably beginning on 4 September, having been proofread by Brown earlier the same day. Eight days later the book, with "copy-right secured," finally appeared.[13] There was no second impression, perhaps because the type was distributed soon after the sheets were wrought off to provide letter for the next half-sheet, as was apparently customary in the Swordses' small shop. Probably between 750 and 1000 copies were printed.[14]

Examination of the proofreading of A helps substantiate what

state that they printed a certain work in half-sheets (AMS, PPHi, Campbell Collection). Other books of theirs in 1797–1798 were printed in half-sheets, as analysis and external evidence from Smith's "Memoirs" (vols. I-II) show. The gathering of A and the watermarks in it are the best internal evidence for half-sheet imposition, though this and the other physical evidence cannot prove conclusively that A was printed by the more normal work-and-turn method, rather than by means of "two half-sheets worked together." However, given the circumstances and what is known about the Swordses, the probabilities lie with their having used the more common method, and whichever they in fact used, the implications for the proofreading outlined below remain virtually the same. Joseph Katz, "Analytical Bibliography and Literary History: The Writing and Printing of *Wieland*," *Proof,* 1 (1971), 8–34, also argues for the view that A was printed by work-and-turn in half-sheets. This method would help keep a forme always "at press"; see Rollo G. Silver, *The American Printer, 1787–1825* (Charlottesville: Univ. Press of Virginia, 1967), p. 89, on keeping the press busy.

[13] For the dating and the external evidence mentioned, see pp. 321–322 and the Table below. A contemporary, John Pintard, quoted in Austin Baxter Keep, *History of the New York Society Library* (New York: New York Society Library, 1908), p. 241, describes the Swordses' shop. The compositor's typesetting rate is based on Uriel Crocker's output in a Boston shop in 1811, mentioned by Silver, *The American Printer,* p. 5.

[14] The size of the edition is a guess based on Caritat's costs (see Silver, *The American Printer,* p. 78, for approximate charges in New York at the time), his payment to Brown (see p. 321), the sizes of editions (see Silver,

a few of its readings suggest about the relative accuracy of its text. Presumably the Swordses and possibly Caritat made corrections before turning over a proofsheet to the author for his approval.[15] The role Brown actually played in the proofing is somewhat unclear. While the initial half-sheets were printing, Brown was busy writing the conclusion to his novel and parts of *Arthur Mervyn* (see p. 321). Dunlap's comment (*Diary,* I, 317) that the first proof "was under [the] correction" of Brown, Elihu Hubbard Smith, and William Johnson is suggestive. If proofreading *Wieland* was indeed a group project, at least at the beginning, "the trio" overlooked the misreading 'designed' for 'deigned' (12.35) in the first half-sheet, which is the kind of error that an author, rather than his agents, is more likely to notice.[16] Thus how much real attention Brown gave the proof—especially in the early gatherings, printed before 25 August—seems problematic. Other editions for which Brown was responsible (either as author or editor) suggest that he was careless, or possibly uninterested, in proofreading (see p. xx, n. 10). Initially, probably much of the

The American Printer, p. 173, and Hellmut Lehmann-Haupt, et al., *The Book in America,* 2nd ed. [New York: Bowker, 1951], pp. 39–41), the retail price of a copy of *Wieland* (see p. 322), and the publisher's risk involved; Rollo G. Silver, in a private letter to the General Editor, arrives at a similar figure. Smith (II, 331–332) says that Isaac Riley acted as "agent" for Caritat in the purchase of *Wieland* and may have been in partnership with Caritat, but there is no evidence that he was more than an agent, whereas George Gates Raddin, Jr., *The New York of Hocquet Caritat and His Associates, 1797–1817* (Dover Advance Press, 1953) shows that Riley was "financially embarrassed" until December 1798 and became associated with Caritat's bookstore only "by 25th of May 1799" (pp. 121–122).

[15] The Swordses were relatively careful printers, who took pride in their work; in the affidavit mentioned above (p. 353, n. 12) they testify to having "carefully read and corrected the proof sheets," and Pintard (see p. 354, n. 13) calls them "the neatest and most correct printers on the continent." Caritat's role in the proofreading is more conjectural, but publishers' practices at the time suggest that ensuring "correctness" would have been one of his responsibilities; see Rollo G. Silver, "Mathew Carey's Proofreaders," *Studies in Bibliography,* 17 (1964), 123–133, and Silver, *The American Printer,* p. 93.

[16] Cf. a similar oversight by Smith, when proofreading the Swordses' edition of Erasmus Darwin's *Botanic Garden* in 1798; in the "Economy of Vegetation," I, 143, the copy (the third London edition of 1795) reads 'widening waves', which becomes 'winding waves' in the Swordses' edition, an error that Smith (who did not read against copy) predictably failed to notice.

proofreading was done by Smith (perhaps in periodic consultation with Brown), who by mid-1798 was an experienced hand at correcting proof for the Swordses.[17] Given Smith's usual practice and the kinds of error which survive in *Wieland,* it seems unlikely that this proofreading would have been done against copy.

Nevertheless, the details of Smith's role in the proofreading remain obscure. Since *Wieland* was printed in half-sheets, there should have been twenty-six proofsheets, but Smith records reading only seven. Dunlap supplements Smith's records, most notably by providing the date for the last proof when transcribing Brown's letter of 4 September in his *Diary.* The following table presents this external evidence.

TABLE
External Evidence of Proofreading of *Wieland* (1798)

Date	Day	Activity	Source
7-23	Mon.	Swordses begin printing *Wieland*	Smith, II, 331
7-25	Wed.	Brown, Smith, & Johnson read first proofsheet	Smith, p. 333; Dunlap, *Diary,* I, 317
7-27	Fri.	Smith reads proof	Smith, p. 334
7-30	Mon.	Smith reads proof	Smith, p. 336
8-2	Thurs.	Smith reads proof	Smith, p. 337
8-6	Mon.	Smith reads proof	Smith, p. 339
8-8	Wed.	Smith reads proof	Smith, p. 340
8-13	Mon.	Smith reads proof	Smith, p. 342
9-4	Tues.	Brown reads last proof of *Wieland*	Dunlap, *Diary,* I, 335

After 13 August, Smith's account of the proofing of *Wieland* breaks off, though he records several later visits to the Swordses (20, 28 August) which apparently do not involve the proofreading of the *Medical Repository*—his usual reason for such visits—and may be connected with *Wieland.* Thus the proofreading, which continued until 4 September, began, in the first few weeks, on a regular schedule that may or may not have been adhered to after 13 August.

[17] Joseph Katz, p. 19, speculates that Brown both corrected proof and revised it (i.e., altered his readings that had been in the printer's copy), but analysis shows that there is no convincing evidence for this theory.

The incompleteness of Smith's account is a bit perplexing because by early 1798 he was keeping quite regular, though not entirely full, records of his proofreading.[18] Had the printing of *Wieland* continued at the rate indicated by these records, it would have taken twice as long as it did.

There are two possible interpretations of the evidence. One is that after 13 August the Swordses increased the production of *Wieland* threefold (as illustrated in Schedule A, p. 369). The second is that from the outset Smith's records conceal the schedule of production, that the production of *Wieland* was in fact regular, and that, roughly speaking, for every proofsheet recorded by Smith in the first few weeks two were seen (see Schedule B, p. 370). There is no way of proving which of these two interpretations is the more accurate. Both raise difficulties.

Several such difficulties arise from consideration of the first interpretation. Although the Swordses were briefly relieved of their usual printing of the *Medical Repository* during August and might therefore have been able to treble their weekly typesetting of *Wieland* from some 24,240 ems to 72,720, there is no evidence that between 2 and 13 August they did in fact increase their production.[19] Nor is there any evidence, in Smith's account of events after the 13th, of any great pressure on himself or Brown to correct proofsheets. (At this time Brown was still completing *Wieland,* was writing installments of *Arthur Mervyn,* and had begun "Carwin.")[20] The arrangements for Brown to finish his

---

[18] Smith, comments his friend Dunlap (*Life,* I, 56), "did nothing but by rule"; however, though Smith certainly tried to be methodical in everything, Dunlap is stretching the point to fit his nice contrast of Smith with Brown, as is shown by a perusal of Smith's journal, his own complaints during various periods about his lack of industry, and attempts to pin down his actions, such as that made immediately below. There is some reason to believe that as 1798 wore on, Smith's practice of writing long meditative pieces in his journal decreased as his worldly activities increased, but there is no evidence that his mere chronicling of these activities declined; see James E. Cronin, "The Life of Elihu Hubbard Smith" (Diss. Yale 1945), p. 326.

[19] Smith, II, 337, shows that the fifth number of the *Medical Repository* was published on 2 August. Producing 12,120 ems (i.e., a gathering of *Wieland*) per day, six days a week would have required the almost undivided labor of two of the Swordses' compositors if Uriel Crocker's output in a Boston shop in 1811 was typical (see p. 354, n. 13).

[20] See p. 321; Smith does record such pressure in connection with the *Medical Repository,* for which he sometimes read two or three proofs a day.

tale that were made on 23 July as well as his industry in completing it suggest that from the outset Caritat and the Swordses
expected publication in something less than two months, not the
three it would have taken had the Swordses printed only two
half-sheets per week.

On the other hand, the theory that Smith's account conceals
facts and that the Swordses really produced about four half-
sheets per week does not explain the incompleteness of the records kept by Smith nor the reason he altogether stopped recording the proofreading after 13 August—neglecting to mention
even the last proof of 4 September. Although in retrospect Brown
said the middle of August was the time the yellow fever began to
show signs of assuming the form of an epidemic in New York, the
increase of the plague that was to take Smith's life apparently did
not significantly affect his writing in his journal until about 15
September, nor his medical practice until around 23 August; he
had plenty of time before that for his usual reading, writing, and
visiting.[21] Nevertheless, his account suggests that, for some
reason, his attention to the proofreading of *Wieland* relaxed
about the middle of August. And this inference from external
evidence finds support in the fact that gathering P (which should
have been in the press about this time, if the Swordses were
printing about four half-sheets a week) contains the first blatant
substantive error in *Wieland* (at 130.25) and that the following
gatherings—especially those (Q, R, T, U, X, 2A-2C) which would
not be connected with Smith's known visits to the Swordses or
Caritat, according to this schedule (see Schedule B, p.
370)—contain such obvious errors as 'foundh er' (169.17), 'A' for
'At' (140.8), and 'not not' (157.29). Moreover, whereas there is
one omission in the earlier gatherings (at 83.17), there are five
(155.22, 164.8, 194.3, 230.15, 239.10) in the later, which also
exhibit a measurable increase in the instances of inconsistency
between tenses of verbs (see the text at 238.20) and between the
number of nouns and their verbs and pronouns (e.g.,
196.19-20)—the kinds of things that Smith was more likely than
Brown to attend to in proofreading.[22]

[21] In a letter to his brother James on 25 August 1798 (Dunlap, *Life,* I,
4), Brown said that conditions in New York had "within these ten days,
given birth" to the epidemic. Brown's other letters to James at this time
(*Life,* I, 4–9) confirm the better evidence in Smith's "Memoirs" (II,
342–356) of the gradual effect of the plague on Smith's activities.
[22] For discussion of the plausibility of A's readings, see the Textual

Although we cannot reconstruct the exact details of the proof-reading of *Wieland*, the little we know has some fairly clear implications for editing the text. The first edition of *Wieland* is, superficially, one of the most accurate of any of Brown's novels. Most of the fairly obvious errors that slipped past Caritat, the Swordses, Brown, and sometimes Smith are easily corrected. More serious is the error at 12.35 already alluded to, for it suggests that similar plausible, but incorrect, readings occur elsewhere in the text. Such errors are the most difficult to pinpoint because they are often embedded in a sophisticated text which has been smoothed out by various hands and which is—though in a sense less authorial than more naive texts obviously less "corrected" by others— by all appearances reliable. The one consolation in such a situation is that the undetected errors which may remain are probably relatively minor, and that probably no major corruption is present. But the fact that there is evidence that the proof-reading relaxed in the latter half of the novel (if not before)[23] suggests that generally more emendation is necessary from gathering P onward.

Given these circumstances, the majority of the present edition's emendations naturally occur in the later gatherings (P-2C). The increasing rate of error that characterizes the pages apparently not supervised by Smith is responsible for the difference in the proportion of changes in the earlier and later gatherings. Emendations of fairly obvious substantive errors, of accidentals to resolve unintentional ambiguities resulting from deficient formal presentation, and of other accidentals, made on the premise that these pages are more likely to misrepresent Brown's intentions, account for much of this difference in proportion. The number of less obvious substantive errors which are corrected increases somewhat as well, especially in chapters 16-18. This edition restores six words omitted in the copy-text and makes fourteen changes of readings that involve graphic similarity or repetition. Some of these are very obvious (130.25, 140.8, 157.29), and one (90.27) involves the *th-/h-* confusion which is especially easy in

---

Notes. Some typographical errors—'seduously', 'hyprocrisy', 'whcih' (28.7, 82.15, 91.1), easily missed when proofreading for sense—occur in the gatherings before P, but they are not of the same order as those cited here.

[23] That is, if the first interpretation, of trebled production, is not chosen (see Schedule A).

Brown's hand and to which the Swordses' shop was prone.[24] However, though it makes these changes, the Bicentennial Edition allows to stand a number of infelicities,[25] on the evidence of their occurrence elsewhere in Brown's writings and on the premise that A's readings derive from Brown himself, who once remarked on the presence of such "slighter inaccuracies" in his work (see p. xx).

The treatment of quotations in the present edition is a final matter needing comment. As a matter of practice, the copy-text encloses direct discourse in double quotation marks and uses single marks to set off quotations within quotations. Apparently the Swordses thus "styled" the text of Brown's manuscript—since there is no evidence that he himself ever followed such a practice—and in doing so naturally failed to note all instances and mistook some others. In accordance with its general principles (see p. xxiii), the present edition adopts the practice of the copy-text and supplies or deletes quotation marks where the printers of A have failed to interpret the text correctly. But though thus treating the dialogue, this edition also adopts the copy-text's general practice of omitting quotations around monologue, which is often indistinguishable from direct or indirect accounts of recollected thought (see, e.g., the passages beginning at 139.33, 209.30).[26]

The present edition of *Wieland,* then, provides a critical text that differs in some particulars from the text of the first edition, but that is based squarely on it, our only witness.

[24] Brown's manuscripts repeatedly show that his initial *th-* and *h-* could be confused, especially when capital letters; in the errata to his *Edwin and Angelina,* printed by Swords in 1797, Smith lists 'the' for his 'he' as one of the three "Errors of the Press" surviving in the text.

[25] Such as possible omissions and graphic errors, inconsistency of tenses and possessives, nonagreement of number between nouns, pronouns, and verbs, and forms (like 'sung' at 24.9) in the past of irregular verbs that were acceptable at the time.

[26] See the appended List of Emendations for the specific alterations of the copy-text's quotations.

"CARWIN"

The history of the text of the "Memoirs of Carwin the Biloquist" begins and ends, for present purposes, at approximately the same times as that of *Wieland,* but its course between these times is different. Whereas *Wieland* appeared almost as soon as Brown had completed it, most of "Carwin"—which was begun while *Wieland* was still in press—remained in manuscript for nearly five years before Brown, as editor of the *Literary Magazine* and apparently in need of material, began publishing it in installments in 1803. Apparently his 1798 manuscript was exhausted after the seventh installment in the *Literary Magazine,* and the last three were written specifically to supply copy for the periodical.[27]

Published by a syndicate of which John Conrad was apparently the leading member, the *Literary Magazine* was printed in octavo half-sheets,[28] with two columns per page, and contained approximately 53,000 words (180,000 ems) per number. Perhaps for this reason alone the type was not left standing to be re-impressed for a second (possibly annual and bound) issue; certainly, no variants indicating duplicate typesetting, correction in press, or re-impression occur in the gatherings containing "Carwin."[29] The text of "Carwin" was sandwiched in amidst others in the first

[27] See p. 336. The installments begin at the following points in the present text: 247.1, 254.3, 259.25, 266.1, 271.11, 278.11, 286.5, 292.14, 298.1, 304.19.

[28] *The Philadelphia Gazette and Daily Advertiser,* 7 September 1803, p. 3, col. 1, contains the "proposals" for the *Literary Magazine,* which mention publishing it monthly, at fifty cents an issue, in "large octavo"; this evidence of format is confirmed by the size and shape of the leaf, chainlines and watermarks, and the gathering of the volumes.

[29] Collations indicate that variation of any kind is rare and textual variation virtually nonexistent in the *Literary Magazine.* The only variant

three volumes over a period of three years. Hugh Maxwell printed the first five installments (those in volume I) and T. and G. Palmer the remaining five (in volumes II and III). In the second volume "Carwin" was the lead item.

Despite its prominence in this volume, its importance in the first three volumes as the only continuing original narrative, and its authorship, "Carwin" received little special attention by way of proofreading. The text of this first printing (M) is full of errors, many of them blatant, and contains some inconsistencies, the most notable being the puzzling alternation between 'Ludloe' and 'Ludlow'.[30] The 'Ludloe'/'Ludlow' variation is analogous to that between 'Benington' and 'Bennington', but the causes of each seem to be different. Only two 'Bennington' spellings occur in M; one in the seventh installment (290.37), which Brown wrote in 1798 and the Palmers printed, and the other in the last installment (310.5), which the Palmers also printed but which Brown wrote as a single installment in early 1805 for the March 1805 issue. In the other two installments, also printed by the Palmers and written, in mid-1804 and in late 1804 or early 1805, for specific issues of the magazine, only 'Benington' appears. Thus the variation seems to be due to Brown's own failure to decide on a single spelling of this character's name and adhere to it from one time to the next.

On the other hand, the variation between 'Ludloe' and 'Ludlow'—though also traceable to Brown's own inconsistency rather than the printers—seems to reflect his failure to execute a predetermined spelling. The spelling 'Ludloe' appears in the outline of the plot of *Wieland* and "Carwin" (see below), where Mrs. Benington either has the name "Louisa" or "Mrs. Conway," or is nonexistent. 'Ludloe' is the dominant form in M, and 'Ludlow' seems to be a spelling into which Brown (influenced by the analogy of "low") lapsed periodically, especially when writing the ninth installment. Maxwell reproduces Brown's unintentional inconsistency in the third, fourth, and fifth installments, but the installments printed by the Palmers have either one form of the name or the other ('Ludlow' in the ninth and 'Ludloe' in the

located in "Carwin" itself is the movement of a *t* to make 'withou tscruple' (286.4), which is probably the result of loose or pulled type. See the Record below for details of the collation and other consultation of copies for the present edition.

[30] For additional remarks on unresolved inconsistencies in "Carwin," see above pp. 337–340.

others). Thus though Brown himself probably continued to lapse into 'Ludlow'—especially when he began writing installments one by one—the Palmers took some care with each installment to present a text uniform in this spelling at least.

In themselves the 'Ludloe'/'Ludlow' and 'Benington'/ 'Bennington' variations are not textually crucial, though of course some decision about the forms to print must be made; however, what they suggest about the printing of M is important and finds confirmation in other evidence. Maxwell's half of M is less carefully printed than the Palmers'. Mere accidental and typographical errors are much more frequent in Maxwell's five installments than in theirs. The fault seems to be traceable to Maxwell, rather than to Brown's manuscript copy. Recent collations of *Arthur Mervyn*, part of which Maxwell set from identifiable printed copy, have turned up the same kinds of error; perhaps this is one reason Brown's brother James suggested that the second part of *Arthur Mervyn* should be printed in New York (see Dunlap, *Life*, II, 100).

Since the Palmers printed two installments of the portion of "Carwin" written in 1798, there is no way of arguing that the differences between Brown's manuscripts of 1798 and 1804-1805 account for the differences in the texts printed by Maxwell and the Palmers. The manuscript of the 1798 portion must have been relatively uniform and was probably the same one that Brown promised on 4 September to send to Dunlap, who records reading it ten days later (see p. 336). Given the time that elapsed between Brown's promise and its fulfillment, his awareness that his foul drafts needed to be recopied and "corrected," and the fact that he had "Stephen Calvert" but neither *Wieland* nor *Arthur Mervyn* to occupy him after 4 September, it seems likely that the manuscript Dunlap received was a relatively fair copy, but of this we cannot be sure. And no matter how fair it was, it no doubt contained at least some of the infelicities of grammar, spelling, and punctuation that Brown knew, regretfully, plagued his work (see p. xx).

Maxwell's proneness to error may well have been one of the reasons that the publishers decided to change printers at the end of the first volume, though there were probably other equally salient causes of the change. In any case, there can be no doubt that Maxwell's five installments contain a larger number of substantive, as well as merely typographical, errors than the Palmers'. A more difficult question is how much editing the Palmers did beyond the reconciling of obvious inconsistencies, such as 'Ludloe'/'Ludlow'. Presumably their alterations would have been confined to such matters of "style," but they might also have touched up the wording itself and thus have produced a text more sophisticated than Maxwell's, though there is no clear evidence that in fact they did intervene in this way.

Despite the clear general contrast between the work of Maxwell and the Palmers, the Palmers' two cases of dittography on a single page (at 290.11, 291.9) suggest that the errors throughout M survive not only because of the printers' oversights but because of defective proof-correction. Exactly how much proofreading there was and who did it is unknown. Presumably the printer, publisher, and editor could have read proof. But that Brown really devoted much attention to it seems unlikely, in view of his other pressing duties—which included not only editing but writing much of the material for each number—his temperament, and the kinds of easily revised infelicities that survive in the text.

Because it was printed directly from Brown's papers with his authorization, the text of "Carwin" in the *Literary Magazine* is the copy-text for the present edition. It is, in addition, the only text with authority. William Dunlap reprinted "Carwin" with minor changes in the second volume of his *Life,* in 1815, but there is no indication that he had an independent manuscript (found by Brown's family and passed on to their friend) or that he had access to any other authority for annotating the pages of the *Literary Magazine* when preparing printer's copy.[31] Some of the changes (e.g., at 258.4-8, 260.33, 302.16) in the text of the *Life* (L) are certainly not attributable to the printers, but they are as certainly not beyond the scope of a man like Dunlap, who knew that Brown's work could bear some correction (see his *Life,* II, 29-30). Besides inadvertently following one of the 'Ludlow' spellings in M's ninth installment while otherwise regularizing them to 'Ludloe', L reproduces several errors of M's (at 261.29, 262.7, 263.18) that are common compositorial slips resulting in plausible but wrong readings; the fact that these readings from M survive in L not only shows that its copy was M, rather than a manuscript, but also suggests that Dunlap had no resource other

[31] See the following paragraph for more comment on the unlikelihood of revisions of M's text by Brown ever having existed in some nonextant document.

than his own ingenuity in preparing the copy for his printer. A busy professional man with a number of other duties and interests, he naturally overlooked some less obvious errors while correcting more obvious ones and, in one case (at 258.4-8), altering a satisfactory but difficult construction that he misunderstood.

When in 1822 Henry Colburn reprinted Dunlap's *Life* as the *Memoirs of Charles Brockden Brown,* he extracted "Carwin," "Stephen Calvert," "Jessica," and "The Scribbler," and made them into the three-volume *Carwin, the Biloquist, and Other American Tales and Pieces.* "Carwin" occupies most of the first volume. The 1822 edition (E) preserves many of the errors in L and unintentionally adds a few new ones, while restoring several readings of M's corrupted by L and correcting M readings independently. It also introduces a host of new variants which, like those in *Wieland* and *Ormond,* cannot be assigned to mere compositors. Theoretically, these variants could represent Brown's revisions, discovered posthumously by his family and made available to Colburn (see p. 351), but that any of E's changes in fact derived from Brown is virtually impossible. Two of these deliberate variants (at 258.4-8, 279.6) follow the direction given by L's alterations and thus depart further from Brown's intentions, rather than restore them. The theory that Brown would have revised an incomplete piece—which he was hard put even to continue—rather than completed it is improbable. That these revisions would not have been discovered and used by Dunlap is unlikely. Finally, it seems incredible that, having the revisions (which must have been in pages of the *Literary Magazine*), Colburn would have decided to annotate a copy of Dunlap's *Life* for the printer, and then have failed to consult it when mending two of L's errors. These changes, like those in *Wieland* and *Ormond,* must have originated in Colburn's house (see p. 352); they, as well as those in L, have no authority.

Although they have no authority, a few of the variants in L and E correct errors in M, the copy-text, and have consequently been adopted here. Other emendations, both substantive and accidental, have been necessary to fulfill Brown's presumed intentions. Naturally most of these emendations occur in the early half of "Carwin" because of the differences in the work of Maxwell and the Palmers, but a few changes in the latter half have been necessary. Many of the emendations correct fairly obvious mistakes, because M is, fortunately, a relatively naive text, and most of its errors are therefore easily detected. Of the seventy some changes, three involve omissions and three graphic errors, including *th-/h-* confusion (see p. 359f.), whereas most concern deficient presentation (at least seven of them clearly substantive).[32] However, this edition rejects a number of other possible emendations, especially of infelicities in grammar and punctuation, on the evidence of passages in Brown's other first editions or M itself and on the premise that M's "slighter inaccuracies" derive from Brown.

Since it appeared serially, "Carwin" lacked any division into chapters, and any such division introduced in an edition must be conjectural. Just how Brown would have divided "Carwin" had he finished it we cannot know; moreover, that he had any clear structure or division in mind is a fact not in evidence. The present edition eliminates the vestiges of serial appearance—the introductory head-title and the closing *'To be continued'* that occur before and after each installment, as well as the ascription of a note to the 'EDITOR' (at 299.38)—and prints the text undivided, as it must have originally stood in most of the printer's manuscript. Given the nature of the 'Ludloe'/'Ludlow' and 'Benington'/'Bennington' variations already discussed, this edition regularizes to Brown's 'Ludloe' but retains his 'Benington' and 'Bennington' spellings.[33]

The system of representing direct and indirect discourse in the copy-text raises difficulties. There is apparently no clear and consistent distinction between direct and indirect discourse in M, and when M is clearly printing direct discourse, it usually sets it off not with quotation marks, but with commas, parentheses, dashes, colons, periods, successive dots, and paragraphing. M's lack of system no doubt reflects the text of its manuscript copy. In accordance with its general policy (see p. xxiii), the present edi-

---

[32] Some of the changes in the copy-text of course concern merely mechanical problems and go unreported in accordance with the general policy of this edition; see p. xxiii.

[33] These changes are made without further note, except for the deletion of 'EDITOR.' (see the List of Emendations). M's 'Ludlow('s)' has been changed to 'Ludloe('s)'—adopted by L (usually) and subsequent editions (except K)—at the following points: 265.25, 274.8, 274.22, 276.13, 298.12, 298.19, 299.7, 299.22, 299.26, 299.30, 299.34, 300.5, 300.26, 300.35, 301.13, 301.17, 301.20, 301.27, 301.34, 302.2, 302.8, 302.24, 302.30, 302.36, 302.38, 303.7, 303.29.

tion follows the basic style of the copy-text by adopting its use of punctuation and various other devices instead of adding quotation marks; in the few cases where emendation is necessary, the general usage of the copy-text as well as the particular context has determined the exact form of the change adopted.[34]

Besides being reprinted in the nineteenth century in the two English editions published by Henry Colburn—which, previous discussion has shown, intentionally altered the text, but without access to any fresh authority—*Wieland* appeared a number of other times during the nineteenth century in the unauthoritative collected editions that began with S. G. Goodrich's publication of the novels in Boston in 1827; "Carwin" was ignored in these same editions (see p. 337). But twice in the twentieth century "Carwin" has appeared alongside *Wieland* in editions by modern scholars. Following its general practices, the present edition has consulted the editorial work of these scholars, neither of whom of course had access to any new authority. Fred Lewis Pattee's edition[35] made some attempt at emendation, which goes unrecorded, and has been collated for the present edition. That by William S. Kable, in the Merrill series, aims to reprint the copy-texts while reporting the few corrections of obvious errors; consequently it has not been collated.[36]

The appendixes that follow contain reports on the substantive variants from the copy-texts in the editions produced by these two scholars and in the nineteenth-century editions examined, on the variants from the copy-texts in the present edition, and on other similar matters concerning the editing of the texts.

S.W.R.

---

[34] See the appended List of Emendations for the changes.

[35] *Wieland, or the Transformation, Together with Memoirs of Carwin the Biloquist, a Fragment* (New York: Harcourt, 1926; rpt. New York: Hafner, 1958). Pattee apparently based his text of "Carwin" on a copy of E (annotated).

[36] *Three Early American Novels* (Columbus, Ohio: Charles E. Merrill, 1970); Kable lists his changes on pp. 16–17, and only these intentional variants are reported here, unless it is necessary to give the history of a reading first emended by the present editors.

POSSIBLE SCHEDULES OF THE PRINTING OF
WIELAND (1798)

[NOTE. The following tables present the reconstructions of the hypothetical printing schedules for the first edition of *Wieland* (1798) which are referred to above (pp. 356–358). The tables assume the work-and-turn method; were twin half-sheets printed, the tables would be slightly more complex—e.g., for quires B and C we would have B&C (inner formes) and B&C (outer)—but the schedules themselves would remain essentially the same.]

SCHEDULE A
Printing of *Wieland* with Threefold Increase in Production after 13 August

Week of (Mon.)	Date	Half-Sheet No.	Quire	Pages	Contents	Source
7-23	7-25	1	B	1-12	chs. 1 & 2	Smith & Dunlap record date
—	7-27	2	C	13-24	chs. 2 & 3	Smith records date
7-30	7-30	3	D	25-36	chs. 3 & 4	Smith records date
—	8-2	4	E	37-48	chs. 4 & 5	Smith records date
8-6	8-6	5	F	49-60	chs. 5 & 6	Smith records date
—	8-8	6	G	61-72	chs. 6 & 7	Smith records date
8-13	8-13	7	H	73-84	chs. 7 & 8	Smith records date
—	8-14	8	I	85-96	chs. 8 & 9	none
—	8-15	9	K	97-108	ch. 9	none
—	8-16	10	L	109-120	ch. 9 & 10	none
—	8-17	11	M	121-132	chs. 10 & 11	none
—	8-18	12	N	133-144	chs. 11 & 12	none
8-20	8-20	13	O	145-156	chs. 12-14	Smith records visiting Swords
—	8-21	14	P	157-168	chs. 14 & 15	none
—	8-22	15	Q	169-180	chs. 15 & 16	none
—	8-23	16	R	181-192	chs. 16 & 17	none
—	8-24	17	S	193-204	chs. 18 & 19	none
—	8-25	18	T	205-216	chs. 19 & 20	none
8-27	8-27	19	U	217-228	chs. 20 & 21	none
—	8-28	20	X	229-240	chs. 21 & 22	Smith records visiting Swords
—	8-29	21	Y	241-252	chs. 22 & 23	none
—	8-30	22	Z	253-264	chs. 23 & 24	none
—	8-31	23	2A	265-276	chs. 24 & 25	none
—	9-1	24	2B	277-288	chs. 25-27	none
9-3	9-3	25	2C	289-*300*	ch. 27	none
—	9-4	26	*A*	[*4*]	title & adv.	Dunlap records date from letter of Brown's

SCHEDULE **B**
Printing of *Wieland* at Regular Rate of Roughly Two Half-Sheets for Every One Recorded by Smith

Week of (Mon.)	Date	Half-Sheet No.	Quire	Pages	Contents	Source
7-23	7-25	1	B	1-12	chs. 1 & 2	Smith & Dunlap record date
—	7-26	2	C	13-24	chs. 2 & 3	none
—	7-27	3	D	25-36	chs. 3 & 4	Smith records date
—	7-27/28	4	E	37-48	chs. 4 & 5	none
7-30	7-30	5	F	49-60	chs. 5 & 6	Smith records date
—	7-31/8-1	6	G	61-72	chs. 6 & 7	none
—	8-2	7	H	73-84	chs. 7 & 8	Smith records date
—	8-3/5	8	I	85-96	chs. 8 & 9	none
8-6	8-6	9	K	97-108	ch. 9	Smith records date
—	8-7	10	L	109-120	chs. 9 & 10	none
—	8-8	11	M	121-132	chs. 10 & 11	none
—	8-9/12	12	N	133-144	chs. 11 & 12	none
8-13	8-13	13	O	145-156	chs. 12-14	Smith records date
—	?	14	P	157-168	chs. 14 & 15	none
—	?	15	Q	169-180	chs. 15 & 16	none
—	?	16	R	181-192	chs. 16 & 17	none
8-20	8-20	17	S	193-204	chs. 18 & 19	Smith records visiting Swords
—	?	18	T	205-216	chs. 19 & 20	none
—	?	19	U	217-228	chs. 20 & 21	none
—	?	20	X	229-240	chs. 21 & 22	none
8-27	8-27	21	Y	241-252	chs. 22 & 23	none
—	8-28	22	Z	253-264	chs. 23 & 24	Smith records visiting Swords
—	?	23	2A	265-276	chs. 24 & 25	none
—	?	24	2B	277-288	chs. 25-27	none
9-3	9-3	25	2C	289-*300*	ch. 27	none [Adv. dated 9-3]
—	9-4	26	*A*	[*4*]	title & adv.	Dunlap records date from letter of Brown's

APPENDIXES

TEXTUAL NOTES

[NOTE: These discussions of the readings adopted by this edition, either by emendation of the copy-text or retention of its reading when emendation is possible, use a short title to refer to the authorities cited in the note on the Bicentennial Texts earlier in this volume (p. xxii, n. 13). The lineation of *Wieland* and "Carwin" cited here is that of the present edition; for other works of Brown cited, the lineation is that of the first edition. The page-line citation alone appears when the reference is to a passage in the work being discussed; when it is to other works, the following abbreviations precede the page-line citation:

AM1	Arthur Mervyn (1799)	*EH*	Edgar Huntly (1799)
AM2	Arthur Mervyn (1800)	*JT*	Jane Talbot (1801)
Car.	Carwin	*Orm.*	Ormond (1799)
CH	Clara Howard (1801)	*Wie.*	Wieland

The sigla listed at the head of the notes identify the editions of the work discussed.]

WIELAND

A: the copy-text: *Wieland; or the Transformation. An American Tale.* (New York, 1798), the first edition

E1: *Wieland, or the Transformation. An American Tale.* (London, 1811), without authority

E2: *Wieland, An American Tale.* (London, 1822), without authority
P: Fred Lewis Pattee, ed., *Wieland . . . with . . . Carwin* (1926)
K: William S. Kable, ed., *Three Early American Novels* (1970)

11.7 this] The 'object' of converting the savage tribes (10.37-38), which the elder Wieland sees as a 'duty' (11.2), is an antecedent somewhat removed from 'this'. It is, nevertheless, perfectly clear, and E2's 'his' seems unnecessary. Although the Swordses could set *th-* for *h-* (see p. 359f.), Brown's *h-* is not as easily misread as *th-* as his *th-* is mistaken for *h-*. Cf. 115.33, 194.19, 196.16.

12.35 deigned] Brown uses 'deigned' elsewhere (*Car.*, 272.19) in the sense that is required here. A's inadvertent, or even deliberate, adding of an *-s-* (an easy misreading of Brown's small hand) to make a more familiar word gives a plausible reading that could be passed in proof; in fact, Smith passed such an error ('winding waves' for copy's 'widening waves') earlier in the year when proofing Darwin's *Botanic Garden*.

19.6 rendered] The passage obviously requires 'rendered', which Brown uses in similar contexts (see 17.35, 51.38); A's 'rended' is a simple graphic error.

27.29–30 family were] E2's alteration to 'was' may seem reasonable, but A's reading is correct; Brown uses the collective 'family' in the plural elsewhere (*Orm.*, 8.33, *EH*, III, 3.3)—as does his friend Dunlap (*Diary*, I, 3)—and here means that the members of the family were acquainted with Mrs. Baynton (see 166.1–2 for another example in *Wie.*).

35.8 flow] A's 'flow' has all the sound of an idiom of Brown's, who uses the verb in similar contexts (35.28, 38.4, 53.25, 94.34), though of course E2's 'follow' is a possibility as a correction of haplography.

42.24 accent] Although he seems to prefer the plural of this word (cf. 52.6, 60.2), Brown elsewhere uses the singular in a similar context (*EH*, III, 121.12); A's reading (followed by El but altered by E2) seems to be true.

62.13 hither] Although A's 'hither' is certainly a possible mis-reading of its copy's 'thither' (see p. 359f.), which was adopted by E2, the context seems to require 'hither'; the point of view has imperceptibly shifted to 'this' (62.12) crevice, where it remains throughout the account—see 'hither' (63.1), 'here' (63.29), and 'hither' (64.33). Cf. 66.12.

65.39 panic-struck] The issue here is Clara's present state of fear in contrast to her usual courageousness, a fact which the absence of a comma after 'confused' indicates. Brown uses the form in a similar way later (163.6) in *Wieland* and elsewhere (e.g., *AM1*, 83.20, 148.30). The break between lines in A could have occasioned the loss of Brown's hyphen, as a nearly identical case (*An Address on the Cession of Louisiana*, 1803, 39.27–28) suggests.

66.12 Here] Again we are in Clara's consciousness as she medi-tates about 'this' (66.7) spot, as if it were physically present (see the same point of view in 'is' at 66.24); Brown's *Th-* could be misread as *H-*, but in this case E2's 'There' seems to be no true correction. Cf. 62.13.

83.17 cannot] The sense requires the negative, even though it is possible to read the sentence the way it stands in A (as the proofreader and subsequent editors have done); 'perhaps' (83.18) shows that Clara could not 'ascertain' exactly when she became subject to phantoms. A elsewhere omits short words (155.22, 164.8, 194.3, 230.15-16, 239.10) while doubling 'not' (157.29).

84.30 these] Clara's 'fears' are apparently the 'apprehensions' just referred to; the 'these' adopted by E1-2 is a probable correc-tion of A's 'those', which seems to be either a misreading of Brown's small hand or, perhaps, a graphic error encouraged by attraction to the similar 'whose' that is immediately above it in A. Cf. 136.1, 222.16.

90.27 Here] The flow of Clara's account, as the 'Here' at 92.5 suggests, seems to require the immediacy conveyed by 'Here' (cf. 168.22). Brown's *H-* can readily be misread as *Th-* (cf. *Car.*, 268.18).

96.31 realized] Clara's fears are 'real', all right (the reading of A and subsequent editions, except E2); the point seems to be that if she yields to them and thus distrusts the 'divinity' that has protected her, she deserves to suffer what she fears (a not uncommon idea, cf. Job 3:25). Had Brown written 'realized.', it could easily have been shortened to 'real."' in A's crowded last line of a paragraph to avoid dangling 'ized."' in a line by itself. Its having been missed in proof is no surprise, given similar oversights of plausible readings (cf. 12.35).

100.30 shut] Although E2's 'it' could have been in Brown's manuscript and omitted by homoeographon with the -t in 'shut', the object of 'shut' seems to be the 'it' at the end of the sentence (100.31); the tension given by this reading accords with the precipitation of Clara's emotions and actions. See 137.9 and 149.5 for similar constructions without 'it', and 210.34 for the function of a single word in two ways.

127.23 received] Brown's intention is clear enough, even though his wording may be deficient; E2's 'all received' catches Brown's sense, but his dependence elsewhere (*Car.*, 276.30, 285.25) on tenuous associations (here with 'none', i.e., all those who had never before seen Carwin) to imply words suggests that Brown, not A, failed to include 'all'.

136.1 These] A's 'Those' is a possible reading, as its acceptance by subsequent editions indicates, but it is probably a misreading of Brown's 'These', which conveys the sense of immediacy maintained throughout Clara's account and continued in this paragraph (e.g., 'these incidents' and 'this house'). Cf. 84.30 and 222.16.

137.9 opened] Like the lack of 'it' elsewhere (100.30, 149.5; *EH*, III, 63.11), this construction seems to be Brown's own— fostered perhaps by the parallel with 'read' (which shifts in function as the object 'it' is understood or not)—and not A's omission (for which no physical cause, such as homoeographon, is present).

137.21 resource] A's 'resource' could well be a graphic error for 'recourse'; Brown uses both words elsewhere (*Car.*, 262.27, 291.35; 202.2). Neither word has such propriety that it rules out the other. With 'recourse', Carwin could be saying that 'the only way' he has 'to repair' his 'misconduct' is an 'interview' with Clara, which she is unlikely 'to adopt' (12–16) because of his former 'folly and rashness' (20–21). With 'resource', Carwin could be saying that he has 'no means of removing any fears that [Clara] may entertain of [his] designs, but [his] simple and solemn declarations' (17–18), in which she is unlikely to have any 'confidence' (20) because of Carwin's former 'folly and rashness'. Since this is strictly a matter of interpretation that depends on whether one thinks the issue of removing Clara's fears has momentarily superseded Carwin's over-all concern with obtaining the interview, we have chosen to adopt A's reading, partly because its referent is more immediate (in the three preceding sentences rather than those in lines 12–15) and partly because the probabilities lie with A being correct rather than wrong in having the reading that is less predictable and more difficult in the context.

138.9 unaccompanied] To say Carwin's letter is 'not accompanied by . . . uncommon earnestness' is to contradict the tone of the letter and the thoughts in the preceding and following sentences. A's erroneous 'accompanied' may be an error of omission by Brown's own pen or, more likely, by a compositor perhaps confused by the presence of the two other negatives in the sentence. The tone of Clara's exclamations, as she contemplates the unthinkable against the normal, seems to require 'not unaccompanied' rather than the plain 'accompanied'.

150.21 befallen on] The double dative could be A's error, but it is probably Brown's own construction. The compositor of A might well have been induced by the graphic similarity of the ending of the preceding word or the beginning of the following to set 'on' as a natural companion to 'befallen' (through analogy with "fallen"). However, even though Brown uses "befall" correctly elsewhere (e.g., *CH*, 62.11, 233.2), the construction resembles others in the novel (e.g., 'await for', 170.27) and emphasizes the idea that 'fate' has mistakenly crushed Catharine.

151.18 camest] The passage obviously requires the past tense, and 'comest' is an easy graphic error for 'camest' in Brown's small hand. Although elsewhere Brown is sometimes inconsistent in his tenses and confuses them in a somewhat similar form (in 'liedest', an especially difficult form given the "lie"/"lay" confusion, at 232.6), this case is so obvious that the 'comest' seems to be A's error, especially since Brown gets the awkward 'besoughtest' (151.15) correct in this passage.

154.14 affected] The context seems to require 'affected' rather than A's 'effected', for Wieland's loss of reason would surely not bring about Clara's safety. It is possible that the 'effected' of A and subsequent editions is Brown's own word for 'affected' (not just a slip of his pen), but his works indicate that he observed the distinction between the two which was established by his time (see Johnson and *OED*). In an area of the text rife with other errors, A's 'effected' is probably a mistake for 'affected'. Cf. 179.35 and *Car.*, 248.10.

154.30 These] A's 'These looks' (i.e., the 'faces') gives the account a surrealism that is appropriate to Clara's paralyzed mind, especially when the 'looks' are pictured as prying into corners. 'These' seems an unlikely graphic error for the more commonplace 'Their' (which has to take 'faces' as its antecedent) substituted by E1.

155.22 a mistress] At the beginning of a new type line, A omits the article which is required by the immediate context and is clearly needed to complete Brown's parallel with 'a parent'; we, therefore, adopt the 'a' of E1-2 (not followed by P or K), even though Brown sometimes omits articles in other contexts where they are less necessary.

162.13 There] Both 'Here' and A's 'There' (retained by subsequent editions) are plausible readings. The sense of immediacy in Clara's account of this conversation does not seem sufficiently intense to require 'Here', and hence it seems more likely that A's 'There' is correct than that it is an error (presumably graphic) for 'Here'. Cf. 90.27.

162.15 compelled] Although it may seem that 'instigations' should have 'impelled' (E2's reading) rather than 'compelled' (A's) the criminal, either word is plausible. The frequency of error in this part of A argues for emending to 'impelled'. However, 'compelled' has the virtue of suggesting the irresistible force which must have driven the criminal to so horrid a crime, and as the less predictable reading is probably Brown's own, rather than A's error.

164.8 a criminal] Although Brown sometimes omits articles in contexts where they are expected, though not required (see *Car.*, 248.31, 249.1; cf. 155.22), the present context demands the 'a' added by E1-2, P to effect Brown's contrast with 'a friend', 'a father' and so on (164.7); obviously, as the next sentence suggests,

377

'criminal' is not to be read as an adjective, and as a noun it clearly functions in contrast to Wieland's other roles.

166.17 those] Given the relative clause that follows 'ideas' and A's lack of a comma before it, E1-2's 'those' seems the correct reading—rather than the possible 'these' (without an immediate antecedent) printed by A, which could easily have misread Brown's 'those'.

179.35 effected] A's 'affected' hardly conveys the total trans-formation brought about in Wieland in a moment, which is the point Clara is concerned with (as the ensuing sentences show). The 'effected' substituted in E1-2 seems to be the correct reading; 'affected' is either a slip of Brown's pen or, as seems more likely in an area of the text characterized by frequent error, A's own mistake, perhaps caused by misreading or recollection (see 179.24).

187.25 my mind] A's 'my' serves to distinguish Clara's from Wieland's state of mind (just discussed). It is a plausible but unusual phrase that only with great difficulty could be ascribed to A's erring rather than to Brown.

194.19 here] E1-2's 'there' is a plausible correction of A's 'here', especially given the possibility of *th-*/*h-* confusion (see p. 359f.). But as elsewhere (e.g., 62.13) the point of view seems to shift as Clara or her thoughts do, and 'here' preserves the sense of her movement from the chair to the closet, and thus away from the door that Carwin's shadow is about to darken.

195.26 clasped] A's 'clasped' seems to be the right reading, though the graphically similar 'clapped' is a remote possibility; in analogous situations Brown has Pleyel clench his hands (see 42.12), and Wieland clasp his (153.20).

196.16 this] A's 'this' obviously refers to the 'deportment' de-scribed in the preceding paragraph, though 'his' is also a possible reading. Since the Swordses sometimes misread their copy's *h-* as *th-* but the misreading of Brown's *h-* as *th-* is not highly probable, though possible, we adopt A's reading, which is preferable literar-ily.

197.26 denounce] It is possible that 'denounce' (the reading of A and subsequent editions) is an error for Brown's 'pronounce'; neither reading is so compelling that it rules out the other. On the one hand, 'pronounce' suits the immediate context in that it carries on Carwin's metaphor of the trial when linked with 'punishment' and gives the desired contrast to 'listen'. On the other hand, 'denounce' does not violate the metaphor or destroy the contrast, and it is apt, as Carwin has been overwhelmed by Clara's virulent denunciations of him. The less predictable 'denounce' is perhaps more likely to be Brown's word than A's substitution for 'pronounce'.

210.34 not having] E2's 'you' (i.e., Clara) is definitely implied, but is awkward and breaks the rhythm, whereas the sentence can be read as is, when 'you' (210.35) does double duty as the object of 'between' and the referent for the participle 'having'. That E2's 'you' was in Brown's manuscript and was omitted by A's compositor seems unlikely, in view of similar constructions elsewhere (see 100.30, 205.23; *Car.*, 265.11–12). Cf. also *Car.*, 295.2–4, 298.8–10.

222.16 these] Again, A's 'those' seems to be a misreading of Brown's 'these', which suits the sense of immediacy and involvement that he creates throughout the account and, specifically, in this paragraph with words such as 'these gesticulations', 'this inaudible prayer', and 'these tokens'. Cf. 84.30, 136.1.

227.30 this] A's 'this ruin' refers back to 'this desolating rage' (227.28) and forward to 'these horrors' (227.31); thus it applies to both Wieland and Clara, not just to Wieland, as Clara's subsequent words show. Hence, E1's 'his' must be rejected, even though Brown's *h-* could be read as *th-* by the compositors of A (see Textual Essay).

230.15–16 not difficult] Although A's omission of 'not' is followed by subsequent editions, it seems to be an error. Wieland's mutterings, though perhaps not fully audible, are sufficiently comprehensible to Clara, who is sympathetically united with Wieland at this point and who proceeds to explain their 'theme' (230.5–6, 16–19). Even Carwin, outside the room, sufficiently understands their meaning to reply to them (230.20–21). A's error of omission makes the passage unintentionally convoluted and obscure. Cf. 83.17 and especially 222.10–17.

232.6 liedest] A's form seems to represent Brown's own lapse due to the difficulties of "lie" (cf. *Car.*, 259.34), the use of this especially troublesome person and number (cf. 151.18), and his general inconsistency of tense; it could hardly be A's unintentional or deliberate alteration of its copy's more proper 'layest' or 'didst lie' (found in E2).

232.12 faintly] If 'now' is emphatic—is to be read as *even now* (i.e., now that Clara is looking back on the experience)—there is no need to hypothesize A's loss of Brown's 'but', or to adopt this reading from E2.

236.26 reverie] The final *-ie* spelling, rather than *-y*, was at least current—if not dominant—by the eighteenth century and need not imply A's loss of Brown's *-s*; the singular is used by Brown elsewhere (42.21), is perfectly idiomatic for the time (see *OED*), accords with 'dream' (236.22), was passed by E1, and seems superior to E2's plural.

239.10 predisposed him] The verb must, of course, have an object, and the short 'him' (i.e., Wieland) is obviously the one who was 'predisposed' by Carwin's actions to the 'perversion of mind' ('maniacal illusion') that Cambridge is discussing. A omits short words elsewhere (194.3, 83.17), though this error may be attributable to the homoeographon of 'him to' and 'Carwin to' in the line above.

CARWIN

M: the copy-text, in *The Literary Magazine* (1803–05)
L: in William Dunlap's *Life of Brown* (1815), without authority
E: *Carwin, the Biloquist, and Other American Tales*, vol. I (London, 1822), without authority
P: Fred Lewis Pattee, ed., *Wieland . . . with . . . Carwin* (1926)
K: William S. Kable, ed., *Three Early American Novels* (1970)

248.10 effect] The main reason for emending the 'affect' of M-L must be literary (although clearly an ill-formed *e-* of Brown's *could* have been read as *a-*): Brown, who knows the distinction between "affect" and "effect" which was established by his time (see Johnson and *OED*), uses 'effect' in similar constructions elsewhere (249.8, 253.8, 286.39; *Wie.*, 176.1, 201.5) and here means "to bring to pass" avoidance of 'censures and stripes' (248.8–9). Johnson and the *OED* have "affect" in the sense of "aim at" or "aspire to" (Jefferson, 1776), but Carwin adopts 'stratagems' to avoid stripes, not just strive to avoid them.

254.9 be at] Although 'bear' is a plausible reading and could have been misread as 'be at' by M, 'be at the expense' is a frequent construction in the eighteenth century (see *OED*) and has a Brownian awkwardness about it.

258.4–8 I . . . them, and . . . I] Though complex and far from lucid, M's construction not only makes sense but is obviously what Brown intended; the sentence divides at 'or' (258.5)—not at 'them' (258.6), as is assumed in L's alteration, which quite naturally leads to E's total revision.

258.31 could I] The addition of 'I', first made in E and adopted by P, is necessary to make sense of the passage in which M omits 'I' at the end of a line; a parallel is M's 'could' (for 'I could') at 263.18, which is similar to omissions throughout M. See the Textual Essay.

259.34 laid] According to Johnson (sig. b4), Lowth (p. 76), and Webster's *Dictionary* (pp. 173, 176), the word should be 'lay'. But Fox's *Instructions for Right Spelling* (p. 89) confuses 'lain' and 'laid', and Brown may have suffered from a similar confusion (cf. *Wie.*, 232.6). Almost certainly he wrote 'laid', with M-L (but not E) following him.

261.29 not uttered] E's addition of 'not' is necessary to remedy M's omission (followed by L), which is probably an example of haplography; the idea that the song came from a human would hardly call for comment, whereas the spectators are so amazed by Carwin's trick that the 'only' explanation they can find is that the source of the song is, like Ariel, an inhuman creature that can rise into the air.

263.18 I could] M once again omits an 'I' that is necessary to the sense and was apparently missed by the compositor reading the MS; a parallel is M's failure to print 'I' at 258.31, one of several omissions throughout M. See Textual Essay.

263.27 strain] Although M's 'strain' may be an error for 'train' (E's reading) caused by recollection (see 263.15), it effectively conveys the sense of a line of thought regarding the deception of Dorothy produced by Ludloe's comments. Probably the word is Brown's, rather than an error.

263.39 supernal] Although this could be M's eyeskip error for 'supernatural', it might just as well be Brown's own word. The reference to the 'quarter' (263.38) from which the voice comes suggests 'supernal' rather than 'supernatural', and Milton writes of "errands of supernal Grace" (*OED*).

265.5 were] The compound subject of 'husband' and (she) 'herself' seems to be understood and to dictate 'were'; such constructions are not uncommon in Brown, even though Murray (p. 88) and Lowth (pp. 104–105) denounce them, the latter criticizing Pope and Swift for incorrectly using "island" and "mankind."

265.11–12 if . . . it] The words "for them" are to be understood as implied in this construction, even though the sentence is awkward as it stands and probably would have been changed had Brown revised; E's change to 'on legal compulsion' is obviously editorial.

267.33 to me] An example of Brown's inversion, where 'to me' would normally follow 'assistance'; M has not omitted 'give' after 'to'.

268.18 His] The *Th-/H-* confusion of Brown's hand makes M's 'This' a likely mistake for 'His'; even though 'This' is a possible reading (as its retention in all editions after M indicates), the context shows that Carwin refers to Ludloe's treatment of him, discussed in the preceding paragraphs.

269.3 topic,] 'This . . . heart' is not a true "case absolute" and thus should not be separated from the rest of the sentence in the way M's pointing implies; 'topic' is the object of 'introduced', whereas 'being . . . heart' is a participial phrase modifying 'topic' which should, in accord with the mode of punctuation dominant in M, be set off by commas.

269.9 motive] Either M's 'motive' (followed by L) or E's 'motives' is a possible reading, but though 'the sordid motives of gain' provides an exact parallel to 'erroneous principles', Brown's inconsistency of number even between nouns and pronouns (283.31–32) and the lack of any clear cases of M's loss of his final -*s* suggest that 'motive' was in his manuscript. Cf. *Wie.*, 89.19; 299.32–33.

269.15 destructive] M's 'destruction' is probably an error (followed by L) for Brown's 'destructive' (the reading in E), which was caused by recollection of 'gratifications' (269.14). Although either reading is possible, 'destructive' seems to fit best the elaboration 'they enervated his frame and brutalized his mind' (269.16–17).

270.1 novelty, however, disappearing.] M's use of a comma after 'disappearing' obscures the fact that 'Their novelty, however, disappearing' is the subject of 'left' and not a "case absolute." The pointing of Brown's manuscript may have been unclear (cf. 269.3, 270.13–14), and M's could be an unsuccessful attempt to clarify the ambiguity or correct Brown's "slighter inaccuracy."

270.13–14 apartments.] The phrase 'his apartments being wholly separate from mine' is a true "case absolute," with 'his apartments ... mine' existing independent of the rest of the sentence. M's pointing suggests that 'apartments' is the object of 'discovering' and 'being ... mine' a mere participial phrase modifying 'apartments', whereas Brown (whose punctuation in the manuscript was probably deficient) meant 'in what ... employed' to be the object of Carwin's 'discovering'. Cf. 269.3, 270.1, for other ambiguous pointing in similar constructions, and *Wie.*, 215.19.

272.31 man] Brown seems to use 'man' in the generic sense here (cf. 274.30 and 'nation' below, 272.37). E's 'men' could be correct (*a* for *e* is a misreading of Brown's hand not too difficult), but the *OED* shows "man" could stand for "mankind" in Brown's time, as L's retention of 'man' and Brown's similar use of the word elsewhere (*Wie.*, 118.37) suggests.

272.37–38 a nation ... their] Here M uses the collective noun 'nation' first as a singular and then as a plural; but Brown often produced such awkward shifts (cf. 283.31–32) and hence E's change to 'its' is unnecessary.

274.27–28 confessors; ... prelate,] Theoretically, the first clause could end after either 'confessors' or 'prelate'. But the contrasts between '*hidalgo*' and 'peasant', 'monk' and 'prelate', 'austere' and 'voluptuous' (which do not apply to 'priests' and 'confessors') imply that the second clause begins with 'the *hidalgo*', as in E and P, just as the introduction of 'the' before '*hidalgo*' (suggesting that the following words are not the object of 'the hearts of') and the grouping of the singulars in contrast to the plurals (resulting from the use of the article) indicate that the break occurs after 'confessors'. The decision must rest on literary grounds alone, since a check of about twenty exemplars of the copy-text verifies that all internal points in the sentence are commas.

278.4 thousands, and thousands,] The phrase 'into millions' does not seem to be intended as an after-thought; the point is that expansion is irresistible under these conditions, and L's emendation of M is necessary to convey this point. For a similar case, see 268.15–16.

281.27 candidate] M's inconsistency between 'candidate' and 'they' resembles the disagreement between noun and pronoun elsewhere in Brown's work (e.g., *Wie.*, 89.19, 89.26–27, 196.19–20), though in "Carwin" itself this inconsistency only involves the troublesome 'somebody' (295.30) and collective nouns (272.31, 272.37–38, 283.31–32). Whereas the plural occurs throughout this passage (281.16–34) and the final -*s* could have been dropped inadvertently at the end of M's line, the lack of any clear evidence of M's loss of final -*s* and Brown's general inattention to agreement between noun, pronoun, and verb both suggest that M's 'candidate' (followed by L and K) was in Brown's manuscript and that E's change (adopted by P) is unnecessary.

283.31–32 fraternity . . . it . . . them] The varying use of the collective noun is Brown's, who elsewhere writes in this manner (cf. 272.37–38); thus it is not due to an error in M, whose reading is accepted by L and E.

285.26 of going] M's reading, accepted by subsequent editions, seems to be Brown's; "discovery" is the subject of 'going' implied in a circuitous way by virtue of the contrast with 'suspicion' and the previous linking of 'unsuspected and undiscovered' (285.23–24). For a similar construction, see 276.30.

301.34 *incognitae*] That the printer missed '*terrae*' (added by E) in his MS seems less tenable than the view that (1) Brown's simple 'a' was misread as the digraph (an easy slip in his small hand) or (2) Brown meant the '*terrae*' of the familiar phrase to be understood. Since the second alternative requires a simpler hypothesis and gives a reading that perfectly suits the context, we retain M's reading.

304.13 will] Presumably, the 'new obligation' would make Carwin a 'new being'. But though M could have omitted 'it' or 'this new obligation' (through eyeskip), a similar construction elsewhere (293.26–27) and the use of 'in which' (subordinating the 'new obligation' and emphasizing 'the moment') suggest that M has indeed reproduced Brown's own construction.

LIST OF EMENDATIONS

[NOTE: This list contains all instances of alterations of the copy-texts, except for the silent changes specified in the note on the Bicentennial Texts earlier in this volume and the few other emendations connected with the regularization to 'Ludloe' and the serial appearance of "Carwin" (see the Textual Essay). Alterations involving quotation of discourse appear separately below, headed by an explanation of the form of notation. Elsewhere in the present list, each note gives the reading of the Bicentennial text before the bracket, followed by a siglum identifying its earliest source (either one of the editions examined, or the present editors) and then by the variant reading(s) of the copy-text and of the other editions between it and the source of the adopted reading. This information is provided for both substantives and accidentals; for a complete history of substantive variants among the editions examined, see the Historical List. An asterisk (*) before the lemma indicates that the Textual Notes discuss the emendation. A wavy dash (~) represents the same word appearing before the bracket and occurs only in the recording of variants in punctuation or other accidentals associated with that word, when the word itself is not the variant being noted; the inferior caret (ᵥ) shows that punctuation is absent. Three dots (. . .) mean that the note omits one or more words in a series, and a vertical stroke (|) marks the break between lines. When the reading of the lemma is a possible compound and is ambiguously hyphenated between two lines in the present edition, a dagger (†) precedes the lemma; the reader may consult Part B of the following appendix for more information on such word-division. "B" following the bracket identifies readings adopted for the first time in the Bicentennial Edition (that is, readings not appearing in the editions examined). Preceding the list for each work are the sigla which identify the editions examined and cited in the lists.]

WIELAND

A: the copy-text: *Wieland; or the Transformation. An American Tale.* (New York, 1798), the first edition
E1: *Wieland, or the Transformation. An American Tale.* (London, 1811), without authority
E2: *Wieland, An American Tale.* (London, 1822), without authority
P: Fred Lewis Pattee, ed., *Wieland . . . with . . . Carwin* (1926)
K: William S. Kable, ed., *Three Early American Novels* (1970)

*12.35	deigned] E2; designed A-E1
18.6	naked;] B; ~, A-E1,P,K; ~: E2
*19.6	rendered] E1; rended A
19.11	structure̬] B; ~, A-E2,P,K
19.28	selects̬] P;~, A-E2
23.18	disordered,] B; ~̬ A-E2,P,K
26.19	England,] B; ~̬ A-E2,P,K
28.7	sedulously] E2; seduously A-E1
28.27	child,] E1; ~; A
30.29	*polliceatur*] B; *polliciatur* A-E2,P,K
37.13–14	advantages, he thought, attending it] B; advantages̬ he thought̬ attending it A-E1,P,K; advantages attending it, he thought, E2
39.38	scheme̬] B; ~, A-E2,P,K
42.9	Yes.] E1; ~, A
42.14	dead!] E1; ~? A
47.19	blossom̬] B; ~̬ A-E2,P,K
65.36	courage.] E1; ~, A
*65.39	panic-struck] E1; panic | struck A
76.23	others:] B; ~; A-E2,P,K
77.20	value,] B; ~̬ A-E2,P,K
82.15	hypocrisy] E1; hyprocrisy A
*83.17	cannot] B; can A-E2,P,K
84.10	lamp,] B; ~̬ A-E2,P,K
*84.30	these] E1; those A
*90.27	Here] E1; There A

*96.31	realized] E2; real A-E1
98.2	augmenting‸] E2; ∼, A-E1
100.29	afraid] E1; affraid A
105.14	night,] E2; ∼; A-E1
119.20	servants,] B; ∼‸ A-E2,P,K
128.26	uncertainty,] B; ∼‸ A-E2,P,K
130.25	it] E1; in A
135.25	it‸] B; ∼, A-E2,P,K
*136.1	These] B; Those A-E2,P,K
*138.9	unaccompanied] B; accompanied A-E2,P,K
139.13	Now, . . . thought,] E2; ∼‸ . . . ∼‸ A-E1
140.8	At] E1; A A
142.17-18	falsehood] E1; falshood A
142.28	*Hut*] B; *hut* A,P,K; hut E1-2
146.26	moment,] E2; ∼‸ A-E1
148.3	shrieking;] B; ∼, A-E2,P,K
*151.18	camest] B; comest A-E2,P,K
*154.14	affected] B; effected A-E2,P,K
*155.22	a mistress] E1; mistress A
156.17	weakness] E1; weekness A
157.29	not] E1; not not A
157.33	*not a*] B; not a A-E2,P,K
159.4	Germany‸] E1; ∼, A
*164.8	a criminal] E1; criminal A
164.27	ones‸] B; ∼, A-E2,P,K
*166.17	those] E1; these A
*179.35	effected] E1; affected A
185.22	execution;] B; ∼, A-E2,P,K
187.29	danger,] B; ∼‸ A-E2,P,K
189.19	heaven,] B; ∼; A-E2,P,K
189.20	virtue,] B; ∼; A-E2,P,K
192.1	*Hut*] B; HUT A-E1,P,K; hut E2
193.1	habitation‸ . . . darkness,] B; ∼, . . . ∼‸ A-E2, P,K
194.3	drag on] E2; drag A-E1
197.34	reason;] B; ∼, A-E2,P,K
202.18	fearlessness] E1; fearlesness A
203.29	foresaw] E1; forsaw A
204.6	intended,] B; ∼‸ A-E2,P,K
208.14	to] B; *to* A-E2,P,K
209.22	hopelessness] E1; hopelesness A

209.24	scheme,] E2; ~ₐ A-E1
219.24	tear] E1; tare A
*222.16	these] B; those A-E2,P,K
223.38	longerₐ] E1; ~, A
225.11	for!] E1; ~? A
227.3	infernal,] B; ~ₐ A-E2,P,K
227.10	heaven;] B; ~, A-E2,P,K
228.16	hurry] E2; Hurry A-E1
229.14	to] B; *to* A-E2,P,K
*230.15–16	not difficult] B; difficult A-E2,P,K
232.23	*Hut*] B; hut A-E2,P,K
238.20	elapsed,] B; ~ₐ A-E2,P,K
*239.10	predisposed him] B; predisposed A-E2,P,K
239.35	*Hut*] B; hut A-E2,P,K

CARWIN

M: the copy-text, in *The Literary Magazine* (1803–05)
L: in William Dunlap's *Life of Brown* (1815), without authority
E: *Carwin, the Biloquist, and Other American Tales,* vol. I (London, 1822), without authority
P: Fred Lewis Pattee, ed., *Wieland . . . with . . . Carwin* (1926)
K: William S. Kable, ed., *Three Early American Novels* (1970)

*248.10	effect] E; affect M-L
250.15	uttered] L; utterred M
250.25	voice,] E; ~ₐ M-L
250.34	scarcely] L; scarely M
252.26	and,] B; ~ₐ M-E,P,K
252.35	habitₐ] B; ~, M-E,P,K
254.12–13	propensities] L; propensites M
254.28	heard,] B; ~ₐ M-E,P,K
255.11	views;] E; ~, M-L
255.13	detection;] B; ~, M-L,P,K; ~: E
255.34	intense,] L; ~ₐ M
257.6	every where] L; everywhere M
258.26	them;] E; ~, M-L
258.28	neighbour's] L; neighbours M
*258.31	could I] E; could M-L

260.10   reputation.] L; ~ₐ M
261.2   lies.] P; ~ₐ M-E
261.21   Cowslip's] L; Cowslips M
261.26–27   succeeded] L; succeded M
*261.29   not uttered] E; uttered M-L
262.7   who was] E; who as M-L
262.14–15   up . . . Dorothy] B; ~.....~ M; ~; ~ L;
                ~. ~ E; ~, — ~ P; ~ . . . . ~ K
262.18   clothes] L; cloths M
262.21   aunt's] L; aunts' M
263.4–5   intercourse] L; intercouse M
*263.18   I could] E; could M-L
264.4   property] L; proporty M
264.16   deter] L; de- | deter M
266.17   inquired,] L; ~ₐ M
266.24   removed;] B; ~, M-L,P,K; ~. E
266.29   expressing,] B; ~ₐ M-E,P,K
266.31   replied,] L; ~ₐ M
267.11   with] L; wth M
267.16   subsist] L; subsit M
267.19–20   beₐ . . . leastₐ] B; ~, . . . ~, M-E,P,K
267.31   in *promises*] B; *in promises* M,P,K; in promises
                L-E
*268.18   His] B; This M-E,P,K
269.2   guidance,] L; ~ₐ M
*269.3   topic,] E; ~ₐ M-L
269.9   gainₐ] B; ~, M-E,P,K
*269.15   destructive] E; destruction M-L
*270.1   novelty, however, disappearingₐ] B; noveltyₐ
                howeverₐ disappearing, M-L,P,K;
                novelty, however, disappearing, E
270.7–8   uncontrouled] L; uncontroled M
270.7–8   uncontrouled,] L; ~ₐ M
*270.13–14   apartmentsₐ] B; ~, M-E,P,K
271.2   thoughtsₐ] B; ~, M-E,P,K
273.8   intercourse] L; intercouse M
273.19   thatₐ] B; ~, M-E,P,K
273.19   rites] E; rights M-L
273.24   transgressions,] L; ~ₐ M
273.35   perfection] L; pecfection M
273.39   principles:] B; ~; M-E,P,K

274.2	intrinsical;] E; ~: M-L
274.6	duty,] L; ~ˌ M
274.15	perseverance] L; perseverence M
274.21	preparation,] L; ~ˌ M
*274.27	confessors;] B; ~, M-L, K; ~,— E,P
275.16	power:] B; ~, M-E,P,K
275.32	heretic] L; heritic M
277.3	force;] E; ~: M-L
277.31	menˌ] E; ~, M-L
*278.4	thousands, and thousands,ˌ] L;
	thousands,ˌ and thousands, M
279.19	wisdomˌ] B; ~, M-E,P,K
282.2	trespass] L; tresspass M
290.11	to] L; to to M
290.13	these,ˌ] B; ~, M-E,P,K
290.14	existence,ˌ] B; ~, M-E,P,K
291.9	which] L; which which M
292.28	it,] L; ~ˌ M
293.34	insuperable,] B; ~ˌ M-E,P,K
298.31	proportions,ˌ] E; ~, M-L
299.38	Cook.] L; Cook.—EDITOR. M
308.15	affirmative:] B; ~. M-L,K; ~, E,P
310.28	privy,] E; ~; M-L

QUOTATIONS

[NOTE: Emendations involving quotation of discourse are listed here; the reading of the Bicentennial text precedes the bracket, and that of the copy-text follows it.]

WIELAND

28.2–3	"Who . . . name?"] ˌ~ . . . ~?ˌ
28.16	ˌMiss] "~
28.26	ˌThey] "~
29.3	ˌIt] "~
29.13–26	ˌNew . . . property.ˌ] "~ . . . ~."
33.16	"'Stop . . . path.'] "ˌ~ . . . ~."
33.22–23	'Who . . . Catharine?'] ˌ~ . . . ~?ˌ
33.24–25	'Yes . . . house.'] "~ . . . ~."
42.16–19	ˌBut . . . company?ˌ] "~ . . . ~?"

391

42.31 silent.ₐ] ~."
43.15–18 'We . . . there.'] "~ . . . ~."
43.25–33 'Suppose . . . subdue.'] "~ . . . ~."
43.35–44.1 'You . . . remain.'] "~ . . . ~."
44.1 'But,'] "~,"
44.2 'when . . . it?'] "~ . . . ~?"
44.10 'No.'] "~."
44.12 'Catharine,'] ₐ~,ₐ
44.13 'where . . . you?'] ₐ~ . . . ~?ₐ
44.16 his.ₐ] ~."
44.17 "'Well,'] "ₐ~,"
44.17–19 'What . . . informed.'] "~ . . . ~."
44.20 "'Yes,'] "ₐ~,"
44.20 'this . . . fancy.'] "~ . . . ~."
44.25 'Yes,'] "~,"
44.26–30 'my . . . silence.'] "~ . . . ~."
44.32–33 'You . . . tomb.'] "~ . . . ~."
44.36 'Who . . . speaks?'] "~ . . . ~?"
44.37 'whence . . . tidings?'] "~ . . . ~?"
44.38–39 'From . . . dead'] "~ . . . ~."
45.7 'Yes,'] "~,"
96.27 ₐSurely,ₐ] "~,"
96.27–31 ₐthere . . . realized.ₐ] "~ . . . ~."
130.10 'Aye,'] "~,"
130.10–13 'that . . . advertisement.'] "~ . . . ~."
147.26 *"hold! hold!"*] ₐ~! ~!ₐ
164.1 ₐTheodore] "~
168.4–7 'Thy . . . fall.'] "~ . . . ~."
168.12 "'My wife!'] "ₐMy wife!ₐ
168.12–17 'O . . . deed.'] ₐ~ . . . ~·ₐ
168.35–37 "'Come . . . me!'] "ₐ~ . . . ~!ₐ
168.39–169.1 'What . . . go?'] "~ . . . ~?"
169.14 "'Follow . . . see,'] "ₐ~ . . . ~,"
169.16–17 "'What . . . her?'] "ₐ~ . . . ~?"
169.18 "'Come . . . yourself.'] "ₐ~ . . . ~."
169.26 ₐwhat . . . matter?ₐ] "~ . . . ~?"
169.27 ₐwhither . . . going?ₐ] "~ . . . ~?"
169.35–36 'Why . . . in.'] "~ . . . ~."
170.17–20 'O . . . worst!'] "~ . . . ~!"
170.24 "'Come then,'] "ₐ~ ~,"
170.24 'let . . . go.'] "~ . . . ~."

170.25	"'I . . . light.'] "ˌ~ . . . ~."
170.26–27	"'Fly . . . return.'] "ˌ~ . . . ~·ˌ
171.3–4	'Wieland . . . you?'] "~ . . . ~?"
171.12–14	"'My . . . wife?'] "ˌ~ . . . ~?"
171.25–27	"'O . . . thyself.'] "ˌ~ . . . ~."
171.31–35	"'Undone . . . die!'] "ˌ~ . . . ~!"
172.1–2	"'I . . . must.'] "ˌ~ . . . ~."
172.6–10	"'Surely . . . help——'] "ˌ~ . . . ~—"
173.39	mother!—' "] ~!—'ˌ
177.21–23	"Such . . . so?"] ˌ~ . . . ~?ˌ
177.25	"is . . . dead!"] ˌ~ . . . ~!ˌ
204.2–3	'hold! hold!'] "~! ~!"
225.10–11	"O . . . for?"] ˌ~ . . . ~?ˌ

CARWIN

266.17	inquired,] ~ˌ
266.31	replied,] ~ˌ
308.15	affirmative:] ~.

END-OF-LINE WORD-DIVISION

[NOTE: The two following lists provide information on the word-division of divisible compounds that are hyphenated at the ends of lines in the copy-text or in the Bicentennial Edition. List A contains, in the form of the established text, such compounds which are hyphenated and divided at the break between lines in the copy-text. A double dagger (‡) precedes the notation if the word happens to be similarly hyphenated in the Bicentennial Edition (see List B for more information on such words). List B contains all examples of possible compounds hyphenated at the break between lines in this edition which are meant to be hyphenated in the established text; the absence of such compounds hyphenated in this edition shows that they are meant to be un-hyphenated in the established text. A dagger (†) precedes the notation if the word is an emendation (see the List of Emendations for further information) and a double dagger (‡) precedes it if the word happens to be similarly hyphenated in the copy-text (see List A of this appendix on such words). Both lists omit words with hyphens between capitalized elements (e.g., North- | American) and those that are clearly mere compositorial syllabication (including syllabication of compound words falling elsewhere than at the point of word-division).]

A. *Word-Division in the Copy-Text*

WIELAND

7.10	fruitfulness	9.22	mournful
8.36	Sunday	10.22	himself

11.17	himself	104.19	disappear
12.6	postpone	107.29	insight
13.15	likewise	110.5	considerable
15.6	nothing	110.32	indeed
16.39	discharged	111.1	dishonor
18.31	somewhat	111.17	outweigh
22.15	sometimes	115.31	myself
22.35	thoughtful	117.3	bespoke
25.18	discovered	117.9	distempered
27.34–35	motionless	118.31	upbraid
31.19	Methought	119.1	myself
33.34	discernable	123.33	worthless
35.12	understanding	124.15	witchcraft
38.14	nothing	127.15	nothing
41.11	unnoticed	129.2	newspaper
41.23	nothing	130.12	republish
‡45.1–2	notwithstanding	131.12	bespoke
50.3	powerless	131.38	Bloodshed
51.37	somewhat	133.35	understanding
53.17	reminded	136.11	myself
54.20	inroads	137.23	disclose
54.28	darksome	138.5	midnight
62.20	cheerful	138.32	themselves
62.36	withheld	139.6	artless
64.33	afternoon	141.3	re-exaltation
75.21	understanding	143.5	Meanwhile
75.32	overheard	143.36	Meanwhile
76.16	summer-house	144.6	understanding
76.29	without	144.6	without
80.36	misapprehension	144.9	myself
80.38	to-morrow	149.15	supernatural
81.2	unforeseen	151.18	mistake
82.36	disappointment	151.24	cannot
85.14	nevertheless	154.15	mad-man
91.31	yourself	161.38	servant-maid
94.1	Nothing	162.4	himself
94.14	unspeakably	163.5	god-head
96.7	without	163.6	panic-struck
99.6	Instead	166.24	without
100.39	moon-light	167.29	nameless
101.15	midnight	169.27	ceaseless

175.16	understanding	207.28	nothing
176.9	myself	207.29	Instead
178.15	extraordinary	208.21	useless
179.36	tenfold	210.20	cannot
180.34	supernatural	217.6	somewhat
182.7	powerfully	217.9	sometimes
183.14	mistaken	222.13	understanding
183.27	herself	225.22	mournful
183.33	friendship	232.19	nothing
186.13	without	233.4	fulfilled
189.10	likewise	233.31	without
190.3	wakeful	234.15	hopeless
198.20	nothing	239.10	predisposed
199.39	however	239.13	himself
200.11	whatever	239.18	usefulness
204.2	powerful	240.19	suitable
205.17	sometimes	240.37	lawless
207.3	however	244.17	double-tongued

CARWIN

247.7	to-day	267.30	hurtful
248.7	outroot	268.27	nothing
250.3	midnight	270.2	myself
250.32	twilight	271.1	overflow
251.32	beclouded	271.10	hitherto
252.13	another	271.25	yourself
253.23	another	272.13	successful
255.9	misgivings	274.5	sometimes
257.35	disobedience	275.9	biloquial
258.33	discovered	275.10	yourselves
260.9–10	extraordinary	275.33	whatever
261.31	viewless	279.17	boundless
262.17	kinswoman	280.32	mankind
262.30	meanwhile	281.25	immortal
262.38	mournful	‡282.1–2	himself
263.35	discovering	282.3	withheld
267.24	myself	283.31	withdraw
267.26	however	285.34	myself

396

286.19	somewhat	299.33	without
‡287.20–21	without	301.5	ourselves
288.38	Something	301.28	sometimes
291.14	henceforth	302.14	whatever
292.12	forethought	302.16	itself
293.14	Indeed	306.20	all-absorbing
294.31	himself	306.27	themselves
295.32	overturned	307.18	doubtless
297.29	myself	307.25	ourselves
298.17	nothing	308.36	something
299.1	outlines	309.34	hitherto
299.23	nothing		

B. *Word-Division in the Bicentennial Edition*

WIELAND

6.18	grand-father	122.32	breakfast-table
9.36	grand-father	157.14	after-scene
11.29	summer-house	173.7	blood-suffused
20.20	boarding-schools	205.25	short-hand
86.26	summer-house	209.21	self-upbraiding
100.20	re-enter	226.28	half-formed

HISTORICAL LIST OF SUBSTANTIVE VARIANTS

[NOTE: This appendix lists only substantive variants from the Bicentennial text in the editions examined; accidentals— including accidental variants of the readings—are not, as such, listed. Thus the report that two editions agree in having one of two readings (e.g., 'apprized' as against 'surprised') implies only that they both have the same word (e.g., perhaps in the spellings *apprized* and *apprised*) and not necessarily the identical form. Each note gives the reading of the Bicentennial text before the bracket, followed by the variant reading and then the sigla for the editions having that variant. A wavy dash (∿) represents the same word appearing before the bracket and occurs when variation involves punctuation associated with that word but the word itself is not the variant being noted; the inferior caret (ₐ) shows that punctuation is absent. In a given entry, the editions are cited only when they vary substantively from the reading of the Bicentennial text given in the lemma (i.e., omission of sigla implies agreement). Preceding the list of variants for each work are the sigla which identify the editions cited.]

WIELAND

A: the copy-text: *Wieland; or the Transformation. An American Tale.* (New York, 1798), the first edition

E1: *Wieland, or the Transformation. An American Tale.* (London, 1811), without authority

E2: *Wieland, An American Tale.* (London, 1822), without authority

P: Fred Lewis Pattee, ed., *Wieland . . . with . . . Carwin* (1926)
K: William S. Kable, ed., *Three Early American Novels* (1970)

Title   Wieland; or the Transformation] Wieland, E2
Head-title   Wieland; or the Transformation] Wieland. E1–2
3.2–3   the favorable . . . publish.] it is the author's inten-
              tion to publish if this production be favourably
              received. E2
3.11   but] and E2
3.17   its] this P
3.20   moral painters] painters E2
3.26   awakened] excited E1–2
3.31   C.B.B.] B.C.B. E1
3.32   September 3] September E1–2
5.7   to] for P
5.18   nothing more] nothing E1–2
5.26   past] part E1–2
6.8   corroborations] corroboration E1–2
6.15   suspended] expended E1
6.21   vacations] vacation E1–2
6.29   mortally] seriously E1–2
6.34   be] have been E2
7.15   child‸] child, my father, E2
7.16   the merchant] Weise E2
7.17   trader] merchant E2
7.20   now] thus E2
7.29   of recreation] for recreation E1–2
8.8   This] The P
8.23   finished] had finished E2
8.25   further] farther E2
8.26–27   light . . . present] sight . . . prelent E1
8.27   it] the volume E2
9.7   were] was E2
9.9   His] My father's E2
9.39   his] this E2
10.16   for] of E2
10.37   ancient] early E2
11.7   this] his E2

399

11.14	a] his P, K
11.31	foot] base E2
12.10–11	but her] but P
12.28	a dreamer] dreamer E1–2
12.35	deigned] designed A–E1, P, K
14.1	he] my father E2
14.8	a more] more P
15.9	it that] it E1–2
15.15	this] his P
15.36	himself] him E1–2
15.39	that it] it E1–2
16.3	they] he E1–2
16.8	toward] towards E1–2
16.19	that she] she P
16.28	An] A E1–2
17.10–11	was heard on the outside] on the outside was heard E1–2
17.24	towards] toward P
19.6	rendered] rended A
21.17	by] for E2
21.27	bounds] bonds P
22.11	beside] besides E2
22.12	an] a E1–2
22.18–19	understanding] understandings E2
22.38	principles] principle E1
23.2	positions] provisions P
23.24	ground] grounds E2
24.9	sung] sang E2
25.20	calvinistic] Calvinistic E2
25.28	an] a E2
25.37	ancient] accustomed E2
26.8	sort] degree E1–2
27.12	resided,] ~ ʌ E1–2
27.30	were] was E2
27.30–31	perform] make E2
29.3	an] a E1–2
29.16	and] or E2
32.16	behaviour. He] behaviour: he E1–2
32.36	more calm] calm E2
33.16	further] farther E2, P
34.15–16	to take away the solemnities] to dissipate the gloom E2

35.8	flow] follow E2
36.5	dark] darkness E2
37.12	establish] re-establish E1–2
37.14	he thought, attending it] attending it, he thought, E2
38.13	at present] then E2
38.18	were] was P
38.28	not only as instruments of misery to others] as instruments of misery not only to others E2
38.39	should] could E2
39.13	but] and E2
40.17	some one's] some one E2
40.26	proposed. He] proposed, he E1–2
40.30	if possible, or prevent] or prevent, if possible E2
40.33	her] its E2
40.38	me] I E2
42.15	her] the lady E2
42.16	agitations] agitation E2
42.24	accent] accents E2
43.17	a while] awhile E1–2
43.28	beside] besides E2, P
43.32	stratagem] stratagems E2
44.20	the fancy] fancy E2
44.20–21	We again sunk into mutual and thoughtful silence.] Again we both sank into thoughtful silence. E2
45.5	inquired,] ~∧ E1–2
45.31	beside] besides E2, P
49.10	shall] may E2
50.6	contemplation] the contemplation E2
50.10	in] at E1–2
50.17–18	his body] a body E2
50.33	pausing,] ~∧ E1–2
50.35	towards] toward P
50.35	house,] ~∧ E1–2
50.38	remained] continued E2
51.14	the acquisition] acquisition P
51.18	and she was a] a E2
51.26	an] a E1–2, P
52.9	The voice was not only] Not only was the voice E2
52.11	an] a E1–2
52.22	it] if P
52.29	an half hour] half an hour E1–2

52.30	and] an E2
52.31	garb] a garb E2
52.33	this] the E2
52.37	sunk] sank E2
53.8	upon] on E2
54.2	this] this event E2
54.3	link?] ⁓. E1–2
54.4	Next] The next E2
54.10	whose attractions] the attractions of which E2
55.15	fortunes] fortune P
55.20	with] by E2
55.23	Cavalier] cavalier E1–2
56.8	afflicted] affected E2
56.15	somewhat] something E1–2
56.38	is] was E1–2
57.22	shewed me] shewed E1–2
57.28	should be] was E2
58.21	sunk] sank E2
59.14	resolved] determined E2
59.23	custom] usual custom E1–2
59.35	voice] supernatural voice E2
59.37	case] cases E2
60.9	ancient] former E2
62.13	hither] thither E2
62.32	at the] the E2
63.6	upon] on E2
63.17	had heard] heard E1–2
63.24	further] farther E2
63.33	umbrage] foliage E2
64.2	unintermitted] uninterrupted E1–2
64.36	impetuosity] confusion E2
65.19–20	Who was there with whom I had] With whom had I E2
65.24	But this sympathy was not] Nor was this sympathy E2
65.39	panic-struck] panic struck A, P, K
66.12	Here] There E2
66.16	but had] —had E2
66.30	and which] and E2
66.35	had met] met P
67.3	mindful, as Pleyel said] Pleyel, mindful, as he said E2

67.3	footing] interest E2
67.4	he had] had E2
67.11	he] Pleyel E2
67.30	catholic] Catholic E2
67.31	and] he had also E2
68.7	this] the E2
68.9	Romish] Roman E1–2
69.10	introduced] produced E2
69.22	by anxiety] with anxiety P
71.13–14	rectitude of articulation] correctness of pronunciation E2
71.14	force] a force E2
71.25	here] at Mettingen E2
72.5	Our sphere, in this respect] Our intercourse with society E2
72.31	incongrousness] incongruity E2
72.35	should] would E1–2
73.6	Empire] empire E1–2
73.12	than] than the E2
73.20	without] without a E1–2
74.5	to] for E2
75.8	an] a E1–2
75.16	was] were E2
75.18	an] a E1–2
75.37	an] a E1–2
76.37	or to] or P
79.2	demean] bemean P
79.6	previous] previously E2
79.13	till] until P
79.20	will] shall E2
79.31	has] had P
80.1	be] have been E2
80.31	An half hour] Half an hour E2
81.4	and his] or E2
81.4	detained him] prevented his coming E2
81.7	him] Pleyel E2
81.8	declining,] ∼ͣ E1
83.10	which this] this E2
83.17	cannot] can A–E2, P, K
83.27	an] a E1–2, P
84.9	book] hook E1
84.11	latter] former E2

403

84.17	aided] unaided P
84.25	towards] toward E1
84.30	these] those A, P, K
84.39	An] A E1–2
85.9	upon] to E1–2
85.20	whose tone] the tone of which E2
85.26	and yet] yet E2
85.27–28	measured, between . . . words,] measured‸ between . . . words‸ E1; measured‸ between . . . words, E2
85.30	fail to have been] have failed to be E2
86.1	to] of E2
86.6	midst] middle E2
86.11	Dark] Darkness E1–2
86.18	with] by E1–2
86.21	to] into E2
88.12	new] a new P
88.14	could] can E2
89.19	motive] motives E2
89.27	it] they E2
89.37	hast] has E1–2
89.38	were] was E1–2
90.5	intents] intention E1–2
90.27	Here] There A, P, K
91.14	museful] thoughtful E2
91.20	restore] might restore E2
91.20	to him] him to E2
93.2	rung] rang E2
93.18	breathings] breathing P, K
94.15	that] who E2
95.24	infantile] infantine E2
95.35	made] had made E1–2
96.6	which] that E1–2
96.25	exceedingly] exceeding E1
96.31	realized] real A–El, P, K
97.7–8	almost the vital motions were] the vital motions were almost E2
97.10	thrust to] thrust too E2
98.16	An] A E1–2
98.17	pulled] was pulled E2
98.33	conceive] have conceived E1–2
98.38	deep] a deep E1–2

99.18	have been already] be E1–2
100.7	an] a E2
100.15	has] had E1–2
100.30	shut] shut it E2, P
101.1	the day] day E2
101.21	give] gradually give E1–2
101.24	of] for E1–2
102.17	that] who E2
103.16	impulse] interest E2
103.21	an] a E2
103.32	seemed] seems E2
104.8	not hatred or envy] nor hatred nor envy E2
104.11	way] means E2
104.11	detestible] the detestable E2
104.21–22	come. This . . . presence.] come. E2
105.3	to follow] follow E2
105.12	the dictate of] dictated by E2
105.15	this man] Carwin E2
105.27	grant] gain E2
106.13	they] these E2
106.18	late] the late E2
106.19	upon] on E2
106.24	not become] become E2
107.6	so unseasonable] unseasonable E1–2
107.16–17	was, in some way] in some way was E1–2
108.10–11	what articles] such articles as E2
108.38	were] was E2
109.1	said he] he said E1–2
109.18	incited] excited E2
109.26	mists] mist E1–2
109.30	suspect] suspected E1–2
110.10	some parts of it] in some parts E2
110.35	power of divinity] human power E2
111.16	in] into E2
111.17	outweigh] outweight P
111.32	may] might E2
112.29	servant] a servant E2
113.4	prevented] preserved E2
113.6	hope] hopes E2
114.32	towards] toward P
115.7	young master] master E2

115.15	towards] toward P
116.6	which I] I E1–2
116.30	but] and E2
117.4	shrunk] shrank E2
118.8	this] the former E2
118.13	for] on E2
118.13	reasons] grounds E2
118.37	man] woman E2
119.8	The] Tho E1
119.20	the] an E1–2
121.15	You] Your E2
122.9	facilitate] facilitated E2
122.12	experienced] obtained E2
124.19	on the] and the P
125.12	*midnight*] and *midnight* E2
125.29–30	recollected] recolleeted E2
126.2–3	afterwards] afterward P
126.19	to condemn] condemn E2
126.23	reasonings] reasoning E2
127.5	doubts] doubt P
127.13	sanctify] sanction E2
127.15	was] were E2
127.23	received] all received E2
127.24	intercourse] acquaintance E2
127.26	he] Carwin E2
128.22	perform] pay E2
129.6	at] on E1–2
129.18	in] on E2
129.36	in] into E2
130.6	Towards] Toward P
130.25	it] in A
131.35	original] origin P, K
132.6	but] except E1–2
132.35–36	opposite to the] the E1–2
133.12	at] were at E2
133.21	an] a E2
134.6	further] farther E2
134.14	with] by E2
134.37	Thou] thou E1–2
136.1	These] Those A–E2, P, K
136.8	and] or E2

137.9	opened] opened it E1–2
137.21	has] have E2
138.9	unaccompanied] accompanied A–E2, P, K
138.36	to] of E2
140.2	overbear] overwhelm E2
140.8	At] A A
141.27	was] should be E2
141.28	fully] have been fully E2
142.23	an] a E1–2
142.28	*Hut*] hut E1–2
142.32	walnuts] walnut trees E2
142.37	They were] They E1–2
143.26	period] time E1–2
143.37	returned] returned to my remembrance E2
144.11	I was] I were E1–2
145.13	toward] towards E1–2
146.19	myself] I myself P
146.25	a flint] flint E2
146.30	had laboured] laboured E1–2
147.18	I will] will I E1–2
147.36	an] a E1–2
148.3	shrieking] shrinking E2
148.10	its] his E1–2
149.5	opened] opened it E2
149.8–9	his iron] iron E2
149.12	was] were E2
149.22	adventure] venture E1–2
150.15	hope] hopes P
150.18	which] that E1–2
150.21	befallen on] befallen E2
150.27	had fixed] fixed E1–2
150.34	at the] the E1–2
151.18	camest] comest A–E2, P, K
152.8	should] would E2
153.23	into] with E1–2
153.36	be] by P
154.3	this] his E2
154.4	towards] toward P
154.14	affected] effected A–E2, P, K
154.15	towards] toward P
154.30	These] Their E1–2

155.9	at] on E2
155.11	considerable] a considerable E2
155.13	Baynton's] Baynton E2
155.16	were] was E1–2
155.22	a mistress] mistress A, P, K
156.7	are my motives] my motives are E2
156.10	have] can have E1–2
156.17	weakness] weekness A
157.19	for] of E2
157.29	not] not not A
159.18	this] that E1–2
160.6	importunity] opportunity E1–2
160.30	grounds] ground E2
161.2	is, therefore] therefore, is E1–2
161.6	my] in my E1–2
162.14	what] what were E2
162.15	compelled] impelled E2
162.17	to] for E2
162.35	was] had been E2
163.2	and that] and E1–2
163.3	to vindicate] vindicate E2
163.10	me alone] me E1–2
164.7	an] a E1–2, P
164.8	a criminal] criminal A, K
164.20–21	his treatment] the treatment E1–2
164.21	is] are E1–2
166.2	were] had E2
166.7	imagination] imaginations E1–2
166.17	those] these A, P, K
167.24	stair] stairs E1–2
168.22	here] there E2
170.27	await for] await E2
170.38	inquiring] her inquiring E1–2
173.26	an] a E1–2
174.17	act] action E1–2
175.3	sunk] sank E2
175.16	the hideous] hideous P
175.25–26	have resort] resort E2
175.36	peruse] pursue P
176.3	shrunk back] shrunk E2
176.6	saluted] met E2

176.9	to] to the E2
176.28–29	this evil] these evils E2
176.31	elude] allude E1; avoid E2
177.28	is] his E1
178.19	particulars] the particulars E2
178.30	an] a E1–2
178.34	company] family E2
178.35	its] the E2
179.7	an] a E2
179.10	headlong] headlong down E2
179.26	showed] shewn E2
179.33	vain] in vain E1–2
179.35	effected] affected A, P, K
184.10–11	new airs] a change of air E2
186.18	will] would E2
186.26	would I] I would E2
188.19–20	he has] has he E2
188.28	whither] where E2
188.32	was now] had been E2
190.34	in this] on this E2
190.35	that] the E2
191.3	and this] which E2
192.1	*Hut*] hut E2
192.14	an] a E1–2
192.17	led me] led E2
193.3	mine] my own E2
193.4	stair] stairs E1–2
193.9	round it] around E2
193.19	this] this was E2
193.31	so enormous a] such enormous E2
194.3	drag on] drag A, E1, P, K
194.18	hasted] hastened E1–2
194.19	here] there E1–2
195.11	round] around E2
196.6	ghosts] ghost E1–2
196.15	lunatic] a lunatic E1–2
196.20	they] it E2
197.19	confess] to confess E2
198.11	apprized] surprised E1
198.40	inanimate] other inanimate E2
198.40	imitated] imitated by ventriloquists E2

198.41	The] Their E2
199.23	successive contemplation] successively contemplating E1; successively contemplated E2
200.1	gone] read E2
200.1	through] through it E2
200.17–18	as I judged by their voices, earnest in dispute] earnest in dispute, as I judged by their voices E2
200.23	enforced] increased E2
202.38	never] never more E2
203.12	this as] this for E2
203.38	Peeps] peep E2
203.38	and cries] To cry E2
205.18	adventure] venture E1–2
206.28	Some] An E2
206.30	father] father's E2
206.31	in] of E2
207.30	an] a E2, P
208.11	once more was] was once more E2
208.20	Further] Farther E2
208.23	and] or E2
208.30	make] allow E2
208.31	resolve to give it] to resolve on giving it E2
210.7	further] farther E2
210.14	whose purpose] the purpose of which E2
210.20	reviewed] review E2
210.23	be] have been E2
210.34	not] you not E2
211.2	I had] had I E1–2
211.26–27	confusion; and] confusion. The E2
211.28	description] description of my person E2
211.28–29	the apprehension of my person] my apprehension E2
212.29	in] of E2
212.31	an] a E2
212.34	opened] open E2
212.36	inconveniencies] inconveniences E1–2, P
213.2	motion] sound E2
213.4	adventured] ventured E2
215.18	was] should be E2
215.19–20	to incite] which incited E2
216.8	situation] condition E2

216.12	an] a E1–2
216.28	an] a E2
216.34	bad] bidden E2
218.22–23	undescribable] indescribable E1–2, P
218.28	Carwin's] Carwin E1–2
218.28	instigation] instigator E2
219.16	Wast] Was E1
219.19	heard] had heard E2
219.21	should] shall E2
219.23	an] a E2
219.24	tear] tare A, P, K
220.10	have easily] easily have E2
222.16	these] those A–E2, P, K
222.27	had deemed] deemed E1–2
223.5–6	Is there … abhorrence? It] Is there … abhorrence, it E1; If there be … abhorrence, it E2
224.23	believed] believe E1–2
224.29	being] Being E2
225.11	for!] ~? A, P, K
225.20	of] by E1
226.15	not] nor E1
226.26	thoughts] thought E1
227.14–15	Remoter] Remote E1–2
227.30	this] his E1–2
227.35	go? leave me! Succourless!] go? leave me, succourless! E1; go—leave me succourless? E2
228.5	to notice not] not to notice E2
228.9	every] ever E1
229.13	depict] describe E2
229.20	flown] fled E2
229.22	execute] prepare E2
230.15–16	not difficult] difficult A–E2, P, K
231.11	thought] thoughts E1–2
231.15	with his] with E2
231.28	be] have E2
232.5	ghastly with death] was ghastly in death E2
232.6	liedest] liedst E1; didst lie E2
232.12	faintly] but faintly E2
232.23	*Hut*] hut A–E2, P, K
232.25	hasted] hastened E1–2
232.37	ferociousness] ferocity E2

411

233.11	will] shall E2
233.26	Go˄] ∼, E1–2
234.22	despair] my despair E2
235.13	derived] indulged in E2
236.11	momently] momentarily E2
236.24	suffer] suffer from E2
236.26	reverie] reveries E2
236.32	hubbub] noise E1–2
237.21	disconnected] unconnected E2
238.19	to communicate] in communicating E2
238.20	elapsed] had elapsed E2
238.29	upon] on E2
239.10	predisposed him] predisposed A–E2, P, K
239.35	*Hut*] hut A–E2, P, K
239.36	hasted] hastened E1–2
240.4	upon] on E2
240.28	county] country E1–2
242.29	to pursue] pursue E1
242.30	made] made by him E2
243.14	was] were E2
243.16	an] a E2
244.1–2	destruction, though . . . manner.] destruction. E2
244.10	these efforts] them E1–2
244.10–14	If . . . catastrophe. If Wieland] ¶ If Wieland E1–2

CARWIN

M: the copy-text, in *The Literary Magazine* (1803–05)
L: in William Dunlap's *Life of Brown* (1815), without authority
E: *Carwin, the Biloquist, and Other American Tales,* vol. I (London, 1822), without authority
P: Fred Lewis Pattee, ed., *Wieland . . . with . . . Carwin* (1926)
K: William S. Kable, ed., *Three Early American Novels* (1970)

Head-title	Memoirs of Carwin] Carwin E
247.1	was] am E

247.11	exertions] exertion L, E
248.3	upon] on E
248.10	effect] affect M–L
248.35	rung] rang E
250.7	the objects] objects E, P
250.7	apprehensions] apprehension E
250.13	hallowing] hallooing E
250.23	In a few minutes] This being accomplished E
250.28	appeared] seemed E
251.2	were surprized] felt astonished E
251.5	was this] this E
251.32	beclouded] o'erclouded E
252.26	were,] ~ₐ L–E
254.12–13	propensities] propensites M
254.17	pertinaciousness] pertinacity E
254.23	enhanced] enchanced P, K
255.13	detection;] ~, M–L, P, K; ~: E
255.17	selected] fixed on E
255.29	wind] winds L–E
256.2	hands] my hands L–E
256.34	an] a E, P
257.31	necessity] circumstance E
258.4–8	I was . . . them, and . . . resolution, to . . . remonstrances, when I] I was . . . them; and . . . resolution, to . . . remonstrances, I L; Whilst I was . . . them, I E; I was . . . them, and . . . resolution, to . . . remonstrances, I P
258.7	opposition] oppositions P
258.12	clothes,] ~, L–E, P
258.22	upbraiding] unbraiding P
258.28	neighbour's] neighbours M, K
258.31	could I] could M–L, K
258.33	maxims] intentions E
258.35	request,] ~ₐ L–E
259.4	the chuser of my] chose my own E
259.12	assiduous] an assiduous E, P
259.12	use] uses E
259.21	associates, and] associates; often E
259.34	laid] lay E
260.16	words] word P
260.28	The] Then the E

260.33	lighted] alighted L–E
261.21	In] Where the bee sucks, there suck I;|In E
261.21	Cowslip's] Cowslips M
261.21	lie,] lie;|There I couch when owls do cry; E
261.26	distance] a distance E
261.29	not uttered] uttered M–L, P, K
262.7	who was] who as M–L, K
262.18	clothes] cloths M, P, K
262.21	aunt's] aunts' M
262.33	to return] return M–L, E, P
262.37	from books] books P
263.8	but he did not] he did not, however, E
263.18	I could] could M–L, K
263.27	strain] train E
264.16	motives of rectitude] motives E
264.16	deter] de-|deter M; have deterred E, P
264.33–34	Lonely and at midnight] In her lonely midnight hours E
265.5	as well as] like E, P
265.5	were] was L–E
265.11–12	if legally compelled to it] on legal compulsion E
265.18–19	have been productive] productive E, P
266.23	Oho!] O! ho! L–E
266.27	uncautiousness] incautiousness E
266.34	fell short, ran beside, or outstripped] ran beside, outstripped, or fell short of E
268.7	beside] besides L–E, P
268.18	His] This M–E, P, K
268.18–19	corporal] corporeal L–E
269.3	topic,] ~ₐ M–L, P, K
269.7	cause] urge E
269.9	motive] motives E
269.12	instable] unstable E
269.14	gratifications] gratification P
269.15	destructive] destruction M–L, K
270.1	novelty, however, disappearingₐ] noveltyₐ howeverₐ disappearing, M–L, P, K; novelty, however, disappearing, E
270.6	suit] suite E
270.13–14	apartmentsₐ] ~, M–E, P, K
270.38	chilling] chilly E

271.2	thoughts] thought E
271.33	an] a E, P
272.5	withdraw] withdrew P
272.24	sprung] sprang E, P
272.31	man] men E, P
272.38	their] its E
273.8	rising] arising L–E, P
273.16	on] to E
273.16	Roman] Romish E
273.19	rites] rights M–L, K; rights [rites] P
274.25	spacious] a spacious E, P
274.27	confessors;] ∼, M–L, K; ∼,— E, P
274.33	were] be E
275.4	scale. Your . . . mine.] scale. E
275.9–14	unemployed. What . . . projects.] unemployed. E
275.15	these] my mystical exploits E
275.20	The] My E
277.5	the individual] each individual E
277.29	are] is E
278.4	thoughts, and thousands,] thousands, and thousands, M, P, K
278.16	would] should E
279.7	it] there E
279.7	reasonable] reason L–E
279.9	were] are E
279.10	excellencies] excellences E, P
280.13	by] only by E
280.25	by] with E
281.25	which] who E, P
281.27	candidate] candidates E, P
282.10	who] which E
283.11	further] farther E
284.18	reserves] reserves were E
284.35	conscious to] conscious of E, P
285.27	his own] his E
287.4	the] the the E
287.24	hasted] hastened E, P
288.11	at] to E
288.19	the bestower] bestower E, P
288.21	at] by E
289.4	greater still] still greater P

290.11   to] to to M
290.19   personal] my personal P
290.39   credulent] credulous E
291.9   which] which which M
291.23–24   fortitude,] ~ˌ E
293.9   occasions] occasion E
294.7   these] those E
294.17–18   in investigating] investigating P
296.9   a] the P
296.13   an end] end L
297.8   of so much moment were not] so momentous had not been E
297.10   way] ways P
297.31   'Twill] It will L–E
298.11   sir Thomas Moore] Sir Thomas More E, P
298.22   lighted] alighted L–E, P
298.23   reasonably] reasonaly P
298.30   faint] feint L
299.36–38   *The . . . Cook.] *The . . . Cook.—EDITOR. M, K; [note omitted] P
300.4   had] made E
300.21   closet] closest L
300.22   which] also E
300.25   certainty] a certainty E, P
300.30   came] come E
301.14   in] for E, P
301.34   *incognitae*] *terrae incognitae* E
302.16   vocal] biloquial L–E
302.21   was] were E
302.36   the way] a way P
305.34   I] that I E
306.4   expected] had expected P
307.5   nor murdered] murdered E
307.8   further] farther E, P
308.22   a blue] the blue P
309.14   be henceforth] henceforth be E
310.17   have] had E, P
310.25   had received] received E

[NOTE: E inserts chapter headings at the following points: 247.13 (I), 259.9 (II), 269.33 (III), 283.34 (IV), 296.18 (V). K inserts chapter headings at the beginning of each installment in the *Literary Magazine* (see p. 361, n. 27).]

RECORD OF COLLATIONS AND
COPIES CONSULTED

WIELAND

Wieland; or the Transformation. An American Tale. (New York, 1798), first edition: A

The following copies have been examined and collated (by different operators) at least twice by machine: OKentU—Spec. Coll. PS1134.W5.1798, Spec. Coll. PS1134.W5.1798, Spec. Coll. PS1134.W5.1798; PSt—T813.B812w (vault); OU—PS1134.W5. Several other copies have been collated throughout once and spot-collated by gatherings a second time: ViU—*PS1134.W5. 1798, copy 2; InU—PS1134.W5; ICN—Case Y255.B814;NjP— Ex3643.7.39.14, copy 1, Ex3643.7.39.14, copy 2;TxU—Av. B812w.1798. A few copies were collated only once: NcU— T813.B877w; PBL—818.4.B8772.T, 818.4.B8772.1798.T. In addition, the punctuation of the passage at 65.36 has been independently checked in the copies at the following libraries: CLU, CSmH, CtY, DLC, ICN, InU, MH, MMeT, MWA, MdB, MtU, MiU-C, NBU, NNC, NN, NNHi, NNS, NNU, NcU, PBL, PPHi, PPL, PU, RPB, ScU, TxU, ViU (2), ViW, WBB.

Wieland, or the Transformation. An American Tale. (London, 1811): E1

This edition has been collated (by different operators) against A three times by hand, and the following copies have been collated (by different operators) twice by machine: ViU—Barrett *PS1134.W5.1811 (vols. 1–3), Sadleir-Black*PZ2.B78W.1811 (vols. 1–3); NjP—Ex3643.7.39.15 (vols. 1–3).

Wieland, An American Tale. (London, 1822): E2

This edition has been collated (by different operators) against A

417

more than three times by hand, and the following copies have been collated (by different operators) twice by machine: OKentU—Spec. Coll. PS1134.W5.1822; ICN—Y255.B815 (vols. 1–3); PSt—T813.B812W.1822. NNHi—PS1134.W5.1822, copy 1 (vols. 1–3) was collated once by machine.

Fred Lewis Pattee, ed., *Wieland . . . with . . . Carwin* (1926): P This edition has been collated against A at least twice by hand and its readings independently checked against E1's and E2's variants with A; no machine collations of this edition were performed. The copies consulted were OKentU—Spec. Coll. PS1134.W5. 1965, copy 1, Spec. Coll. PS1134.W5.1926.

William S. Kable, ed., *Three Early American Novels* (1970): K This edition was not collated, as a list of editorial changes appears on pp. 16–17; it was consulted to complete the history of substantive variants in the editions reported on here and, when necessary, the history of emended readings. The copy used was OKentU—Spec. Coll., uncatalogued.

CARWIN

The Literary Magazine, volumes I–III (1803–1805): M
The gatherings containing "Carwin" in the following copies have been collated (by different operators) twice by machine: Volume I: OKentU—Per. Spec. Coll. *Literary Magazine,* v. 1, c. 6, Per. Spec. Coll. *Literary Magazine,* v. 1, c. 1; OO—094.1 1803 L712; IU—051 LIM, v. 1; MiD. Volume II: OKentU—Per. Spec. Coll. *Literary Magazine,* v. 2, c. 5, Per. Spec. Coll. *Literary Magazine,* v. 2, c. 3; OO—094.1 1803 L712; IU—051 LIM, v. 2; MiD. Volume III: OKentU—Per. Spec. Coll. *Literary Magazine,* v. 3, c. 6, Per. Spec. Coll. *Literary Magazine,* v. 3, c. 5; OO—094.1 1803 L712; IU—051 LIM, v. 3; MiD. The preceding OKentU copies of volume I were also collated throughout once by machine, as were the following copies at OKentU—Volume II (rectos only): Per. Spec. Coll. *Literary Magazine,* v. 2, c. 3; c. 4 (pp. 241–319 wanting); c. 5 (pp. 241–320 only, rectos and versos); Volume III (pp. 1–240 only): Per. Spec. Coll. *Literary Magazine,* v. 3, c. 2; c. 4. "Carwin" alone has been collated once in the following OKentU copies— Volume I: c. 4; Volume II: c. 1; Volume III: c. 1, c. 3. In addition, the punctuation of the passage at 274.26–29 has been independently checked in the copies at the following libraries: C, CtHT, CtY, DLC, FU, ICN, IaU, MB, MBAt, MH, MWA, N, NN, NIC,

NNHi, OKentU, PPAmP, PPHi, PPL, PPiU, PU, Vi, WHi.

William Dunlap, *Life of Brown* (1815): L

The text in this printing has been collated (by different operators) against that of M at least three times by hand, and the gatherings containing "Carwin" in the following copies have been collated (by different operators) twice by machine: OKentU—Spec. Coll. PS1136.D8.1815, v. 2, c. 1, Spec. Coll. PS1136.D8.1815, v. 2, c. 3; OU—Spec. Coll. PS1136.D8.1815.

Carwin, the Biloquist, and Other American Tales (London, 1822): E

The text of this edition has been collated (by different operators) against that of M at least three times by hand, and the preliminaries and the gatherings containing "Carwin" in the following copies have been collated (by different operators) twice by machine: OCU—PS1134.C2.1822; NjP—3643.7.324, v. 1; ICN—Case Y255.B811; NNHi—PS1134.C3, v. 1, c. 3, PS1134. C3, v. 1, c. 4 (copy 4 collated once only).

Fred Lewis Pattee, ed., *Wieland . . . with . . . Carwin* (1926): P

This edition has been collated against the text of M at least twice by hand and its readings independently checked against L's and E's variants with M; no machine collations of this edition were performed. The copy consulted was OKentU—Spec. Coll. PS1134.W5.1926.

William S. Kable, ed., *Three Early American Novels* (1970): K

The consultation of "Carwin" in this edition was the same as that of *Wieland*.

"OUTLINE" OF *WIELAND* IN
ELIJAH BROWN'S JOURNAL

[NOTE: The *Wieland* "Outline" appears in a notebook (No. 14) among the Brown papers at the Historical Society of Pennsylvania (MS. 03398). The date of its writing is uncertain, but it seems to represent a pre-composition, planning stage of Brown's work on the novel, and must have rather closely preceded composition. The fact that his father, Elijah Senior, had copied into the notebook newspaper and journal extracts bearing dates of 1800 and 1801, for example, only means that Elijah likely took the notebook over after Charles had committed his "Outline" material to it and wrote around the "Outline," not that Brown was afterwards trying to reconceive *Wieland* as a play.

Our transcription is literal. Thus inadvertent misspellings like "guardeaness," "yieelding," "cheearfully," and "dungion" are preserved even though Brown also has a correct spelling of like words—e.g., "guardian." Additionally, we do not tamper with peculiar or archaic deviations from common usage in such spellings as "cloathes," "ventrilloqually," and "ventriloquizm." Inconsistencies of capitalization ("Schyylkill", "schuylkill"; "saxony," "Saxony"; "Savoyard protestant") along with inappropriate punctuation are likewise given as they appear in the MS. However, where context all too obviously indicates that what looks like a period had to have been a comma shortened through haste and carelessness, we provide the intended comma. Where—given Brown's inattention—there is genuine doubt as to whether or not he intended a comma, we give the sign—usually a period—as we find it.

Authorial excisions are placed in brackets; editorial interpola-

420

tions are given in angle brackets. A few words seem illegible beyond recovery. For these we offer our best guess, and the reader is free to supply his own.

Our transcription begins with the "Outline" proper on page 6. The word lists on the three preceding pages seem legible enough. The lack of a page 9 doubtless was caused by Brown's having misnumbered. There seems to be no special explanation for the gaps between pages 11 and 18, and 19 and 24, the intervening pages being taken up with Elijah Senior's notations. The speech on page 18 may be compared with paragraph 13 of Chapter XX (pp. 176–177 in this edition) which comes toward the end of Wieland's response to the jury's verdict.]

3.

Conway	Lee	Kilby.	L m r
Dartrey	Wynn	Metcalf	Morley.
Wilmot	Weir	Moreland	Romney.
Barwell	Ede	Strangeways	Monro
Bertrand	Hyde	Smalley.	
Carew.	Bowes	Speke.	
Caster.	Bragge	Spearing.	
Ingle	Byrd	Weyland	
Trycroft.	Clough	Alstrop	
Astell.	Dayne		
Ayout	Erle	M Kea	
Blackett	Eyre	Melbourne – 2 Bedloe	
Baynham	Edge	Monro. –	
Bendyshe	Goffe	Lorimer – 2	
Baskett	Hane	Assburge Armidale	
Bawlby	Hitch	Davis – 2 Dudley	
Blencowe	Howe	~~Wyndham~~ – 3 Pleyel	
Cooksey.	Reeve	Edny	
Cardwell	Hayes	Wyatte	
Clerrall	Keene	Gorran	
Cowther	Mayne	Inglefield Camberton.	
Conthwaite	Poore	Baynton	
Dansey	Rees.	Pleyel.	
Tormer	Rowe	Armidale	
Eadowes			
Foley			
Gilchrist			
Gower			

423

4

(From a Paris paper)

Weyland	
Beddowes	
Conway	
Gower	
Foley	
Dormer	
Fillingham	
Tavistock	
Tylney	
Medway.	
Marcreeve	Beckwith
Bedloe	Welbeck
Harington	Caring
Carling.	Carey
Charlton.	Carton
Carlingford.	Caxford.
Carlington.	Carfield
Carlourg.	Caxbury
Carsey	Carttoleen
Carlette.	Carney
Carwin.	Carhill
Carrell.	Carlhurst
Cardale.	
Carrylle.	
13. Carhuyson.	
Carry.	
Carborough.	

The Cap. presented by the Turkey Company to L.d Nelson ... of an oblong form, on either side ... emblematical decorations, the ... crocodile, the Lotus, & other appropriate ... the laurel in ... on its apex. ... on the names of the ships, ... Relations; specifying the names of ... & the names of the ... when they saw ...

Lady Hamilton's handkerchief

Among the distinguished personages who hastened to pay their respects to Sir W.m & Lady Hamilton, and Lord Nelson on their arrival at Hamburgh, was Dumourier. During their short stay in that city the ex-general was invited to one of the parties. After supper Lady Hamilton sung "God save the King", at the request of Lord Nelson, when she came to the couplet reflecting on France she was interrupted by his Lordship, Dumourier, who had listened with ecstasy to the ... melodies of the delightful warbler, deeply affected by the act of Delicacy, and filled with gratitude burst into tears. Lady Hamilton fancying she saw the tears of a Royalist, of a heart overflowing with Love for its country glistening in his eyes wept in excess of softness Lord Nelson soon began to weep from Sympathy, and old Sir W.m Hamilton, in constant activity wiped away the tears of the Admiral with her handkerchief fondly; then those of her husband slightly, then those of Dumourier kindly, then her own delicately. And then Dumourier, falling on his knee implored, as the greatest possible favor, that the charming Lady Hamilton should make him a present of the handkerchief.

Lady Hamilton softened into compliance the favour was granted and Dumourier having on the handkerchief with a holy respect, retired to meditate upon the miraculous destiny which had deigned to unite in his favour in the same handkerchief the relics of so many great personages. To see, to touch and kiss this famous handkerchief, are now considered on the continent the proudest honours; and as such are sought with all the enthusiasm of superstition. —

Speaking of France

1766 — 27.

5 — 17

4 — 7

1739 — Bert. born

35.

1759 —

1766 — 21.

J. Mordaunt

A tyrant of antiquity ordered men to be laid on a bed of iron; stretching those who were shorter to the full length of the bed and amputating the legs of those who were too tall; so that all were brought to equality by the tyrant into the bed. This tyrant was fond of equality: and such is the equality which the tyrants who now torture us with their mad desires, would subject us to. —————

Sky-walk, or the man unknown to himself

Wieland, or, the Transformation.

Carwin, or, ~~the~~ ~~of~~ ~~wit~~

Bedloe, or the self devoted.

Gower, or, the dead recalled. ————

Wieland. Charles

————— Caroline

————— Charlotte

Marcresse Philip

Conway. Mrs.

————— Henry

C

Robert —— 61 — Jan.

Susan —— 62 — Jul.

Mary —— 64 — Jan.

James —— From the same author: *Bedloe* as above

I overheard a curious Dialogue between Anacharsis Cloots at Paris between him & a plain sensible looking man, who drank Coffee at the same table with him one day after dinner at Roberts. This man happened to say something, I dont remember what "was as certain as that God made the world."

"Pshaw!" said Anacharsis snappishly, he did not make the World. —

"No!" cried the man, staring with surprise; Who made it, then?

"Why nobody, It never was made, answered Cloots."

see page 11.

6.

Act 1;

Wieland was of saxon origin. He was born 1700. He was apprenticed in London at the age of 15 — He contracted a gloomy & religious spirit from the perusal of the works of the first reformers. He built up a system of his own. The savoyard protestant faith was his. See Chambers Cyclopaedia. At the age of 22. He retired to America with a view to enjoy his tenets unmolested. He was an orphan, with enough secured to him, to purchase an estate in his new own country. He bought ground & built an house, on Schuylkill. He lived a batchelor & farmer till 1734. Then married a girl of 18. With a fortune. Amiable & devout. X They died 1749. Their son 10 yrs old. Their daughter 6 — A guardianess. their mothers sister. a maiden lady. living in the city. A domestic education. not devout. was enjoyed by them. Devotional impressions were already made upon the son. he. at the age of 24. married. a woman of 23. Charlotte. Her character; as little devotional. as Carolines. Considerable resemblance of character. Between the woman. Gayety of spirits in them. A certain gravity & gloominess in them. In solitude deepening, in society & in consequence of efforts. yielding. affectionate, guileless inoffensive. After 4 yrs wedlock. happy. serene. enjoying 4 children. The oldest six yrs old.

An orphan girl. 14 yrs of age. adopted & cherished by Charles.

Act 1.   6.

Wieland was of saxon origin. He was born 1700. He was

apprenticed in London at the age of 15. He contracted a

gloomy & religious spir[r]it, from the perusal of the works

of the first reformers. He built up a system of his own. The

Savoyard protestant faith was his. See Chambers

Cyclopædia. At the age of 22. He retired to America,

with a view to enjoy his tenets unmolested. He was

an orphan, with enough secured to him, to purchase an

estate in [his] [own] new country. He bought ground & built

an house, on Schyylkill. He lived a batchelor & farmer

till 1734. Then married a girl of 18. With ^out fortune,

[but ⟨?⟩] amiable and devout. ⟩⟨ They died 1749. Their son

10. Yr's old. Their daughter 6— a guardeaness. Their

mothers sister, a maiden lady, living in the city.

A Domestic education, not devout, was enjoyed by them

Devotional impressions were already made upon the

                                              Rimband ⟨?⟩
                                              Charlotte
son, he, at the age of 21. Married, a woman of 23. ^ ⚡

        Ch.2.

Her character, as little devotional, as Carolines. Considera

ble resemblance of character. Between the woman.

Gayety of spirits in them. A certain gravity & gloom

iness in them. In solitude deepening, in society & in

consequence of efforts, yieelding. Affectionate, guileless

inoffensive. After [4 ⟨?⟩] 6. yrs. wedlock. happy, serene,

enjoying 4 children. The oldest six yrs old.

        An orphan girl. [13 ⟨?⟩] 14. yrs of age. Adopted & cherished by

Charles.

427

7

Marcreeve is introduced to them. A form & mind, cultivated, enlightened. Arrived at Philadelphia from Hull. Single & unknown. Resides in lodgings— Walks on the schuylkill Is sometimes seen near Corfield.

Ch. 4 One occasion wanders here at night. Takes his post at the summer house. Philip & Charles come hither. to plan a certain affair. They are overheard by Marcreeve. They fear Charlottes disapprobation. This is ventriloqually given. A voyage to Europe; to Saxony. to claim an estate— Charlotte & Caroline at that time together at Cardale.

Previously to this. Marcreeve in the temple. sees Charles approaching. desires his absence. Therefore calls to him from behind.—

5

Marcreeve introduced. Characterized. Parallel between him & Charles. Deportment. Conversation. Suppresses his story. Conjectures founded on the hints afforded them — Scenes tending to impress Charles with an opinion of invisible influence. designed more ly to excite surprize. & sport with credulity. 3 of these goes a journey— whither he conceals. July 6.

Act. 2nd

Words audible to Charles alone. Assumes the character of guardian Angel. Warns of danger to a rise from going into his chamber. Commands him to save a tenants house from the flames. 3rdly, Summer house. the scene; death, conditional, on performing some precept to be given

428

7
Marcrieve is introduced to them. A form & mind, cultivated

enlightened. Arrived at Philadelphia from Hull. Single

& unknown. Resides in lodgings— Walks on the schuylkill

Is sometimes seen near Carfield.

Ch. 4.
　　　One occasion wanders here at night. Takes his post

at the summer house. Philip & Charles come hither,

to plan a certain affair. They are overheard by

Marcrieve. They fear Charlottes disapprobation. This

is ventrilloqually given. A voyage to Europe, to Saxony,

to claim an estate—Charlotte & Caroline at that time

together at Cardale.

Ch. 3.
　　previously, to this, Marcrieve, in the temple, sees

Charles approaching. Desires his absence. Therefore calls

to him from behind.—
　　　　　5
　　　Marcrieve introduced. Characterized. parallel

between him & Charles. Deportment. Conversation.
　6
Suppresses his story. Conjectures founded on the hints
　　　　　　7.8.9.10.
afforded them.— Scenes tending to impress charles

with an opinion of Invisible influence. Designed mere

ly to encite surprize. & sport with credulity. 3 of these

goes a journey—whither he conceals. July 6.

Act. 2nd

[The scenes] Words audible to Charles alone. Assumes
————————————————————1
the character of guardian Angel. Warns of danger to a

　　　　　　　　　　　rise from going into his chamber
　2
Commands him to save a tenants house from the flames.
　rdly
3　　—Summer house, the scene; Death, conditional, on

　　　　performing some precept to be given

429

a month forward.

Act 2nd

11 Evening Aug: 6. Carol. Charl. & Charles together
Tranquility pleasure, congugal & parental tenderness. Accom
=panies his sister home. ~~Returns~~

12. Return. Conference.

13. Carol. visits & ~~examines~~ examines.

14. Returns. Mr. Uatzel & four neighbours. Confined in Philad
prison.

15. Arraignment & incidents.

16. 17. 18. 19. 20. — Confessional speech.

4. 5.
2 Rupture from prison. ~~Connivance of Caroline~~. goes to meet
=ham. Endeavours to gain access to Philip. Kills a faithful
negro who withstands him. Philip escapes. Maniac
searches his chamber. Flies to Carlhill. Knocks at the
door rouses his sister. Conference from a window. Persuades
her to descend. About to do so when seized by officers
whom Philip has sent & conducted. Borne to his
dungeon —

9. 2. 3
1. Rupture. Connivance of Caroline. Finds her in
her chamber midnight. Expostulation. Saved by her
presence of mind. Escapes. Search after him desired
1 prohibition. & reconvey to prison.
2 Injunction.
3. Warning.
9 10.

a month forward.   8

Act 2nd

11 Evening Aug: 6. Carol. Charl. & Charles together
Tranquility, pleasure, conjugal & parental tenderness. Accom
panies his sister home. [Returns.]

12. Return. Conference.

13. Carol. visits. & [inspects] examines.

14. Returns. M^r. Hatsel & four neighbours. Confined in Philad
prison.

15. Arraignment. & incidents.

16. 17. 18. 19. 20.— Confessional speech.

2 Rupture from prison. [Connivance of Caroline.] goes to Men-
ham. Endeavours to gain access to Philip. Kills a faithful
Negro who withstands him. Philip escapes. Maniac
searches his chamber. Flies to Carlhill. Knocks at the
door rouses his sister. Conference from a window. Persuades
her to descend. About to do so when seized by officers
whom Philip has sent & conducted. Borne to his
dungion—

1: Rupture. Connivance of Caroline. Finds her in
her chamber midnight. Expostulation. Saved by her
presence of mind. Escapes. Search after him descried ⟨desired?⟩

1. prohibition. & reconveyed to prison.

2. Injunction.

3. Warning.

            10.

431

10

Desore. Summer House. Time 12 oClock.
Returing to his family. 1st Object to his chamber. Deportment.
Conversation to his wife & children. Affectionate, solemn
forboding misfortune. The hour having arrived. of 11.
goes to Summer house

Vocal sounds, light. figure.
Dialogue. Forewarns against Idolatry. 12 to 4.
4. Hours. Destroys some favourite inanimate. object.
an organ.   2. Greyhound.   200.

                             3. Children 2.

                             4. Wife. Ward

men   5. ~~Ward~~. Wife.
Command
Repugnance   6. Sister.
Resolute
~~Interval of~~
Relenting

~~Narrative.~~ birth, education. Acquaintance
Conway. In love with a beautiful woman but
Conway he introduces to her. Loves & seduced by
~~Conway~~ headlong. & prevailed upon to aid him in pursu
ding m. to concur with C. scheme
        Carwin,
        m. made unintentionally instrumental in
terrifying mr C. Efforts of this kind ineffectual.
prevailed upon fully to adopt the scheme of
destroying Mr C. by means of faith. This done.
likewise her daughter. Residing at a distance.
Discovers the perfidy of Louisa. Colvill aroused
by

10
Scene. Summer House. Time 12 oClock.

11 oclock
Returns to his family;   to his chamber. Deportment.

Conversation to his wife & children. Affectionate, solemn

forboding misfortune. The hour having arrived, of 12—

goes to Summer house

    Vocal sounds, light. figure.

    Dialogue. Forewarns against Idolatry. 12 to 4.

in-
4. Hours. Destroys 1 some favourte animate object.

an organ.
           2. greyhound.

                200.

           3. children 2.

           4. [Wife]. Ward.

omen
Command   5. [Ward]. Wife.
Repugnan⟨c⟩e
           6. Sister.

Resolute
[Interval of]
Repenting

    [Marcrieve.] birth, education. Acquaintance **2** ⟨sign for with?⟩

Conway. In love with a beautiful woman <u>but</u>

Conway he introduces to her. Louisa seduced by

    Ludloe.
[Conway] & prevailed upon to aid him in persua

ding M. to concur with C. scheme

    Carwin,
[M.] made unintentionally instrumental in

terrifying M^rs. C. Efforts of this kind ineffectual.

prevailed upon fully to adopt the scheme of

destroying M^rs. C. by means of faith. This done.

likewise her daughter. Residing at a distance.

                Colvill
    Discovers the perfidy of Louisa.   accused
                            by

Ludloe
~~Conway~~ of murdering M.ʳ C. Circumstantial evidence
strong. before trial. escapes prison. by changing cloaths
with Louisa. Comes to Am.

Inducements. Affluence. marriage with Louisa who
is poor. Relief of distress.

Tales. passions pourtrayed.   37. 38. 1 - 2/3.
Hallucinations   2 - 3. 1/3.
           ulation
Somnamb: memory.   4 6 2/3.
{ nam. simil ~~personal similitude~~.
{ Melanomia   12.
Hallucinat. Ventriloquism.   8 . 12 1/3.

Love of Country. Dissimulation.   24.

Conflagration. of mil. preparations. naval. Timber Hemp
                                       { Ships.

Carwin.   "How came it here then," said the other.
Colvill.   "How came it here. Why it has been here from eternity"
Ludloe.   "I should never have guessed it to be so old" rejoined the
                   man but still you have not inform'd me how it exists
Conway. sen.   "By Chance" said Clvits. . . . .
Conway. jun.   "By Chance — exclaim'd the other. . . . . . .
                   "Yes, unquestionably by mere chance" added Clvits
Pleyel.   & If you have no notion of the power of Chance
Weeland. Ch.   The power of Chance!" repeated the other. Chance is blind
              "Blindness, does not diminish power" cried Clvits.
   — Char.   with an air of triumph. for even according to your bible
   — Car.   Samson was able to pull down a house and kill another
5000 ~~in times~~ in these times after he was stone blind . . . .
     "Sneering is one thing M.ʳ Clvits, and reasoning is another
     "Then let us reason, resumed Anacharsis. "I speak for the power of Chance
Give a 1000 dies put into a Box, and thrown out often enough there can be no doubt, 6000
would be thrown out at last; nay if 100,000 were to be rattled, & thrown without ceasing
600000 would appear in process of time at one throw. Who then, we may ask this world just
as we find it, have been each of by the mere rattling of atoms. ———

434

Ludloe   rs   11.
[Conway] of murdering M^{rs}. C. Circumstantial evidence

strong. Before trial, escapes prison, by changing cloathes

with Louisa. Comes to Am.

Inducements. Affluence. Marriage with Louiza who

is poor. Relief of distress.

Tales. passions pourtrayed.   3[8]7.   38. 1–2/3.

Hallucination   2– 3 .1/3.

Somnamb.^{ulation}	Mimicry	4⟨7?⟩ 6 2/3.
{ person. Simil	[personal Similitude.]	
} Melanæma		12.
Hallucinat.	Ventriloquizm 8.	13 1/3.
Love of Country	Dissimulation.	

                           24.

Conflagration. of Mil. preparations. Naval. Timber—Hemp
                                        { Ships.

Carwin.

Colvill.

Ludloe.

Conway. Sen.

Conway. Jun.

pleyel.

Weiland Ch.

_____ Char.

_____ Car.

18

Tales of life.

{ 2. particular transaction. some moral.

Misfortune. Self depravity } Moral.
            another's depravity }
            Physical —— Direct.
                  { Indirect.
            Death.   qr. 20   20.6.
            Pain.   Rut. 24.
         Personal.   Ong —12.

Here, omnipotent truly! thou wast the prompter of my deed. My hands were but instruments of thy will. I know not what is crime. If what virtue and vice is the ultimate result. Thy knowledge as thy power is unmeasured. I lean upon thy promise. I cheerfully sustain the load of pain or of infamy hatred whatever men may lay upon me. In thy arms of thy protection I entrust my safety. In the fulness of thy justice I confide for my reward.

You say that I am criminal. presumptuous man! thou deemest that the aim of vengeance should reach thee. Thus impiously to usurp the prerogative of thy creator. To count this easily in the comprehension of thy views. in the full pervading property of thy thought!

I am not commissioned to be thy punisher. Tis well for thee. I am not. The wrong thou hast defeat of prevent is immense to government. A space is allowed thee for repentance.

If I were, how would thy shadowy security vanish. I am filled of surrounded. There and I cannot reach thee while thou art, but let the commission be given. If in spite of chains & walls & interposing multitudes, my hands should snatch thee from thy

18
Tales. { 1. life.
{ 2. particular transaction, some moral.

Misfortune.   Self depravity   } Moral.
               Another's depravity }

               physical. _____ { Direct.
                                 { Indirect.

                    Death.   gr. 20   20. 6.

                    Pain.   Rwt. 24. ⟨?⟩

          personal.   Onz —12.

Thou, omnipotent & holy! Thou wast the prompter of my deed.
My hands were but instruments of thy will. I know not what
is crime. Of what action caused ⟨?⟩ evil is the ultimate result. Thy
knowledge as thy power is reverenced ⟨?⟩. I lean ⟨?⟩ upon thy promise
I cheearfully sustain the load of pain or of [infaming] hatred wh.
erring ⟨?⟩ men may lay upon me. In thy ⟨the⟩ arms of thy protection
I entrust my safety. In the fullness of thy justice I confide for
my reward.

    You say that I am criminal. Presumptuous man! Thou deserv

                 rightious⟨?⟩
est that the arm of vengeance   should crush thee. Thus impious
ly to usurp the prerogative of thy creator! To count thus rashly on
the comprehension of thy views: on the fall ⟨*sic*⟩ pervading property of
thy foresight!

    I am not commissioned to be thy punisher. Tis well for
thee, I am not. The learning ⟨?⟩ thou has defied ⟨?⟩ & spurned is common
to resen⟨t⟩ment. A Space is allowed thee for repentance.

    If I were, how would thy shadowy security vanish. I am fettered
& surrounded. [Were not ⟨?⟩] I cannot reach thee where thou art, but
let the commission be given, & in spite of chains & walls & inter
posing multitudes, my hands should snatch thee from thy

437

real Shuve thee to death.

1700   Philad.ᵃ 3 mo 9. 1801   1 lb wt of gold

Mr Poulson.   Annually Extra — 500 — 6,500 Guin.

"Mr Jefferson's speech at his inauguration" conveys to the mind of every real friend to this Country much pleasure and satisfaction — the sentiments expressed in it are purely republican & federal; with such principles as a basis of conduct, and with such ends in view Mr Jefferson will meet the firm support of every American whatever his opinions relative to the administration of his predecessors may have been — it is truly a matter of rejoicing to find in our chief Magistrate so extensive a spirit of reconciliation; and it is to be hoped, that, so long as he endeavours to maintain the true dignity and Interest of the American Nation — the friends & supporters of the administration of his worthy predecessors will accompany him in his — with all the firmness and patriotism which has heretofore so strongly marked their Conduct for "We Are All Republicans We are all Federalists" ———   Willins

An Earthquake was experienced at Salem (M) on Sunday afternoon the 1 of March 1801. ————

[When the good humoured Dibdin cheerily calls to honest pleasures & innocent mirth, none but the austere discuss les of ——— will refuse to read & relish the following.]

While wisdom & glee & jest and song,
  Display their charming treasure,
Mingling in gay Laughter's throng,
  Come to the Camp of Pleasure?

All human beings have their cares;
  Life's made of joy and sorrow;
To balance life then our affairs
  Should of our pleasures borrow

Youth's joys season, so is age,
  Each temper, sex, complexion
In mirth may harmlessly engage,
  As well as in reflexion.

You who proudly roll in wealth
  You whose means are slender,
You, whose lungs proclaim your health,
  You whose frames are tender.

You who wear grave wisdom's wigs,
  You who deal in folly,
You, who merry are as grigs,
  You who are melancholy.

Where's 'mongst them all the Cynic elf,
  Of joy the open scorner
But doff'd the sage and to himself
  Took pleasure in a Corner.

turn over

seat &hurl thee to death.   19.

24.

5. male & 5 female characters.

Extremes of virtue & vice. in both sexes

virtue matured by suffering. Vice triumphant

Pleyel followed by Carwin. Former passes the S.U. latter
stops & descends & recals P. by mimicing Leon: laughter.
P. cautiously descends, listening to a diallogue. An half-hour
elapses. P. goes to his chamber. Talks with Wieland in
the morning. Returns to town to Mrs B. Meets Carwin leaving
the house. C. left a letter for Leonora. Pleyel opens it.
confirmed by it in his mistake

Leonora returns. Stops at her lodgings

		Fire at Manchester
Balfour.	Thorold	Letter from thence of Decemr 13. 1800
Menso. Carlowe.	Carlowe.	The square is completely inclosed by
Loisnes. Wortley	Percival.	high buildings chiefly ware houses
Windham. La Hoo	Audley.	the streets & lanes very narrow —
	Harley.	it consisted of 10 large & lofty ware
Davis. Dudley	Macde.	houses — the loss is computed at 5,000
Cleves.	Cecil.	pounds — but the principal part of the
Avonde.	Sydney.	property was insured. what was particularly remarkable is —

the following account given to wit — . . . . .
During the raging of the fire and whilst the whole appeared as a quad
furnace. Several persons were struck with the singular incident of seeing
the word GOD in large Capitals high upon one of the Walls. The circumstance
of the time and the singularity of the place made it impressive. The word is
now to be seen — and must have been written probably during some moments
of leisure. —

Doctr Drake says; — I have read the Farmers Boy with a mixture of astonishment
and delight. There is a pathetic simplicity in his sentiments and
descriptions that does honour to his head & heart.

His copies from nature are truly original and faithful, and are touched
with the hand of a master — His versification occasionally displays an
energy and harmony which might decorate even the pages of a Darwin

24.

5. Male & 5 female Characters.

Extremes of virtue & vice, in both sexes

Virtue matured by suffering. Vice triumphant

   pleyel followed. by Carwin. Former passes the S.H. Latter

stops & descends & recals P. by mimicing Leon: laughter.

p. cautiously descends; listens to a diallogue. An half-hour

elapses. P. goes to his chamber. Talks with Wieland in

the morning. Returns to town to M^{rs}. B. Meets Carwin leaving

the house. C. left a letter for Leonora. pleyel opens it.

Confirmed by it in his mistake

   Leonora returns. Stops at her brothers

   Balfour.   Thorold.

   [Menro.] Carlowe.   Carlowe.

   [Lorimer.] Wortley   Percival.

   Windham. [Smither ⟨?⟩]   Audley.

   Davis. Dudley   Harley.

   Cleeves.   Maude.

   Avonedge.   Cecil.

                                   Sydney.